The Return of the Phantom

Etienne de Mendes

Le Couer Loyal

Etienne de Mendes

Based on characters and events created by
Gaston Leroux in The Phantom of the Opera

Bloomington, IN

authorHOUSE®

Milton Keynes, UK

AuthorHouse™
1663 Liberty Drive, Suite 200
Bloomington, IN 47403
www.authorhouse.com
Phone: 1-800-839-8640

First published by AuthorHouse 6/13/2007

ISBN: 978-1-4343-1637-0 (e)
ISBN: 978-1-4259-9492-1 (sc)
ISBN: 978-1-4259-9485-3 (hc)

Printed in the United States of America
Bloomington, Indiana

This book is printed on acid-free paper.

Cover design by Scott and Mitzvah Williams

Library of Congress Control Number: 2007901335

Dedicated to

SCOTT WILLIAMS
&
MARK GARFINKEL

The loves that heal the soul!

The Return of the Phantom

Le Couer Loyal

Everything in this world can be imitated except truth,
for truth once imitated is no longer truth.

Take care of your own soul and of another man's body,
not of your own body and another man's soul.

Menahem Mendel "The Kotsker"

PROLOGUE

The three story French provincial house stood on the corner of *Rue du Renard* and the Boulevard of Ships, several blocks up a hill from the boat docks in the industrial section of Paris. At night the lights from the vessels docked below were a pleasant and reassuring site – post Napoleon commerce in France was alive and thriving. Through the Palladian windows of the home's first floor, one could view a well-appointed ballet studio. Polished oak floors and large ornate mirrors with gold painted frames greeted the eye. To the left stood a small stage with a doublet of heavy, red velvet drapes tied back on golden cords.

The canvas scene filling the rear of the stage area depicted a harbor under the approach of a storm. On its waters a three-masted schooner, flying the colors of France, wrested the whitecaps. Past the ship, a quaint village lay nestled at the foot of a hill, cast in the shadow of ominous clouds. Rays of pinks and oranges encircled the edges of the thunderheads, like the coming of a strong clan of dark-skinned gypsies touting brilliant scarves about their heads.

On the afternoon of October 15,1873, a young woman sat on a simple wooden chair to the right of the stage, cuddling a tiny infant and cooing to it softly. Her mother, in a comfortable gray training dress, stretched on an exercise bar nearby. Behind the young woman a door opened, and a cloaked figure, wearing a black mask over the upper right quadrant of his face, filled the doorway. Beyond this noble and silent man, lay the beginning of the back staircase ascending to the next two floors of the home. He nodded briefly to the two women. When they returned the greeting, he was gone.

Madame Giry, the former mistress of ballet at the Paris Opera House, said to her daughter, Meg, "This devotion of his never ceases to amaze me."

Meg touched her nose for luck. "He's happy just to see her in the street, Mama. His spirit isn't in such a bad place. Last night he sang to little Claude, the most beautiful lullaby, so sweet. The baby smiled at him and he smiled back. When he's not out playing ghost, he's writing stories and composing. His mind seems balanced…at least he's in one complete piece. Not cut up like the corpse the three of you left in the cellars of the Opera for the *gendarme's* to find!"

Madame Giry frowned, remembering the stench of the mutilated body they'd burned to trick the police into surmising that the Phantom was dead. *That nauseating, acrid smell never quite leaves one's senses, does it? But one must always be willing to sacrifice for the plan.* Then outloud she mused, "It's true. At least he doesn't return to the tunnels and that dismal hideaway of his under the Opera House anymore. Maybe someday, he'll give voice to this mute love that holds him so deprived. Come, do some stretching. It's good for you after the birth. When will your husband be here to fetch you?"

Meg gently placed the baby in a wicker laundry basket at her feet. "Jean said he'd come around four, Mama. You are so correct…who knew that any man, anywhere, was capable of this kind of love." The two women laughed lightly as Meg joined her mother.

Out in the street the cloaked illusionist disappeared into the fog. This was Wednesday, Christine's day for light shopping.

1 HERALD BACK THE DEAD

Hearts take warning here. Let this tale of woe and triumphs unfold to those whose allegiance to the myth enshrouding the truth proves them loyal. And know this brave soul, the Phantom's voice calls thee 'friend'.

In the early spring of 1871, Christine Daae, a promising young singer and dancer in the French opera, married into an ancient and noble Parisian family. Since the girl was a mere seventeen years of age, and her groom a vigorous twenty-two, one might suppose that this was the beginning of a long and happy vocation for the new bride. The presumption would be incorrect. The Countess de Chagny endeavored to be a dutiful and loving wife to her husband, Raoul, but her relationship with the Count was complex. The mysterious haunting of a ghost at the Opera House had marred their courtship. Actually, the ghost was more of a tangible Phantom who reigned over the theater, and controlled its managers through a variety of unexplained pranks. The apparition came and went as it pleased, making demands and causing irritating mishaps with the productions and staff if its orders weren't obeyed. Taking advantage of the wraith's attraction for his fiancée, Raoul had utilized her as bait to end the tyranny. The Count took great pride in his apparent success, and was actually unaware of the depth of knowledge the Phantom possessed about his precious bride.

Indeed, the specter knew the girl as well as he knew his own face, and carried upon its dark personage a large portion of the young performer's deepest, most unvoiced secrets.

For years Christine had known her husband's adversary as a most beloved, but unseen mentor. At some point every day the creature's dulcet voice had filled her dressing room, singing his musical instructions and inspiring her voice. Because she could not see her tutor, she believed him to be the Angel of Music sent by her dead father to be her companion and teacher. She discovered too late that the angel was a man, a graceful powerful man, keeping to the shadows and watching the theater troupe's performances. A musical genius with a grotesque facial deformity, but one gifted with a voice so talented and so exquisite, that the sound of it, once loosened, could fill the heart and make the very heavens weep. A man choked to overflowing with the sadness of loving her for years in undeclared silence.

Even though the entire world of Paris believed the Phantom dead, Christine was certain he was much too clever to oblige his enemies with a timely demise. Haunted by his songs, she sensed with every fiber of her being that he was still alive. Deafened by the absence of his music, her eyes searched for him everywhere she went. That she never saw him ripped at the fabric of her mind. She imagined him hiding somewhere close by, alone and in sorrow. In her chambers at the chateau she grieved, privately tearing at her clothes and pulling her hair in despair. Penitent, she begged God to forgive her for throwing away the Angel of Music so callously, and to mercifully bring to an end the anguish of her spirit.

More than two years of this torment passed and then one autumn day in 1873, while out shopping with her maid, she was astonished to see the elegant form of the Opera's ghost facing her from a corner across the street. The man wore a gray hooded cloak in the light rain, but she sensed it was him, she knew it – for she would recognize him anywhere. He raised the front of his hood back briefly and allowed their eyes to meet. The part of his face not covered by the mask was lean, but strong and healthy. Stunned, she read in his eyes that his hunger for her burned as brightly as ever. In the street a horse and covered carriage passed between them. She remained transfixed, unwilling to take her eyes from the spot where he stood. When the carriage cleared from her vision he was miraculously still there! Impulsively, she wanted to rush to him. Her body gave a small involuntary jerk forward. Seeing her dilemma, he raised his gloved hand and lowered his hood as a signal that she should stay put.

Her servant, following her employer's line of sight, thought her mistress wanted to go into the shop next to the Phantom, and inquired if they should cross the street. Forcing her mind to focus, Christine replied as if in a trance. "No, let's go in here." The ladies turned and entered the lamp store behind them. Distracted and impatient, Christine emerged within a few short minutes.

As the women proceeded from shop to shop on the winding street, the man followed slowly at a distance, watching from beneath his hood. Every time she glanced out a window and saw him loyally near, disbelief and elation flowed through her like electricity. Each uplifting bolt quickly devoured by the numbing realization that he might easily disappear, and leave her to her abhorrent suffering. Her troubled thoughts made it difficult to pretend an interest in the items for sale, but she tried to keep up an appearance. She needn't have worried, on this particular day everyone in the shop was busy. No one seemed to notice her distressed preoccupation with the weather, or the visible shaking of her hands as she moved about gently fingering the items on sale.

Carefully, she contemplated her options. *If only I could bolt from this store into your arms!*

The Countess stood a slender five-foot eight, and walked with the grace of a former dancer. Her bright eyes were hazel, more green than blue. Her supple skin reflected the mixture of ethnic cultures in Europe, even in the coldest months of the year, it boasted the palest of tan colors. The highlights of her brown wavy hair were ash, and her brilliant smile, when she could muster one, lit up the room around her.

Christine made a decision to somehow have contact with the Phantom, and was spurred into action when she looked into the foggy rain and no longer saw his figure. Her muscles tensed fiercely, almost painfully, as her mind screamed out in silence. *No, don't be gone! Let me see you!* Her eyes glassed over in tears.

From the street, where he held his body in perfect stillness, he read her sad face like a book. In comprehension, his head slowly leaned toward his shoulder, his lips parted to breathe in the surprise.

The mists swirled and suddenly he became visible to her again. He stood next to the molding of a storefront, close by, almost blending in. With his hood turned her way, she wondered, *how well can he see me inside this store?* Her eyes darted nervously around the shop, and she noted with satisfaction that for the moment, not even her maid was paying attention to her. Quickly she wrote in the dust on the counter top:

FATHER'S TOMB NOON

She strained to make out his face but could not. His hooded head nodded ever so slightly. When she moved to another area of the store, he entered, his face still covered. His booted steps made no sound as he walked to the counter! *Is he gliding?* He coughed into a linen handkerchief and read her message. The Phantom wiped the dust away with his gloved hand and bent over as if to view the figurines within the glass case. From this position his eyes moved to where she stood when he entered, but now she was gone! He straightened up abruptly and saw her getting into a carriage out in the street.

She glanced back. *Yes, he is standing where I wrote the words.*

The rain continued into the following day. She went to the cemetery by carriage and asked her driver to return in an hour. Christine used a skeleton key to open the metal lock, and pulling on the double set of open grillwork doors, entered the mausoleum of her father's repose. She closed the doors quietly and turned to face the inside. Sighing deeply, she was surprised that the only smell was that of the rain and wet earth. In the cool air of the tomb, she lowered her head and placed her gloved fist over her heart, strengthening her resolve. Then looking up, with eyes grown more accustomed to the semi-light within, she saw his outline standing deep in a darkened corner. His arms lay folded across his chest beneath a cloak, his head bare.

In the hollow of the tomb she softly spoke the words she'd practiced so many times since yesterday. "I have never known your given name, but from my orphaned youth you defined the very context of my soul. My thoughts, my very self, are not mine alone...they are the labyrinth that is you. I cannot tell where I end and you begin. I am bereft without you in my life. And the music, your music, sings in my head more real to me than life itself. Our beginning was spawned in mystery because you knew no other way to approach. Our parting all too hurtful, too full of confusion."

Her words broke off as emotion brutally tightened her throat, effectively silencing her rehearsed words. Choking in her own tears she could not continue, but kept her eyes on his illusive shape, fearing he might vanish. Her chest heaved, sucking in a painful searing breath over her partially closed throat. Beneath her cloak her hands knotted into fists. In an attempt to regain speech her mouth opened, but her lower lip only curled inward over her bottom teeth. Awash in misery, only a jagged sob escaped. Surrendering to grief, she closed her eyes and turned her face away from the man, wiping her tears with the back of her glove. When at last she was able to force her voice and look once more at the elusive presence, the grievous truth poured forth.

"Oh Phantom, now you stand before me and I long to know you still!"

From the corner, in perfect pitch, he sang his lament. "Christine, I love you."

She held her head in dismay, replying in a coarse whisper. "Every fiber in me trembles to hear you once more. Your exquisite voice rolls like thunder across the black night that has become my heart. It calls to me, allures me, as if time had not passed between us." She tapped her sternum with her fist. "I am suffering, Dark Angel, what am I to do? Married, yet still yours. Wed to another and wanting you...longing for you every moment. Like a pitiable soul interred alive, I thrash for air. I feel I am cursed to die in this! If I am to die, I welcome the curse. I cherish it. Only let it mean that somehow you are again a physical part of it."

His teeth clenched shut and ground together, as he heard her speak of her death, and although he had a readiness to move, he did not. Silence filled the tomb. The empty space gradually engulfed with the sound of rain striking stone in the cemetery.

"Erik, my name is Erik."

The sound of his name seemed like a beacon, drawing her willingly to its solace. She took one brave step forward and seeing his sleek figure more clearly, entreated the man wrapped in shadows. "Erik, can we two share just moments, and be satisfied that those brief shreds of time are worth the pain each parting will bring? Reach to my hand and I am yours for the taking, yours sweet angel, yours my friend." He offered no response. From her soul she pleaded in a breathless whisper, "Please…please."

She removed her gloves, letting them fall to the floor. From inside her cloak, her right arm rose slowly with her palm upward. The rain pounded against the tomb. Patiently she waited as several heartbeats passed. He did not take her hand. Instead, they came together quickly in a blur, air and time standing still, for indeed neither of them was initially breathing.

They trembled in the power of this first hidden embrace.

Erik's strong hands on the middle of her back pressed her to him, moving in circles as if to relearn their sense of her. The tips of his fingers grabbed into her clothes, massaging, celebrating, feeding his brain with a stimulus almost too painful to endure, but deeply gratifying. On some primitive level too compelling to resist. *Oh, the feel of her!* He was dizzy. He turned his face toward the ceiling of the tomb and gasped, as one just freed from a pit. Lowering his imperfect lips to hers they kissed in thirst and recognition. She felt the sweet warmth of him enfolding around her. He no longer smelled of the dank cellars beneath the Opera House, now he smelled of Persian musk. His arms moved deftly to beneath her cloak, one around the middle of her back and the other low on her waist. She lifted herself up into his six-foot two frame, hugging him tightly. He stood, booted feet set apart, with the strength of his erection pressed on her abdomen. The purest sensation of joy spread throughout her. Their kiss continued, full of wonder as they hungrily sought to know each other.

No other place yielded such gladness, even as the kiss ended she bestowed a series of several, smaller kisses on the lips of this phenomenal creature vested in shade. To each he responded in kind. Bowing her forehead onto his chest, she began to sob with relief. Feeling the agony of her pain easing, she sensed his start afresh because she'd separated just a little from him. She rested her hands on the front of his shoulders and gazed into the Phantom's golden eyes, his face half hidden by a gray leather mask. She reached to touch the facial covering, but his hand took hold of hers, delaying the removal of his protection. Her softened face waited in anticipation. He took the mask off himself and let it fall softly to the flag stone floor.

In the darkness, Christine kissed his deformity and cried. She could not stop. She kissed the normal side of his face, but moved back again to the right – to comfort the cause of so much torment and anguish. He held her tenderly as this strange ritual continued, kissing her hair as she buried her face into his abnormal cheek. His body throbbed, demanding satisfaction. He pleaded for relief by rubbing her scalp with his hands, his fingers lingering deep at the base of her curls. Mastering control of himself, he pressed her hair to his nose and mouth, breathing in the fragrance. *Lavender, she always liked lavender.* His breath in her right ear caused an almost excruciating tingle to run down her back and both her arms to their fingertips. This time their lips found each other in intoxication, and something wonderful happened, something that rarely occurs among men and women. A transfiguring event so momentous, that its incidence upon the earth causes angels to stop and stand in silent admiration. Erik and Christine's souls fused. They were simply one person, one entity. The rift of self-awareness dissolved away by the magic of sheer ecstasy. Their tears dried and Erik triumphantly lifted Christine off her feet into his arms.

He moved her to the top of the sarcophagus. There they spent the next hour together, tenderly fulfilling what their hearts and bodies demanded, laughing softly as they repeated their union again, and yet again.

When she returned to the estate, Christine spent the next few days virtually locked in her rooms. Whatever food was brought to her she scarcely touched. She sat in a chair in her private parlor looking out the window, desperately wanting to be left alone in her world of dreamy revelation and hope. She refused to bathe and remove whatever traces of him still lay upon her. Over and over she relived their meeting. She ran her fingers through her hair and across her body, imitating his touch. *Alive, he is alive!* Carefully she placed the garments she'd worn to the sepulcher on her bed and knelt beside them. *He was near these clothes…he felt them.* She vowed to guard ferociously the secret meetings they'd planned. *Raoul must never know…I will tell everyone only the simplest of words needed to enlist their aid.*

Leaving the tomb that afternoon had been the most difficult thing she had ever done in her life. Like a child she had clung to Erik's jacket and risked all by keeping her driver waiting impatiently at the front gate of the cemetery. Erik had been obliged to gently take her to the iron doors and reluctantly push her from him, promising to meet her again in the mausoleum. "Where have you been all this time?" She had begged plaintively for response. He assured her he would answer all her questions at their next meeting. But when she refused to release his lapels from her grasp, and he looked into her eyes brimming with lustrous tears, he weakened, explaining that he knew her routines well. Over the past thirty months he had kept up with the movements of society by reading the papers, and had managed a glimpse of her several times a week. Like a lamb she had finally obeyed. Blindly trusting that she would hold him again, she walked down the path to the carriage.

When the driver opened the door for her and settled her onto the seat, he thought her the most truly miserable, morose woman he'd ever met.

Left alone in the tomb, Erik sat behind the sarcophagus, surrendering his own shipwrecked soul to the agony of skepticism. He'd lived so much of his outcast's life in fantasy, that he had to pry open a place in his mind and permit the simple truth of this clandestine reunion to exist. Yesterday, he had decided to reveal himself to her on the slim chance that she might acknowledge him. Acknowledge him! He had no idea of her tormented lonely thoughts, of her constant devotion to her teacher, and her accelerating grief over the loss of him. Now there was no running from reality. The truth of her unhappiness was gutted and laid waste for him to view. Thinking she was comfortable was his delusion – not knowing how he fared had been killing her! A taste of bile rose in his mouth as he chastised himself bitterly. Shrunken in the shadows for over two years, waiting for a chance to see her pass by on the streets of Paris, he had only perceived that she was growing gradually thinner, becoming a mere wisp of her former self. *All those lonely, wasted hours waiting and I knew nothing of her sorrow! She* **will** *take an interest in life again! I mean for her to be happy, and will content myself with whatever bits of her I may yet know.*

For a few minutes he permitted himself the outlandish vision of healing her by giving her children. He ordered himself to subjugate his natural needs and stay away from his own progeny. *Erik, will not speak with them, will not play with them as they grow! Perhaps he will allow himself to watch them from a distance at their games, or at school. Yes, that will suffice for Erik!* He would wrestle himself into being at peace with this arrangement. He sat there for hours mentally playing in a make-believe world he knew could never exist. Then he began to study the interior of the sepulcher, and his creative mind envisioned another world, one of more practical circumstance. Should he show her what secrets this tomb already held?

As twilight took the sky that evening, a cemetery worker walked a German Shepherd on a chain through the tombs. Twenty feet in front of the Daae mausoleum the animal stopped and refused to move forward. Bolted to the spot, it wagged its tail excitedly, its tongue spilling forth in happy greeting. In shock the caretaker watched as an unwholesome creature with the face of a skeleton, loomed in the entrance to the mausoleum. The sight of this fearsome apparition brought the very hairs on his neck and arms to stand in fright. His jaw dropped downward, but no sound chanced uttering for he was totally unprepared for what happened next. The specter knotted its fists and throwing out its black caped arms toward him, opened its fingers and its mouth, releasing the most soulful wail the man had ever heard. The singular cry of an alpha wolf over the loss of its mate could be no more plaintive and unnerving. The dog at his side sat down and tightening its throat joined into the dirge with its own ear piercing, high-pitched howl. The laborer dropped the chain and ran pell-mell for his very life. On his way off the grounds, he passed his employer, screaming out almost incoherently as he flew by, that he quit! Years later, the worker would still deem himself the most unfortunate of human beings for having lived through this unexpected, surreal experience.

Safe from the worker's sight, the caped figure emerged from the tomb. Coming over to the dog he undid its leash and rubbed its furry head. As Erik turned to walk away into the rain, the animal simply followed, its tail lowered, its keen pointed ears up and on alert.

2 AVOW THE UNSPEAKABLE

Eager anticipation mounted steadily within Christine as their next meeting approached. Months of desperate depression peeled away, leaving her with an almost euphoric sense of weightlessness. She found her true emotions difficult to control and even harder to conceal. On the following Tuesday she lay in her bathtub surrounded by pleasant smelling bubbles, trying to imagine how Erik would be preparing for their second meeting that afternoon. Despite multiple attempts, no image of him bathing would come to her. She stretched back into the soothing water and allowed her mind to drift. In her reverie she pictured herself on the Opera House stage the last night she performed there, her arms lifted upward, her voice singing gloriously. *Holy Angel, in Heaven blessed…my spirit longs with thee to rest…*when suddenly the stage all around her went dark.

In the middle of a rendition of 'Faust' during the month of March 1871, she had evaporated mysteriously from center stage during an unfortunate black-out. Investigators at the time were drawn to the conclusion that the two males in the de Chagny household, Count Philippe and his younger brother, the Viscount Raoul, had vied for the affections of the young soprano, and one of them had succeeded in carrying her off. Days later, Philippe's body was found on the banks of an underground lake beneath the Opera House, near the entrance off the *Rue Scribe*. The authorities determined that an ill-fated fall caused his demise, and ruled his death an accident. Nothing was heard of the young Viscount until mid-April, when the local papers heralded the news that he had wed the performer, Christine Daae, in a private ceremony at *Sainte-Chapelle,* beneath its dozens of richly hued red and blue stained glass windows.

The public was not informed of the team of detectives the two married de Chagny sisters sent out to discreetly locate their missing younger brother. The de Chagny family held dear the time honored tradition of primogeniture – the eldest living male de Chagny had sole right to control the estate and the family's holdings. So the sisters spared no effort, or expense, in locating their missing brother and insidiously bringing him back to the chateau. In return for Raoul establishing himself as the head of the family, they gave their blessings to his proposed marriage to a commoner. The sisters believed that Raoul had spirited Christine off the stage like a love struck puppy. They were never told the odious truth of her abduction. Never told that in the blink of an eye, a love crazed man, known to the theater troupe as the Opera Ghost, stole her from beneath the watchful eyes of an entire audience. The kidnapper dropped her through the center stage trapdoor and carried her to his house of stone beside an underground lake, thinking that time would meld her heart to him. For days he restrained and cajoled her, only to recant when she finally surrendered and pledged herself to him. In an unexplained act of self-effacement, he freed her to be with Raoul. Dumfounded and bewildered, Christine left with her 'normal' suitor, leaving the pariah desolate and consoling himself with the knowledge that he had returned her to the possibility of a happy life, away from him and his eccentricities.

The traumatized young starlet married into one of the oldest and most distinguished families in France, one whose coat of arms originated in the thirteen hundreds. Her new husband brought her to live on an estate outside of Paris, consisting of a mere forty-one hundred acres. An estate that boasted a twenty thousand square foot chateau surrounded by stone patios, manicured geometric gardens and opulent splashing fountains. On the north and east side of the mansion stood dense woods of pine, oak and beech trees; to the south, a lake stocked for fishing, and beyond that, grasslands with cows and sheep.

Christine became a living example of how money cannot buy happiness. Not that the chateau wasn't handsome to behold. The current house was built in the seventeen hundreds on a rolling piece of land, to replace an earlier structure on the same site. Its asymmetrically laid out elevations could be viewed just off a well-traveled road outside the city. The private entrance was approached through a simple opened gate and lined with lush shrubs. A circular driveway brought visitors up to a two story mansion in the style of the French Renaissance, but one whose architectural touches paid obvious homage to the designs of the Middle Ages. Its granite and limestone façade was graced with tall windows of diamond-cut lead glass. Its massive front doors beckoned from between two columns that held up an arch of carved stone towering to the second floor. Symmetrical balconies off the second floor suites afforded impressive views of the gardens and the spectacular woods beyond. To the right of the structure, a *porte cochere* attached a guest house which Count Philippe had remade into a hunting lodge, for the lands were home to red deer, wild boar, pheasant, fox, ducks, and geese. The architect intended for the home to embellish its environment, but instead of invoking a sense of grandeur and mystery within Christine, she felt it dreary and overpowering.

Inside the chateau the main foyer rose to a vaulted ceiling, one whose dome terminated in the attic. A great staircase fashioned from Italian marbles of blacks, whites and deep greens, with railings of ornately carved woods and wrought iron decorated with gold leaf, flowed to the left in a sweeping curve. A tremendous effort had been made by the designer to employ ancient geometric principals within the structure. The architect tied together the square, octagon, hexagon and circle into a three dimensional experience, creating a house of elegant beauty and grace. A house of grand expanse and expression, a magnificent cage for a woman who felt her wings safely clipped against any attempt at flight.

Indeed, everything in the house spoke of ownership to Christine; the wine cellars, the servants' quarters, the arches and columns that delineated passageways and framed views, the hand carved crown moldings that were meant to arrest the eye. Room after room of elaborately painted ceilings, murals, tapestries and statues, nauseated her. Everything in the chateau was proportioned by deliberate plan and spoke of the immense male ego that had conceived it. To her the mansion blistered of exaggeration. Its carefully manufactured designs sought only to portray an image of prestige and stature, allowing no space for the cozy warmth she craved.

She found herself housed in a palace fit for a Countess, a woman of noble birth and bearing. Not the daughter of a humble, country violinist. She sighed in her bath, remembering the melancholy father who had raised her and told her to wait patiently for the Angel of Music, the celestial being who inspired artists and guided their performances into the realm of the ethereal. "I will send him to you after my death Christine, watch for him, sweet child."

Orphaned at seven, she had clung stubbornly to the hope that the angel would come, and how a child perceives the world speaks volumes about what strengths they will demonstrate as an adult. When the angel finally spoke through the walls to the child Christine, she welcomed him with a loyal, open heart, obeying his every instruction and basking in his visits. As a teenager, even the repulsive vision of his true countenance and the desperate captivity he'd enforced upon her, could not mar the place of majesty he so solidly held within her mind. Without an ongoing relationship with her 'angel', the adult Christine had become distraught, almost soul-less in the vacuum created by his absence. No chateau, with all its amenities and overstated affluence, could fill the void relentlessly sucking the joy from her soul.

With distinct clarity, she understood her motivations, and was fully aware that she had crossed the line preset by law into adultery. She firmly dismissed any consideration of penalty as she prepared herself for this second meeting with Erik. Her rooms had belonged to Raoul's mother. Their walls bore heavily embellished, crimson velvet wallpaper with *fleur-de-lis* and pompous lions wearing crowns. The detailed woodwork that graced the doors and accented the walls was of darkly stained cherry wood. Even the fireplace of simple river stones, which did not fit with the elaborate nature of the rest of the décor, offered no appeal to her except for its heat. The former Countess had died giving birth to Raoul in this massive bed. Christine shuddered when she thought of it. The only thing she liked about her personal quarters was the privacy she was afforded upon entering her own domain.

She spent the morning hours carefully choosing her clothes and toiletries. Nursing a bottle of Tokay and humming in rhythmical freedom, before going down to the carriage and driver who awaited her arrival at the precise time she'd requested. Safely settled on the vehicle's leather seat, she secretly relished the thought of escaping the intricate puzzle box that held her, for the arms of the man who had won her heart, precisely because he had taught it how to fly with feeling. Then as it soared – set it free.

An anxious Christine approached the cemetery on that cool, crisp afternoon. She wore a dull, rust colored wool dress and waistcoat with a small, feathered hat upon her head. Over the last year she had taken to wearing only dark colors, a reflection of her spirit one would suppose, but if truth were to be told, today she actually wanted to wear a bright blue, and had resigned herself to appearing bleak. Just as she forced herself now to walk slowly, in a dignified measured pace to her father's grave, when all she truly wanted to do was run. Run quickly to the tomb. She was early, by her watch thirty minutes early for their appointment. This time she wanted to be waiting for him, as added proof of her determination to keep him in her life.

When she entered the mausoleum and locked the door behind her, she scanned the interior closely. *Good, I am here before him.* As she removed her hat and placed it on a small shelf intended for flowers, she began to plan. *Where shall I be when he enters?* Smiling, she hugged herself and twirled in a *pirouette,* almost unable to contain the excitement she felt rising within her. Coming into a ballerina's pose, her right foot circled to end behind her – her arms forming a graceful circlet at chest height with the tips of her middle fingers almost touching. She surprised herself with a short vibrant laugh. She had not danced in over two years. Dropping her arms, she implored, "Oh, do hurry!"

His melodious voice resonated throughout the tomb, "Is this quick enough?"

She was near the back of the singular room, facing the door and could view the entire space with one scan of her eyes. He was not there! Slowly she turned in a complete circle, unable to pinpoint the source of his voice, and as she came around to once again face the metal doors, he stood before her, barely a yard's length away, appearing out of nowhere. Frozen like a wide-eyed statue, she stared quizzically into his endearing half masked face. "*Inamorato.* Where did you come from?"

The Phantom went down on his left knee and dramatically swept his right arm outward. "Madame, I am your obedient servant." His right index finger pointed straight to the ceiling. "Under the roof of the mausoleum is a hollow space and I have made a place for us to be together, like a garret. Close quarters and tight, but private and comfortable."

Puzzled, Christine turned her face upward. There she saw a black opening made by the removal of four, eighteen inch squares of stone. "What a unique magician you are, once again the ingenious architect. You dropped down from there so silently?"

"Hmm," he responded, enjoying the moment immensely. He smiled broadly at her inquisitive face of surprise. For years as she grew from a child to a young woman in the Opera House, he sang that face to sleep each night, lovingly watched it change and blossom. He could close his eyes at any moment and behold her as if she were actually before him. *But why do that now? She is here!* "Christine, do you want to go up there? The stones slide shut like a trapdoor, and the entrance is not visible to the eye once the door is closed."

Christine went to her knees before the Phantom, who was still down on one of his. "This is a wonderful, imaginative gift. We will investigate it together, but please remove your mask and hold me first. Every part of me aches for you. I don't wish to wait a moment longer."

The man sighed deeply, he would have preferred to remove the mask once they had entered passion, but he honored her request. He sat on the floor with his back resting against the sarcophagus, the length of which hid them from the world. Removing his shield he angled the right side of his face away, watching her reaction. The absence of his protection made him feel edgy and vulnerable. He hated being without it, and tended to keep the deformed part of his face concealed whenever the mask was off. The mental slap of rejection was all too familiar, its impact a dreaded fact of life. Would this afternoon be different? Driven by fervor to know the truth, he left his face exposed. Was she feeling something genuine? All the risks were worth the taking if she was truly accepting him!

Instinctively she understood Erik's posture. The sight of his natural face was repugnant to people, and he had suffered greatly from the abuse of others. Had his features been uniform he would have been quite handsome, a striking Adonis, with his pale skin and thick raven's black hair. His eyes were the most astounding color of gold and pale green. A copper colored ring surrounded each pupil, and a thin line of blue-gray encircled the outer edge of each iris. But the upper right quarter of his face was not much of a face at all. It bore the appearance of chopped raw meat placed over a prominent skull, with a living, inquisitive eyeball peering from a socket. Tiny veins, like dozens of fetal snakes, traveled through the underlying translucent skin. He fashioned the masks to form the right side of his nose. Without them, or an appliance that he sometimes wore, there was only a hole, exposing the tubular structure of the right nasal passage. His right upper lip lacked muscular strength, and was pulled slightly upward, leaving the tips of his right incisors and canine teeth visible.

She decided to go slowly and sitting back on her bent legs, took his right hand in hers, rubbing her thumbs across the palm to soothe him. His hand was no longer the bony, cold vice she remembered from her abduction. Living above ground had warmed him, and he showed the good health that proper nutrition brings. The muscles of his arms and legs were well defined and powerful. She knew he could climb theater ropes with ease, and snap a person's neck like a dry twig.

Oh, but the left side of his face, that face which was before her now, was full of mournful expression and hope. He shaved this morning in preparation. She smiled briefly, trying to picture him shaving in front of a mirror. Carefully she placed her hand upon his gruesome right cheek, he leaned into it even though he could only feel the part of her hand that touched his lips and chin. His sad eyes echoed years of pain as they concentrated on every emotion registered in her face.

She spoke gently, her voice light, as if sharing a secret with a playmate. "There was always such a fuss made over your appearances at the Opera House. If the little ballerinas spotted the slightest glimpse of you, they scurried off in exaggerated fear to hide with the older dancers. They cried for protection from the walking skeleton. No matter what trifle went astray, or what object went missing, you were always blamed for it. You and I know that your mystique helped preserve your existence. When word spread that you were roaming about, everyone fled in terror, clutching their good luck charms...hoping to avoid you. They never stopped to question who you really were, or what you wanted."

He did not answer her, preferring to let his actions show his intent toward this woman. He took her in his arms and cradled her head on his green woolen vest. Once she settled up against him, he stroked her face. "Your heart is beating like a sparrow's."

Holding her tenderly he began to kiss her. At first the kiss was gentle, almost polite, but they hastened to explore and let it evolve in form. The kiss melded them, carried them effortlessly down the path of a singular soul intent on desire. His tongue stroked the roof of her mouth to tantalize her. In response, her body sent forth a tiny spasm of arousal. Excited by the investigation of his tongue, she placed his hand on the lace ruffles adorning her bodice. His agile fingers moved to free her from her buttons. Skillfully he caressed the sides of her breasts, drawing them delicately out from within her clothing. The backs of his long fingers brushed over them. Soft, like silk, their nipples erect in anticipation. The moistness between her legs and the aching of her crotch was intensifying. Her back began to arch, and she separated her legs. He broke the kiss but his lips remained close, so close. His breath was still upon her face as he laid her flat upon the floor. He raised himself up to unfasten his trousers, then reached under her petticoat for her underwear, only to discover she was wearing none. His hands moved up and down her inner thighs until she moaned a plea. He placed himself over her, supporting his weight off her chest with the strength of his arms and shoulders.

In invitation, her legs spread wider to receive him, her knees bent wrapping him in her thighs. She intoned a solemn declaration. "I love you, Erik. I take you to me again, but this time let it be for all eternity."

Such simple words, 'I love you.' Words uttered, swiftly – easily, by thousands of people every day. Words never spoken to Erik before this moment. He believed he was dreaming. Here on hallowed ground his obsession lay beneath him, and from some foggy place of sleep she was telling him what he had not heard before. Never assumed to be true. With a start he realized that the roaring in his ears was his own blood rushing through his arteries.

Poised to enter her, he contemplated her lovely green eyes. "Where does this love reside?"

She drew him down upon her, squeezing him with her arms and thighs. "In my being…it breathes of love for you."

"Oh, how I need you, Christine. Whatever love I possess is yours… for all my life. I pledge it." He kissed her mouth, her nose, her forehead, and slid himself inside her. As he moved back and forth in a rhythm that sent rapture throughout them both, she welcomed him with an accepting purr and kissed his neck. Her hands traveled up and down his sides and across his back, ardently insisting that he continue his mating with her. He lifted his chest off her, moving his pelvis in circles, back and forth. He was the embodiment of a *portamento*, imparting a passage of pleasurable physical tones within her. Gliding his instrument. Guiding her. Moving her from one pitch to the next with the smooth progression of a masterful musician.

Nearly delirious she acknowledged his gifts as a lover. With every thrust she arched up to him, pushing as hard as she could against his hair and pelvic bone in sheer delight. As her pleasure spiraled upward, he refused himself a climax until she was deeply in the throws of hers. Then as her body eased down, he slowly and with deliberate intent built her up again to experience another intense crescendo, and then another. The *Da Capo al fine* he brought her to was more a satisfying promise than a close. Biting her lower lip, she put her hands behind her head and pulled her long curls up off her neck. Stretching like a cat, she smiled gratefully.

As one unit, he rolled them onto their sides facing each other, and continued to remain within her should she not yet be satisfied. Holding her tightly in his arms, he whispered into her ear his most private thoughts. Christine listened intently, her hand resting upon his neck.

When he became silent, she answered with a voice full of earnest determination. "I feel alive because you've returned to me, most beautiful creature. My marrow no longer the dust of desiccation, I am awake once more to hope and vigor. The world, with all its trickery, shall not strip this love from us. I vow to keep it! You can tell me anything that's in your will to tell me, and like the shore receiving the waves I will take you to me. You are free to be as the summer breeze, or as the raging hurricane. Be gentle or fierce. I will leave Raoul for you, Erik, and go anywhere you want. All I ask is that I am never in the state of being alive without you again. I call on those who reside in the celestial realms to bear witness to my words. The love I feel demands they listen! May I be struck dead if I've not spoken my heart's utter truth!"

For a time he traced her lips with his fingertips, studying the feel of her breath while considering her words. Finally, he voiced his thoughts. "I believe it would serve you well to remember that Raoul has proven to be generous and kind, but more importantly, his mind is stable. I know by the world's standards I am insane. But possessing your love and ministering to myself inside your body, has cooled the heat of the savage feelings that once compelled my actions. I want you to be anchored in a safe harbor…secure and protected by the de Chagny name, should I loose control of my actions, or the *gendarmes* come to arrest me. It is enough to have you in these moments. I am…content. I do not see this as a double life for us. Just a life lived by our choices." He pulled her closer and breathed in deeply, filling his nostrils with the smell of her. *I deserve only the scraps off the table. Let them be enough to sate me.*

Shaking her head in disbelief she remained obedient to him. "Erik, it will be as you will it, whatever you declare, but I doubt we are finished with this discussion. Let's leave this subject open for future debate. Now, kindly show me what you've done to the attic of this tomb."

Sighing deeply, he chuckled and stood up to fasten his pants. He reached to take her hand and when she rose, he positioned them both directly beneath the opening in the ceiling. "See here," touching the top of a decorative metal torch affixed to the wall, "push this to the right."

As she turned the torch, another area of four stones in a square lifted off from the floor beneath their feet, carrying them up into the ceiling. When it came to a standstill he quickly moved them off the platform, and it receded noiselessly back downward into its place in the floor below. Standing in the cool black air with her hands on his waist, she marveled, "How did you accomplish **that**?"

"Some of the pipes which carry water into the city run beneath the cemetery. When opened, a valve with a metal ball in it diverts water into graded pipes that are collapsed inside each other. I adhered their end to the bottom of the platform. For a few moments we are pushed upward by hydraulic pressure. At maximum extension the valve, still opened, allows the water to return to the main pipes, and the platform back to its original position. We just need to step off before it commences its return. It's really quite simple."

He reached over to a little table and striking a match lit a candle. Then he pushed a wooden lever on the wall to the left, and without a sound the trapdoor in the ceiling slid shut. "When you enter the tomb, turning the torch below to the left will cause the ceiling door to open. There is a painted screen depicting stones hiding the ropes and pulleys in the room. I'll show it to you when we go down. To open the trapdoor and raise the platform from here, push this lever to the right."

Trying to grasp his explanation, she sat on the side of a bed he had placed next to the table. The space they were in was small but adequate for their meetings. In the center of the room they could even stand erect under the apex of the roof. She noted that air was entering from two vents, one on the front and the other on the back of this level of the structure.

Watching the direction of her eyes, he said, "Those were part of the original masonry."

"And how did you get this bed up here?"

"In pieces, then I put it together. Very few people come to this cemetery during the day, and from dusk to dawn there's no one here. I worked mostly at night. My eyes are accustomed to the dark and the half-light of candles. Does this please you?"

She stretched out on the mattress of the rope bed, feeling the blue velvet coverlet with her palms. "We met here only five days ago. It is beyond me that anyone could have accomplished all of this in so short a time."

He eased back into a dark corner, contemplating her resting form. "You are making an assumption. I worked on this a long time ago. Getting into the sewers and waterways was easy for me, just wet. I simply adapted what I found and brought in what I needed."

Startled, she raised her head. "You've been here many times?"

"I come here to lie among the dead and think."

"Were you ever up here when I was…?"

"Praying below? No. I was never lucky enough to enjoy the vision of a young Countess in supplication for her father's soul."

"If you had seen me, would you have revealed yourself?"

"Am I not here? Look at this, Christine. It is my latest addition. Done this past weekend as a present for you." He pinched out the candle's flame and the entire ceiling of the attic became aglow with hundreds of phosphorescent, hand painted stars.

Her eyes immediately comprehended the touching simplicity of his painting. It appeared that they were under a nighttime sky somewhere, alone. She turned to her side, barely able to make out his form in the strange light of the stars above. Patting the bed, she beckoned him. "Come here and get your reward, my genius."

Smiling wryly he advanced.

That evening, at the house on *Rue du Renard*, the Phantom sat with Madame Giry, and over a dinner of roasted pork and potatoes, decided to tell her he had revealed his existence to Christine, and of the location of their budding affair. Madame Giry had been his closest friend and confidant since his arrival in Paris from Constantinople as a teenager. Without reservation he trusted her with his life. She had saved him many times and repeatedly proven her friendship. She simply accepted the news of his decision, and without hesitation asked what she could do to help. "The happiness love brings has been a long time coming, and you, its all too patient servant. I suggest that the two of you create some kind of signal to alert us should she need you. Written messages can be traced and might place her in jeopardy."

The person he dreaded telling was the man who'd engineered his escape from Persia, the friend who had followed him here to Paris, and had helped them hide the truth that the Opera Ghost still existed, the Daroga – Khalil Echad Salim. The Daroga was one of the chief reasons Erik had released Christine from captivity. He was the nagging voice of conscience during her abduction, and although the Phantom dreaded listening to him, his civil words about responsibility entered into Erik's brain, and would not be dismissed. Erik decided to put off telling Khalil that he and Christine were involved with each other for as long as possible. Without doubt the Daroga would be most unhappy, but there was no getting around it, he would have to be told eventually if their friendship of decades was to survive.

The Persian made it a little easier for them when he showed up at the backdoor of the ballet studio a few mornings later, unannounced. His tall, dark skinned form stood on the stoop holding a bag of dried apricots and cheese. "*Bon Jour!* I've come bearing gifts," he proclaimed, handing the sack to Madame Giry with a flourish. She thanked him and ushered him into her kitchen where she offered him coffee or tea. "Neither for the moment, perhaps later on. Is our boy in?" He said this despite the fact that Erik was thirty-seven.

"He's upstairs."

The former head of the Persian secret police rubbed his hands together in anticipation. "May I go by way of the passage? It delights me so to use it."

"Of course, but make sure you…"

"Holler before opening it upstairs," he asserted.

"Yes, do." She reached over and discreetly pulled a string at the side of her kitchen curtain. A soft bell jingled upstairs.

The lanky Persian touched his hand to his forehead and to his heart before bowing. He proceeded into Madame's living room where he stood before a painted Japanese screen that possessed a peculiar three-dimensional quality. It depicted a room with two Asian ladies enjoying tea at a short-legged table. The plants around the pond at the bottom of the picture overlapped onto the floor and their cushions. These cushions overlapped onto the bottom of the ladies' robes. Their hairdos, in turn, overlapped onto the wall behind them, and so on. Each layer slightly on top of the next, as in a fan, all the way up past the trees and the clouds, into the sky at the top of the screen. The Daroga pulled the header of the screen's frame toward him and slats, like louvers, appeared in the painting. With only a minimal effort he continued to pull downward and the slats came forward, forming the six steps of a stool that could fold back upon itself. Its highest step revealed the opening of a secret entrance. He bent over and climbed upward, reaching a ladder hidden in the wall within a space that easily accommodated a man's girth. He turned and pulled a rope, returning the slats to their closed position, and moved up the ladder until he felt the second set of slats on the floor above. But before he could bellow out a greeting and push them open, they unfolded, dropping down into the third floor living room.

There stood the Phantom, grinning, "Still not using the stairs, I see."

The Daroga entered, clasping Erik's hand firmly within his own and patting him affectionately on the shoulder. "What's going on? You really seem rather perky, almost pleasant. Have you created another book of regulations for someone to live by?" He was referring to the codex the

Opera Ghost had given to the managers of the Opera House. In it Erik had defined how the theater was to be run during his haunting.

Erik openly studied the expression worn by his alter ego. *All decent human communication comes directly from the face, even the face of the foolish in love, so here we go. Positives first.* "Hardly, I've no inclination to attend to rule books right now. Life seems like a dream to me, I'm walking around in a pleasant, sensuous dream."

Greatly intrigued, the Daroga asked, "What kind of dream could have ensnared our ghost so peculiarly?" He stood with his hands on his hips studying the Phantom's brilliant eyes. "Perhaps we could have a cup of coffee and you can tell me more."

While Erik busied himself with making the brew, Madame Giry quietly entered through the apartment's backdoor, and took a seat at the kitchen table next to the Daroga. After they were served, Khalil inquired, "All right, does someone want to tell me what's going on?"

Madame Giry laid her hand upon the Daroga's arm and calmly informed him, "It seems that Christine will have our Erik now."

"Hell's flames!" He exclaimed slamming his hand down flat upon the table. For a few moments he was mute, looking from Erik to Madame, then back again. He removed his Astrakhan wool hat, and ran his fingers through his hair as if to loosen his brain cells and accept what he had just heard. "Erik, I have sworn to always protect you in payment for the many services you bestowed upon my family, and I understand full well that the world has conjured against you over the years, but I am compelled to tell you that this is madness and will lead to some further tragedy, probably of the worst kind. You tread too near the flame that royalty can ignite."

The Phantom sat in silence, his face thoughtful, and Madame Giry spoke. "She says she loves him, and she wants to leave Raoul. But Erik will not allow her to come here. He feels she is safest on the estate."

"Little brother, this is a game of diabolical mayhem you are playing. Raoul must suspect that Philippe fell at your hands while you desperately attempted to persuade Christine to be your bride."

Erik's voice was calm, almost apologetic. "Truly, that was an accident. The Count's blood is not on my hands."

The Daroga could barely comprehend that they were sitting at a table casually discussing the nightmarish events of two-and-a-half years ago, like this type of horror was a common occurrence. His mind searched frantically for a change of subject, he needed time for his equilibrium to adjust, since apparently they'd all gone daft. "What did you do with those sad bits of furniture you had from your mother?"

"You cut me to the quick, since it's all I have of her," answered Erik.

"Sorry, no sense of hurt was intended."

"The furniture is still in my house by the lake."

"It's sealed up?" asked the Daroga.

"No the furniture is not sealed up. It's still sitting in the rooms."

"I wasn't referring to the furniture. I meant, is the house sealed up?"

"Yes, I don't go back there anymore, too many unhappy memories."

"So something above ground has engaged your interest enough to keep you from burrowing into the ground! Great!"

"Not exactly," Erik's left eyebrow rose in amusement.

"What part is 'not exactly'? You're tunneling again? Where?"

"The cemetery."

"The cemetery? Of course, why not, that makes perfect sense. You'll soon be dead when Raoul gets wind of all this, so why not fashion a special egress right into a tomb." He growled in frustration. Then it dawned on him how close he must be to the truth. "Whose tomb?" He shouted as his buttocks rose up off the seat.

Madame Giry intervened. "Shh, sit down. Maybe it would be better for you to mind your own business and not know about these affairs." She knew how to prick him for a more constructive response.

The Daroga pulled himself up officially. "It's much too late to cut me out now. Whose tomb have we tunneled to?"

Erik answered in a low, reverent voice, "Gustave Daae."

"Well, at least we're keeping it in the family," Madame Giry could hardly contain the giggle that was creeping to the surface. "Khalil, why don't you just admit that you're in this with us?"

The Daroga joined the conspiracy with a nonverbal response. He raised his hands to heaven in mock prayer, then took Madame's hand and kissed her fingers, and turning to Erik, put a hand on his shoulder and gave a fatherly squeeze.

Two nights later, The Count and Countess de Chagny attended a performance of '*Le Danse Macabre*' at the Opera House. The first act displayed the martyrdom of Hannah and her seven sons. Christine thought the little ballerinas very cleverly dressed in black, with luminescent white skeletons painted on the front and back of their costumes. In the second act, Black Death, played by the lead adult dancer, was to lead a troupe of souls from all walks of life down into hell. During the intermission, Raoul excused himself, saying he would fetch refreshments. Waiting in the hall the Persian saw his opportunity and entered their box in the grand tier, closing the door behind him with a defining click.

Christine was delighted to see his face. "Daroga, you are the picture of health! It has been too long, please, do be seated."

"For only a moment, Madame, and only to warn you that this is a perilous game you have undertaken."

Her face darkened and she withdrew her proffered hand. "We don't owe you an explanation. This time you should keep your distance, Daroga."

He feigned agreement. "I have no choice, Madame. One must always keep their distance where the Opera Ghost is concerned, or be forever holding their hand up at the level of their eyes to avoid strangulation."

"You don't fool me. You know he would never hurt you. Perhaps you're worried that I'm throwing away a perfectly good reputation, but I'm glad we've started this. Truly, I love him. I was his wife before I was Raoul's."

"I beg your pardon, Madame. I don't get your meaning."

"I gave myself to him body and soul by the lake. I agreed to be his living bride! He tricked me into leaving with Raoul. No doubt your influence played a heavy part in that decision. I was stupid and confused. I didn't understand that he had no idea how to court me, and I certainly had no concept of how to accept his idiosyncrasies. But I am not a naïve innocent any longer. Time has allowed me to comprehend that he poured himself out to me through his music. Had he known any other way he would have employed it. As it was, he risked everything to place his affections before me, even his friendship with you. I can not, and I will not, deny that I love him. I swear to you that I will do all I can to protect him, and keep harm away from his door."

She looked to be on the verge of tears, and the Daroga surprised himself by taking her hand to comfort her.

"Please, Daroga, you are his friend, don't cover my hopes with a cloud of despair. There will be enough worry ahead to fill an entire ship, but I won't throw these times with him away again. I would rather die."

He saw the firm resolution in her eyes, and knew something of the depth of her feelings. "All praise to *Allah*. I think I understand, Madame. I am stunned to hear your words this night. May you stay true to them, for his is a most constant and tender heart. I don't care to see him shattered ever again. The revenge I will administer to the one who carves another hole into his soul will be most distasteful. I assure you, it will be something akin to a slow boiling in oil. He lives today because his friends pleaded with him not to leave this world. The fiasco of stealing you only to present you back to Raoul, sent him to the very depths of hell." Christine's eyes grew round in revelation. The Daroga stood to leave, "But I am your friend too, and will help you where I can. I fear you are going to need all the assistance you can get."

"Thank you, Daroga, one adversary is quite enough."

"Indeed, you speak a most profound truth. It would be a grave mistake to underestimate a de Chagny." With that he slipped away out of the theater to return to the house on *Rue du Renard*.

3 *NASTY RUB*

Providence smiled on Christine and Erik over that first winter, for they managed to see each other once a week in the mausoleum. They varied the days and times somewhat, but she firmly believed no one really cared about her visits to a graveyard. The realm of household matters at the de Chagny estate appeared to move forward at its normal, mundane pace.

Inwardly, she felt her spirit happily nourished. She kept her feelings to herself and took no one in as a confidant. Insulated by this secretive bliss, she failed to appreciate what the staff of the chateau saw happening to their young mistress. Before their eyes a woman of regal beauty and bearing seemed to be returning from the grave. It was hard to miss the significance of the change, but for a time her husband succeeded.

The Count managed his lavish ancestral home through the talents of his financially astute secretary, Victor LaPointe. Raoul spent most of his time occupied with the building and selling of merchant ships to the Italian and English gentry. The trade routes to America and the Far East were booming, and money was there to be made if one applied oneself.

After his marriage to Christine, Raoul seemed content to abdicate his role as the most available of Parisian bachelors, and settle into the newer one of businessman. He made it a rule to never speak harshly to his wife. Believing her to be mentally fragile, he feared that any hint of the unfortunate events in her past would cause her to plunge into an emotional withdrawal. Shortly after their wedding it became obvious to him that his angelic young bride did not seem comfortable at soirees, so gradually the frivolous parties of the privileged failed to hold his interest as well. Instead, he began to enjoy sumptuous dinners with business associates, surrounded by their lively discussions regarding supply and demand. If she were asked, Christine would attend any function, or act as hostess for any dinner.

Whenever a guest inquired about her days performing at the Opera House, she artfully turned the subject to some current affair of the day. Certainly, no one was ever so rude as to inquiry about the Opera Ghost or his ghoulish dealings with Christine. At the time, every one in Paris assumed that the charred and divided body found by the police in the convoluted tunnels beneath the theater, was indeed that of the man masquerading around as the Phantom.

On the surface, the whole ghastly affair seemed far behind the young couple, but despite the positive nature of their outward lives, the new Countess became more and more disinterested in conversation and human involvement. She was most content to just sit quietly during waking hours. Her handmaid would talk her into weekly shopping trips, but as the months passed, her mistress seemed to grow further and further away, into some vacant inner world. And though Christine's pretty mouth would smile, her eyes belied a sadness, vast and growing, within her soul.

She became so dismal and anemic in the second year of their marriage that Raoul feared her pleasant, happy affect gone forever. He turned his attentions away from his vapid wife and focused on his business. In the initial days of December 1873, he finally noticed her emerging from her rooms and engaging the servants in conversation. Delighted to see her taking an interest in the life around them once more, he began to dote over her. The tall, blond haired Count showered Christine with clothes and trinkets. It seemed that whatever she desired he would bless and allow. At her request, he ordered Victor to have her rooms in the chateau completely redone with fresh wallpaper, drapes and furnishings – the very finest that could be obtained in the French world of the day. Everything was to be replaced except for her commodious mahogany bed. Victor was given explicit instructions from his employer to leave the canopied four-poster undisturbed.

Pleased to have a second chance at marital happiness, Raoul took great pride in mentally numbering his accomplishments. He lived on the magnificent estate of his ancestors, orchestrated a brilliant business steadily amassing him gain, and could bed his starry-eyed, delicious wife any time he wanted. She was finally back from whatever wasteland she'd thrown her mind into over these last two years! So what if she wasn't the most responsive of lovers? She always permitted him entrance into her quarters. He reminded himself that she'd been put through quite a lot: orphaned at the tender age of seven, sent to the opera to grow up in the ballet, and *Mon Dieu,* kidnapped at seventeen by a madman bent upon twisting her mind! No wonder she sometimes still seemed distant and in her own world. Whenever Raoul grew fretful over Christine's attentiveness to his needs, he would amuse himself hunting in the glorious woods around the chateau. As he rode back to his stables, with his gamekeeper towing whatever animals he had killed, he would assuage his doubts.

Do I truly have her heart? Yes, of course I do! She is my wife, the Countess de Chagny! She does love me. Look at her, she's happy once again. She wants to be here!

Everyone on staff at the chateau knew of the mistress' mental rebirth, and the renewed relationship between their employers, but the early weeks of winter ticked by without a hint of an announcement regarding the upcoming birth of an heir to the estate. The discreet servants were too respectful of their sweet Countess to mention it openly – they only whispered of the peculiarity to each other.

On a December morning, one week before Christmas, Raoul entered his well-appointed office on the ground floor of the mansion to find his secretary already hard at work. LaPointe was a thin man of medium height, with high cheekbones, dark reddish hair and a straight even smile. His penetrating brown eyes did not miss much around the chateau, but he was generally fair and even-handed with the staff. He had a fondness for rolls and butter, crimson cravats, and unexplained weekends away from the mansion and its grounds.

As Raoul entered, Victor pointed to an elaborately carved mahogany sideboard situated beneath a large painting of fruit and bright yellow flowers. "The coffee and crescent rolls are here, my Lord."

"Good," Raoul responded, moving toward the food. "And what of the shipyards today? Any news from our three builders down there? I'm particularly keen to know how we're progressing with our fast little honey of a ship with the three masts." He clapped his hands together, his fair angular face the very definition of confidence. "Delightful, the foremast and mainmast to be square-rigged and the mizzenmast fore-and-aft rigged. I'm tickled every time I think of her."

Victor continued to write in a journal. "I have arranged for a carriage to be brought around at eleven. I thought a surprise visit to the builders would keep them on their toes."

"Excellent idea!" Raoul picked up a linen napkin, but eyeing the prodigious plate of fruit depicted in the painting above, threw the napkin down impatiently. "Appetizing rolls, but why have we no cheese and fruit as well? Must I go to the kitchen to be properly fed?"

Victor, dressed in a dark brown doublet and pants, was quickly on his feet and as he came around his desk to head for the hallway, said to Raoul, "I'll have the cooks prepare a more satisfying tray."

"See to it, man, I'm famished today!" Taking his coffee to his desk, the Count hollered after him. "Let's go over the reports from the *Banque de France* this morning as well."

Victor returned in a few minutes carrying a tray laden with an abundance of fruit and cheese. "The butler will be right here with some fresh coffee." Setting the tray down on the sideboard, he walked over to the window and considered the frigid, frost-covered patios, and the leafless trees with their empty branches rocking in the winter breeze. The steel-gray sky hinted of coming snow. Taking out a handkerchief, he wiped the sweat off his hairless upper lip and moved back to the desks. "Did you find the bank reports in their folder?" The butler entered, and after replacing the coffee pot and creamer on the sideboard, stood waiting. Victor impatiently waved the man away. The servant bowed politely and left the room.

Raoul's head was in that very file. "Yes, they appear to be in good order. This is the largest amount we've had on deposit. Good job holding down the shipyard's expenses, Victor. You are most efficient! Shall I reward you by increasing your Christmas bonus?"

Victor brought a fresh cup of coffee to his employer and sat down in a chair beside the desk. "The amount of my bonus is left to your honest discretion. As you see from the pages before you, I have only your best interests at hand. May I take the liberty of discussing with you a matter that has come to my attention?"

Raoul looked up at his secretary and saw the blush across his face. *Damn weakling!* He couldn't control the subtle arrogance of his voice. "What? Get it out, Victor, before you choke on it. It can't be the stays in your collar turning you red."

"Everyone has noticed how much brighter the Countess' spirits seem these days, and no one can account for the lift in her mood." He cleared his throat. "I have inquired of all the maids and they tell me that her routines are all the same, as well as her preferences for food and clothes. Nothing seems altered before their eyes, except of course, the new decorations to be placed in her rooms. The change is rather peculiar...and a little suspicious. Of course, my concern is for you. We wouldn't want anything adverse under foot now that everything is moving so splendidly in our finances."

Ah, the asp slithers home. Raoul took a sip of coffee and smiled condescendingly at Victor. "Let's put it right out there, shall we? She doesn't have to answer to you, but let me reassure you that Christine is a respectful and loyal wife. If her outlook has improved it's to the benefit of the household and the business. Give her anything she wants." He rapped his knuckles sharply on the desk. "When I am away to England or Italy procuring contracts, you are to take full responsibility for seeing that she is cared for in every aspect. As long as she is doing well and her temperament remains happy, I will be satisfied."

"Yes, yes, her reputation is immaculate, and you may rely on me to see to her good affairs." Victor took out his handkerchief again and wiped his upper lip. "There is yet another matter I must bring to your attention. The members of the staff confide to me that sometimes they hear the most incredible singing coming from our woods. Strange don't you think? Perhaps our pines and maples have become infested with sirens ominously echoing each other. The staff tells me that they see dark foreboding shapes outside, like spirits moving through the trees, or crawling up the walls."

With his back straightening, Raoul demanded harshly, "Voices? They hear voices? Women's voices, right? You said sirens." Victor nodded. "Perhaps my wife has once again found the beauty of her voice! She was a marvelous performer, you know. She always loved the melodramatic, and the house staff has always been a childish, superstitious lot. Christine is not to be disturbed in any way. Do you hear me? You, and the rest of the staff, are to ignore her movements and her motives, or be excused from my employ!"

"But, I…"

"No buts, Victor. Christine is honor bound to her family responsibilities and she will perform them at my bidding, of that you may be assured. She leaves this house only a few times a week, and regularly one of those trips is a morbid visit to a cemetery. If my wife wants to brood over her dead father, you let me worry about it. And if her optimism has improved so much that she has reclaimed her voice, well that's just excellent!" *It thrills me to see her alive again, and these damn fools are not going to destroy it!* Raoul pictured his hands on her hips and her mound of feminine curls. *Damn, I want to go upstairs!* He rubbed the palm of his hand vigorously on the edge of his desk to intensify his thoughts. His next words were assertive and precise, but Victor detected the undertone of sexual tension they contained. "My God, man, she deserves her privacy. Don't pry!"

Seething with indignation at the rebuke, Victor itched to place a sound slap across Raoul's face. He reigned in the urge, opting to bide his time. To soothe Raoul he replied meekly, "I meant in no way to imply that Madame is disloyal or has a bad conscience. No indeed, she does not!"

Raoul was effectively placated. "Well then, this news of yours is all for the better. You're much too good a managing secretary to replace." He playfully wagged his finger at Victor. "But I will if I have to." Raoul suddenly smacked his hand against his thigh. "I have a wonderful idea. Have a harpsichord sent round from Michelin's. Communicate to them that they are to send the best they have as soon as possible. Expense is of no issue. Have it installed in the southern salon while Christine is out. Do you think she might be persuaded to do some shopping today or tomorrow?"

"I believe so, Sir. I'll speak with her personal maid."

"Good, I shall gift her once more with music. I want this to be a surprise for Christmas, so tell the staff to prepare for the instrument's arrival. Move furniture, clean, do whatever. I want it placed in a sunny spot. This time of year there's a good deal of warm light in that room. Call for the carriage now and be about this errand. I'll take the one at eleven to the shipyards and apprise you of the builders' progress."

Victor was up and moving to the door to do his employer's bidding as Raoul checked his watch. *Eight-thirty...she might not even be dressed yet!* He took the steps two at a time and knocked at Christine's door. *No answer!* He tried the knob and it remained fast, so he took a master key from his pocket and entered. He found his wife in the bath, with her personal maid, Justine, waiting close by with a robe and heated towels. Raoul dismissed the girl, saying he needed time to speak with his wife and would call when he was ready to have her return.

Christine sat in the bubbles listening to him, wondering what he could possibly want to discuss. Usually at this time he was down in the office immersed in business with Victor. When Raoul started to pull off his jacket and remove his boots, she held no doubts about what he was after. "Do you want me out of the tub?"

"Well I can't do you properly from here can I?"

She arose, bubbles clinging to her curves; the sight drove his appetite further. He was quickly down to his pants and socks. As she reached for one of the towels, he said, "Don't bother." He lifted her into his arms and carried her to the bed before she could measure out an appropriate delay tactic. Dispensing with foreplay he climbed on top of her. He was moving too quickly for her to cope well, and she shivered involuntarily, wanting to crawl away. Thinking she was chilled, he offered reassurance. "I'll warm you up, give me one minute." *Be my wife, Christine! Be my wife!* His hands went around her buttocks and pulled her to him.

She tried to invoke an image of Erik. None would come to her. It was as if her angel, having no place in this act, had somehow lapsed into oblivion. Left alone to handle Raoul's exuberant aggression, her mind went blank. Had she willed it, she could have wrapped her arms around him in an embrace, but her limbs were oddly heavy – outside her power to control them. They remained immobile as he took her. The bath oils made her slick so there was no pain, despite his abruptness. He was forceful and forgot her, thinking only of his absolute delight at being once again inside his Countess. After a minute, he removed himself and rolled her over onto her abdomen. Drawing her slender frame up onto her knees, he steadied her position with his hands and entered her from behind. Disheartened and invaded, she buried her face into the perfumed pillow, grateful for the lack of participation required of her.

A moment later, he withdrew and placed his finger in her, twirling it in circles. Then sticking it in his mouth, he savored her essence. "The bath makes you taste so sweet."

Resigned to the degradation, Christine folded her arms beneath her pillow. "I'm glad I please you, Raoul." Her tone was flat, distant, but she was compliant.

He separated her cheeks and inspected her openings, so inviting. The timber of his hard mast pulsated, clamoring for attention like an insolent toddler. He took his thumb and index finger and pressed diligently at its base to calm it. *Good, let's not do this too fast. I've got time.* She was drying quickly, but the oil from the bath stood out in little beads in the hollows of her spine and neck. He rubbed his hand across her rump, then brought his fingers to her most tender circle. *Mine, all mine!*

She stiffened and squeezed her eyes shut. "Raoul, don't!" But he was already there, dragging himself in and out, moaning loudly. Christine refused to scream. Denouncing him, she told herself she would not permit a single tear to escape from her eyes. She tried to take refuge in the thought that this ordeal would soon be over. She was wrong.

He pulled out again and rolled her to her back. Still on his knees he leaned over her. Running his hands from her throat to her *mons veneris,* he paused to play in her hair. He took her breast in his mouth, sucking hard and flicking her nipple with his tongue. When he bit down on her areola, she finally attempted to shove him off. *At last, she shows some spirit!* "Sorry, I know, too rough." Smirking with satisfaction, he moved her arms aside as if she were a doll, and entered her again. He began to sweat with the effort of doing her in a proud and proper fashion.

Because she didn't want him and she wasn't aroused, she became dry, making coitus uncomfortable. She ordered herself to relax and placed her arms around his back.

"That's it, Christine, sail with me. Are you almost there?"

How in the hell do I...? She tried to fake some audible pleasure, but only high-pitched, little whines issued from her throat, and he still didn't climax. *The man is a damn ox!*

He put his arms under her back and brought his hands up and over her shoulders, securing her in a human harness for his next strategic maneuver. With every inward thrust he pushed her torso and pelvis down onto him. The heavy sturdy bed began to rock, its joints creaking with the aggressive, pounding motions.

She felt as if she were being devoured by Satan's phallus. This form of intercourse went on for several minutes. Christine lost her restraint. Mentally pleading for a *discant finale,* she angled her face away from him, painful tears soaking the pillow. He didn't notice, and she doubted that he would have stopped even if he'd seen them. Finally, blessedly, he shoved himself into her as deeply as he could, and expelled a muffled scream into her pillow. With a playful, satisfied snort, he jumped up and went to her bathroom to wash. She pulled the covers over her head, curling into a ball on her side. The entire ordeal had taken only twelve minutes. Twelve minutes of sheer, goring hell.

In a few minutes he returned, buttoning his jacket. "Madame, I thank you. That was a most exhilarating experience. You're an extraordinary lover." He reached over and pulled the downy quilt off her head. Kissing the top of her hair, he added, "I wish I could stay so that we could have at it again, but I've matters to attend to at the shipyards. We can meet later tonight." He kissed her crown once more and started to leave. Pausing at the door with his back to her, "I'll send the maid in to warm the bath for you."

From beneath the sheet she insisted, "No, don't. I want to rest a bit."

"Yes, after that who could blame you." He opened the door and disappeared.

Feeling loathsome and unclean, she got up and went to the bath. The water was cool but she stepped in, lowering herself down gingerly. She was sore and positive he'd rubbed her raw. With her body placed in the cleansing ablutions, she allowed a sob to escape. *Oh, Erik…if you only knew.* She submerged her entire head, knowing she would never tell him what kind of wife Raoul fancied. She wanted Erik to be her husband of his own choice, not because she had manipulated him by demanding to be removed from this physical sorrow. *How? How do I get him to say 'leave'?* The problem seemed insurmountable. She emerged from the water and hid her face in the wash sponge.

As quietly as a church mouse, Justine entered the bathroom and knelt beside her mistress. One look into the sorrowful eyes of the Countess told her that the Lord of the Manor had brutalized her. He ruled with too strong a French hand – never asking, only taking and expecting cooperation all along the way. Silently Justine took the sponge and began to wash Christine's shoulders. When the wounded doe let out a deep reflexive sigh, the maid leaned in closely, whispering into her mistress' ear the details of a trick that could be used during sex to quickly satisfy the Count, and bring to an end each sadistic session. Amazed and enlightened, Christine took Justine's palm and pressed it to her lips in gratitude.

Raoul was gone all that day and Christine took an early supper in her room, telling the staff she was weak with a headache and wanted to be left alone. She prayed for the tenderness to ease and slept fitfully in naps throughout the night. In the morning she awoke before dawn and left with her maid, saying she would take breakfast in Paris and do some shopping. She did not return until late afternoon, having spent the greater part of the day at the dressmaker's. Her plan was to hurry upstairs to her room, complaining of fatigue. But as they entered through the front doors she was greeted by six of the servants standing in a formal reception line. She willed a degree of gaiety into her voice. "What are you all doing here in such a perfect row?"

In answer, they all smiled respectfully and bowed or curtsied. Raoul stood at the end of the line and addressed her. "My dearest wife, we are all here to witness your expression at our new arrival."

"What new arrival?"

"The one in the southern salon." Raoul brandished his arm toward the room just down the hall.

Christine moved to where her husband stood and passively took his arm, allowing him to lead her to their favorite winter gathering place. The house staff followed, like ducklings trailing in cue behind their mother. The first thing she saw as they approached the room was the head butler, standing very erect and holding a tray with glasses of sherry and a cigar for Raoul. The sherry was given to each individual as they entered the double doorway of a room saturated with the fragrant, resinous smell of Swiss pine. When everyone had a drink she was asked to look into the corner by the fireplace. There stood the great, ten-foot Christmas tree, decorated in an aura of multicolored ribbons and delicate ornaments, but no sooner had her eyes seen the conifer, then they fell on the beautiful instrument beside it. Cream colored, awash in elaborate painted flowers, its music stand and keyboard cover open to greet her. She walked over to it slowly, allowing her fingers to brush the keys.

Standing behind her, Raoul had the butler assist him with cutting the end of his cigar. He lit it, inhaled deeply, and then allowed himself the prestigious moment of bestowing the gift. "Merry Christmas to you, my darling wife. Merry Christmas! What do you think of it?"

She pressed a key and the full tone of its note vibrated in the room. "It's beautiful and amazing. Is it mine?" She turned to Raoul, "You are so thoughtful. I never dreamed I'd have a harpsichord, but I don't know how to play it."

Grinning at his great triumph, Raoul answered, "Then we shall hire you a teacher. We'll make an inquiry at Michelin's and engage the most talented individual they recommend."

It seemed to the staff that they had never seen Christine's face radiate as it did at that moment. Her eyes danced. Lifting their sherry they all toasted, "*Salute*". The Countess downed her entire drink in two continuous swallows.

Christine secretly hoped that in some wondrous, holiday miracle, Michelin's would send Erik to teach her. Disguise had never been an issue with him. He was proficient at the organ, the piano, and the violin – surely the harpsichord would fall into his repertoire. To her aggravation she was unable to formulate a discrete method of inquiry that would not raise an unwanted, questioning eyebrow. She strolled along the hallways of the house, resolving to discover exactly how many instruments Erik could play. *What other talents does he possess?* She knew he was an architect, a ventriloquist, a magician, a composer, and painter. *I wonder if he cooks or tends a small garden? All I do is sit around in my finery and shop, my theatre career...gone,* she snapped her fingers and her thoughts returned to Erik, as they always did. Perhaps her greatest function in life was to earnestly love the ephemeral and accept her polyandrous role.

The teacher Michelin's sent to train Christine was a young Jewish man named Benjamin DeVille. He stood five-foot eight with curly dark hair, had a neatly trimmed beard, and wore a dark blue velvet suit with a vest of blue brocade beneath. She liked his sparkling eyes and the way he held his hat below his waist as he introduced himself. He was obviously a modest man, quiet and well mannered. She ushered him into the southern salon where she reviewed her background as an artist with him. He told her that his specialty was keyboard instruments, although he enjoyed playing a variety of others, and that he did a little composing in his spare time. Teaching seemed to come easily to him. He was sure she would do exceptionally well, since she already possessed a solid foundation of musical knowledge. They went to the harpsichord and he showed her where the notes were to be found, and how to position her hands. He gave her simple scales and hand movements to practice everyday, and in an hour that seemed to fly by, he was finished and excused himself.

She stayed at the harpsichord for another thirty minutes and then suddenly felt like a walk on the grounds. The butler assisted her into her cloak and offered to have one of the footmen accompany her. She thanked him and explained that she wanted to venture out on her own. Asking where she might find the de Chagny's private cemetery, she was told that it was located approximately two miles to the north. If she followed a footpath that entered the woods directly off the north wing she would walk right to it. The family had placed the cemetery in an isolated spot, allowing privacy for the mourners, not at the top of a hill like many graveyards. The butler told her to look for several black metal hitching posts at the entrance to the footpath. The family had an old, out of use, tradition of tying their horses and walking to the graves out of respect.

"How would a hearse enter to bring in a coffin?" she asked.

"It's not reachable from the main road in any direct manner, but there's an access road to it. There are access roads to all parts of the estate. Madame will find it if she hunts for it. Are you sure you don't want an escort?"

"I'm safe on the grounds, am I not?"

"Oh yes, Madame, quite safe."

"Then I'll explore a little." She took a bottle of port from the kitchen and left by the north side of the house to find the graves. In ten minutes she was to the edge of the woods. She turned to look at the mansion, estimating that she was just about where the servant had directed, but she couldn't see any hitching posts. Scanning carefully, she spotted them – six metal statues of stable boys holding up rings in their hands for horses' reins. Standing about eight feet back in the brush, they were nearly covered by overgrown branches and decaying leaves. She oriented herself by studying the perspective she had of the chateau from this spot. Identifying her bedroom windows on the second floor toward the front, she visually followed the driveway downhill to the public road, about a half-mile away. She tromped into the trees. Deliberately crackling leaves beneath her feet, she searched for the path but was unable to locate it. Returning to the metal boys she hunted twenty paces to their left, and then to their right without success. *Obviously no one has been here for a very long time.*

She stepped backward onto the winter lawn and then she saw it, almost imperceptible, but there, an arch formed by some of the tree branches to the right of the posts. She walked straight to it and picking up a branch with dead leaves started sweeping. The dirt path appeared. She walked and swept, walked and swept, and was soon out of sight from the mansion. Coming to an opening where the path was clearly visible, she listened to the chorus of wind gusting in the trees. The dappled sunlight that hit the pines and lit the ground in patches somehow imparted a sense of belonging. Taking in the grandeur of the woods, her eyes came to rest on a deer with a majestic set of horns. It stood grazing and turned its great liquid eyes to her for a second, before springing off into the woods. She wondered how she had managed to come so close to it, and thought about what direction the breeze might be in. *How would one tell?* The smell of the winter woods filled her nostrils and enticed her onward. With her spirit stirred by the adventure, she looked to the sky. The sun was still high above in a nearly cloudless arena. She came to a halt when she saw that the path traveled between several, thirty-foot smooth granite stones. Coming straight up from the ground each monolith was a proud colossus of nature. She moved between them in silent admiration, her hand passing over their wind polished sides.

Passing the guardians, she entered a large clearing and found the graves. She started counting and finished when she got to fifty-three. Centuries of de Chagny's were laid to rest here. There were no mausoleums, no walls, just this field of tall grass filled with tombstones and grave-covers. It seemed almost a natural part of things, the cycle of life. She began to walk the rows and read the names. She came to a tall headstone with a tree carved into its side, its branches protecting the name inscribed below:

PHILIPPE GEORGES MARIE COMTE DE CHAGNY
APRIL 2, 1830 - MARCH 3, 1871
A BROTHER GONE TOO SOON

She stood looking at the grave of Raoul's brother and uncorked the bottle of port. As she raised it to her lips she heard from behind, "*Requiescat in pace.*" She smiled broadly, the words had been sung in his irresistible voice. The man who had mended the breach in her heart was present once again. She turned to see her dashing Phantom in full black funeral attire, cape blowing to the side, white mask over his face, left hand resting on the hilt of his sword, the other placed lightly on the front of a black brocade vest. What a fine figure he cut, dressed for evening in the middle of the tombs.

"Wine, maestro?" She offered the bottle to him.

"Please, after you." He stepped forward. Drinking deeply, she wiped her lips with the back of her hand and passed the bottle to him, but before he lifted it to his own mouth, he poured a little on Philippe's grave. "*Requiescat in pace,*" he repeated and then drank, but he held the final swallow in his mouth and came up to her. One arm went around her waist and the other to the back of her neck. He lowered his lips to hers, supporting her head with his hand as he filled her mouth with the wine from his own. She swallowed and as she did his tongue briefly entered her mouth. "*Sui generis,*" he breathed into her ear. "There is no other like you." He pulled away from her, and a fleeting expression of disappointment fell across her countenance. It did not go unnoticed by him.

She longed to be back in his arms. "How did you know I was here?"

"Music and **you** are my business." Effortlessly he returned and swept his cape around her shoulders. Hidden in its folds he kissed her deeply and swayed with her as if the cemetery were filled with some unearthly music only he could hear. "The purchase of a grand harpsichord does not go unnoticed among musicians in Paris. I know Benjamin DeVille, and he told me that today was your inaugural lesson. I called you from the mansion with my mind. You might say I lured you here, but I offer no apology. You seemed most determined once you started out."

She cuddled into him, resting her head on the strength of his chest, feeling the protection and warmth of the Angel of Music.

The sound of a hawk screaming in flight flashed through his mind, and he brought the imaginary orchestra to a discordant halt. "What's wrong, Christine?"

She allowed herself a few more seconds of his blessed comfort and then separated herself from him. "Nothing, all is well. I felt exhilarated by my first lesson and was glad to come out for a walk." He detected the sadness in her voice, but did not acknowledge it. "This is a very deserted spot," she commented.

"You have no idea," he said. "Come with me back into the woods, I want to show you something." They left the tombs and went east, away from the sun and into the trees. After a few minutes they came upon another colossus of stone, but shorter, maybe twenty feet in height. As they rounded it, they stood on the banks of a pond. It looked to have been undisturbed for decades. The Phantom's black horse was tied to a nearby tree. He went to stroke its neck and gave the steed a lump of sugar he produced from his pocket.

"What a beautiful spot," she exclaimed. "How did you find it?"

"I've had many an occasion to roam around and explore after you moved in. I've never seen anyone here. If you like, I'll make a firepit, this can be a place for us to meet. Learn to ride a horse, Christine. These grounds will speak to your soul."

Certainly the house doesn't, she thought.

Standing behind him she touched his shoulder and he turned to hug her again. The only place she felt absolved and truly pure was in the refuge of these arms. She would have been content to stay in them and just relax, but he vetoed the pleasure. "You should return to the mansion. It's your first time out on your own, they're probably watching, anxiously waiting for you to pop back out of the woods." He rubbed his hands across her back and kissed her cheek. "Come on, let go of me. I'll walk you to where you entered."

When they parted she felt her heart almost ripped out from within her. There would be no Christmas presents between them, no letters or notes, nothing that could be traced, only these moments, these shreds of time as she had called them, little chips of castoff tile to form the mosaic of their life.

Feel the pain. Relish the pain, she told herself. She knew he watched her as she crossed the lawn, but she did not look back. Her hands were clasped behind her and she swung the bottle gently by its neck like a pendulum, creating an imaginary smile for him. *Learn to ride a horse!*

Erik walked back to Philippe's grave and sat down to converse with the dead. "Sorry for the intrusion, Count, you understand. You were a man once, a good man. You sought to protect your brother, and your family name. No honorable man would have done less. I wish I had a brother half as good as you. Raoul must find you a difficult example to follow. Do you know that I lived for a time without any conscience at all?" He reached up reassuring himself that the mask was still in place. At times it became so comfortable he couldn't perceive its presence, especially if he focused on a subject, as he did now. "It seems, Philippe, that when we murder we change events forever. But there's all kinds of wrongful death, isn't there? She was dying slowly without me, and I seem to be simply incapable of leaving her alone. She made a tomb of every place she sat, while I was so lovesick I crawled around like a rat, seeking whatever crumbs of her I could manage."

The word rat reminded him of a dungeon in Persia. A distasteful memory, unbidden and unwelcome, intruded into his consciousness – one of him placed in shackles and whipped with his unholy face pressed against a sooty wall. His mouth and left face contorted in the pain of the vision. He wrung his right hand around his left wrist. To this day it still ached. The sound of the jailors' laughter flooded his mind, along with the smell of their excited sweat as they snapped the lash across his body.

"Beaten, but not broken," he proclaimed. "There must be something truly wrong with me. I feel absolutely no remorse over coming back into her life. She is like succor, so what am I to do, Philippe? What am I to do?"

The wind picked up again, an ungodly fuming in the trees. Retreating from nature's grating rendition of mocking females wailing in ecstasy, he returned to his horse and left the grounds for Paris. Christine was already at the horse corals, talking to the head stableman about learning to ride, and a spineless Victor LaPointe stood at the office window spying on her from the edge of the draperies.

When Christine entered the house she went to the main foyer. There she began to play one of the several odd games she employed to help her cope with the long abstinences from Erik. Because the main staircase had so many polished marble steps, she used them as a mental journal. She stood on the floor at the bottom of the stairs and relived the shopping day in mid-October when he appeared to her in the street. The first step represented their first meeting at the tomb. She would move to it and recall its vivid details in her mind, the second step – their second meeting, and so on. Today's experience of him placed her on the tenth step. *Ten meetings in as many weeks!* She eyed the staircase curving upward and to her right in its ostentatious splendor. *May it be so*, she thought. On the eleventh step she sat down and placing her face in her hands, remembered the week of her marriage with all the specifics she could rally, her marriage, not to Raoul, but to Erik.

The staff watched her discreetly whenever she performed this ritual. They called it 'The Time of the Pearls', because the head butler, who had a brother working in a jewelry shop, estimated the amount of time she spent standing on each step was about the length of time it took to bore a pearl, polish it, and string it onto a strand. Justine called the last step – the one Christine chose to sit on, 'the clasp'. The servants had no idea how close to the truth they were, or how much this strange way of moving up the stairs intrigued Victor's officious imagination.

4 TORMENTING REVELATION

Hope and wishful yearning motivated Christine to write the following veiled words on the morning of Christmas Eve, 1873. She sent the letter by messenger, along with a crate of oranges, to her former ballet teacher and sponsor, Madame Giry, knowing that amber eyes would read it.

Dearest Friend,
I write these words to you in the most thoughtful of hours as the winter sunshine graces the lawns about me, warming my heart. Historically we have shared so much. Certainly any life could be rationally measured by the number of days and weeks within it, but what if we strove to perceive our existence in a different manner? What if we considered each singular conscious moment separately, the way a dying man does? If we could gather those moments like jewels, and string them one upon the next to form the necklace of a lifetime, no doubt we would be boggled by its length and hopefully by its beauty. My harpsichord teacher tells me there are mystics who endeavor to live in this fashion. In the space of each and every moment, they renew themselves to inner peace and joy, while still remaining acutely aware of the physical world surrounding them. In this contemplation they seek to bind themselves to the very Seat of Love within the universe - a worthy endeavor, indeed. I ask you, if genuine love runs afoul of moral law who among us is qualified to judge its merits? Rather than lay judgment to it, would it not be better to place that love on a higher spiritual plane and simply acknowledge its presence here upon the earth? For is it not true, that real love is a scarce thing, and its occurrence to be prized and celebrated?

Undeniable love is a thing mankind strives to extinguish, therefore it warrants diligent protection. I am interested in your thoughts. I send you my exceptional fondness and hopes for your continued health in the New Year.

As always I remain your devoted student,
Christine de Chagny

Sitting in his apartment Erik broke the letter's seal and carefully studied her message. His fingers traced her pen strokes as he memorized and considered her words. *How eloquently she states her case.* For a few minutes he allowed himself to toy with the idea of going directly to the chateau and permanently stealing her away to some far-off land, but the image of adapting to a totally new culture broke through his wishful hopes, forcing a more honest evaluation upon him. He knew himself to be mentally unbalanced, and if provoked, ruthless and unpredictable. The thought of a lifetime spent hiding from Raoul angered him, and he sincerely wanted Christine to have her current position of wealth and prestige. He understood his need for the stability of Paris – it provided a place for him to make a living.

As if to torment him, the Daroga's words rang out in uncelebrated chorus. *This is a game of utter mayhem!* In one motion he withdrew a dagger from a shoulder scabbard and without sighting it, threw it firmly into the kitchen doorframe. Resolving to keep her as safe as he possibly could, even though he knew full well he no longer possessed the strength to resist her. Weekly visits with her barely satisfied his urges, and the idea of sharing her spirit, and her body, with Raoul was evolving into a most tender boil. One pressing to be relieved.

Sensing their peril under the laws of church and state, only served to heighten their needs. Like Adam and Eve indulging in the succulent tastes of the forbidden fruit, they loved each other with great abandon at their next meeting. But in the end the reality of their imminent danger won the day. As rational beings, they were compelled into difficult discussion. They agreed to institute Madame Giry's suggestion and designed a simple signal should Christine need to alert him. Her rooms in the chateau were on the second floor, in the northwest corner of the north wing. The large window in front of her desk faced a busy road coming from Paris, the windows nearby gave her a view of the woods on the north side of the mansion. If the curtains of her desk window remained closed in the daylight hours, events in the chateau required she meet with him at her father's tomb the following day. If they remained closed with an unlit candelabra on the sill, she had left the house of immediate necessity and Erik should fetch her at an agreed upon spot. She was to walk out of the mansion wearing warm clothes and carrying nothing. Once a day, usually in the late afternoon, either Madame Giry or Erik would take a carriage ride and check the desk window.

Despite the comforting knowledge that a signal was in place, the consequences of breaking the stringent moral order were proving an odious pressure on Christine's mind. She feared the retribution that would come to them if they were caught. She longed to end this sham with Raoul and spend her days at Erik's side. But how does one change so strong and tenacious a heart as the Phantom's? She had no idea, and found herself at a loss to formulate a tactic until a day in mid-January when she sat at her harpsichord with Benjamin. Her mind had been continually wandering away from her instructor's words, willfully leaving her lesson to mull over Erik's immutable decisions.

When Benjamin repeated a finger transgression to her twice, and saw her determined eyes focused somewhere on the wall, he patiently touched her motionless hand. "If I may be so bold, Countess."

"Please, call me Christine."

"Christine, you are not here in this room today, are you?"

"Forgive me, Benjamin. No, my mind lies with a friend and his troubled thoughts."

Benjamin looked at the frown of her mouth and the way her eyebrows were drawn together. *Perhaps she refers to her own mind.* "I have an uncle who helps people whose thoughts disturb them. He is a physician of sound repute, but he employs a technique he saw demonstrated in a carnival act. I know that sounds odd, but he uses it to help treat his patients. It's called hypnotism."

"Can you explain it to me?"

"Won't the house staff think it peculiar that no sound is coming from this instrument?"

"Why don't you play, and talk to me while you demonstrate."

"All right." He renewed the music with his own fingers, but played a simple soft tune so that he could talk to her. "My uncle saw it done as a young doctor and was most impressed with its effects. He says there are many components to the human mind that we do not understand well. During the performance a hypnotist brought people from the audience up on stage and verbally drew them into a state of profound relaxation. Their ability to make selective judgments was bypassed. They could no longer distinguish between hot and cold, sweet and sour, large and small. My uncle thought it was a trick and said so…quite loudly. The conjurer called him to the stage and invited him to assess the condition of each individual's mind. He discovered that although they appeared to be in a trance, they could respond to him normally and appropriately, but each was highly opened to suggestion. He immediately saw the therapeutic benefit to this technique. A person could be brought to review a past traumatic experience and their perceptions about it altered. Someone who felt anxious, subjugated by terrors, could be guided to lessen the terror's destructive hold, and learn to function normally. Sometimes he uses a drug, like laudanum, or a little alcohol, to help the patient relax, but often he achieves positive effects without any adjunct at all. He says that hypnosis opens up the patient to a hastened healing."

Christine placed her hand over his, stopping the music. "What is your uncle's name?"

"Abraham DeVille."

"Is he here in Paris?"

"Yes, he has an office in the home where we live together. It's not far from the boat docks in the industrial section. He says he likes the activity of all the commerce, but I know of another reason why he's there. He's…"

Christine was already on her feet. "Please, take me to him right now. I will triple your payment for this afternoon. It's urgent that I speak with your uncle."

"You don't have to give me more money. I'll gladly take you to meet him. He loves people." Christine had already retrieved Benjamin's coat from the sofa and taken hold of his arm. "My hat," he exclaimed, hastily grabbing it as she hustled him out the door.

By February of 1874, Erik's physical health and mental outlook had greatly improved. He practiced some form of calisthenics everyday, and authored musical plays prolifically under the pen name E. D'Angelus. Often, when the ballet lessons in the studio below were concluded, and the young students whisked to their respective homes by their parents, he would sing to Christine in his apartment. Rather he would sing to the many drawings of her that filled his walls, or to the life sized mannequin he had created of her. The 'immobile Christine' sat at the table in a dress of silk indigo with a matching lace apron and a cup of coffee in front of her. Her delicate porcelain face offered up an approving smile for him to bask in at any hour of the day or night.

He and Madame Giry purchased the building on *Rue du Renard* while the good Madame was still employed at the Opera House. The sturdy, stucco-over-brick French provincial structure appealed to them because of its ample three floors of space, and its shallow, second floor balconies. The shuttered Palladian windows of the home were modest in size and easy to manipulate. Each contained twenty-four panes of glass held fast by sturdy metal strips. The arched top of the second floor windows broke symmetrically through the unadorned cornice of the steep, gray tiled roof. The dormered windows of the third floor, which was actually the attic, were evenly placed across the front and rear of the home, and would afford an accessible exit route for any fleeing wraith. A basement ran underground the entire expanse of the dwelling, and a detached carriage house stood slightly recessed and off to the right. Three stone steps with wrought iron side rails decorated in acorns and leaves led to the centrally placed front porch. The entrance was a sturdy rectangular door of oak and beveled glass, set within an arched opening artistically trimmed with decorative slate. Should the unavoidable need for the Opera Ghost and Madame to permanently leave the theater ever arise, Erik and the Daroga had prepared the home by remodeling it into a suitable residence for an artist in need of concealment from the law and his collaborating friend, the dance teacher. The two men converted the first floor into a proper ballet studio, the second into a spacious apartment for Madame, and the third into Erik's personal domain. In early April of 1871, amid the turmoil created by the police and the irate managers over the disappearance of a performer and the myriad of accidents blamed on the Phantom, they faked Erik's death and occupied the home full time. With Erik safely removed from the fray at the theater, Madame promptly resigned from the Opera House and opened the ballet studio, where she began to enroll young female students. She tried never to speak of the occupant on the third floor of the dwelling. If pressed, she would simply say that the kind gentleman living above was her half-brother, a recluse, overcome by a lingering childhood disease.

On a chilled, gray afternoon in February, Madame Giry returned from her carriage ride outside of Paris and immediately proceeded up the back staircase to the third floor apartment. She knocked on the door in a prescribed, coded knock. Without hesitation, Erik opened the door and welcomed her in. Taking the coat from off her shoulders he hung it on a coat rack and escorted her to a cushioned sofa. The way she urgently pressed his hand as she sat down told him that she had news, but he was not inclined to pressure her by asking. All things would come forth in time. The loyalty and friendship Madame had bestowed upon him over the years was priceless, and meant the world to him. They were second in value only to his feelings toward Christine. He might very well be insane, but he knew who cared for him, and he unabashedly loved them back. He asked if she would enjoy a glass of cognac and she accepted. As he stepped from the room to his kitchen area, she looked through the open door of the *salle de bains*. The only mirror he owned hung there, draped with an opaque white cloth. After he returned with the cognac, he settled onto the chair opposite her – stretching out his long legs and folding his hands across his abdomen. She was never prone to idle chatter, so he simply waited as she sipped the warmth held in the glass.

Madame spoke first, "Are you calm, with your mind in order?"

"*Oui,* I am in a state of profound serenity."

"The signal to meet her tomorrow is present in Christine's front window. I had the driver go by twice. It is plainly there." Before she completed her sentence he was already on his feet and heading to his heavier coat. Anticipating his immediate departure at hearing the news, Madame hurried to the door. Using her entire five-foot four-inch frame, she tried to fill the exit before speaking again. "This is only a signal to meet with you, she is not in peril." Placing his second arm into his coat, her words were enough to give him pause. "She wants to tell you something special, not leave the chateau. She is not in danger so don't place her there. She needs nothing more than to speak with you."

"Do you mind if I check it?"

"No, not at all. Let's take a carriage ride and go together."

"No, I'll go alone, by horse. It's quicker. I'll be back before the moon's risen to mid-sky."

Madame moved gracefully to the side allowing him room to pass. "Take a scarf at least."

He swept one around his neck and pinched her check with a smile. Kissing her forehead, he hid the tenseness in his gut. "Louisa, always the fret. Please don't worry, I'll be careful and swift. I promise."

By the time the winter sun stretched low into the sky, beckoning on the tendrils of night, he stood in the woods to the north of her rooms. He could not see her inside, but their signal was in plain sight. Noting well the hour, he decided to move around to the eastern side of the mansion where the woods lay closer to the dining rooms. Like a panther quietly stalking its prey with ease of facility and skill, he took up a new position, invisible to the windows of the chateau. From this new vantage point she was poignantly visible, sitting at a dining room table, apparently disinterested in food.

As Christine attempted to take supper, she gazed listlessly outside, studying the geometric gardens and the lawns beyond them. The patches of snow under the bushes and in the corners of the lower balustrades foretold of a frosty night ahead. In her mind she wondered if he had seen her signal. Surely he must have, but how could she know for certain? *Tell yourself that you will see him tomorrow. Be confident. Trust him.*

Suddenly filled with an urge to move, she pushed away from the table and told the butler standing discreetly by the wall, that perhaps she would catch some fresh air before the sun set completely. Fetching her cloak and gloves, the servant stood waiting to escort her.

"I'll just go out for a few minutes. I'll be fine." She walked onto the stone patio and watched her breath suspended in the air. Reaching out like a child she tried to touch it, but the mist dissipated too quickly. Her next breathe had no sensation whatsoever on her hand, and she wondered what it was that Erik's fingertips sensed when he placed them in front of her nose. Tucking her fingers into her leather gloves, she spotted the walkways cleared of snow and decided to walk toward the central fountain. The air felt crisp and clean. It flowed like cold silk into her lungs. She heard her name sung ever so softly, its two syllables enticing, almost imperceptible. Sitting down on a stone bench she tried to pinpoint where the sound came from. Knowing that she must maintain her posture and show no surprise or excitement should anyone from the house be watching, she straightened her back and made herself appear perfectly relaxed. They'd played this game many times in the Opera House – she loved the memories it evoked.

From the woods to her right a flock of birds took off in hurried flight. Her eyes studied the trees at their trunks. *Yes!* She could see the Phantom's outline. He appeared as only the extended side of an oak, but it was her love. He had disturbed the birds to alert her of his position. She understood that the Opera Ghost was allowing himself to be seen, so she shielded her fingers and pointed to the south end of the lawns where a boathouse stood near the water. She got up, stretched leisurely and walked over the frozen brown grass to the boathouse.

Standing at the water's edge, she did not look behind her as she heard his alluring voice again. "Christine, what is wrong?"

"Nothing really, I'll see you tomorrow at two and tell you of my news."

"Do not ask me to wait! You have never used the signal before and I know you all too well. I entreat you to tell me." His melodious and princely voice was like an aromatic balm, so soothing, so compelling in the deepening shadows of twilight that she almost gave in.

She dug a thumbnail into her palm to break the spell. "Tell me why the dogs are not barking their heads off at your presence so close to the house?"

His lips vibrated as he blew out a frustrated sigh. "As you wish. I am no stranger to your dogs, Madame. They know me very well, as I have fed them many times."

At this news she spun around and saw him in the doorway of the boathouse. "What?"

"I am the simpleton they call George. Victor LaPointe hired me to work when your groundskeeper is away for personal reasons. By the way, you don't pay me very much."

She pinched her nose, stifling a laugh into her glove and turned to face the water, appearing to just be enjoying the view, but actually savoring the thought that he was apparently about these grounds quite often. "Is there nothing locked away from you?"

Christine began to speak to the ripples on the water, as if telling them a splendid secret. "I'm in the beginning of a pregnancy and since I know well the last time Raoul touched me, I am absolutely sure, beyond all doubt, that this is your baby." Only the wind whispered in her ears. He offered no reply. "Did you hear me, Erik? Please answer me."

"Come to me."

She rotated slowly to face the entrance of the boathouse expecting to see his smile, but the doorway was empty.

"Over here." His voice could have easily been mistaken for only the air swirling in the trees around them.

Her eyes looked to the stand of pines at the right of the boathouse. The wind rocked their branches in a requiem for winter. With her heart thumping out of rhythm, she walked in the fading light straight to him, stopping six feet from where he stood. "Can you hear the pleading *tremolo* of my heart, Dark Angel? I want to leave Raoul and come to you so that we can raise this child together."

He did not touch her, but caressed her with his eyes. "*Enceinte!* Would that I could hold you, my love, but the butler stands even now on the patio looking for you, and I dare not place the mother of my child in jeopardy. It is taking all my control not to gather you in my arms and let my lungs sing out in joy. Please, keep our appointment tomorrow. I will be there sharply at the hour you bid me to come. Pick up the stone at your feet and walk away from me, back to the house."

She looked down. In front of her shoes lay a white piece of granite the size of a small lemon, worn smooth and round by the waters of time.

His voice implored her, "Wait. Hesitate a little before you leave me. Pick up the rock and study it in your amiable hand. Let me assure you that I am bursting with happiness and gratitude for this great gift. It is taking every bit of will power I have not to clasp you to me. Go! Go quickly. Leave me to deal with the heavy weight of my restraint."

Without hesitation, Christine did exactly as he directed and returned to the house.

The following day, as she entered the mausoleum's attic and stepped off the platform, she found herself, for the space of a few seconds, covered in a shower of red rose petals. They floated in front of her face and alighted on her hair and bodice. Smiling, the Phantom said, "You cannot take the flowers home, so I may as well bathe you in them. Sit, please, and tell me how a woman knows she's pregnant."

She wanted to play with him a little. "Before I offer explanations you must wish me good day and kiss me."

He placed his hands in prayer before his lips. "Forgive my callousness and abrupt ill manner. How indelicate and boorish this monster must seem to you."

Christine came to him, stricken with sadness to hear him refer to himself as a monster. She placed his hands upon her breasts. "My nipples are so sensitive and tender, they feel like little tiger cubs have been nursing. Vomiting has become my first occupation of the day. I bled in a feminine way six weeks ago and Raoul has not touched me since. Only you, my Most Exalted Prince, have raised your scepter near me."

"He has not touched you in over six weeks?"

Exasperated, she threw up her arms. "I don't know how I feel about him anymore, so through a variety of ploys I have managed to avoid his intimacies."

"And risk his angry disappointment?"

"And his shameful effronteries!"

Humbled, he pressed her to his chest, gravely perplexed and unsure of how to ask about her last statement.

Lifting her mouth to his, she kissed him in expectation. His response was pallid, but she was developing an arsenal of weapons to breach his summits. Studying his responses to her actions was her most favorite subject. Placing her mouth on the side of his neck, she breathed across the skin below his ear and felt the muscles in his arms grow tense. He bowed his head down to her shoulder.

"Do I smell different pregnant?"

As he inhaled he lifted her off her feet and she rejoiced. Thirst for her was replacing the mountaintop where his mind had fled! Her tongue explored his mouth in sharp, *staccato* like movements and exigency seized him. He began to clutch at her, his body demanding possession. She giggled in the delight of knowing she had his full attention. Repeatedly he had proven to her that he was a man of focused and purposeful intents. One who would not claim release for himself until she had appreciated hers. While he poured over her body that afternoon, she told him she wanted to leave the chateau and be with him, anywhere. Under the assault of her avid kissing and stroking, he found it difficult to verbalize his concerns. She was actively assailing his senses. Proving herself a formidable mate, one readily determined to overpower his rational decisions.

He finally relinquished any hope of serious discussion and moved to the assertive position of attending to her flesh first. When she writhed and wiggled wildly beneath him, he told her that not only did pregnancy change her scent – it apparently intensified her responses as well. No sooner had they ended their lovemaking, intertwined together in a sweaty mass, than she moved against him again, pleading for more. The word 'insatiable' crossed his mind as he carefully stretched her arms out to their fullest extent. Her skin felt hot to him, and he blew on her face to cool her. *Pregnancy must also increase body temperature,* he surmised. This was an entirely new creature, one he was most interested in exploring, that laced her feet over his calves and spread his legs apart, grinding her pelvis seductively against him. Her mouth opened beside his, forcefully sucking in air away from his cheek. For the first time in his life, he knowingly surrendered to someone else and found himself pulled into a fast moving torrent. With his defenses swept aside, past all thought of care or caution, Erik lay consumed in the ardor of her love.

When he watched her dress he thought her beautiful beyond words, and strange, so brave to risk so much to ease him. He bid her sit on the stool with her face away from him that he might comb her hair. A deepening need to protect her at all costs cracked open like a crater of conflict within him. The resonant sound of his voice compelled her to listen as he explained. "How can I let you go back to Raoul when my baby grows within you? Mine!" His fingers moved gently, following the path of the comb. The single tear drying on his left lower eyelash went unseen. "But how can I bind you into a dark and uncertain future with Erik? He does not know the cause of his deformity, only that he was born with it. He is so hideous that his own mother rejected him. Made him wear a cloth sack over his head, and ordered him to stay away from her. What if the child is born with it too? What if its personality is also unstable and lacks remorse?" He finished with her hair, his fingers passing over her drying curls, and told her to think of the child's welfare. Raise it a de Chagny, rich and stable, with all the advantages titled position could give a youngster. Every word he spoke descended like an ice storm. His final thought, painful and crushing, etched the frigid depths of his pain into her. "Erik does not want the youngster to suffer nightmares over the horror of his father's face."

She looked sadly at her sweet, imbalanced gargoyle, and started to believe that her dreams of a life with him might never become a reality. The road to a permanent place beside him seemed so unclear. Taking his long, skillful fingers in her hands, she kissed them. "If the child is born deformed I will love him and teach him to be strong, for the world does not know how to value true beauty." With great reluctance she conceded to his wishes. "It will be difficult, but I will play the part of the Countess as you wish, but promise not to withdraw from me because I am pregnant. Swear it!"

He took her hands and placed them over his own heart. "You have my solemn oath, I will not forsake you."

"And I swear to you that I did not foresee this, although I probably should have. I want this child very much. A precious piece of you is seeded within me and we need to guard it. I can be brave if I know you won't disappear. But I shudder when I think about giving birth in the same bed where Raoul's mother died giving birth to him."

"If my presence gives you comfort, then I shall devise additional ways to give it. I did not know that Raoul's mother died in your bed. Order another and replace it immediately. Tell Raoul it is an imperative."

5 *OMENS*

A silent Christine suffered a myriad of cascading emotions over the next few months. One minute she would soar with exhilaration, and in the next plummet into a mire of resounding worry, but at the base of all, an abiding joy held her fast – Erik's baby inside her! At last, a descendent to carry on something of the genius and tenderness of this noble man, a living piece of him to grace the world.

Even as she celebrated this unspeakable fact, a malicious fear crept into her thoughts, robbing her of confidence. *Would the little one be physically and mentally sound?* Erik seemed to think the child's welfare in real danger. If the baby were damaged facially, Raoul would know her secret. Raoul! Hanging over all this mental upheaval, churned a tremendous struggle laden with bitter stress – how to tell Raoul she was pregnant without being forthright about the baby's origin. *Perhaps the infant will have Erik's eyes and solve the issue for me.* All other normal attributes could be explained away. *Oh, he looks like your grandfather's painting in the hall upstairs, or he favors my side of the family. But those eyes would be a different matter entirely. Brilliant yellow sapphires are hard to miss!*

Since the fate of the baby's appearance was sealed until its birth, she decided to present a deliberate picture of serene happiness to the world. She would simply keep herself occupied while inwardly struggling to control the labile rushes of elation and vexing uncertainties. The groomsman taught her to ride on a gentle, chestnut colored mare named

Venus. Three times a week, in the company of one of the stable hands and a member of the female staff, for the sake of respectability, she ventured out over the estate learning its geography and becoming acquainted with those employed beyond the chateau. She shopped, practiced her music, visited with Meg, and continued to meet with Dr. Abraham DeVille.

In the beginning of her fifth month, when the evidence of her confinement was getting difficult to conceal, the doctor advised her to stop riding horses. She knew she had no choice but to tell Raoul. She simply informed him over breakfast one morning while he sliced a sausage. His nonchalant reaction was not what she anticipated.

He sat at the head of the table placidly studying her. "Congratulations, Christine, you're having a baby, how wonderful."

"We're having a baby, Raoul, hopefully an heir to this estate."

At that he smiled, "Of course, it might be a boy. Are you feeling all right?"

"Yes, I'm doing well. The baby should be here in four months."

"Then I imagine you have much still to prepare. Come upstairs with me. I want to show you something very special to my family." Without speaking he took her to the second floor and unlocked a door down the hall from her rooms. Inside a nursery greeted her. She ran her hand across the delicate bassinette and the wooden cradle, opened the chests of baby clothes, and smiled at the small, elaborate bathtub inside a carved walnut changing station. The room had been closed up for some time, but with the curtains drawn back it would be a bright, sunny place to raise a child during the initial years of its life. She already knew those of higher stature hired nannies, so the close proximity of the room to her own pleased her very much.

"This is lovely. Were you in this room?"

His affect was indifferent, devoid of even the slightest notion of cheer. She thought perhaps he had his mind on business. "Until I started walking and talking, then I was assigned a valet and my own quarters. We'll have the staff freshen this room, and you can prepare it by purchasing anything new that you desire."

"Raoul, do you mind if I make a request?"

He stood very straight and strangely expressionless. "Certainly, what do you require?"

"Could I please order a new bed to replace the one in my room? Your mother died in it. Not a good omen, as omens go."

An astonishing scowl crossed Raoul's face, he lifted his head even higher, glaring down his nose at her. "Your room and that bed have been occupied by loyal de Chagny women for generations. You will not replace its venerated boards with another. Buy a new mattress if you want, but the bed stays." He turned on his heel and headed abruptly for the door, leaving Christine rattled and staring at his coattails in surprise.

"I didn't mean to insult tradition. I'll only replace the mattress, Raoul." *Did he say the word 'fine' as he stomped down the corridor?*

Raoul's business trips to Italy and England became more frequent, but he always returned with some new present or trinket for the baby. He seemed accepting, almost happy, about the coming addition to their family – asking for progress reports about her preparations and thoughtfully inquiring as to her health. Gratefully, he stopped coming to her private rooms to service his sexual needs. Christine enjoyed the distance and the peace. She would have submitted to him, the Church and Erik said she should, but after his defilements it took days to feel cleansed. Perhaps the sight of her growing abdomen was repugnant to him. With her fingers she would place a kiss upon the sheltered child and thank him. *Even unborn you defend me.*

On the surface all seemed well. Although Raoul no longer pressured her for intimacy, he would readily take her arm to escort her, or hold her hand as they sat together. For the most part Christine was bored, so she taught herself a new game. She found a shop in Paris that specialized in carved ivory pieces and began to purchase human skulls, each smaller than a peach, with vacant black eye sockets and prominent teeth. Since she couldn't take excursions on horseback anymore, she exercised with frequent walks to the family cemetery. There she memorized the names on every tombstone. Upon returning to her room, she would line up the respective skulls of the dead and recite the names of the de Chagny ancestors. Before the birth she had the task completed and could recite them correctly in the order of their burials. Fifty-three graves and fifty-three little skulls in neat rows, exactly as they lay entombed beyond the behemoth stones. The staff referred to this morbid occupation as 'The Time of the Skulls'.

Erik spent the days of Christine's pregnancy alternating between incessant worry and work. He tried to steer his thoughts away from the health of Christine and the baby, but the unwelcome serpents of doubt plagued him, as well. Too many women died in childbirth and he had only to look in his mirror to view congenital aberration at its finest. The ballet studio was booming, keeping Madame Giry busy during the day, and in the evenings she occupied herself with the practical task of making intricate baby clothes. All her attempts to console Erik's troubled mind failed. He would pick up a tiny shirt, or a bonnet, and despondently announce that the child might never get to wear it. So Madame asked the Daroga to increase his visits, but Khalil's counsel proved of no assistance whatsoever. Khalil had never married, never fathered any children, he could offer no words of genuine solace except to pull out his backgammon set and encourage Erik to play a game or two with him.

It wasn't until the middle of May that a real diversion occurred to help them all weather the last trimester of the confinement. Ballet lessons were given in two sessions Monday through Friday; ten to twelve in the mornings, and one to three every afternoon. Around noon on a Tuesday, a thirty-five year old police detective, and his little girl, rang the front door chime of the studio. Madame greeted them and invited them to sit on some chairs in front of the stage. The gentleman introduced himself as Mr. Thomas Edwards, and his brown-eyed daughter as Kate. He explained that he was a British police officer on loan to the *Surete* for a six-month period to exchange ideas on the newest methods for detecting and analyzing crime scenes. His French wife passed away last year of pneumonia, and he wanted his eight-year-old daughter, who was very bright, to augment her studies by taking dance lessons. He brought Kate to Madame Giry's ballet studio on the high recommendation of a fellow officer's wife.

"How are you finding Paris, Monsieur?"

"It's not as damp as London, and I'm definitely not looking forward to the coming summer heat. I don't find excessive warmth agreeable. Madame, please pardon my directness, but I am a man of few words. Will you teach her?"

"Eight is rather old to start, but she seems eager. Yes, she can learn with us in the afternoon sessions."

After the lesson on Thursday afternoon, Kate sat alone on the studio's stage rubbing her sore leg muscles and waiting for her housekeeper to come pick her up. She didn't like being the last child to leave and decided that sitting was much too uncomfortable. She needed to move. Through the open door of the office, she could see Madame Giry writing at her desk, and understood that the ballet mistress could see her as well, but she wanted to explore and snoop a little. Still in her white practice leotards, Kate went to the wooden door to the right of the stage. Curious about what adventure might lie beyond, she turned the knob and found it unlocked. Opening the door enough to peek into the back hallway, the smell of boiling meat and potatoes cooking atop some unseen stove tantalized her nostrils. As her eyes traveled over the polished wooden walls, and up the red painted banister of the staircase, they came to rest on the back of a man, standing perfectly still like a statue. He had thick, wavy black hair, a white shirt tucked into doe colored leggings and he was barefoot! His arms were up at his chest as if he carried something in front of him. She could not make out what he held so protectively. She too stood frozen, expecting to see the man's face as he turned to scold her. As she started to work up the courage to say hello, she heard a young cat meow at her feet and glanced down expecting to see a kitten, but none was there. Looking back to the stairs the man had vanished. *How marvelous,* she thought, *I didn't even hear him move.* As she shut the door to return to the stage area, she was startled to find her ballet teacher right behind her, frowning in disappointment. Madame retrieved a ring of keys from her pocket, locked the door and tested the knob.

"Well behaved pupils mind their place and don't go about spying. You should concentrate more on your new ballet steps." Madame took Kate's hand and led her away from the door. "It's good to respect people's privacy, don't you think? Curiosity killed the cat."

Kate responded glumly, "Sorry mistress, it won't happen again, but who is the man who stands so still?"

Madame appeared quite disinterested and brushed the front of her skirt with her hand. "Perhaps he is only someone from your own mind. Did you get a good look at him? No? Well you are not here to practice imagining shadows into people are you? Come, I will show you how to loosen your sore muscles."

Over dinner that evening Louisa told Erik who had opened the back stairwell door behind him – a British police officer's daughter, no less. She asserted that they should renew their vigilance securing the doors. "The locks provide us with precious seconds." He casually inquired if the girl was pretty, and Madame set her fork down on her plate with an impatient clang. "Really, that's what you want to know? She's too curious, pretty does not enter into it."

The following afternoon, little Kate huddled the other students around her and told them about the man she had seen the day before. The heads of the other girls bobbed up and down in excitement.

"You're so lucky," chided Anne, "that door is always locked!"

"We've all tried it at one time or another," added Helene, "but we've never seen him."

"Him who?" asked Kate.

The smallest, a little cherub named Ruth, with bright blue eyes and blond pigtails, saw her chance to jump into the cluster. "You must have spotted Madame's brother. He lives on the third floor. She'll never talk about him, but our mothers have told us that he's ill and keeps to himself. Perhaps he is contagious!" Her last word was pitched high and drawn out for emphasis.

All the other girls giggled. "Don't be ridiculous, Ruthie. He's not contagious, he's old!"

"As a matter of fact, he's quite handsome and he's certainly well enough to carry packages!" Kate conferred her intelligence with an air of superiority, pleased to add information to the treasure trove of knowledge about the mysterious man of the dwelling's upper floors. Kate's eyes grew wide with the promise of revealing secrets, and her fellow students drew in closer, begging to be told everything she saw. Hidden behind the side curtain of the stage, the Opera Ghost smiled at her description. "He's a tall, prince of a man, muscular and strong, with thick wavy black hair...and carries a ruby handled sword sheathed at his side. He wore the softest of black boots going up to his knees, and was just returning from banishing brigands out in the street." The little girls were spellbound at Kate's amazing tale.

Ah, women, mused the eavesdropper, *it starts so early!*

From her office, Louisa gazed at the curtains to the right of the stage. Tapping her desk blotter with a letter opener, she smiled mischievously. She knew he could not resist the attention once she had the students' curiosity peeked about him.

All a quiver with expectation, the girls rushed to try the side door and found it locked tight.

"Try the front," shouted Helene.

A flock of pink flamingoes in tutus ran to the front entrance of the studio and out into the foyer. In unison the girls looked to their left at the oak door which opened to the street.

"No," said Anne pointing to another door in the rear of the reception area. In their daily hustle to get inside for dance practices they had never bothered with it, but it had their full attention now. The heavy wooden door with the decorative bronze knob and keyhole plate, stood sentry before the world of forbidden adventure. Kate walked up to it and boldly tried the knob. Locked out again! Their expectant little faces fell in disappointment.

"Oh, well, let's go practice," declared Ruth. The young ballerinas hurried back into the studio.

Madame Giry emerged from her office, and clapping her hands together sharply, announced that they should take their positions next to the bars. "Promptly, girls. Line up, let's go."

Behind the stage curtain the Opera Ghost touched the head of a nail and a secret door in the wall silently slid open, revealing a small dark room – the size of a broom closet. It contained a ladder going upward with the weighted ropes of a pulley beside it. In a flash he was gone, and the girls began a rigorous workout under the firm direction of their mistress.

Later, as Kate sat in a carriage waiting for the driver to take her home, she studied the third floor windows. Intrigued, she told herself that she would find a way to meet the brave handsome prince inhabiting the castle towers.

The residents of the house suspected that the inquisitive eight-year-old would remain interested in the mysterious man upstairs for some time. To track her curiosity, Erik screwed a series of half-inch bridle rings from the front and back studio doors, up the walls of the stairwells into his apartment. To each of the first floor doorknobs he affixed a metal eye. Then traveled a string, attached to two little bells on his upstairs desk, down the series of rings. At the strings' first floor end he secured a toggle. Before a ballet session commenced, Madame Giry would walk to the two studio doors, drop the toggled end of the strings through the metal eyes on the knobs, lock the doors and check the locks. If someone attempted to jiggle the knob of either door, the bells on Erik's desk jingled merrily. Consistently, Monday through Friday, at some point during the afternoon session, the back hall bell would ring, and occasionally the front bell a few minutes later. He would pause from his writing and look up amazed at her persistence. At worst, she was a minor irritation disturbing his concentration, but most often he thought it downright amusing and had a splendid laugh.

The warm, sticky months of summer passed with Christine counting skulls and stairs, Erik repulsing Kate, and only Meg making worthwhile plans. Crafty and innovative, Meg shunned the gloomy portents issuing forth from Erik and Christine, telling them both that the child was probably a prodigy and would excel to heights past his parents' wildest dreams. The versatile Meg believed in tackling problems head-on, and always worked hard to find agreeable solutions. She favored outcomes that were both subtle and momentous. In loyalty, she kept her hand on the pulse of the situation, and watched for an opportunity to come to the aid of her friends. Fortune cooperated in the final month of Christine's pregnancy, when Raoul announced he would be leaving for Italy to personally present several business deals for closure. He assured his wife that he would return before her delivery in mid-September. Immediately after Raoul's departure, Meg initiated a plan that would allow Christine to give birth away from the chateau and with Erik close-by.

On the first day of September, two weeks before Christine's scheduled due date, Meg sent her husband Jean, the Baron Castelot-Barbezac, to pick up Christine for a visit to their estate. An unpretentious and affable nobleman, he proved to be a most willing confederate in his wife's enigmatic plan. Soon after Christine and her luggage arrived safely, Meg gave her a potent tonic of herbs and mineral oil to induce labor. In two hours it took effect, Jean went quickly to fetch Madame Giry and Erik. Initially, Christine was overjoyed to see them, but as the contractions intensified, it became obvious that she was going into hard labor. She told Erik she could not maintain her composure and asked him to wait downstairs. Jean took him to a private, family parlor, leaving Christine with the midwife, Meg and Madame Giry. The women started to give the burgeoning mother small doses of laudanum and alcohol to help cope with the pain.

As the hours ticked by, the tense atmosphere in the parlor increased. When the duration of Christine's labor reached ten hours, both Erik and Jean began to pace the room anxiously. Starved for reassurance that she was doing well, they decided to send Jean upstairs to inquire at the door, while Erik waited downstairs, running his fingers in distress through his black hair. In a few minutes Jean returned with a request. "Christine is asking that if you can bear to see her as she is, she would like to have you with her. The baby is almost here. She's fared well, but is close to exhaustion."

Grateful to be of some useful purpose and for the chance to see her, a determined Erik silently followed Jean up the stairs. Louisa's tired eyes greeted him at the door.

Resolved to be of help, he took the chair close to the head of Christine's bed. She was pale and wet, her hair matted to her head, but great determination and love for him filled her eyes.

"Labor is not for the feeble," she proclaimed.

The midwife, a little stooped over with age, her wispy gray hair pulled back neatly into a puffy white cap, handed him a wet cloth. "Glad to have you here, Sir."

Erik began to wash Christine's face and hands. As a contraction bit down into her, she fixed her eyes on his and stifled the scream emerging in her throat. The lack of strength in her hand grasp caused him endless concern. As the contraction started to ease his agreeable voice vibrated in her ears. Under its hushed and euphonic spell, Christine closed her eyes. He told her to sleep and regain her strength, the way was almost clear now, there was only a little work left to be done. He started to sing to her as she slept:

> "The joy of life, to suckle a child,
> To suckle a child, at its mother's breasts,
> To suckle, to nurture, to kiss and caress,
> The newborn child at its mother's breasts."

The midwife, who had served this household for decades, told him his treatment was excellent, whatever he was doing, the baby's head was fully crowned. "If you'll help her, Sir, I'll birth the child."

Erik nodded and told Christine to open her eyes. "Sit up my darling and let's greet the baby, shall we?"

Meg and Erik lifted her shoulders off the bed and Christine clung to their hands like a tigress. In three mighty pushes she had the baby out and they helped her lie back, drenched upon her pillows. The midwife helped with the afterbirth, while Louisa smiled at Erik and mouthed the word 'perfect' to him. Erik stayed with Christine while the three women washed the peaceful infant's tiny face and body. After wrapping it in a white blanket, Madame Giry placed it tenderly in Christine's arms, telling her in reassurance, "It's a boy, a perfect little boy."

Brightening, Christine took the child. "He's so beautiful and so quiet! I shall call him Michael, after the first of the archangels who guard the passage to heaven."

"And I shall call you very brave and most precious. Come, let's wash you up and let you sleep." Erik's eyes danced in relief.

A week later Raoul returned from Italy. Upon his arrival Victor greeted him in the marbled entrance of the chateau. "You have a son, born just last Sunday morning," his secretary informed him. "But your wife is not here. The child came early while she visited the Castelot-Barbezac estate. She is there still."

Raoul's look was strangely distant, yet something savage seemed to play behind his eyes. "Tell Justine I need her and call for a carriage to take us to Christine. Send for the nanny we hired and have her brought here."

Victor thought him tired from the trip. "The nanny is already upstairs waiting. Everything is prepared."

"Good, then we go to fetch the mistress of this house back to her place. Apparently she's forgotten where she belongs."

6 *MARRED AND FESTERING*

Nestling Michael in her arms, and nursing him to the extent that the decorum of titled nobility would permit, Christine recuperated under the vigilant eyes of the staff at Raoul's estate. Life at the house on *Rue du Renard* began the easier process of returning to a more pleasant atmosphere. Energized and happy that the child was finally here and in good health, Erik worked on his musical plays unfettered. While Madame returned to the routine of giving ballet lessons to her pupils. It was the custom of women in those days to confine themselves to bed for a period of six weeks after giving birth. Before Erik left Christine's side, she asked him to be at the tomb every Sunday, on the chance that she might be able to come to him. He promised to be there, but encouraged her to complete the period of 'laying in' before restarting her visits.

Fourteen days after the birth, he was in the crypt ready to install a removable screen behind the grillwork of the metal doors. The screen depicted an exact image of the vault's interior. With it in place, anyone passing by and glancing at the doors would see only the inside of the room. Off in the distance, at the very beginning of the walkway into this section of the cemetery, a woman wearing a simple, light blue jumper and a white blouse approached the tomb. *Christine?* Setting the screen aside he waited, and as she unlocked the door he opened it for her. He gathered her in his arms and held her to him, a lost treasure returned. She seemed so small, this young mother, her heart beat too quickly from her walk to the tomb. It worried him. Her brow was wet with sweat from the exertion, and the small tendrils of hair surrounding her face matted in place by the moisture.

"Christine, you're supposed to be in bed. Come and sit."

"Hello to you, too. Yes, sitting would be fine. I am well, so please don't vex yourself. Feel me." She put his hand on her arm. "See, I'm quite strong. Let's go up to our world."

When they were safe in the attic, she sat carefully on the edge of the bed. He took a less comfortable position on the floor directly in front of her, sitting cross-legged. "Please, tell me, what has possessed you to come out so soon after Michael has entered the world? Why endanger your health?"

She scanned his face and body with her eyes. He was eating and his color was good. He wore a simple bone colored shirt, unbuttoned over his chest in the September heat, and gray leggings. *His shoes must be somewhere else,* she thought, *he's barefoot. The cool stones of the tomb must feel pleasurable to the soles of his feet.* With her right hand she massaged her forehead, thinking. Then lowering her hand to her lap, "How can I explain this? Love, Erik, love for you brought me here."

"What kind of love brings a brand new mother to a cemetery to view a ghost?"

"Please don't say that. You are not a ghost to me, no curling wisp of smoke, no fleeting shadow dissipated by the light." She sighed – sometimes being with him was so difficult. Smiling she rubbed the stubble on his chin with her thumb. *He has hidden for so long, hiding is all he knows.*

Erik's voice bordered on mockery, "We do meet in a tomb."

"We meet in my father's tomb," she stressed. "The father who sent me the Angel of Music just as he promised. His blessing rests upon us." Grimacing, she shifted her weight on the bed and straightened her jumper, still somewhat sore from the birth. "It does me good to see you, to know that you are still loyally mine and still quite touchable…not some spirit eluding me through a wall at the Opera House. And don't worry, little Michael is fine. I just fed him. He's asleep with his nanny close beside his cradle. I told them that if I didn't get out of the house

I would go mad. I needed air. They scurry about when I speak like that...rushing to get my carriage ready. Sometimes I wonder why no one questions my wanting these visits, but it's just as well. They are all about their duties and show me great respect, but I digress. You asked me what kind of love this is and I am happy to tell you, if I can only find the words." As she hesitated her eyebrows drew together in earnestness.

"Oh Erik, the baby gurgles and pushes his legs as I hold him. I study his face and I see your petulance there. I hold his tiny fingers and imagine they will someday play the violin and the organ, like his grandfather and his father. Then I start to wonder how you're doing, and **what** you're doing. I try to picture you working or resting, and I long to tell you everything I'm thinking...to assure you that there's no place within me hidden from you, nor would I ever want there to be. Since I am not supposed to send you notes, I had to come here and tell you these things myself. You see, my love, you possess my mind."

While she spoke so candidly, Erik continued to sit on the floor. He attended closely to her words but was keenly aware of the odor of clotted blood flowing from her body. She had bathed and washed her hair before coming to the tomb, and wore clothes recently removed from a closet, or drawer, containing a fresh sachet of cedar chips. He was unaware that his acute sense of smell was quite unique. He believed that everyone could detect the odors that so frequently permeated his nostrils – he just thought most people didn't pay any attention to them.

Christine asked, "Are you listening to me?"

He answered in a nonchalant manner. "Oh, yes. You were telling me that the parts of you that really matter, that what is indeed the very essence of you, belongs to me, and you would like to reassure yourself that I am still here for you. Christine, the train carrying my heart left the station a long, long time ago. It roared its way to you with all the love I'm capable of...I couldn't get it back now even if I tried." Then, as if he were once again assisting the midwife, he added, "Let me get you some water, perhaps you should lie down and rest."

Impatient with his request, she waved her hand in dismissal, her words shooting out rapid fire. "I'm fine, please let me continue. I want you to understand what's been happening in my mind these past two weeks. It has occurred to me that you and I are spared the trivial arguments husbands and wives share over household matters. We are past the tumult and fearsome mysteries of those years in the Opera House. Here in this space and time, I find myself full of a bewildering amount of joy over this baby you have given me, but the joy is accompanied by an equal amount of fierce longing…for you. You are always in my thoughts, Erik, and in my queer reality you are always around me."

As she paused to take in a few deep breaths and readjust her position again, Erik sat amazed at the stream of words coming from her. He simply said, "Please, go on."

"During the day, I relive the times we've been together over and over. I imagine you speaking to me as I move about the house. In my mind we hold entire conversations! Three years ago you set me free, and that very freedom has enslaved me. Ironically, the whole world has become my prison. At times, it feels like I actually float with love for you. I kiss our little son and know in my heart, that at a moment's notice I would put my life at risk for the two of you. You are dearer to me than my own soul, and before God, I vow that no other shall have the place in me that you hold. I would never surrender it."

He opened his mouth to speak and Christine raised her hand. "No, please wait, there's more. Let me finish." Tears appeared in her eyes and started to trail down her cheeks. She wiped them with a linen handkerchief and forged onward. "I want you to know that this sacrifice you've made for my welfare and for Michael's is too great, too unselfish. I would like to sing of it to the world, to write of it in huge letters, and place it on display for everyone to read and review at their leisure." The salty taste of her tears was in her mouth. "I know that people would shake their heads in disbelief. How could someone be this self-effacing? It saddens me that no one beyond our tiny group of friends will ever know of the greatness of your soul, and yet, just having your love fills me with such pride. I could burst I am so full. Can you feel what I'm feeling? Can you picture what I am trying to say to you? If I thought I could get away with it I would emboss the name, Erik D'Angelus, across my chest and be...and be..." Christine's face grew puzzled and her mouth drew into a tight line as she searched for the words to finish her thought.

Erik sat in wonder. It seemed to him that her emotional state had gushed forth like a broken fire hydrant and filled the air in the room with love and wild frustration. His left eyebrow (the only one he had) rose upward and a sly expression crossed his face. "You'd be an invitation, a delicate, but formal invitation. One with gold letters, announcing the gala of life...a chance to come and dance the most splendid of dances."

Flabbergasted, Christine responded, "Erik, are you being funny? Your humor has returned, Sir! And those worried furrows on your brow are gone! Please don't tease me. I concede. Come and lay beside me. Hold me for a while. That will have to sustain me for another week."

Erik took his place on the bed and holding her hand told her a wonderful story about a big plodding bear in the forests. One who searched and searched for a magical orb to be its lifelong friend, and when the bear found the orb, he understood the value of his treasure and guarded it ever so well. Never did the bear abuse it or intentionally disobey its wishes.

Christine drifted beneath the sky of phosphorescent stars as he told her the tale. At the end of the narrative she praised him. "What a marvelous story! It reminds me of the ones my Papa used to tell me as a little girl. What a mind you have, so clever, so capable. I saw the screen downstairs. You are such a mystery to me. I want to know you, to understand, to hear with my own ears what you've experienced. Can you tell me about your past?"

She felt his muscles grow rigid and his body shrink on the bed beside her, as if he were ready to pounce from it. "Don't go there, Christine. My mind and my experiences are a foul sewer, not a very inviting place for a lady of your quality to go wandering. I am lecherous and pagan, a monstrosity whose character has been drained of all good cause."

Christine moved closer to him, despite the tightness of his body. "I'm wrong to want you to recall pain in anyway. I only ask because I love you, and want to understand the person who has taken my love so completely captive. Think of the baby. Let Michael's tiny life tell you how much I love you."

His body shuddered as he exhaled a slow, jagged breath, then rolling to his side to face her, he hissed into her ear. "You want to know what Erik thinks? Never leave Paris! He would not tolerate it. He would never stop hunting for you. Wherever you went, he would find you…even if you entered the cloistered halls of the Vatican itself, with a hundred guards to ward him off."

Without hesitation Christine answered in a demure, monotone voice. "I pledge that I will never leave Paris of my own free will. Only the Lord of Death shall separate us – and he needs to bring an army with him. The disparate, icy fingers of the Grim Reaper acting alone are not powerful enough to tear us apart, because I would bargain deviously and fight to remain with you." She kissed his hand. "I don't want the father of my baby to be an enigma to me. If you are willing to share it, I still want to know everything there is to know about the man who holds my soul such a willing prisoner."

He swallowed hard, his mouth felt dry, his skin prickled of ice. "My past has ripped me into pieces. I lay here torn and full of wounds, a condemned man, tied to a wall…cut through with arrows, and at the whim of the executioner, not allowed to die. The wounds fester and ache. The poison sears my veins, and I cannot move to end the torture because I am held fast by the ropes of my own loathsomeness. The only ray of light is you."

His voice took on an unreal, almost feral undertone. Together they entered a bizarre reality of turbulent recollection, arduous for him to handle, onerous to share.

"The first time Erik saw you at the Opera House, his mind fixed on you as the way to his release. You were seven, so small in the bed where Madame placed you. He perceived you were an angel, but one wounded like him because your father had died and left you an orphan. Your innocence heedlessly trampled over him. Like a thousand maddened horses cresting a hill, you stomped his despair and chewed on it – as if it were a trifle! With no regard for his wishes, you fed on Erik. Sacrificing him to Hope, to Love, to the dark goddess Nyx."

He seemed to curl further inward, pale, his muscles cold as stone and hard. The fingers of his hands moved, playing notes on unseen keys. "The crazed music Erik pounded in the cellars began to change. At first it spoke cautiously, shyly, of what he was feeling for you, but your presence in the theater above drew his intentions upward. His efforts, his body, were nothing but meat hooked through the shoulders and hauled toward you. Unwittingly, relentlessly, you trespassed his self-inflicted isolation, demanding his presence near you! When the organ, the bench, his heart were unmercifully afire, when all he cared for was you, the music changed in a rush he could no longer withstand. It developed a life of its own. Wisely, he let it have its way, and guarded you with his murderous heart of darkness from the gloomiest corners of the playhouse. Delighting in your growing up became his only balm."

His voice grew clearer, more like a man. "Do you know that you never frown when you pray or read a book?"

Determination returned to Christine's voice. "No one can stop the tempest once it hits the shore. When the storm comes, it comes, enveloping all that stands in its way. Your brave words tear into me. I regret every cruel thing I ever said to you. I just didn't understand who you were." She kissed his fingers. "Thank you for telling me these things. To open your heart is difficult, I know. The executioner is the guilty party, not the poor soul tied to the wall. You always acted out of self-defense to preserve your life and your home, you never hurt others for amusement."

A few moments passed, each contemplating what had just transpired.

"You said that taking a life for amusement is not the same as taking a life out of self-defense, but what about revenge? Does revenge justify taking a life?"

"I suppose it would depend upon the crime. Surely not for insult or robbery, but if murder occurred, revenge might be just."

"Because I would kill anyone who threatened your life."

"Of that I have no doubt, Erik. Did you ever feel happy when you killed?"

"No, only relief. I didn't even try to conceal the bodies, I let them decay where they fell. Except for Philippe de Chagny." He grew silent again, his muscles partially relaxed as a thought occurred to him. "Your complexity astounds me. You're a new mother, the mistress of a chateau, a budding legalist, the..."

"Devoted lover of E. D'Angelus!" Christine broke in. "I am not a child anymore, Erik. The stench of the wounds you bear does not drive me away from you, it draws me to you." He thought of the blood flowing from her and how it did not repulse him in any way. "My heart belongs to the man who is tied to the tree," she continued. "Maybe together we can take the arrows out, and start to heal the angry wounds caused by Fate and the searing inhumanity of all the rest of us."

"Does the 'not knowing' about my past stand between us?"

"Picture a wall, a solid stone wall, too high for me to climb, and in the wall a metal gate gives access, but before the gate lies a pit of poisonous snakes. I want to enter but cannot. I'm not afraid, but I don't know how to pass the snakes unscathed."

"Unscathed is more accurate than you can imagine. Those snakes are in my head and I fear that if I let them out, they would come forth screaming, loosed upon you. Who knows what they would do? When their strength intensifies and they grow too numerous, I keep them in check with a dozen tricks."

Christine turned to face him. Placing her fingers beneath his chin, she lifted his face so that she could look directly into his disconcerted eyes. "I do not fear you. You are not a mad man riling in a corner. Everything I have ever seen you do has had purpose and intent. Your actions have shown me that your mind has direction, self-preservation and love as its goals. What causes you the most fear if the snakes are loosed?"

"That you would reject me again, turning away from me in dismay. I couldn't bear it another time...your disapproval and the loss of your presence in my life."

As he spoke these words he gripped her upper arm so tightly it caused her pain. She took care to show no expression on her face, lest her grimace give him remorse. She understood the depth of despair behind his words so she controlled her response. *He's testing me. He has to, I used to feel only fear and pity for him.*

Thinking past the pain that now traversed her whole arm, she spoke in the kindest voice possible. "What happened to you in the past was genuine, palpable. Your wounds are deep and very real. Please, ease yourself...just a bit. I know that life has dealt you torment, but try to see yourself as I see you. To me you are masterful, perfect in form, my welcomed, sweet addiction. I hunger for the man you are, not just your body, but your mind as well. I don't know if I'll ever have enough of you. We are bound to each other now because of Michael. Don't you feel the bond?"

He released his grip on her arm, and could see the mark of his hand on her sleeve. He rubbed her and berated himself mentally for being a vicious cur, but he did not whimper and he offered no apology. He reminded himself she wanted the man, not the dog who used to drool after her footsteps at the Opera House.

Still placid and calm she said, "Let's not talk about your past now, I want to enjoy being here beside you."

Erik thought for a moment. "Perhaps we could pretend that I have read a novel and you could ask me questions about the story. I will answer you truthfully, for I have never lied to you and don't wish to start. But you must always act as if it's only a book we're discussing."

"Good, that sounds good, and if you don't feel like answering my questions tell me. But I have a condition."

"What's the condition?"

"That you get to ask me questions as well, whatever you want. I'll let you into the mind of a woman, this woman – no secrets, no veiled answers."

He brushed his hand across her cheek and kissed her lips timidly, like honey to a bear. "You have an agreement."

Patting his arm, she completely reversed the momentum of their conversation. "I feel the need to move. Let's get up and dance."

Stretching his arms and legs to loosen them, Erik replied, "I don't think I'm a very good dancer. I've never had the opportunity to become proficient."

"Then let's pretend." She stood up in the middle of the little room and he joined her. She placed his hands upon her waist and rested hers on his forearms. In a gentle, deepened voice she whispered something into his ear, then leaning back she said, "Let me hear your music, Erik. Close your eyes. Can you hear it? Where is the tympani of the drums? Yes, there it is, now add the violins and horns. Let me tell you where we are..."

Their bodies simply swayed side to side as they joined together in the task. From some distant corner the music commenced and began to rise in their ears. They stood in an opalescent ballroom, with shimmering, multicolored lights and laughter all around. The music of celebration swirled and faded, only to increase again while other couples twirled about them, moving to the tempo. Erik was a young nobleman, no mask, no disfigurement, totally whole and handsome. Christine smiled and hanging on, followed his lead as they danced around the ballroom. Gay and light hearted, they chuckled at the scenes of other couples obviously amused and in love. Erik looked to a domed ceiling painted with angels singing in an azure sky full of cumulus clouds and wind. A chorus of angelic voices blended into the music. He basked in the grandeur of it, wave after wave washing gloriously over his ears. And here in his arms was Christine, a vision in a dark burgundy ball gown with a choker of black velvet holding a droplet of pearls at her throat. She touched the pearls and grinned broadly at him, love blooming full upon her face. They continued the dance, and as the music faded to a softened end of violins, he thought himself enchanted. *I have never seen her more radiant than tonight, those pearls revel in her beauty, as do I.*

When she opened her eyes his face was full of wonder, his skin warm and pliable beneath her hands – the disconsolate man calm and at peace. "You fill me with love, Erik, let me fill you." The briefest of smiles blessed his lips and his head rocked back and forth gently. She paused to let him bathe in the bliss of this moment, and then whispered something else to him.

His eyelids flickered. Returning to the attic he beheld her, still in his arms, cheeks flushed from the dance, a soft expression of love and acceptance upon her face. She was looking at him so closely, drawing him in with those blue-green eyes of hers. He stood trying to comprehend what had happened. *Where have we been?* Where indeed, for as he watched, Christine's fingers traveled up to her throat, to exactly where he had pictured the pearls, and smiling sweetly, her fingertips moved upon them as if they were still there!

They lingered over their parting that day, fingers entwined, their foreheads pressed together, as they waited by the sarcophagus for Christine to depart first. Reluctant to leave him, the smallest of tears coursed down her cheek and he kissed it, savoring its priceless taste. He reached into his pocket and showed her a little gold ring. She recognized it immediately. He had given it to her at the Opera House. Renewed hope welled within her. She took the ring and slid it onto the smallest of his left fingers. Looking up into his brilliant eyes she declared war on his immutable decisions. "This puts an end to innocent aspiration, Erik, so prepare to offer up your best defense. You may not always be able to hold me at bay."

"I love you so very much," he twirled the ring upon his finger.

"I know you do. We can have a life together, I love you, too." Before she cleared the door she began to calculate the amount of time until she could be with him again. She wouldn't see him until a week from the morrow. *Eight days, about one hundred ninety hours to go!*

Erik watched as she walked away and pragmatically counted the widening distance between them in feet, knowing all too well that soon he would measure it in miles. His guttural words were feral again, low in pitch and drawn out. "Each time I see you, I rejoice as the space between us melts away. Now I wait in desolate grief until I can hold you again and listen to your voice, not a voice held in my memory but your true voice.

I curse every inch that lies between us, for only you possess the power to soothe the vicious beast and coax him from his hole. And you think you're the prisoner!" He sobbed as the last of her disappeared from view, retreating into the mausoleum he felt destitute and terribly alone.

The next day Christine went into Paris and visited the de Chagny's lawyers. She signed a document stating that she wished to be buried near her father's grave when she died and not in the de Chagny ancestral plot on the estate. She also wrote that she wanted to be buried in her plain blue jumper and white blouse. She went directly from the lawyers' office to the very throne of hope itself, the home of Dr. Abraham DeVille.

7 SUMMON A GOBLIN

The utilization of ardent work as a profoundly therapeutic release had not escaped the Phantom's appreciation. He knew well that obsessive devotion to a profession could afford an effective escape from whatever problems a person experienced. During the first few months of Michael's young life, music began to pour forth from the maestro. In the past, some of his stage presentations had taken years to compose, but now he turned his heightened energies into his artistry, producing skits, and shorter three-act plays with accompanying scores by the multitude. When he completed a presentation, Madame Giry would send a note to their lawyer, Monsieur Pierre Toussaint, to inform him of the opportunity to sell an additional piece of work. The lawyer promptly sent his agent, by appointment, to the ballet studio office to receive the newest creation from E. D'Angelus. Monsieur Toussaint would then alert the local playhouses and theaters that an intriguing drama, or a delightful comedy, was now available and up for bid. The bids arrived by certified letter at the lawyer's office before a designated deadline. Toussaint reviewed them and notified the winning bidder. When payment was procured and the play or skit delivered, the good lawyer subtracted his fees and placed his clients' share in their designated bank account. The system worked smoothly for years, giving Madame Giry and Erik no cause to ever want for funds.

Initially, Erik didn't care how a theater's management produced his works. He never attended any performances. As long as the money kept coming in he was satisfied, but eventually curiosity and his ego got the best of him. So Madame purchased tickets for a musical comedy he'd written. Disguised as an elderly gentleman, he and his dedicated friend took their places in the audience. He was quite pleased to see the play portrayed so accurately. The story was about a drunken friar who constantly mixed up people's appointments and their troubles. In the first act, the error prone monk tried to wed a brother and sister having an argument over ownership of a prized heifer. While the complaints of the boisterous pair further addled his brain, he attempted to reconcile a betrothed couple, quarreling over who they should invite to their wedding, by awarding the intended groom with 'the cow'. The audience laughed as the confused characters romped about the stage, trying vainly to comply with the friar's instructions. Amid the flurry of questions, and the ensuing accusations, attractions started to grow between the brother and the prospective bride. The irate sister, flustered because she had not received her just recompense, started flirting outrageously with the promised male. He, in turn, found himself haggling loudly with the monk over the appropriate worth of a milk cow, and prancing around trying to avoid the sister's remonstrations. The clergyman took another drink and screamed at the young man that unless he had a case of St. Vitus's dance, he should stand still during a dispute!

Erik felt a deserved sense of pride for his abilities, but as his eyes furtively scanned the seats he took note of all the couples in the theater. Most were young people, but quite a few were elderly or middle aged, and all with gaiety and delight registering upon their faces, happily sharing an evening's entertainment together. He felt himself nullified and angry to be without Christine on a permanent basis. *Why not be with her? She wants to be with me!* When he realized he was about to spoil a singular night out with sour humor, he put the thought from his mind by arguing with himself. *Selfish lout, you have no intention of removing her from the chateau.*

Madame Giry could sense him tensing beside her and said into his ear, "It's very funny and articulately sung. You've done a superlative job. Congratulations!"

"Thank you, Louisa, above all others, you could certainly be the judge of its merit." He sat back in his seat brooding and a plan began to form in his mind. He would create a living theater and work out some of his loneliness by staring himself in a play. It pleased him greatly that he could orchestrate the entire scenario without troubling the two women he cared most about, and in a manner which would allow him to vent the tempestuous rage of an invalidated male. The author began to compose a bar fight, a raucous drunken brawl of a fight. *Now to find the appropriate stage,* he mused.

Deep in the recesses of an establishment for drinking and billiards near the waterfront, sat an old man with brown tobacco stained teeth, gray disheveled hair, and dirty clothes. His untucked shirttails lay visibly over his trousers, and the lining of his shoulder pad peeked through the fabric of his broadcloth coat. He kept his eyelids half closed to hide the alertness of his exotic eyes, and looked to his shoes, worn and stained, but with toes safely covered. For the past two hours he'd studied the inside of this bar and was well into his third shot of bourbon and stein of beer. Although he acted somewhat drunk he was far from it. Kerosene lamps provided him with a dim, smoky kind of light, more than adequate for his surveillance. Dusty fishing nets and washed out pictures of ships cluttered the walls. The actual bar itself was fashioned from used planking and ran down the left wall, halfway into the room. Tables and chairs of rough-hewn wood filled the rest of the floor space. The saloon was attached to the brothel next door, and prostitutes came and went with their clients through an entrance to his left. On his right, a double set of doors allowed for deliveries. An earlier inspection revealed that those doors led out into an alley wide enough for a horse drawn wagon to drop off goods.

The atmosphere inside the bar had been gradually heightening. The level of people's voices growing louder, their speech more slurred, as an occasional drinking song broke out, first at one table then spread throughout the room. As the liquor flowed, the women got freer with their favors, exposing more of themselves, and a sexual tension had begun to develop. The whores all wore dresses with low cut bodices, a point of petticoat tucked into their belted waists, exposing a portion of suggestive thigh. After targeting a potential customer, a prostitute slithered into place at the man's side, or onto his lap, rubbing herself provocatively against him. The Phantom had not seen any such favor refused, the potential subject being allowed to feel a breast or thigh, before the woman stated the cost of continuing into his ear. If the man agreed to the price they left together, usually returning in about twenty minutes, immediate needs gratified.

No proposition had been offered to the Phantom; for as a prostitute approached this unkempt being in the far corner, she smelled the horseshit he rubbed on his pants earlier and withdrew in hasty retreat. He sat quietly, enjoying the mild buzz in his head and carefully watching the interchanges, ever the panther stalking its prey in the dimness. He had decided upon two characters at his end of the bar. They were well liquored and fit for an adventurous brawl. He discretely tossed a couple of coins beneath their stools. Right on cue, the pair heard the distinct tinkling as they landed. Jostling each other, the men argued over which one should retrieve the money from the filthy floor. With instincts numbed but not absent, the larger of the two saw the flash of Erik's eyes scrutinizing them. He smacked his compatriot on the arm to get his attention, and pointed to the old man with the astounding eyes. "Hey, wah'cha lookin' at fish face?"

The Phantom's pulse quickened, his hand closing around the handle of a knife in his jacket. Without dropping his gaze he leaned forward and spat. The sticky spittle landed squarely on the shoe of the sot who addressed him.

Responding to the challenge, the man faltered a leap from his bar stool then angrily approached. "You mus' be deaf and ugly as sin. I'll teach yah some manners, an' yah won't be thankin' me."

Erik's lips vibrated in abrasive contempt. Up on his feet, and with a hand now in a leather glove, he landed a powerful punch on the left side of the man's jaw. The drunkard staggered back. His drinking buddy grabbed an empty chair and hurled it at the old man, who deftly stepped to the right. The loud crash of wood hitting the wall drew the attention of others in the bar. At a nearby table a man hankering for a scuffle rose, spilling the prostitute on his lap to the floor. She shouted a curse of surprise at the oaf who dumped her, and a fourth man punched the one who dropped the woman before he could join the fight breaking out in the back corner. Wiping his hands in disgust on his apron, the bartender started to leave his post to intervene, but took a punch directly on the nose from someone waiting impatiently for a drink. With blood spurting, the bartender changed direction and went after his attacker. A woman threw a bottle at the bartender's head but missed and hit a wooden post, showering the clients at the table beside it with alcohol and glass. Two of the bartender's friends joined the fight escalating in the front of the bar. Furniture started to fly. The women in the room either took to screaming profanities, or began pulling at the hair of the nearest man involved in a ruckus.

In the back of the bar, the Phantom pointed to his two distracted assailants and beckoned them to bring it on. The brutes rushed toward the old man, and in the ensuing shoving match all three fell through the double doors into the alleyway – just as a withered, toothless woman threw urine from a bucket out a second story window. With his olfactory glands on alert, the Phantom avoided the waste by jumping backwards to the other side of the space. The odious liquid showered the head of the larger man, who immediately wiped his eyes with his large, grubby fingers.

The hag cackled at the sight, "Sorry, gentlemen!"

"Bucket of piss, my friend?" mocked the Phantom who feigned weakness by leaning up against the wall on the other side of the alley.

"You slimy cock! How'd you get such a young voice? Come here and taste this for yourself!" As the two drunks attacked, Erik skillfully slid between them, pushing hard on their chests, throwing them out and away from each other. One hit the wall beside the door and staggered, the other fell through the open doorway back into the bar. Almost immediately, the later came flying back out, propelled by the thrust of someone inside. Regaining his footing he reached to help his friend stand back up. Their heads bobbed from side to side searching for their insulter.

"Where is the cockroach?" asked the smallest.

They heard the roach speak tauntingly. "Perhaps you two gentlemen are not as nimble as you think! Besides, you shouldn't be yoked together like two oxen, should you?" Their heads went round in all directions, but failed to locate him. "You know what's nice about fighting drunks? They're numb from the drink and can get the crap beat out of them without feeling a damn thing." The Phantom stepped forward from the darkened end of the alley into their view. "Drunks are relaxed and they don't stop coming, even if they're badly damaged. You two aren't ready to stop yet, are you?"

They dove toward the old man again. The first got the back of Erik's elbow full into the teeth, stunning him. Erik pushed him into a wall where he groaned and slid down onto his butt. The second, reaching for Erik's neck, received a kick placed so hard into his crotch that he fell to his knees. With a moan he rolled to his side, his face plopping into a puddle as he passed out.

"Sorry to fight so dirty, but I'm protective of my precious neck. Besides, the point is to get you down as quickly as possible in a decisive win. You give in don't you?" The Phantom rolled him over. "No drowning in a puddle tonight, that would upset my ladies." He turned to look at the other fellow who was sitting on his ass, head folded forward onto his chest. "Apparently you're loosing momentum, too. This is a fine kettle of fish!"

Suddenly the fight inside the bar overflowed through the delivery doors into the alley. Men shoving and hitting each other enveloped the Phantom so quickly that he found himself unable to break free of them. Someone yanked him by the jacket collar and a fist the size of a mallet smashed into his jaw. His head snapped backwards with the fury of the blow, but the thick press of people pounding away at each other kept him upright.

He addressed the three directly pushing in on him, "Gentlemen, if we must scrap...well then, we must!" He couldn't get his arm up high enough to hit one Goliath in the face, but managed to land a decent punch into the man's beefy chest. Avoiding a jab from a second brute, he thought gleefully, *perhaps this is my night after all!*

Another fist came hurling toward his left eye. Instantly, he relaxed his neck and let his head move without resistance as it landed, lessening the impact. As he recovered position, his jacket sleeve was torn by a pair of rough hands trying to take hold of him – effectively locking his elbow from movement. With his opposite hand he reached up and finished tearing it off. He stuck the sleeve into the mouth of a grizzly man swearing in his face. "Here, eat this! I won't be needing it." The density of struggling bodies remained tight upon him, so he drove both his fists as hard as he could into the chest of the man with the sleeve in his mouth, trying to create a small space to maneuver out of the fracas. Unsuccessful, he shouldered himself against the bulky human obstacle and moved one foot forward. The stalwart mass abruptly twisted sideways. In the six inches of open space created by the rotation, someone's booted kick landed with full force into the Phantom's chest. The momentum from the fierce kick moved him, and the entire human wall attached to him, backwards. Air expelled from his lungs in a rush, leaving him momentarily unable to breathe and lightheaded.

Behind him a man swore a curse on his mother and pushed him forward. He felt a solid, hard jab into his right kidney. *Not good,* he thought. Then he was head butted by the man with the sleeve still in his mouth, and went down to the cobblestones, unconscious.

In the early dawn a simple farm cart drawn by a single horse drew up to the alley. The driver and two women hurried from their seats when they saw Erik's body face down in the alley.

Despondent, Meg asked, "Is he alive?"

Jean turned him over as Madame Giry knelt beside him. Placing her ear near his mouth she ascertained that he was still breathing. She touched the thick, flesh colored grease paint on his face trying to comprehend what he had done. Erik's deformed right eye was crusted shut, the left eye and jaw darkly bruised and swollen. He appeared to be a beggar, beaten, dirty and discarded – a homeless castoff with the left sleeve of his jacket and shirt completely gone.

Jean told Meg, "He's alive and stinks of manure!"

"*Mon Dieu,* he's like ice," Madame said taking his hand in hers. "Quickly Jean, place him in the cart." Bending Erik over his shoulder, Jean heaved himself to his feet, grunting under the weight. As he put Erik in the cart, Meg tearfully held his head – guiding it down to the hay. Madame covered him, face and all with a blanket, then climbed up into the cart and tucked herself beside him to provide some warmth with her own body. From beneath the wool blanket she ordered, "Quickly now, let's get him home. When we get there, you two send a messenger to her. Say that I am ill and need her to come to me at once."

The pleasant view from the third floor kitchen table was to the southwest. Out in the street people strolled the boulevard, carriages passed by, and boats moved up and down the calm waters of the river beyond. The early afternoon sun made the outside world seem so inviting. She tapped her fingers rhythmically on the table and looked at him still unconscious on the bed. A cool wet cloth covered his eyes in an attempt to help with the swelling, just until they could get a plaster applied to his face. This was Christine's first visit to his small apartment. The open, singular room spoke of an artist with simple material tastes. She saw the pictures of herself on the walls. In the majority she was happy, but a few portrayed her with a questioning, hopeful expression. His bed, armoire and a round table with a lamp filled one wall. On the wall opposite sat a red French provincial sofa, two cushioned chairs and a low, oval entertainment table painted with flowers. An elaborate Japanese screen set the sitting area off from a massive, carved kneehole desk that filled the front corner. His apartment took up only a small portion of the third floor. She believed the adjacent area, which was entered through a locked door to the left of the sofa, probably contained his library. She imagined it crowded from floor to ceiling with musical scores, books, and architectural layouts. The only musical instrument she was aware of was the piano in the ballet studio. She wasn't sure where he kept her father's violin.

From some distant area in his brain Erik heard the pounding of horses' hooves. His mind pictured them running free, their manes and tails rippling majestically behind them. *No, not horses hooves, incessant rhythmic fingers!* Throwing the cloth off his eyes he sat up, drawing back his right arm, ready to punch the imagined foe in front of him. Only his left eye would open and he saw with blurry vision one of the pictures he'd drawn of Christine on the wall opposite the foot of his bed. *I'm in my room!* He flopped back down with a moan, his head throbbing from the pickaxe hammering into his brain.

For a few seconds he lay perfectly still. *Foot thumping?* The Cyclops-Reborn abruptly opened his one functioning eyelid, and turned his head to the table where the manikin of Christine drinking coffee usually took up residence. There rested the genuine article in a dark green dress with a matching puffed shouldered jacket, hat and bag on the table. His eye opened wider to focus. This version was definitely not smiling!

In a high-pitched, sarcastic voice, Christine's words dug their way into his conscious state. "Awake I see…do we have a little headache?"

He curled up into a ball on his left side, holding his head. "Shh, woman, my head hurts and you sound like a wife."

She moved to the bed with a glass of water and some headache powders folded inside a wrapper. Offering a firm directive she instructed him. "Here, drink this. Your head will hurt less. And I am your wife, just probably in the most distorted, weirdest possible sense of the word one could possibly fathom!" In a huff she sat down on an ottoman next to the bed.

He drank the liquid in the glass and asked, "How did I get back here?"

"Madame Giry, Meg and Jean, hunted for you most of the night. They paid a few prostitutes to send out messages and the word came back that a body was lying in an alley by a bar called The Fish's Mouth, about six blocks from here. You were located before dawn. They brought you back here in a livery cart, like a burlap of smelly field potatoes, I might add."

Erik closed his wretched left eye. "God, you sound like a shrew and I love it. Just *pianissimo* would be better. My brain is three feet outside my skull and clamoring to get back in. Did the good Madame send for you as well?"

"Yes, and I want to talk to you when you're ready to hear me."

"All right, but let me take leave of you to urinate."

"You already did once, all over yourself, and it was quite bloody."

"Hmm, well it's burning like meat on the fire now." He threw his legs over the other side of the bed and used a pitcher. When he finished he returned to the middle of the bed with his muscles making little uncooperative jumps. "Ouch, ouch...ow! All right, my ears are yours."

"What are you doing? You're trying to cope aren't you?"

"Softer, please," putting the wet cloth back on his forehead.

"What kind of life is this for you?"

"Can I have the mirror in the bathroom?"

"No, you can scrutinize your image later when you're alone. You never see what I see anyway."

"It must look pretty bad, huh? Like a full-fledged goblin?" He let his tongue droop out the side of his mouth and studied her reaction with his one functioning eye.

She was not amused. "It looks like you, but entirely smashed up! The left side rather favors the right at the moment. And to what good purpose is all this? I want to bring our son here and live with you, and do you want the same? No. You want to waddle in the mire of the lower classes, drink in a beerhouse and get into bar fights. If you raised one finger in invitation I would come to you," her hand sliced the air, "permanently. So why deny yourself what could be?"

"You **are** sounding like a wife. Please take a moment and turn your back to me." She used her feet to circle round in the ottoman without getting up. "My dear woman, I am well aware that if Michael was a little older, he would run from me in horror at the sight of my face." He opened his nightshirt to find a huge bruise running down his sternum. Shaking his head he whistled, "No wonder each breath cuts like a cleaver."

His words about Michael seared her. She bit back the tears. Looking over her shoulder she saw the ugly bruise. "Good, I hope it hurts and you have to go see a doctor. You could get your ears checked, too. They're not working! Apparently you think you're listening, but my words aren't registering in your brain. I said I want to bake bread for you, but you'd rather get pummeled by drunkards."

"Who washed me?"

"You were washed when I arrived."

He cleared his throat and with his right index finger made a circle in the air. "Please turn around again." She obeyed, turning her face from him. He swung his legs over the side of the bed then pulled her and the ottoman backwards toward him, wrapping his arms around her. "Do you remember this...in the caves, my asking you to trust me, holding you like this?" She closed her eyes and rubbed his forearms. "Do you know what I think is the great truth of life?" She shook her head. "No? Well, let me tell you, it's that life belongs to the persistent, to those who come everyday, faithfully, to the job at hand. I know my job and I know where you need to be. I slipped for a while, that's all. I'm sorry. Sorry to worry you all so much, sorry to make my dear friends stay up all night while I slumber out in the street." He slipped his right index finger under her jacket to the small of her back, rubbing lightly to tantalize her. The sensual effect was immediate, but not what he expected.

She stomped her foot in anger, and stiffening pushed her elbows back into him. "Stop it! You're deliberately refusing to allow my words to get through that thick skull of yours!" She tried to turn toward him again, but he held her fast.

Moving his bruised lips close to her ear, "Listen carefully, Christine, I am absolutely aware of what you want, and I want it too, more than you can ever guess. No amount of drink is enough to erase it from my conscious thought, but your welfare is ultimate. I know you are also sacrificing. I want you to love Michael, perform your wifely duties to Raoul, be the head of that grand household...and stay safe!"

"And continue to leave you in emotional poverty? Nice choice, I almost understand the desire for drunken stupor."

"I am richer than you might think, certainly more than I ever dreamed I would be." He decided to tease her. "Did you know that I have perfected the art of disguise? Color and texture are the keys. Like a chameleon I could stand in any of your rooms tomorrow and watch you, and no one would know of it."

"Not with your chest and waterworks burning like they are!"

"You cut me to the quick, Madame, but your point is well taken." He kissed the back of her neck as best he could and released his grip enough to let her turn around to face him.

"Now it's your turn to listen. You stay hidden in the shadows, cast away from the world because no one outside this house appreciates the beauty inside you. And with the inescapable passage of every minute, I am becoming your mirror image. My inner self swims in a vat of horrendous worry. When people see me smiling politely, they know nothing of the distress gnawing at me. Give me your faithful promise that you will stop deliberately putting yourself in danger. The cost if you don't? Me living here, your full-time nagging wife!"

Concentrating completely and without realizing it, Erik had been holding his breath while she spoke. As her words gained clarity in his head, he exhaled in her face, forcing her to close her eyes. She fanned the air in front of her. Apparently he needed to do something about his breath too. He kissed her forehead. It wasn't that he didn't want her constantly with him, as the stars shone in the heavens, he did, but what she said about the mirror image troubled him. He made her an offer, "Perhaps we should take a little time and go do something fun together. Do you agree? Where is Raoul?"

"He's in Italy for at least two more weeks."

"Give me one week to mend. Tell the household that you need to take care of your old ballet teacher for a day while her daughter Meg is away somewhere. Better pleasant memories, than nagging and worry, *oui?* You have my faithful promise. I will not deliberately seek out another fight." Adding mentally, *I will do all in my power not to get the shit kicked out of me like this again!*

After she left, he went to the kitchen table and picked up a folded sheet of music paper from his desk. In Christine's delicate handwriting he read the note she'd written while he slept:

Teach me to live in this pain, Erik, or it is I who will go insane. Torn between two worlds is proving more than I can bear. Knowing you could so easily harm that which I hold so dear, I sail sightless to a precipice where once again I confront the possibility of a life without you. Shall I embrace the horror of despair yet again? Help me, Love, it is I who lists distorted, sheets twisted to the main.

He took a match from a box on top of the table and striking it, burned the note. When he looked up Madame Giry was standing inside the room at the back doorway. "She needs a break, and perhaps you, too." Madame Giry nodded affirmatively. "I'm sorry, Louisa, I will never do this to you again. I promise."

She knew him to be speaking the truth, but her apprehension was not relieved. "Tell me about the grease paint."

"I couldn't go as myself in a mask. It would draw too much attention, put us at risk. And I knew they wouldn't spar with me in my own face, they'd run from the bar in terror."

"You, needed a street fight?"

The wall clock beside his head loudly ticked off a few seconds before he answered. "Not any more. I'll use our other tricks to control him."

Madame nodded sadly. "You need something to eat, come downstairs. I have a roast."

In a week Erik took Christine on a day trip. In the early morning she came to *Rue du Renard,* and they left immediately for the train station. They dressed in casual clothes. He wore a tan colored mask and a large brimmed straw hat suitable for a French country gentleman. Since the weather was still warm, Christine went in a pale-yellow cotton dress and carried a white shawl. She held a parasol to hide her face. They took a two hour train ride northwest to Les Andelys on the Seine. When they arrived at the small town, he purchased a basket lunch and hired a carriage to take them to a spot where he had arranged a surprise for her – a hot air balloon ride over the countryside. They watched as the multicolored balloon, filled with heated air, started pulling at the ropes anchoring it to the ground. When they climbed into the basket Erik placed her in front of him, away from the pilot. They listened to the swishing sound of the burner being fired up, and the cheerful well wishes of the assistants as they untied the ropes. As the balloon floated upward the tops of trees appeared below them, the glorious fields and the curling river spread out upon the vista. The homes and animals clustered about were but tiny children's play things, and the open sky surrounding them, endless and serene. The ride lasted for over an hour, an hour of feeling unattached and unencumbered, no cares, only joy. When the balloon returned to earth, the helpers brought them in a wagon to a pleasant spot. Under the shade of an old elm tree the couple picnicked alone on chicken and rolls.

They decided to remove their shoes and dangle their feet in a nearby creek. As they sat feeling the coolness of the water, he sang to her a little song about the bear lumbering through the forests searching for the magic orb. The smell of the country grass, the lush fields of flowers, even the simple sound of insects buzzing, helped to allay the strain of their lives in Paris. It seemed another world entirely. Wiggling her toes, Christine asked, "How did you find this place?"

"I was born in nearby Rouen, the son of a master mason." Deep furrows formed across his left forehead. "Occasionally a very lonely, little boy could see these balloons from his bedroom window."

She didn't want the past to cloud this day, but the ripeness of the opportunity was irresistible. The desire to know more about him urged her to push a little further. "Lucky me. Where did the little boy go to from here?"

"He ran away to the traveling fairs to learn their tricks, and then to Persia, where he became useful to the Daroga and the Sultana."

"And where did he learn to fight?"

"The guards of the Shah taught him the art of the Punjab lasso." He reached into his pocket and pulled out a long piece of thin, braided catgut with a noose. She felt it – soft and supple, in a coil it hardly took up any space at all.

"How does it work?"

"Lift up your hand and hold it before your face." As she did so the noose flew from his fingers, and in the blink of an eye wrapped itself around her wrist. It moved so quickly she didn't see it catch her. He snapped his wrist back. Her captured arm instantly drew her torso to him. He reached over and kissed her playfully, slipping the lasso off her hand.

"No fair. I didn't see it work. Please, do it again."

"All right, but every time you must pay the fee."

"Bargain!" She moved away from him with her feet still in the water, but as soon as she had her hand before her face he had it in the noose. "No fair again. I wasn't ready."

"Hmm, still have to pay the fee though," he scooted over and she rendered the kiss.

When the wagon dropped them off in the town, they wandered through its quaint streets window-shopping. They spent some time in a park of giant maples, enjoying the paintings done by local artists on display there. The influences of Monet and Degas abounded on their canvases, and Erik spoke with some of them about the French Impressionist's use of vivid color to portray only what the eye actually saw. No one asked about the mask, perhaps they thought him a knowledgeable soldier wounded in the service of his country. For a while they sat at a café, taking in the sunlight and the chatter of strangers. It occurred to him, that for once she was not full of questions and thoughts she wanted to share. *Perhaps all she needs is enough time for me to listen to what she has built up in her head, and then she is content.* He watched her facial expressions and counted the number of curls she had twisted into her hair before allowing it to cascade down her back. When they went to the train station he purchased a private compartment for the ride back to

Paris. Inside they curled up on the suede upholstery like two contented house cats, and surveyed the scenery passing by.

"I might be able to live the rest of my life on the memory of this day," she told him.

"You won't have to." He took a candy from his pocket, "Peppermint?"

8 *VASSALS FOR SCHEHERAZADE*

Onward and upward was the motto young Kate Edwards adopted for herself after the premature death of her mother. Strong willed and determined she stifled her grief, and endeavored to be the very picture of persistence and patience in every situation her widowed father placed her. She was not thwarted by her many unsuccessful attempts to gain access to the two floors above the ballet studio, only delayed. It occurred to her that locked doors were not the only passageways to the prince. After some deliberations she decided on an alternate, more devious attack. For in the end, appeasing her own curiosity proved more appetizing than continually pleasing her father with her virtue of industriousness.

On a Sunday afternoon in October she sat at dinner with her Papa, waiting for his usual litany of questions. She was not to be disappointed.

"How are your ballet lessons going, my dear?"

With a flushed face the words tumbled forth from Scheherazade's disciple. "Papa, did you know that a prince lives on the third floor of the ballet studio? He wears a sword and carries packages, and he is very handsome and strong!"

The detective wiped his mouth, pricked by the magic of his daughter's excitement. "No, I didn't know that. Have you met this prince? What is his name?"

Looking dramatically downcast for a second, she responded, "No, I haven't met him...but I've seen him! He'd just come from a fight out in the street. He defended the house from thieves who wanted to break in and steal his treasures."

The detective was definitely interested now. "A fight you say, and you don't know his name?"

"No one knows his name. It's so sad, Papa, he has no name, but he's gorgeous and so brave! The girls say he's Madame Giry's brother."

"My, a handsome prince who fends off thieves and doesn't have a name. What happened when you saw him?"

"He disappeared right before my eyes, Papa! Did you know that princes could do that? They can you know, when they want to, because the fairies bless them and hide them."

"My, my…indeed, a magical prince with fairies watching his back, perhaps we should investigate and learn more about him. What do you say, hmm?" He brushed her hair with his hand, enjoying her imagination.

"Oh please, Papa, I told the other girls that I would introduce them to him. Could you arrange a meeting? Please, Papa, do it for me."

In the early evening, the detective left Kate with a neighbor and went for a carriage ride along the nearly deserted Sunday streets. He had the driver stop a block away from the ballet studio and walked the remaining distance to Madame Giry's. Putting his back up against the wall of a house down the street from the dance school, he lit his pipe and studied the cream colored house with the gray tiled roof. Lights were lit in both the second and third floor windows on the dwelling's left side. As he watched the shadow of a man passed over the third floor curtains. *So there is someone up there.* After waiting a few more minutes, he moved around to the back of the house, and continued his survey from the alcove of a carriage entrance across the alley. A seven-foot wall encircled the back yard. A solid metal gate prevented him from viewing the ground level, but he had a clear view of the second floor windows and the gabled windows of the third floor. Fetching a couple of wooden crates from a trash pile, he stood on them by the gate and peered over.

He noted several clotheslines stretched between poles, two brown wicker chairs, and a concrete stoop going up to a wooden door on the far right corner of the house. The light was on in what was most likely the second floor kitchen. There the curtains were a lighter lace, and he could make out the figures of a man and a woman sitting at a kitchen table eating. The light from the third floor on this side of the house was dim, as if the only lamps turned on in that area of the dwelling were at the front. In a few minutes the couple finished whatever they were eating, and after placing the dishes in the sink the man draped a shawl about the woman's shoulders. *Perhaps they are going out!*

Edwards returned to the front of the house as the man, with Madame Giry's arm tucked into his, walked up the street to the boulevard. *Taking an evening's walk after supper, no doubt.* Returning to the back gate, he picked the lock and was pleased that it opened without the squeal of metal on metal he had anticipated. *Well oiled.* Proceeding to the backdoor he picked its lock, entered as quietly as a snake hunting a mouse, and found himself in the first floor stairwell. The soft glow of a gas lamp attached to the wall helped him to make out his surroundings. Looking up the stairwell he observed the same light fixture positioned on the second and third floor levels. The walls of the stairwell were of a dark symmetrically grooved paneling. A red banister ran the length of the stairs. The stairs themselves were wooden, with three-foot wide red carpeting. The first eleven stairs curved gently upward and to the right, ending on a small landing. From there they continued to curve around to the second floor where he could appreciate the kitchen door. An identical double set of stairs proceeded from the second floor landing to the third. He could not make out the door to the third floor from where he stood.

To his left he found the back entrance to the ballet studio. He reached to test the knob and came upon the metal eye with the toggled string through it. His eyes followed the string to a bridle ring, and then on to a second, going upward until it disappeared into the darkness. *Simple, alerts them to the prying snoops of little girls.*

The detective stood in the back entrance unaware that he was already being observed. The two he saw leaving were Madame Giry and Jean, who had come to escort his mother-in-law to his estate for a Sunday evening's visit with her daughter. Working at his desk on the third floor, Erik had smelled the tobacco smoke on the detective as he trespassed through the door. He turned off the two lamps that were lit around him and closed the heavy drapes. Re-masked, the Phantom stood in the shadows of the third floor landing watching the intruder closely. His weapon of choice, the Punjab lasso, rested in his right hand. A razor sharp dagger lay ready to fly from a shoulder scabbard. He did not know the intruder's identity, but had a strong suspicion it was Kate's father, the English detective, as Kate carried the same smell of Virginian tobacco in her clothes and hair.

With great care the detective moved up the stairs to the second floor landing. His soft leather shoes made only the barest of noises, something akin to taffeta rustling against itself. The average person would not have heard it, but to the Phantom it sounded like the man stomped his way up, with the encroaching smell blaring the announcement of his advance. The mildest film of sweat broke out upon the detective's brow; in contrast the Phantom was dry, his skin once more like ice to the touch.

Achieving the second floor, the detective saw the door to Madame's apartment, tried the knob and found it locked. A door to his left intrigued him. Opening it cautiously, he discovered her brooms and brushes, a mop with a bucket and other various cleaning utensils. He closed the closet door and looked up the stairwell to the third floor. The same unusually grooved paneling covered the walls above. He ran his hand over the ridges and indentations, but before he could consider its curiosity, realized with chagrin that the stairwell lamp on the third level had gone out. Not knowing how much time the couple would take for their walk, he decided to proceed upward, even in diminished light, and investigate the identity of this brother.

As the detective stealthfully climbed the final set of stairs, the Phantom backed up into the blackness of his apartment, keeping his eyes trained intently on the staircase. With his face constantly forward, Erik retreated in an unusual undulating walk. His right shoulder and hip moved in unison with his right leg and foot, one-step backward.

Then the left shoulder and hip moved as a unit with the left leg, one-step backward. The effect, if one could visually record it, was that of a human snake withdrawing effortlessly in a rhythmic, winding manner. He matched each step the detective took on the stairs to a step of his own, until the Phantom was twenty paces from the wall on the street side of his apartment. The Japanese screen was on his right.

Rounding the newel post of the landing the detective paused. The soft light from the floor below shone dimly behind him. He was surprised to find the door of the third floor wide-open and hesitated to enter, sensing something oddly sinister in the room before him. As he gazed cautiously inward he could see only as far as the little kitchenette and the outline of a large bed directly beyond. *Sparsely furnished, as a man would have it.*

Invisible to the detective's eye the Phantom marked the distance between them and tested the strength of the thin lasso in his hands. *Get within twelve feet of me and you are mine!* Every fibrous muscle within him remained poised for the deadly strike that would end the detective's life should he choose to take it. What he had not told Christine was that once the lasso was around the neck and lifted upward, the weapon deprived the brain of blood, rendering its victim unconscious in seconds. Continuing the pressure caused suffocation and death within minutes, but if the windpipe or spine was snapped, death was virtually instantaneous. A skillful user of the Punjab lasso could apply just enough pressure to keep the victim paralyzed, but still conscious enough to hear the final taunting address of his killer. The Phantom had the strength and the expertise to do all of these, and had done so many times. *Merde, why keep coming? Be smart and stay out, think of your daughter.* The Phantom decided to try one other alternative. Using his skills as a ventriloquist he made the sound of muffled voices come from the street.

Thinking he heard people returning, the detective retreated quickly, leaving the house the way he'd entered. The Phantom watched through a window as the interloper opened the back gate and disappeared down the alley.

The following morning Detective Edwards reported for duty at the police station where he was assigned. He mentioned the brother living on the third floor of the ballet studio to a fellow officer, Andre Davier, whose curiosity was peeked as well. The French officer knew of Madame Giry's past employment at the Opera House, but had never heard of a brother. As best he could recall, he explained to the Englishman the tragedies that occurred at the theater during the winter months of late 1870, and early 1871.

At the time, the managers of the Opera House claimed they were plagued by the haunting of a malicious ghost. A truly sad affair as a number of people had lost their lives. Some deaths were caused by the accidental crashing of a massive crystal chandelier, that was attributed to the poor inspection and maintenance of its chains. While still others succumbed to an unidentified form of strangulation – no actual rope was every found near a victim. Along with the deaths, the current Countess de Chagny, who had been a dancer and singer at the Opera House during those months, had mysteriously disappeared for a time, vanishing right off the center stage in the middle of an aria. She reappeared a few weeks later, and in short order became the Count de Chagny's bride in a very private ceremony. The Count alleged that the same Opera Ghost persecuting the managers had abducted his fiancée. A sort of mass hysteria had gripped the theater. The officers in charge of the case believed the young man fed into the mania. He was madly in love with the girl, and competing with his own brother for her attentions. They found his statements wildly exaggerated and his claims unfounded. Most likely the performer, feeling pressured into marriage, had gone off somewhere to consider her choices. In retrospect, the whole affair seemed curious, what with so many still unsolved strangulations and their possible perpetrator still at large. The officers in '71 felt that some were suicides, but certainly they couldn't all be. The case remained open but inactive. The French officer also remembered that Madame Giry was on somewhat friendly terms with the so-called Opera Ghost, and of some usefulness to him, if there truly was a ghost at all. Remarkably, since that time, all had been well at the theater, except for the occasional pickpocket lifting a purse or a lady's jewels.

An older officer, who sat quietly listening to Davier's recitation, spoke up chidingly. "That's probably because we found whoever was playing the ghost all chopped up and burned, don't you think?"

"You're referring to that body they found in the tunnels?" asked Davier.

"The way I see it, someone laid hold of the rascal and gave him what-for in a nasty way," explained the older detective. "Wouldn't surprise me if it was the managers, or the Count himself...anyway, things are quiet now, like you said. We have bigger fish to fry than three-year-old cases colder than a witch's tit."

Just to be on the safe side, Davier and Edwards agreed that they should do two simple things, even though no crime was currently being reported. The French officer would go to the de Chagny estate and make an inquiry with the manager, Victor LaPointe, as to the health of his employers and the tranquility of the premises. Detective Edwards was to dispatch himself to the ballet studio and question Madame Giry regarding the brother living upstairs.

When Edwards came to pick up his daughter that afternoon at three o'clock, he settled her into a carriage and told her to wait outside. After offering Kate a book to read, he returned to the studio and requested a conversation with the good Madame. She promptly complied and led him through the alcove leading into her office at the rear of the dance studio. He noticed that he was in a room without windows, the walls covered with the same symmetrically grooved paneling as the back stairwell. In the center of the office stood a deeply carved walnut desk, with cabriole legs and an elaborately tooled leather top, protected by a heavy piece of glass. In contrast to the desk, the chairs were a simple country design with thick round seat cushions. Her choice of furniture told him she was a pragmatist who acknowledged, and deeply appreciated, elegance. The room contained more than enough space for the desk and its few chairs. Several cupboards were about the office, most likely for papers and such.

Airflow apparently occurred as a result of leaving the office door opened to its view of the studio beyond. The detective quickly recalled that there were no windows on the outside of this particular corner of the house.

Edwards settled himself into one of the chairs after the ballet mistress took her seat behind the desk. With a composed demeanor Madame Giry inquired, "And the nature of this conversation, Monsieur?"

"Madame, please excuse this intrusion. I know you must be tired from the class, but I need to discuss with you a most curious incident my daughter related to me. Incredible as it may sound, she thinks she glimpsed a gallant prince who resides in this establishment. What she saw came and went before her very eyes, something like a ghost." As he spoke he carefully watched the woman's face for the slightest change in her pupils or expression. She was so placid he wondered for a moment if his words had registered at all. He was suddenly struck with the realization that he had never noticed, up until this very moment, the extraordinary beauty of her countenance. Her long blond hair was braided and fashioned like a crown atop her head. The end of the braid, drawn forward and draped over her shoulder, rested lightly over her bosom. Her eyes were a brilliant blue, the color of Kashmir sapphires, her smooth pink skin showed good health and proper attention. Below her small, straight nose lay a mouth and chin of dignity and repose.

"Little Kate must have gotten a glimpse of my brother. He lives on the third floor."

"Might it be possible to meet him?"

"He is a recluse, Monsieur. In his adult years he has suffered the residual effects of a severe childhood disease. He is often too weak for any real measure of activity. He was in a hospital for many months, cared for by the good Sisters of Charity. When he regained some of his strength they allowed him to be brought to my home."

"I'm so sorry to hear of his ordeal. Is he in the house now?"

"No Monsieur, he is at the healing baths of Lourdes, praying for the Virgin to cure his ailments."

"I see. Was he the elderly gentleman that accompanied you two weeks ago to the theater?" There at last, the hoped for reaction, almost imperceptible except to the trained eye, she blinked in veiled surprise.

"Yes, Monsieur, he experienced a brief period of energy and we took advantage of it to have a rare excursion out. A most enjoyable evening. I hope it will not be our last."

Keeping up the momentum of what was bordering on an interrogation, he asked, "And what is your brother's name?"

"Imel Grey."

"Grey?"

"Yes, he is my half-brother, born from an indiscretion on my mother's part before she was married to my father. Grey being my mother's maiden name." All this was delivered with the same composure and vocal tone she held when she first sat down behind her desk.

"Did he have a trade?"

"When he was a younger man, he was a printer."

"A good one, I would imagine. I've one last inquiry, Madame, if you would be so kind as to humor me."

"Please, be my guest."

"Do you ever hear anything from the Opera Ghost?"

At that Madame Giry's face brightened and she let out a little chuckle. "Sadly no, I enjoyed his antics in the theater very much. He was accustomed to haunting box five in the grand tier, but I've had no preternatural disturbances since I moved into this house in the early spring of '71."

The detective seemed pleased with all the responses she offered. Since he knew he had no business requesting an inspection of the third floor, he resigned himself to further questioning his daughter as to what exactly she had seen. He now suspected Kate guilty of flagrant fabrication and a brazen attempt at manipulation. He stood to leave, fidgeting with his brown bowler hat, and hesitated for a moment.

Madame paused inquisitively as she came around the desk, waiting patiently for him to voice yet another thought.

"Would you ever be interested in going out to dinner with me?"

After a second her face reflected poised disinclination, and she responded, "I thank you for your kind invitation, but I have only been in the private company of two men in my lifetime, my husband and a dear friend who passed away some time ago."

"May I leave you my card, should you ever change your mind and need an evening's respite from your duties?" She took the proffered object from his hand and laid it on her desk.

She escorted him to the front porch, locking the door to the main entrance as he left. When she re-entered the ballet studio she locked its door as well. Before returning to her office she went to the first of the studio's seven-foot Palladian windows and began to untie the cord to its heavy velvet drape. Anyone who came up to the glass could see past the lace curtains into the studio, and she thought to keep the prying eyes of a detective, still hovering out in the street, away from them. Reconsidering her actions, she left the heavier drapes tied back. Since she knew him to be watching, she didn't want to appear to be hiding after his interview.

When she returned to the office she went to a picture hanging on the wall and removed it. The nail it hung on was situated inside a groove of the polished paneling. As she pressed on the head of the nail with her thumb, a three-foot piece of the wall moved back an inch and slid smoothly to the left, situating itself in a pocket. The foot high threshold of the opening remained immobile as the wood moved without a sound. Out over the threshold stepped Meg and their Phantom from a three-foot wide hallway that encircled Madame's work area. The office was essentially a smaller room within a larger one. The later could be entered from the concealed door she had just opened, or from a ladder running up to a secret closet in the library on the third floor. Small holes in the paneling allowed for an almost three hundred-sixty degree visual access of the office by anyone standing in the outer shell. The only area not available for spying was that of the recessed alcove doorway. Hearing conversations taking place within the office from the hidden corridor had never proved a difficulty.

After the invasion of the night before, the three presumed that the detective would, at some point the following day, question Madame. They calculated the most opportune time would present itself as he picked up his daughter from class. When Meg and Erik saw the detective come back into the house after putting Kate into the carriage, they simply climbed down the ladder and waited in the room's unseen sanctuary.

The three made themselves comfortable in the chairs. The Phantom, after stretching out his long legs, laced his fingers together and cracked his knuckles. Folding his hands in his lap he spoke matter-of-factly. "Lourdes, Louisa? I'm not even Catholic."

"I thought I did quite well for someone thinking on her feet. Don't crack your knuckles again. You know very well it piques me."

"You were amazing, Mama, I was impressed. He even wants to take you out to dinner!"

"You enchanted him with your striking features, Louisa," teased Erik. "And cracking my knuckles feels good."

"Yes, I did indeed." She smoothed back the side of her meticulously combed hair, took warranted pride in her performance and ignored his comment about knuckles. "The Detective remembered all his questions, and forgot I performed on a stage."

Meg asked seriously, "How easy is this going to be to contain?"

"If he ever connects the compositions of E. D'Angelus with this house, not easy at all. I could not risk telling him my brother was a composer," her mother answered. "The managers used to pay the Opera Ghost twenty thousand francs a month for his creations. It frosts my cake that this vile man had the gall to enter our home without invitation and poke around as he saw fit. Not only is it beyond compromise that he may discover you," she raised her eyebrows and shot a smile at Erik. "But he has now seen the inside of my broom closet...a grievous breach of etiquette and simply unforgivable!"

Erik snorted a short laugh and Meg candidly added, "I think he wants to inspect more than your broom closet, Mama."

Bouncing her open palm off the desk, Madame announced, "Let's have a sherry!" Burrowing into a cupboard she emerged with a bottle and three glasses. After pouring a drink for each of them, they toasted, "*Bonne sante!* Good health!"

Erik swallowed then swirled the remaining liquid in his glass. Setting the glass on the desk he made a suggestion. "I could go back to the Opera House and live in the caverns again. No one expects the persona of the ghost to reappear."

Madame quickly objected. "No! Regression is not an option. Besides, I would not permit you to return without me, and I will not work again for those lecherous men who use the dancers sexually as if they were a private harem. Summoning them at their beck and call!" She took a bit more sherry and after delicately wiping just the smallest of drops from her lower lip, continued demurely. "We may have to kill you again."

"Killing me is getting to be something of a habit, but it always seems to have its merits. We could purchase a gravesite near Daae's mausoleum and bury me there." He drifted off, his mind rolling into construction mode.

Watching him Meg smiled mischievously. "You know, the house could do with a few more deceptive renovations."

Her mother winked at her and poured more sherry into the glasses. "We must watch this detective and his little girl closely. In a couple of days I'll make inquires about a gravesite. It will be new black dresses for us, Meg. We need to prepare for the unfortunate, but expected funeral of your uncle."

Meg sat back and responded over her drink. "Let's see the dressmaker discreetly in the beginning of next week and casually mention the foreboding ill-health of your brother." She raised a silent toast to them both.

The following day the two police officers crossed paths, each with news of a nonproductive nature. Disappointed, Davier reported that he'd seen Victor LaPointe. The chateau was bustling with the birth of a new son and heir to the de Chagny estate. Both mother and infant were doing admirably and the baptism was to take place the following Sunday. "By the way, we're invited to the party afterward. Do you want to go? The place is really something to see."

Detective Edwards accepted the invitation. He went on to explain that his daughter, in a moment of impolite weakness, had entered into the private quarters of the residence and caught a brief glance of the ballet mistress' ailing, fragile brother. She had been severely reprimanded and made to give her solemn promise to mind her own business and respect the privacy of others. The detective also added that he had hopes of someday taking the good Madame out for dinner. Davier wished him luck, and since there were actual murders to solve, they both returned to their active cases.

After supper that evening, Erik rolled out design sketches on Madame Giry's kitchen table. Presenting them to Louisa, the Daroga and Meg, he explained the obvious. "The house is modest and adequate enough to meet our needs, but could do with a few more concealed entrances and exits."

They all agreed and leaning forward to consider the drawings, vowed they were up for the task. They rejected the idea of sealing the doors to the third floor apartment, but loved the addition of a trapdoor under one of Erik's rugs. Through it he could drop down to the second floor and flee through the back or the front. They also approved of the construction of thick black screens to go over his windows; so that at night it would appear that no one was ever on the third floor. Erik would also install a system of buttons hidden in arabesque ornaments. When pushed, the buttons would activate an assemblage of coordinated chimes that sounded like soft horse bells out in the street. The bells would alert them that Erik needed to go into the walls. The best idea, *la piece de resistance* of deceptions, was a sketch for a set of vertical, three sided blinds to conceal an escape ladder leading to the roof. Although going up was never a desirable option, it would create an additional place for hiding. The first of the three sides to each vertical piece would be the color of the wall it stood before, the second of a Japanese countryside, and the third a slender concave mirror. The confusing effect, to anyone viewing the movement of the sectioned parabolic mirror, would be that of a person spreading-out and disappearing in a shimmering vitreous luster. Erik and Meg did a comic imitation of the befuddled police and they all enjoyed a laugh. An enthusiastic Daroga produced a bottle of Tokay from a briefcase and wanted to know when they could get started on the projects, and which one should be paramount!

"The screens," shouted Meg, as she went to wake up Jean, who was snoring in an overstuffed parlor chair, with one-year-old Claude asleep on his chest like a little frog.

Pleased with their further acts of misdirection, Madame Giry began to serve crepes with berries and whipped cream for dessert.

9 ONLY A DREAM AND A DRAGON

Musing over a virtually untouched plate of food in the chateau's dining room, Christine was informed over dinner of Inspector Davier's odd visit. Unaware of the defensive plans already taking a foothold with the group at the ballet studio, she thanked Victor and retired to her chambers. A growing fear rose within her that the law officer's inquiries and the circumspect existence of the Phantom were somehow related to each other. She paced her room in anxious worry. *Perhaps the police have new information and are starting to sniff about again.*

She tried to settle at her desk and write additional instructions to the household staff about the baptismal party, but couldn't get her thoughts to cooperate. Her mind refused to do anything but tumble about over Erik. In frustration she laid down her pen and climbed into bed.

Attempting sleep was useless. In a few minutes she jerked back up and pulled the cord for one of the servants to attend to her. She asked for a glass of peach liqueur and inquired after the baby. When the alcohol was brought to her she was told that the infant was sound asleep. She drained the contents of the crystal glass and returned to bed. Lying on her back with her eyes wide-open and focused on the ceiling, she fretted over Sunday. Everyone, all their family and friends, would be at the church and then back to the estate for the celebration, everyone but Erik. She accepted that he would not come, even in disguise, for he knew that in her tempestuousness she would walk right up to him and place the baby in his arms. *Here, hold your son!* She missed him and ached for him. They had not been intimate in months. On Sunday she would look everywhere for him. Even knowing he would not be there, she would still search the crowd, wishing for the slightest glimpse of his engaging eyes and handsome figure as he walked around, speaking to the guests. Instead, it would be Raoul strutting about like a peacock. With his sharp, angular features and high cheekbones, the proud father would be talking business and openly eyeing her breasts.

A foul taste of acid rose to the back of her throat as she remembered Raoul demanding to experience suckling like Michael and her flatly refusing him, determined that he would have none of her until she could be with Erik. With his pride wounded, the haughty Raoul had insisted that she stop feeding the baby from her breasts and hire a wet nurse at once. Folding his arms and lifting his head to talk down to her, his vehement words still rang in her ears. "It's not becoming for a Countess to give milk like a cow!" For the sake of peace she finally acquiesced to his demands, and when he'd had his fill at her nipples, he went and hired a wet nurse anyway! To add insult to hurt already received, Erik had not even noticed on the day of their hot air balloon trip that she had stopped lactating. *Oh this is crazy, what a way to live!* She took one of the pillows and vehemently threw it to the floor.

Her rational mind told her to rest, tomorrow was another day and nothing could be accomplished tonight. She willed herself to relax. Punching another pillow with her fist and repositioning it under her head she turned to her left side. A sense of Erik's embrace came to her. *Why does his mouth always taste so distinctly sweet?* She would have to ask him. In so many ways he was still such complex mystery.

Thinking about all she still did not understand of him, brought back the memory of a conversation they'd had in the mausoleum. In the flickering light of one guttering candle, he had told her that he was often reticent to speak of his love for her. The words never come out bearing the true depth of how he felt. To reach the precise truth was painful. He had to lay open a wound within his heart to get even the merest expression to come forth, but telling her in a song proved to be a different matter entirely. For some reason, honestly unknown to him, communicating to her through the discourse of music was easy. He gave her an immediate example. Closing his eyes he caressed the empty air in front of him as if he were holding her, and began to sing in his rapturous voice of his love. She would never forget the song.

"Come with me, my darling, come.
Dance with me among the tombs,
A slow dance into midnight,
A sensuous dance of purpose and pleasure,
One of considered thought and measure.
A slow dance into midnight,
Until you moan, sated in my arms."

His alluring words and the crescendo of his voice, the fervor with which he sang to the imagined Christine he held before him, had thrilled her – and it did again here on this bed of restlessness.

She replayed his love song in her head over and over, letting the words soothe her worries. Gradually she drifted off into its echoing phrases when suddenly her eyes flew open again. She could actually hear him singing the song, but somewhere off in the distance. She hastened to a window to view the woods to the north. In the moonlight, the grass before the wooded area appeared to be a lake of silver. Her eyes canvassed it, moving upward to the trees and there he stood at the edge of them. Despite the distance, she could easily make out his black evening cape, white facemask and evening attire. His gentle mouth above his cravat began again the song of her dream.

"Come with me, my darling, come.
I wish to dance with you, a slow dance into moonlight."

She threw a woolen cloak over her white sleeping gown and left the house through the breakfast room, walking straight to the spot where she saw him standing. She reached the young boys with their metal rings and although she couldn't see Erik, his agreeable voice was still audible in her ears. Stepping into the trees she placed her back against a trunk and listened to the grace of his voice. When he stopped she whispered breathlessly, "Angel of Music, I have brought you a living body to dance with, and my love to succor you in the night. Where are you, my Phantom? I have come."

Not hearing a response she stepped onto the path. Looking back through the thick leaves only a few lights burned through the windows of the chateau, she fretted that she might be alone and thought to return, but the moon shone brightly and welcomed her visit. A barn owl hooted and as it cooed her name she drew courage. *Things are not as they seem here.* She walked down the path searching for the slightest hint of the maestro. As she attained a clearing she saw him laying on the ground, arms folded across his chest. *How dramatic!* She ran to his side, abruptly stopping in horror about a yard away. The crater of a bullet hole lay carved into his pale forehead. Behind his head a dark pool of red blood extended outward, growing in a widening circle.

In disbelief she spun around, seeking an answer in the surrounding trees. The fury of a primitive rage rose within her. She looked to the stars and screamed at the top her lungs, "No! No! Who took this life? You had no right! No right at all!" A low growling sound at her feet sent a prickly chill of fear through her body. Cautiously she brought her head back downward and beheld a wolf-like creature, fangs exposed in a snarl, crouched in attack position on the other side of the Phantom's body. Saliva drooled from the side of the animal's mouth, its retinas shone like satanic discs of red. Still snarling and fixed on her, its snout came forward to smell the bullet hole. It growled a further threat and began to lick the blood pool.

The predator seemed to be declaring Erik truly dead. She shivered and went to her knees before the menace of the beast.

In the air beside the wolf a warm yellow light, about the size and shape of a pear, appeared and brightened. Strangely numb, she watched the light hover and pulsate beside the thirsting creature. The luminescence rose to the level of her eyes and moving midway across the corpse seemed to study her for a moment. Then it returned to where it had first appeared. The wolf stopped its incessant feeding and hunkered down on its abdomen, its devilish eyes still glaring at Christine. The light extended itself vertically, taking on the figure of a delicate young individual. The golden being gaining shape before her was neither male nor female. It had a straight nose and kind almond eyes, with a head of ear-length curls. Softly, and almost as if the sound were only an echo vibrating in her own head, she heard it speak without opening its mouth. "If this form is acceptable to you, I have been instructed to inquire, who is speaking for him?"

In a small voice Christine answered, "I am." Her hand passed protectively over the inert body of her love. "Who is he?"

"Among the celestial beings he is known simply as The Voice. He chose to come here bearing his great gift of sound, but with a curse of equal strength bound to him. His task was to learn to love the curse, to love the gift of ugliness. He has not succeeded."

Christine was perplexed. "I don't understand."

"There is more to living than what you perceive through sight or touch. Life is more than you imagine, more complex than what religion teaches. To hear of it you must un-tether your mind." The entity pointed to the Phantom's mask. "The prescribed curse included his parents' disdain and rejection, and the scorn of the world poured out upon his head. Several times in this life, The Voice has approached loving himself exactly as he is, but it's proven to be too difficult a task. He has met with failure."

"He had to accomplish this goal alone?"

"No, we sent a guardian, but even it lost its way. For a time it valued the material things of this world more than love. It is my job to return The Voice to us. He may yet seek another space and time to attempt this task."

Christine, hoping to create time to bargain, made a request. "Can you send the wolf away, please?"

"I shall. Do you wish to know who he is?"

"Yes, who is the horrid thing?"

"He is a component of The Voice, the earthly manifestation of his physical deformity. He has won the day and as the victor licks his life's blood. For the moment time is suspended. I need to hasten and return with The Voice."

Christine studied the face of the wolf closely and sensing he was indeed part of Erik reached across the body to rub its ear. Whimpering, the animal bent its head sideways leaning into her touch. "He doesn't want to return. Who has the right to speak for The Voice? Surely not you, angel? Let's let love speak for him, shall we? Do you love him? You're here to do a job, so let me help you complete it. Take me in his place and restore life to him. Do you have the power to do that?"

The radiant figure responded, "I have. Is it that you feel pity for him?"

"No, I am him, we bound our souls together. Give him back his life and take mine."

With a mild frown the entity began to pulsate once more, as if it were thinking, or listening, to others. "This is an exceptional thing that you declare. Do you mind if we test it?"

"Be my guest."

The immortal passed its hand in front of Christine's face and her eyes closed. A loud crack of thunder split through the sky and her eyes shot open in fear. She was adrift in a creaking rowboat with the wind howling around her. Pelted by sheets of rain, she grabbed hold of the gunwales to secure herself as the waves rocked the boat precariously back and forth. Another deafening roll of thunder ricocheted through the heavy clouds overhead. Off in the distance a jagged lightening bolt, like the bony fanned-out fingers of an evil hand, hit the water. In disbelief she saw the multiple charges it created heading straight for her boat! A hundred electrical scintillations snaked toward a helpless victim. As they approached, they drew back and gathered again into one fearsome, crackling mass of lightening that lifted itself above the waves in the shape of a dragon's head. In a roar that hurt her ears, the dragon lunged forward butting its forehead against the side of the boat in an intense shower of electrical sparks.

Amid the sounds of planks cracking and wood splintering, she was thrown, thrashing, into the water. She cried out for him. "Erik, Erik!"

Then remembering the test, she stopped flailing and calmly put her head back, allowing herself to be submerged by the storm. Under the water the malice of the tempest was no longer audible and she heard him singing once more. She blinked repeatedly struggling to see him, and there he was, again in the white mask, offering up the nectar of his sweet music. His face rippled in the water, blurry, but truly there.

"Choose to live, choose to live.
    I am with you.
Entwined in purpose,
    We are one forever.
Forbid this ending. Stay.
Teach me to love me. I shall listen,
    Even in the probing light of day."

She kicked furiously and pushed against the water with the strength of every muscle she possessed. Determined to survive she surged upward and broke through the surface gasping for air. The mask of the Phantom was adhered to her face. Amazed she reached up with her hand, acknowledging its presence.

Christine awoke coughing and spitting, her hand pressed tightly to the right side of her face. There was no mask beneath it. She sat up, frantically feeling her nightgown and hair. *I'm wet, drenched in sweat. A fever?* She touched her forehead. *No, I'm cool to the touch but so wet. Hair and clothes soaked as if I were standing in the rain…or swimming in a storm!*

In a flash of revelation she got up and went into the *salle de bains*. Gazing into the mirror she pulled her brown curls straight back into a ponytail and tied them with a black silk scarf. Then she dumped perfumed talc from an orange glass container into the sink. Adding a little water and some facial cream, she made a paste with her fingers and started to smear the white substance onto her face. She covered her right eyebrow and working upward concealed the area of forehead directly above it. Forming a semicircle beneath her eye, she proceeded to cover the cheek below, pulling vigorously at the skin as she worked. Riveted, she stared at herself in the mirror. Even with homemade maquillage she had created quite an authentic facsimile of the mask. Breaking out into a broad smile she blew a kiss off her fingertips to her image.

Someone knocked hesitantly at her door. When she opened it, a startled nanny handed Michael to her. "He's just been fed, Mame. I thought you might want to hold him?"

"Thank you," Christine responded. "Can you bring me a bassinette so that he can sleep beside my bed tonight?"

Six weeks old, little Michael smiled at his mother's face.

She closed the door. *You look more like your father every day.*

10 *IN THE STRANGENESS OF CHRISTINE*

Placing Michael beside her bed did nothing to ease Christine. On Wednesday morning, she awoke feeling just as nervous and tense as when she retired. After placing numerous kisses on the baby's plump little fingers and toes, she dressed and brought the infant to the nanny. Back in her room, frustrating uncertainties fermented inside her, she felt like exploding but had no where to vent. Her mind could fathom no logical reason for Inspector Davier's visit, except that some evidence to confirm the continued existence of the Opera Ghost had presented itself to the authorities. *If only Raoul had not said so much to the police! They have the memory of elephants!*

Taking off like a swan in flight she set forth from her rooms to pace the house. Descending the curved marble staircase she cruised the outside of the main entrance, ignoring its grandeur, and moved on to the perimeter of the large reception hall like a racehorse charging to a finish line. *This is not helping!* One of the cook's assistants startled her when he blocked her path, asking for her Ladyship's choice of meat at the evening meal. Christine tightly clasped her hands behind her. "Lamb, sacrificial lamb." Bewildered by the curtness of his mistress's reply, the servant bowed politely and returned to the kitchen.

Almost immediately, Christine regretted her tone and followed the man to offer an apology. When she entered the cook's domain everyone was busy chopping and stirring, washing pots, and chatting. Her appearance brought the entire congregation to a stand still. Everyone paused to give her a small bow or curtsy. Embarrassed that she'd interrupted their work, she smiled and waved apologetically for them to go on about their duties. She thought to take leave of them but stayed in the doorway. Seeing her thus, the chief cook stepped forward to inquiry if she wished to take breakfast.

Christine's eyes opened wider. "Have all the servants eaten?" It was the practice of the owners of the estate to feed their employees three meals a day. The staff serving the house and the immediate grounds ate in a simple dining room just down the hall from the main kitchen.

The cook responded, "Yes, Madame, quite early this morning."

"And who is working here today?"

"Who, Mame?" Christine nodded and the man listed the thirty odd servants who had taken a meal.

"And what of Armand who keeps the fowl and stocks the lake, or George who tends the dogs? Are they not here today?"

"No, Madame, they are not here. Do you wish to speak to the groundskeeper?"

"No, thank you." She turned away to pursue her agitation and decided to check on Michael. Taking a back staircase from the kitchen to the second floor, she marched down the blue carpeted halls past pictures of elegantly dressed ancestors staring down at her. Coming to the nursery, she opened the door softly to find the baby wrapped in linens and lace, rocked to sleep in the arms of his nanny. As she entered the pleasant, sunlit room the woman smiled and offered to give her the infant. Christine considered the peaceful face and in a hushed voice said, "No, let's not wake him. Did the wet nurse feed him?" She couldn't resist running the silk of his dark hair between her fingers. *So like Erik's.* She kissed the air above his forehead and then looked into the eyes of the nanny.

"Is everything all right, Countess?"

"I was bored last night so I played at some theatrics. I've too much pent up energy and need to work it off."

The nanny smiled knowingly. "A Countess lives from one event to the next, and Sunday's plans are all but complete I hear."

"There's nothing left for me to do except attend the christening and welcome the guests."

"Holding sleeping babies or embroidering won't help the time to pass for such an active woman as yourself. Perhaps Madame would enjoy a trip to the dressmaker's." Christine nodded and left the room to continue her occupation of wearing the carpets down to their mats.

As she walked she continued needling herself, searching for the motives behind the inspector's visit. She simply did not have enough information. *I need to know what they know, how do I discover it?* Without consciously realizing it she was marching up and down the hall outside Raoul's office on the first floor. Raoul sat inside with Victor going over the sale of a ship to a group of Italian nobles. He was surprised to see her form appear in the opened doorway, disappear, then reappear, never hesitating to even say good morning.

The second time she passed Raoul asked, "Restless, Christine?"

In the corridor she froze in her tracks, suddenly aware of where her steps had taken her. She turned to face his office door, her mouth agape in surprised alarm. Fortunately, Raoul could not see her expression.

His words continued, "Why not make one of your visits to the cemetery?"

She did not step to his doorway. "No, not today. I think I'd rather burn off this burst of energy with a horse ride."

The sound of Raoul's voice indicated he was at his desk. "As you wish, my dear, but a day dress might not be the most suitable attire. I'll join you for dinner this evening. Victor and I have a great deal of work to accomplish."

From the hall she heard him continue his discussion with the secretary and knew she'd been dismissed. "All monies received in payment shall be in French notes, the amounts to be delivered in thirds to the *Banque de France* by the following three dates..."

"Fine, I'll see you later," she called out and ran upstairs to her rooms. In a flurry, she threw off her dress and entering her closets donned riding pants, shirt, jacket and boots. Telling her personal maid, who scurried behind trying to keep up, that she was going out for a ride.

"Alone!" Setting forth to the stables she grabbed a riding crop left at one of the backdoors. As she trooped off to the horses she smacked the whip soundly into her left palm. Sucking in her breath, she clenched her fingers shut over the sting of it. Opening her hand in hesitation, she saw a nasty red welt forming. She curled her fingers again, digging her nails into the angry mark to intensify the pain. Then paused to hiss out a swear word and stomp her foot before continuing on.

The October morning was bright with sunlight, the sky a vivid blue streaked with autumn's stratus clouds. The flying insects had not filled the air at the stables yet. She entered breathing in the invigorating smells of hay and manure. The groomsman greeted his mistress, who hurriedly asked for her mare with a horned saddle so she could straddle the animal decently. He prepared the horse and helped her to mount. Christine and the mare emerged from the stables slowly. She stroked the animal's neck and spoke to it as they cleared the buildings and corrals. In the open grass they picked up speed and began to trot south to the fields in harvest. They traversed the lowlands at a steady gallop, Christine enjoying the ride and glad to be away from the cloistered walls of the mansion. As she came to some rolling hills she glanced to the right and there, up on a ridge, saw her Phantom, dignified and princely astride his black horse, his mask giving him the appearance of a highway robber. He sat facing her, deliberately shaking his head, then turned his horse north.

He rode ahead but always in sight and took a more easterly direction than the one she had just traveled. Eventually they came to a dirt road of dual tracks formed over the years by the wheels of passing wagons. The woods appeared ahead and he waited for her in the concealment of the trees.

She greeted him with a sly smile as she rode up along side. "Good morning, maestro!"

"Good morning. Out again without an escort?" He tipped his black gambler's hat in her direction.

"You're a fine one to talk. You take great risk displaying yourself in the open like this."

His golden eyes flashed in the scattered light beneath the branches. "Some people have reward without ever taking a risk. They are called 'the privileged'. I myself don't prefer the life style. All my rewards have come at the cost of immense risk. Do you think me insane for taking this one?"

"Is this the access road?"

"It's one of many on the estate."

"Who is near?"

His horse kicked the ground and moved backwards as it raised its head, snorting and pulling on the reigns, wanting to run. He held the animal in check for the moment and chuckled. "Absolutely no one."

"Then I guess you're not insane, just foraging for reward. Let's go to the pond near the graves."

"Every time the road comes to a fork, go left. When you start to see the tall rocks you are near and I'll move you inward off the road. You lead. I'll give you a head start."

Following his directions, she spurred her mare and galloped off, her spirits lighter knowing him to be so near. For a minute she pressed her advantage, then hastily looking back over her shoulder, saw him coming at a rapid gallop – still at some distance. She urged her mare to go faster, noting that now he earnestly took up pursuit, racing his horse in an attempt to catch her. She laughed with unfettered excitement and reaching up, untied her hair to let it fly in the wind. At full tilt he came round a clump of trees beside the dropoff of a ridge. His horse had closed the distance between them. There were thicker woods ahead and he edged her toward them, pointing in the direction of several tall rocks. Understanding his meaning, she slowed and entered the trees as he rode on past.

The welcome smell of the dense pines and moist earth immediately nourished her sense of well-being. Christine let her animal pick its way through the trees and stayed mounted. Listening to every sound other than the mare's hooves and bending to study her surroundings, she tried to spot him. The anticipation of hearing the timbre of his voice and once again feeling his touch on her skin, stirred her into lust. She continued to give the horse its head as they rounded a cluster of rocks covered in moss. There in the distance the pond's surface glistened amid the pines. "I knew you'd find the water, Venus." She stroked the mare's neck affectionately. The horse made her way to the bank and started to drink. A fall breeze swelled through the trees, the branches of oak and pine moaning as they rubbed against each other. Sensing his presence somewhere near, she closed her eyes to enjoy the sensuous sound, like couples in the throws of sex.

In the dense evergreens on the opposite side of the pond, he stood beside his great black horse, rubbing its snout with his gloved hand. Watching her as she sat with the sunlight on her face and her eyes shut, he ached with desire, but chose to wait and memorize the tender picture of her laid before him. When she opened her eyes again, he took the horses' bridle and moved out into the open. Biting her lower lip, she watched him approach. Removing her gloves she mentally renewed her purpose. *Give me strength of will!*

He tied the reins to a tree trunk and walked to the side of her horse. It was not uncommon for them to come together in total silence, letting every form of communication but speech draw each to the other. As she swung her leg over the saddle, he reached up to her waist. Resting her hands on his shoulders, she slid down to the ground. Remaining at the side of the horse, his strong fingers pressed into her, his thumbs at the base of her ribs. Their foreheads came together, their noses touched. He swallowed hard and angled his head slightly, but hesitated to kiss her, his lips not an inch from hers.

His breath was so pleasurably sweet. It brought the memory of anisette into her mouth. Her lips came forward to his, soft and full. They kissed as if they were adolescents, in total politeness, lips closed. She let him lead the way. In invitation his tongue touched the front of her teeth and ran the underside of her lower lip. She brought her hands to the sides of his face at the ears, her middle fingers encircling the outside of the canals, brushing the skin. The sensuous effect on him was instantaneous. She met his tongue with hers, kissing him long and deep, unbridling his passion.

He would never get enough of kissing her, but the discomfort in his crotch was intensifying. She seemed to want him fiercely as well. Not taking her within the next few minutes was rapidly becoming out of the question.

Feeling the keenness of his arousal, Christine ended the kiss and saw with satisfaction his eyes clearly brimming with desire. She contorted her facial muscles into a scowl and issued a demand, "Cut me!"

The upper part of his body pulled away from her in shock, but his feet stayed planted, his hands fast upon her upper arms as he probed the fierce expression on her face.

She repeated her words like an army officer sending forth a decisive order. "Cut me! Take out your dagger, Erik, and cut me. I want a ragged slice...here." She made a slashing gesture with her thumb down her right forehead, across her eye and cheek. "If you don't cut me, I'll cut myself. Then I'll permit our thirsting bodies to drink."

Horrified at her directive, he stepped backwards, away from her and her crazed command. Yanking off his mask he pointed with disgust at his disfigurement. "You want to destroy the perfection of your own countenance and look like this?"

"Exactly! If you relish the feel of me, do as I bid!"

His icy words discharged like a gun. "Tell me why I should do such an odious thing!" He put the mask back on and turned sideways, showing her only his natural face.

Stepping away from her horse in hot pursuit of the walled-off space he now occupied, she explained. "My mind has funneled down to one primary topic, you! My spirit writhes against the ropes that keep it tied, just as you described those that hinder you. The more I struggle, the tighter they grow. If I cannot live with you, I want to be like you. So cut me, Erik! I welcome the world's rejection. The pain of it will be exquisite! I the recluse!"

In disbelief the Phantom's mind began to race. He could not cut her. He could not physically harm her in any way. He was sure she did not understand the slavery into which she so willingly wanted to sell herself. There would be no escape, no redemption. "*Christine ~* "

The tremor in his irresistible voice filled the air around her – her knees were buckling! She was like hot candle wax, rapidly melting in the vibrato he placed within the song of her name. Nearly somnolent, she mentally fled to an alert corner of her mind, seized determination and straightened her back. She would not succumb to the melody until she had her prize!

"You ask too much of me. I cannot take a dagger and slice into you. Is it not enough that one of us has the appearance of raw meat?" Afflicted and ashamed of his detestable appearance, his words trailed off, loosing the momentum he intended. He turned to face her. His fingers spread apart, pleading for a more agreeable discourse.

Staring at him with eyes fixed and wide, she lowered her head, like a bull about to charge. Through her teeth a peculiar, husky voice emerged. "Our fates are combined. Join us together." In steeled determination, her hands came before her chest in a loud, crisp clap. The defining sound echoed off the trees around them.

He looked at her stiff stance in amazement. Every muscle in her body said she meant it. "Viewing a scar every day is no replacement for a husband and his vows!" She made no response. "Do you think that the physical pain of this cut will be greater than the mental one you feel over me?" She nodded slightly. "You truly believe that one will override the other?" The wind blew the ends of her long curls away from her. It was his turn to spit out a rock-hard directive. His voice was grating, almost crushing. "Remove your clothes!"

She tore at her shirt and pants. Stripping herself bare she stood naked in front of him.

For a moment he considered her shape then came swiftly to her. Taking her buttocks in his hands he lifted her up to his waist. As she encircled him with her arms and legs, he crushed her into the trunk of a thick pine. Holding her in place with the vice-like strength of his body, his pelvis met hers. During their coitus her back rode up and down savagely on the rough bark. She screamed her orgasm to the sky above and once satisfied folded over onto his shoulder, spent and sore. In a blinding moment of ecstasy, his body declared Christine his consort and he gently took her down. In a patch of sunlight he laid her on the inside of his cloak and wrapped it over her. From his saddlebag he brought a blanket and a flask of liquor. Regaining her composure, she took the offered drink, returning the flask when he stroked her face in silence. He opened the cloak and rolled her to her side, surveying the damage to her back.

"You are already deeply bruised. The marks will be dark and ugly for some time. A mirror will show them to you." He rubbed his forehead in consternation and regret. "I wish you had not wanted this, it reeks of strangeness."

She raised an index finger to his lips. "Shh. Don't think. Don't speak. Cut me! Don't hesitate this time...cut me!"

He removed a dagger from the inside of his boot and a handkerchief from a pocket in his jacket. "Let me chose the place." Silently she agreed. He took a match and burned the blade, then waved it in the air to cool it. Holding her left wrist he made a deep, diagonal cut high up on her inner forearm. She did not withdraw in any way, and kept her gaze fixed upon his face. Tears glazed his eyes. "You will be scarred, but function will not be hindered." Wrapping the handkerchief tightly around the six inch wound he counseled her. "Tell them you were attacked in the woods and ran."

Again in the voice of the little bull, she replied, "I will tell them nothing! This is my life, and I do this out of my own free will. My will, my body! This is of us. If I were brought to this choice over and over again, I would still chose to do this." *Even the little fox that finds himself caught in a trap gets to chew at its own leg, let me live with the scar of being Raoul's wife and not yours.*

"I knew nothing of the depth of your stubbornness. You could take on an army regiment before noon."

From the ground her face softened. "My sweet, obedient Phantom, thank you. Don't think that you have harmed me. Your cut has actually helped. I may not have your wedding ring, but I will have your scar." She laughed softly. "The bruises on my back are an added bonus." Her eyes closed and a heavy sigh escaped from its place of confinement. "If only there could be more moments with you. I'm forced to survive on little crumbs of time."

Carefully he placed the blanket over her. He seemed to have no choice but to acknowledge the tremendous sadness in her voice. "Could you see me and not react? Could you stay perfectly still…inside, and let that perfect stillness radiate outward if you saw me?"

Her mind perked up with the intrigue. It appeared a new game was afoot. "Yes, I could develop this skill of perfect emotional stillness."

"Then I will show you when I am near."

He spent the next fifteen minutes telling her all that he knew of Detective Edwards' movements, and she informed him of Inspector Davier's visit to the chateau. When they had ascertained that she would not openly bleed, he stood her up and dressed her, kissing and touching each part he covered with cloth, while she practiced not reacting. As he manipulated her, he talked about the larger reactions people project, such as shrugs, head movements, and changes in stance. Then about the smaller perceptions, those visible to only the highly trained: pupil dilatation, sweating, skin prickles, nipple erections, and stray finger movements.

She listened and learned to restrain her body.

"The person who controls himself is often quite fearless," he told her. "Have you been feeling fear, Christine?"

"Yes."

"Subjugate fear. Swallow it, my love. Swallow it whole."

"It will be my toy."

She rode back to the chateau the way he suggested, turning to look at the woods as she left them. She couldn't see him in the umbrage of the trees, but knew he must be there, hidden from sight, watching. Beneath her sleeve she felt the tightness of the handkerchief, but for some reason, nothing on her back bothered her. She rode the horse at a trot back to the stables, no longer fearing the actions of the police. If the plans he had outlined didn't work, they would meet the authorities head on and boldly deal another ruse.

After she was gone, he returned to the pine where he had held her captive. He smelled the bark and rested his face where her back had been abraded. *She is such a strange mixture of tenacious courage and fulminating passion, but violence? What she feels, she presses to feel completely.* Ruthlessly, he gouged his dagger across the trunk of the tree as if to punish it for bruising her. Before he left he studied the area around the pond. This was indeed a pleasant, sheltered spot. He would build a firepit so they could return to it.

By mutual agreement, they would not visit the cemetery that week or the next. They agreed to wait and let her practice the art of stillness. On Friday evening, she and Raoul attended a ball given in honor of the engagement of a local noble to a lady of rank. Christine wore a ruffled dress of purple satin encrusted with pearls. Feathers dyed to match the satin graced the curls she'd pulled atop her head. Long evening gloves of cream colored doeskin extended to her upper arms. She danced with Raoul on the ballroom floor, but when they announced a Quadrille would be next, the Count escorted her to a chair next to the baroque marble fireplace. Apologizing, he took his leave of her to go converse with some jocular young men. She was disappointed but happy to be left with her own thoughts. Fanning herself, she watched the couples pairing off.

The lively Quadrille started out in the French Court ballet and had steadily gained popularity. A prompter announced dance moves to cell-groups consisting of four couples each. The spirited dance was done in three to five sections with decided breaks in between, allowing time for dancers to catch their breath and flirt. A gentleman with curly chestnut hair and a darker beard and mustache approached her. Impeccably dressed in a swallow tailed coat and a gold cravat, he bowed and asked in a formal manner if dancing the Quadrille would please her. Graciously she accepted his offer and took his hand. The moment her gloved fingers occupied his familiar grasp, a surprising degree of warmth moved over her. She showed no reaction, but as they faced each other to begin the dance there was no mistaking the identity of her partner. He held her at a most respectable distance, and addressed her in a polite nonchalant voice. "Don't you think it's interesting that my manhood is so aroused at the very sight of you, I can hardly walk, much less dance? Nice gloves by the way. Hiding something?"

She smiled reservedly, her face composed, but inwardly she was thrilled to know that he would be her partner for the next fifteen minutes. "Good, all the more for me at the tomb. I thought you didn't like to dance and had no time to practice."

"Well it seems I live with a mistress of ballet who is most willing to teach her favorite subject to me any time I'm ready."

The music started and they began to glide together. Christine's voice was flat. She might have been ordering a platter of fish at a restaurant. "Your delicate eyes are more exquisite than any carving in this elaborate room, Erik." The gentleman's face stayed emotionless as she calmly informed him, "In my mind you are having your way with me right now. I feel you inside me...continue to do it...yes, yes, my love. Feel me accepting you, wanting you." The tempo of the music accelerated and they spun around the dance floor, their eyes locked for the few seconds that the mental explosion went on inside them. The caller of the Quadrille gave a directive and the Phantom calmly passed her into the arms of another. When the dance ended he escorted her to her seat and bowed. She did not see him again until Sunday morning.

The baptismal area of the cathedral was crowded with guests as Michael Philippe de Chagny was christened in the arms of his godmother, Raoul's oldest sister. Christine looked around discretely and found her lover in the shadows of two pillars near the altar of St. Joseph, the father who raised Jesus. She lowered her head, smiling at the irony. Certainly Joseph was no slave to concupiscence. Erik had trusted her to control her impulsive urges. It was sufficient that he was in the room. She placed her left hand over her heart with her right hand on top of it, knowing full well he would understand her deliberate gesture.

Several nights later she sat in the formal dining room of the chateau with Raoul and several of his English clients. She wore an empire dress of lilac and muted green brocade with long sleeves. A choker of polished marcasites at her throat. With her soup bowl untouched before her, she bowed her head and thought of Erik's surprising appearances at the engagement party and the christening. She would have to ask him how he managed the invitation to the ball, and was willing to bet that Meg and Jean played a part getting him in. *Clever deuce.*

Seeing her in quiet reflection with their guests chatting around her, Raoul asked if she were well. Without engaging his eyes she apologized for her lack of conversation, saying she was fine, just a little tired, perhaps in need of some rest after these hectic days. Believing her to be uncomfortable in their present company, Raoul offered to escort her upstairs. She turned her head to him, explaining that she was enjoying the meal with them. For the briefest of seconds she thought she saw Erik's eyes flash like two additional candle flames from inside the textured wallpaper to the left of Raoul's head. The entire wall behind that end of the massive table was a semicircle that contained a great window of frosted Italian glass at its center. Heavy, honey-colored drapes spilled from ceiling to floor. Deeply embossed Italian wallpaper proceeded from beneath the drapes, covering the entire room with swirling plumes and scalloped ridges.

She handed her soup bowl to a servant who took it and disappeared through the door of the butler's pantry. Her eyes went from the door, back to Raoul and there was the flash again! She asked Raoul about the next phase in the sale of the merchant vessel to these good gentlemen.

Pleased that she was taking an interest in his business, Raoul began to tell the company around them of his latest endeavors. He explained that tomorrow they could all travel to the shipyards and watch the vessel being fitted with ropes and sails. One of the men at the table asked Raoul to elaborate on his dealings with a firm in Rome. As all heads turned to the one offering the question, Christine remained focused on the wallpaper. Erik's eyes reappeared. The left one winked, then both were gone. *He is behind the wallpaper!* Taking on the relaxed air of an interested hostess, she joined the conversations around her, glancing occasionally at Raoul as an excuse to study the wall behind him. Eventually she discerned the panel Erik had created. The left side of it curved almost imperceptibly into the wallpaper and was matched perfectly to the patterns of it. The space he stood in was only the depth of man standing straight up against the wall. *How ingenious, the panel must open behind the drape and he slides in.* His view of the room was unhindered. No waiter would stand in so recessed a spot and give the appearance of not being readily available for service. She marveled at his inventiveness and his total disdain for danger. *He wants to show me how close he can get without being detected!* She looked lovingly past Raoul, who mistook the tenderness in her eyes as encouragement to visit her chambers that night. When the men got up to gather in a salon for cigars and talk, Christine moved to the window, and resting her hands on the elaborately carved sill, addressed the night, "How precious you are to me, how much grander than anything else I have ever known in life."

Later when Raoul knocked at her door she offered no protest whatsoever, her only request was that the lights be put out – preventing him from viewing the bruises on her back or her bandaged arm.

The following evening she stayed up late reading. Around ten she went up the stairs with her maid following behind. In her rooms Christine started to unbutton her bodice and told Justine, "Go to bed, I'll prepare myself for rest."

Wishing her mistress the sweetest of dreams, Justine closed the door behind her and walked softly down the halls to Raoul's rooms.

Christine locked the door and went to the foot of her bed to finish removing her clothes. On the corner of the mattress she found a pair of folded men's pants lying atop the covers. The pants were of the same material as her jacquard bedspread. She picked them up and beneath them found a matching jacket of the same dark material and a black shirt, all of her size. Saying nothing she removed her dress and put on the clothes, waiting with her body motionless beside the bedpost.

In the quiet she reached out with her senses. The first thing she heard was her own heartbeat. She had no idea that a person could actually hear it if they listened closely enough. Then off in the distance she heard a few servants' voices. They were bidding each other good night after locking up this part of the house. Her hands remained on the notched lapels of the jacket, and she became aware of the layer of sweat between her skin and the cloth. *Can I hear him breathing?* She stretched her concentration as far as she was capable. *He must be close by, else why are these clothes here?* The second this thought registered in her mind, she heard the softest of foot falls come from her bedroom drapes. She turned around whispering breathlessly, "If this is what stillness feels like, it is wonderful to be alive!"

The Phantom stepped out from the shadows twenty feet away, wearing clothes identical to hers. He stood taking in the cuteness of her form in the outfit he had the tailor sew for her. *Women in men's clothing can be most enticing.* He replayed in his head the vision of her as she took off her dress and donned his gifts. Enjoying her approbation for his lessons, he ran his tongue over his front teeth as if to relish the taste of a fine orange goose. He reminded himself that very soon her surprise would fade, and be replaced with a worry that his presence in her rooms might be discovered. She started to come to him. With his hand he told her to halt. "No rest for you tonight, Countess, you will need your boots. Mess up your bed." His hands were not on her until they were ready to leave.

He removed her from the chateau through one of the corner windows. Using a slat-board seat attached to a rope running off a pulley affixed to the roof by furniture movers, he lowered her to the ground. Keeping to the shadows they walked to the road where he had a covered, two seated carriage waiting. He took her to a hill to view the lights of the city below and made love to her on a blanket beneath the coupe. Filling her ears with songs describing the depths of his feelings for her, his relentless hands roamed over her breasts, abdomen and thighs exactly as she directed him. He took out her father's violin and played the sweetest of tunes, not of melancholy, but of arduous love. She spent the night with him, but long before morning broke he returned her to her bedroom. Sitting on the board outside her window he explained that when he went down to the ground he would remove the rope and take it with him, but the pulleys on the roof would remain should she ever want another nighttime jaunt through the country.

She understood what he was telling her. Even though she was the mistress of this mansion, she was not tied to it and could have an adventure whenever she wished it. Wanting him to linger just a little longer, and knowing that she would have to wait until the next week in the cemetery to touch him again, she kissed him one more time and softly said into his ear, "Jewel that owns my heart, thank you for these memories."

"Oh, we are far from done, woman, and you are the jewel that owns mine. Look under your pillow." She watched as he lowered himself to the ground, bundled the rope seat and departed. When she felt assured that he was safely away, she returned to her bed. Running her hand on the sheet beneath her pillow she felt an icy, oval shaped piece of glass about the length of a finger. She removed it and instantly recognized the droplet-shaped piece of Bohemian crystal. It had come from the fallen chandelier at the Opera House. Lighting a candle, she let the prisms of light from its perfectly cut facets splay a rainbow of colors across her room. The fact that he had placed a trophy there, and not his body, told her two things about his heart. First, he was far more sensitive and romantic than she had imagined; and second, he would never take her sexually here in this room, for this space belonged to Raoul and in some odd, yet to be clarified way, he honored that.

11 CAVORTING WITH SWORDS

Luxurious balmy weather, akin to that of the Caribbean, blessed the country of France in the end of October 1874. The winds picked up, but were mild, and the deciduous trees changed color, their leaves a riot of yellows and reds, enough to please the eye of any forlorn soul. Christine tried, as best she could, to settle into the schedule of weekly visits with Erik, and attend to the duties of wife and mother. Her arm healed without infection, and up to this point she had managed to hide the scar from anyone's eyes but her own. As she walked the grounds, she often found herself heading to the kennels or the stables, in the hopes that she might catch a rare glimpse of 'George'. To see him, even for a moment gave her great joy. If she clandestinely ascertained George's presence on the grounds, she would take Michael, a strong and vigorous two-month-old, out into the sunshine on one of the patios, affording George the opportunity to walk by with some of the dogs. No one seemed to find it odd that the leashed animals never pulled the caretaker along. They walked beside him or behind him, acknowledging their keeper as the leader of their pack. One beautifully groomed German Shepherd stayed particularly close to George's heels. When the troop passed, the illusionist would tip his cap and wish her good day in a queer, slurred form of speech – all the while studying the glorious little boy she played with in her lap.

During her visits with Erik at the mausoleum, she would faithfully tell him of the boy's growth and development. Michael easily recognized her now and smiled often, taking her finger with his little fist and holding it tightly. Erik continued to teach her the art of stillness while developing her senses. She expanded her abilities, listening to the smallest of sounds, tasting subtleties, feeling a breath as it moved through the air from a foot away. She asked him to also teach her the art of swordplay, explaining that she wanted to keep herself occupied and be capable of defending herself. Every time he declined, her lips would draw into a annoyed pout and she would implore him, "Teach me to fight with a sword. Please, agree. I want to learn."

No amount of begging succeeded. Erik's response was always the same. "You know it's not done for women."

She would continue to beg until he finally buried her thoughts of the blade with his rapt affections. He particularly loved the way she shivered as he kissed her neck or suckled her earlobe. If he moved his mouth to her breasts, she quickly grew ravenous for him. Keeping her sated proved a wonderfully challenging mission. It stirred him deeply to watch her face during their unions. Her shuddering, tiny screams, the ardent dragging of her pelvis against his bones, allowed him an accurate sense of the pleasurable summits she was able to attain. Cocooned in the artful magic of her repeated acceptances, Erik began to change. When he was inside her, he no longer perceived himself as deformed and mal-created, but saw himself as whole and handsome, his virility boundless upon her. Every time he exploded within her, she reached up to him, showering him in turn with warmth and love – healing him with the balm of intimacy. Comforted by her body, he swam past the scabrous rocks of ridicule and shame into the ocean of silk that was this woman, Christine.

As difficult as it was to deny her anything, he still refused to teach her the sword – refused until the events of a Thursday late in October changed his mind. Neither of them would ever forget the day. Indeed, its consequences haunted them for years. About ten o'clock in the morning Christine went to the stables. Taking in the smells that never ceased to please her nostrils, she walked past the numerous stalls to find her mare in the back. She greeted Venus with a carrot from the kitchen, making the horse nuzzle her for the treat. Christine picked up a brush and began to groom the animal's coat. In a few minutes, Venus neighed and tensed beneath Christine's strokes. As she pondered the raw strength of the mare's muscles, her instincts told her that someone was quietly entering the stable through the wide double doors at the front. She froze, the hairs on the back of her neck and forearms rising. Searching her senses she tried to identify the newcomer. The smell of him, mingled with those of the horses, came to her, Victor LaPointe. She began rubbing the mare's forelocks and waited.

He entered the stall behind her, about eight feet away. "Yes, Victor, what do you want?"

"How clever of you to recognize me without even turning around. Permit me to dispense with pleasantries and get directly to the point."

"What do you want?" Her voice was a monotone, his words held distasteful implications. She knew they were alone and now he was blocking her only exit. He stepped closer. *Where is this going? Do I have the strength to stop him if his intent is physical? Should I scream?*

She felt his breath on the back of her neck as he spoke. "I know you're dabbling in tricks. You went from a morose little mouse to a happy doe, prancing around the estate like you own it. You have some kind of secret going on at the cemetery, don't you? I haven't told the Count of my suspicions, but I will unless you cooperate and give me what I want."

Deciding not to taunt him, but to definitely face him, she moved Venus further into the stall. Rotating her body, Christine answered modestly, "I have already asked, Victor. What do you want?" Seeing the glint in his eyes and the sneer on his mouth, her heart began to pound within her chest. Somewhere in the back of her mind she willed it to calm down so she could process the trap she found herself in.

Sensing he had her effectively cornered, his words proceeded in sarcasm. "Why just a word, Christine, just a word and perhaps a taste, a *petite* taste. Before you and that little brat of yours showed up, Raoul paid more attention to me, and I do so miss his attentions."

"You and Raoul..."

"No, I was working on him and gaining ground I might add. The prospect of a physical relationship held promise, but was not fulfilled. We were at a fragile, unrequited stage during your dreary depression. With the return of your nauseating gaiety and the arrival of the little prince-ling, Raoul has proven less compliant, less receptive to my favors. Instead of provocative touches I get edicts. He tells me that if I don't insure your privacy and comfort, I am dismissed. So, my rejection, and my protection, will have a price! And I want my payments to start."

"What an unpleasant and malevolent mind you have, Victor!"

"Is it unpleasant to want what Raoul possesses? If I can't have him, I'll have his treasures. It's only normal to crave the things others prize. I prefer my recompense in two forms. Money certainly. I have made this estate richer than it has ever been, and the cost of my silence will be dear. And you, Countess, will let me take that luscious body of yours whenever the Count is abroad. He is rather fond of taking trips, isn't he?"

Christine's pupils constricted at these final declarations. The all too familiar presence of fear descended upon her like an unwelcome river of ice, chilling her skin and paralyzing her muscles. When the Angel of Music kidnapped her, taking her five stories below the Opera House to his home in the cold, damp stone she had known this kind of fear, a dread awareness of pressing danger that stifled the senses and blocked the mind from comprehensive thought. In her head she screamed to herself. *Don't faint! Stay upright!*

Victor drew a pocketknife from his jacket, pressing its sharp point against her neck. She angled her face away from the threat. "Hold very still, my pigeon, while I taste you." A gooey tongue licked her cheek. "Good. Good. You may well enjoy being tasted as much as I enjoy doing it. Pleasure comes in many forms."

Her eyes caught a shadow moving forward over the framework of the stalls. *Hurry!* Victor's breath smelled of coffee. She pictured hot cups of the aromatic liquid. Steaming coffee in delicate porcelain cups with eighteen carat gold rims, cups with roses, daffodils, and pansies encircling their sides and saucers. Mentally she put a cup on a table top, then another. Her expression became one of indifference – her body limp with non-resistance. The change infuriated Victor.

His free hand moved to the laced cords of her bodice and began to untie them. The cups of coffee vanished. The menacing shadow out in the stables moved closer. He pulled at her blouse and her chemise. His voice the threatening rasp of a wasp in her ear, "Not so haughty after all. When you strut around, lost in your solitary thoughts, what are you thinking about? Tell me. What is your little secret at the cemetery? No one could want to be in her father's tomb lighting candles and praying as much as you are." His hand took her breast, rubbing the tender nipple with his thumb. Intrigued, he pinched it and released it quickly, watching her stiffen in the pain, never pausing to wonder why she did not cry out. With the knife still at her throat, he took his tongue to her nipple to lick it. As he commenced a forceful sucking, the Phantom, disguised as George, rounded the door of Venus' stall.

She purred to Victor, "Aren't you afraid I'll disembowel you while you're preoccupied?"

Victor looked up in surprise. Instantly the heel of her boot came down hard onto the toe of his shoe. As Victor howled, she saw the coil of catgut leave Erik's left hand. In a blur the Punjab lasso passed over Victor's face and took him by the throat, cutting off his outcry. Erik pulled so hard that he lifted the secretary onto his toes. His victim's eyeballs bulged outward and the face turned a frightening shade of purple-blue. Caught off guard, Victor didn't even reach for his neck. He barely thrashed as consciousness receded into disorienting blackness. The entire time that Erik strangled the life out of the offender, his brilliant eyes looked directly into Christine's.

Expressionless she stood before him, mesmerized by the unquestioning fierceness of her protector. No court, no trial, just death – swift death for touching her body without permission.

As Victor died Erik arched his back and let him lean against his chest. Waiting patiently as the body became flaccid and the arms dropped useless at his sides. Still fixed on Erik's eyes, Christine took her right hand and calmly shoved Victor off her lover. Erik simultaneously released the lasso and the body thudded heavily to the floor. Christine pulled her bodice up over her breast and looked at the corpse. She drew her foot back to kick him in the face, but Erik's hand came to her shoulder.

"Don't. He's dead. I'll teach you the art of the sword and the dagger, too…and if you develop the strength, the Punjab lasso."

She acknowledged his concessions with a rise of her left eyebrow. "What shall we do with the body?"

"In a hole with some lye, an isolated place, but somewhere we can check regularly."

"*Bien.* I was never very comfortable around Victor. He was more like pond scum than I'd imagined. What shall I tell Raoul?"

"Nothing, keep your association with Victor to a minimum. On weekends he likes to visit a macabre hotel in a quarter down by the docks, men take turns with other men there…fishing for flesh. Perhaps he's taken an unexpected fishing trip."

"I rather like that." Christine let out a soft cry of surprise. "We have to stand him back up!"

"Why? No one saw him enter here but me. The staff is at lunch." Erik looked at the body and understood. "The Punjab lasso is the Opera Ghost's trademark."

"A very distinctive weapon. If the body is ever found and examined by the police the secret of your existence could be at risk. Let's put lye all over his neck and head, and the hole of a dagger in his back. Make sure you nick a rib."

"It appears that you must die again, Victor, so that I may live, *la Comtesse* requests it." Together they lifted Victor and held him against the side of the stall. Erik pictured Victor's mouth on Christine and plunged the dagger in with such vehemence that the head of the corpse bounced against the wallboards with a thump. They laid the body in a cart used for carrying refuse to a dumping area, and covered it with manure and hay. Christine rinsed off the blade at a water bucket as Erik hitched her mare to the cart. Thoughtfully he told her, "It's a good thing Raoul is away to London. Our web grows thin, Christine."

"Not to worry, it will not break, and if it does, we spiders know how to mend it."

The following day Madame Giry canceled ballet lessons on Mondays, announcing to her students that she was going into semi-retirement. The little girls were happy at the extra time off, whether their parents were, was of no concern to Madame. Christine and Erik began their afternoon sessions the following week. In the morning Christine went to visit Doctor DeVille, supposedly for a massage and hot packs to aching muscles, from there she hired a carriage to take her to the ballet studio where she met with Erik in the third floor apartment. Wanting genuine weapons, she chose to learn with the flexible two-sided blade of a rapier, rejecting the foil with its blunted end. Erik presented her with a blade of highly polished steel and a black scabbard. She drew it forth taking in its sublime beauty. "It's lighter than I thought it would be." Around the hilt, four sturdy metal bars curved in a delicate cage to protect her hand. The grip was of black leather. He showed her how to unsheathe and sheath it. As she practiced the technique an unpretentious happiness spread across her face.

"Always hold it with respect. Do you want to name it?"

"Anubis shall be its name."

"The Egyptian god of death, how very appropriate. I have more to give you. Keep your eyes on mine." From inside the sleeve of his jacket a six inch dagger in a leather sheath slid down onto the top of his left hand. Extending his arm he offered it to her. Concentrating on his eyes she reached for it, but his hand deftly turned and lowered, dropping the sheath into his palm. In one smooth movement he withdrew the dagger with his right hand and had it back, next to his head, poised to throw. She grinned broadly. He had never taken his eyes away from hers. His words were firm, "Practice, over and over. It is the key." She smiled with delight as he returned the dagger to its case and let her take it. On the handle of the perfectly balanced blade the craftsman had carved the design of a pouncing winged lion.

He watched her closely. "We'll practice throwing it later in the carriage house. Out there I'll show you how to sharpen both blades. Keep them clean and well oiled. They are tools in need of conscientious care. Learn their feel and make them a part of your body. How far does the tip of your sword reach with your arm outstretched? How far with your right shoulder and right leg thrown forward?"

He brought her over to the kitchen table where a cloth covered several items. They had decided to practice in costumes should any uninvited eyes observe them. Telling her he had fashioned something quite unique he unveiled their outfits with a flourish. She clapped her hands in jubilation, "This is too good!"

They dressed and he pulled a string to alert Madame Giry that they were ready. Madame went into the ballet studio where she drew the curtains closed and lit the ornate wall lamps around the room. Then she sat in a chair on the stage and waited. With an air of austerity, teacher and pupil emerged from the back stairwell and took a position in front of her. Their faces were covered in identical skull masks, the mask of Red Death that Erik had worn at the Opera House. Long sleeved white shirts with loosened ties, red leggings with burgundy sashes, and comfortable but sturdy black boots completed their attire. Their hands went to the sheaths resting at their hips. Their swords sang out as they removed them. Extending their blades to the right, they bowed low then brought their swords before their faces in a grand salute to Madame. She had not thought to ask about their choice of practice attire and was greatly pleased, "*Extraordinare, mes Amis!* Good Luck!"

Erik stepped about ten feet away from Christine, his attitude and demeanor instantly serious. He became the instructor, imparting information and advising in an almost taunting voice. His new goal was not to train her as a lover, but as an opponent. She was not surprised at the change, there was so much more to him than she had fathomed, so many layers, so much talent. The point of his sword was presently in her face calling her thoughts to attention. He began to flow sideways, deliberately circling. "Begin by acquiring basic skills. Allow specific techniques to follow naturally. Your background as a dancer will help you, but no degree of proficiency with the blade will be acquired without devotion to the art.

"First, you must concentrate. Clear your thoughts. Your mind must be in the battle and not elsewhere. The experienced swordsman stays focused, sensing moves and reacting on an intuitive level. Practice until you block a strike and deliver a quick counter without consciously considering each individual action. Believe that your opponent intends to kill you. Do not engage your adversary's eyes, they will be a distraction. Stay aware of your surroundings on a secondary level. The time you spend learning to extend your senses will be of use.

"Second, always breathe. Never hold your breath under stress. Refuse yourself the option of breathing in a shallow manner. Lack of air produces rigid responses and slow thinking. If you tighten up, or loose focus, inhale deeply and let your breath out slowly. You are taking control, dictating to your mind...and your body...that you are calm and powerful. They will obey you. You will get more force behind a strike if you execute it as you exhale. A loud shout at the moment you lunge forward will help you focus and may startle your antagonist. Third, is balance, and balance is more than just not falling down."

She started to turn as he circled her, always facing him. Attending intently to his every word, but with the point of her sword low and pointed toward the floor. As his instruction continued she found herself studying his sword, the arm attached to it, the position of the body beyond.

"Maintaining your balance is paramount to staying advantageously upright. Keep your two feet in contact with the ground, a shoulder's width apart. Slide your feet forward and back, never more than an inch above the floor. Don't lift your boots and plant them back down. The closer your feet are to the ground, the less likely you are to be off balance as your enemy attacks and you counter attack. Never cross your feet, or bring your feet together, as you move in a fight. You may go off balance to deliver a strike, but recover. Recover quickly."

The female version of Red Death separated her feet, spreading her weight, and as she did so she saw how his left torso was angled away from her, protecting his heart and one lung, but exposing the liver, if it were to be penetrated.

"Fourth, is timing, and timing is the most critical factor in your attack. No matter how fast or energetic your shot, if it is not timed so that it hits your adversary, he will remain unhurt. Timing must become instinctual for you. The more you practice the more your body will know how to move so you can succeed. Develop fast reactions. Speed is of the utmost importance. You simply cannot get too fast. Experience will help you develop an intuition for movement...and speed...speed...will get you where you need to be. Study your opponent's movements carefully, looking for opportunities. You will start to anticipate what he intends to do, and then defend, or even better...attack before he has a chance to act. The perception of what is about to happen is truly significant. As you improve, so will your ability to read the encounter. Stay flexible and open for anything that might occur. Anticipate. Anticipate. How will your attacker strike? Block it in you mind and execute the counter strike. If done well, your opponent will picture the block, but not your counter. Remember, your adversary is watching you too. So do not allow shifting your weight, or dropping your shoulder, to become a signal for a particular move of yours.

"The next element is the very body you reside in. It also is a tool. Stretch and exercise your muscles to stay strong and flexible. A swordfighter needs stamina so she can endure. You might win on the sole merit that you managed to outlast your antagonist. Never fight in confining clothes. I recently had a torn sleeve prevent me from landing a great punch in that bar fight. A lesson painfully relearned.

"And finally, the mental game. Never enter a fight thinking you cannot win, you have already defeated yourself. Don't think about the outcome or the strength of your foe. Be confident. It is not about what natural talent you possess, but what you do with that talent that will make you victorious. Engage the toad and make him wish he'd never messed with you. Lunge!"

His sword came forward and hers came up automatically to meet it. "Parry!" The sharp clang of metal resounded in the studio as she warded off his blow by blocking it, pushing it to the side. "Riposte!" She made a quick retaliatory thrust, which he avoided by angling his chest enough for the blade to pass in front of it. "Lunge, parry, riposte, lunge, parry, riposte!" For several minutes they moved around the floor in a drill, the sound of swords swishing through the air and coming together. He took a chair and stood on it. "Lunge, parry, riposte." He jumped down and she went to the chair, learning the feel of throwing a strike from uphill going downward. As he deflected it the male reaper demanded, "Put on your warrior face!" She scrunched up her eyes and mouth. He did not laugh at the absurdity of trying to look fierce beneath a mask, total control.

Trying to be barbarous, she yelled, "I shall plunge my dirty blade into your blood and wipe it with my filthy handkerchief, scoundrel!"

He acknowledged her effort calmly, "Still in need of a trustworthy housekeeper?" He paused to wink at her. "Try insulting me with fewer words and make me the filthy one."

Christine drew her rapier upward in a salute then swung it down and to her right, the point inches above the floor. "Monsieur, I concede, you win the match." She licked the salty sweat from her upper lip and dramatically sheathed her blade. As he housed his weapon and bowed, she leapt off the chair and came straight into him with the hilt of her dagger pushing into his lower right rib cage.

He feigned a wince and looking at the mirror image of his own mask smiled broadly.

In her husky voice, she commanded, "Wipe that smile off your face, brigand. You may have won the match, but I win the prize! *Oui?*"

"*Oui.*" He stole a quick kiss and started moving backward, hands in the air in surrender.

Practicing indignation, she retorted, "How dare you trifle with me! Onward, swine, or I'll take your life." He continued in his sinuous, snake-like walk through the doorway to the rear staircase. Leaning forward to kiss her again she pushed the hilt harder into his ribs. "How dare you presume to take advantage of me! Back, back I say!"

The male version of Red Death laughed, lost his focus and tripped, hitting the floor on his butt. From the stage Madame Giry heard the thud and knowing him to be unceremoniously on the floor, could not resist her own laugh. She hollered out, "There's roasted chicken for dinner." Shaking her head in amusement, she left to go upstairs by the front.

The male Red Death waited where he fell and shrugged his shoulders. He began to lower his arms but his counterpart directed, "Get up, you have been captured." He jumped to his feet and faked a jerk to her right side as if to slip past and return to the studio. She turned to grab him and he hauled her up onto his shoulder like a load of russet potatoes. She howled in protest and kicked, then thinking more strategically pretended a faint and went limp. Her arms dangled down his back, her hand still holding her unsheathed dagger. He took the stairs to the third floor two at a time, and at the door of the third floor apartment set her on her feet.

Her voice was higher and more melodramatic as she teased him. "Unfortunate fellow, you have attempted to foil Red Death and shall pay dearly for your arrogance!"

"Since I grew impatient for you to extract your prize, I had to lug your body upstairs. Do be gentle."

"I shall be as rough as I please. You should fear my every move!" She brought the tip of the dagger painfully close to the underside of his chin. Holding his head perfectly still he reached around her and opened the door. Spinning on the toe of her boot, she turned quickly and let the dagger fly through the air. It landed solidly into the wooden framework of a cabinet on the opposite wall.

He let out a low whistle. "Nice throw!"

Mimicking the gravelly voice of a drunken pirate she said, "It will be all the worse for you my pretty if you..." She broke off speech as she faced him. He had opened the front of his shirt to bare his chest to her. He took her trembling hand and placed it over his heart. She stood there feeling it beat beneath her palm. *Such a fine, strong heart, and here before me stands The Voice.* She winced as she saw a trickle of blood oozing down his clean-shaven chin. She had nicked him with the dagger. "I've cut you," her normal voice was full of regret.

"Oh woman, you will never know how deeply you've cut me."

She licked the blood with the tip of her tongue and kissed his chin. "You are the most handsome, fearsome creature I have ever met. The very sight of you causes trepidation and appetite." Walking backward into the room she took his hand. "Come, allow me to make amends."

When they finished, Christine dressed and left him sleeping face down on the bed. The enticing aroma of roasted chicken filled the entire house and she followed her nose to Madame Giry's kitchen door. Knocking softly Madame let her in and hugged her tightly. "He's asleep isn't he?"

Christine nodded, "Oh, Mama..."

"I know, Sweetheart, your ambitions lie here. I think I'll show you something." Taking her to the sink, Madame lifted up a plate of plant cuttings she had cleaned and rinsed. Christine chose one and inspected its slightly curved, dark green leaves, its tiny yellow flowers. Madame broke off a leaf for her to smell. The delicate sweet scent of cinnamon and licorice combined together came to Christine.

Madame explained, "This is tarragon. It's an herb the Persians call *tarkhum* meaning 'little dragon'. Its oils can soothe a toothache. I use it to add a pleasant fiery taste to chicken and dressing, but he uses it for something else entirely. See here, don't the roots resemble little serpents? The ancients believed this dragon herb could cure the bites of venomous snakes."

Christine put the broken leaf on her tongue and moved it around. *This is the taste in his mouth!*

Madame said, "Take some with you. If you ever need to send us a hurried note, sign yourself, 'Tarragon'."

Christine asked for paper and pen and wrote a quick message for Madame to give Erik when he came down to dinner. It read simply:

Professeur, until next week, live well. Tarragon loves you.

Later that evening he read the note several times. After memorizing her pen strokes and her words, he burned it. If the miscreant were ever arrested he wanted no trace of her to be found around him other than what dwelt safely in his heart.

12 EULOGIES FOR IMEL GREY

Early the next morning Christine dressed in riding pants and requested that breakfast be sent to her sitting room. The blasts of imaginary French horns filled her ears as she practiced her strikes and blocks. Attempting to pierce the chest of an invisible foe, her jab was neatly foiled. She twirled a short cape in his arrogant face and spun around. Leaping to the tapestried seat of an armchair, it rocked precariously beneath her feet. She gasped. Steadying herself, she tried to think of an appropriate verbal torment to mask her awkward misjudgment. A knock at the door broke through her exercise. Barely distracted, a sudden hiss of steam in the recently installed heating pipes returned her to the conflict. She took a defensive crouch. Bending her knees she stretched her sword straight out. *Look there, they retreat into the fog. I will pursue them for they cannot evade my cunning skills of smell and hearing!*

A second later, a louder knock broke the spell of the game completely. Frustrated, she called out, "Just a minute." She sheathed her delitescent blade and went to the door, unlocked the polished brass latch and opened up. One of the butlers stood in the hall and gave a small bow.

"Yes?" inquired his mistress.

"Madame, Victor LaPointe did not come into the office yesterday and he has not returned again today. This is most unlike him."

"There have been no notes?"

"No, and he does not respond to a knock on his door."

"Take me to where he lives and have the housekeeper's keys brought to us."

The butler led the way into the eastern wing of the chateau where Victor had a small apartment of four rooms on the second floor. When they entered they found the bed made and the apartment in order, but some of his clothing and toiletries, as well as a valise from his closet appeared to be gone.

The butler asked, "Should we report his absence to the authorities?"

Christine inquired, "Do you know where he spends his weekends?"

"No, my Lady. He leaves the chateau Friday in the late afternoon and returns on Sunday evening, generally around eight. He has no family that any of us know of, we have no idea how he spends his free time."

Christine told the servant that most likely Victor would return to them soon. "Perhaps wherever he is, he's a bit under the weather. At any rate, Raoul can address the issue of his delinquent secretary when he returns from England on Friday."

When Raoul arrived at the chateau three days later he found Christine sitting at Victor's desk going over the mail. He was greatly agitated to learn that no one had seen his secretary in a week. He explained to Christine that he would have to leave immediately for his solicitors' office as some documents and payments needed to be expeditiously addressed at the bank. She offered to go for him, but Raoul told her the affairs were complex and since she had no knowledge of their history, he would prefer to handle them.

"This is most troubling," he informed her indignantly. "I will inquire at the solicitors' about Victor, since they are the ones who sent him to us. Perhaps they have some idea of his current location. I will also ask for the name of someone they might recommend for a temporary secretarial position. We cannot be without one." Raoul paused only to visit Michael for the briefest of times and then promptly sped off for Paris with several bulky folders tucked under his arm, saying that if it were needed he would remain in the city over night. As the carriage raced to Paris, Raoul sat in the coach thinking about the last time he saw Victor. He had not seemed troubled in the least and all their business affairs appeared to be in good order. Raoul did return that night and the weekend passed without incident at the mansion. On Monday morning the temporary secretary reported for employment at seven, immediately impressing Raoul with his promptness, and straightforward 'let's get down to business' attitude.

At about ten o'clock that same morning a tall, slender young man of about sixteen alighted from a carriage and went up the steps into police station number seventeen. He approached the day officer's desk in the main lobby and asked where he might report a missing person. The officer on duty escorted him to the detectives' area and introduced him to one Andre Davier.

Scanning the young man from his head to his feet, the inspector noted that he had a full head of curly hair, appeared to be clean and neat, and possessed a smooth face still containing some of the younger appearances of a child. He wore a linen shirt with a tight fitting silvery jacket over matching pants. His shoes were rather fancy, adorned with ornate buckles, but appeared to be in good repair. Indeed, the only distracting attribute about the teenager was a syphilitic chancre on the edge of his upper right lip. The visitor had tried to conceal it beneath a generous amount of makeup but the sore had not slipped passed the inspector's scrutiny. Davier placed a fresh piece of paper on the desk and picked up a pen. Poised and in charge, he asked, "How may I be of service to you, Monsieur?"

"I am most distressed to tell you that I have not seen a good friend of mine for two weekends. I believe that something must have gone amiss with him for he is a most prompt and loyal companion to me."

"Your name, Monsieur?"

"Alexander Constantine. I live in a hotel called The Marching Drum. I hope you can locate my friend for me."

Inwardly the detective smiled at the young man's unmistakably effeminate gestures and the lilt of his voice. Inspector Davier knew the aforementioned hotel to be a place where people of higher rank in society housed their mistresses and male lovers, and where sexual favors of the widest variety could be discreetly purchased. Rarely, if ever, was there any kind of reportable incident from the establishment. The prevailing attitude of the police was that as long as the peace was maintained, the owners and their clients could conduct their business in any way they chose.

"When did you last see your friend?"

"Three weekends ago. He came to me as he always does and we spent from Friday evening through late Sunday afternoon together." There was genuine apprehension in the fellow's voice. Davier's face took on a well-rehearsed expression of acceptance and concern. Seeing it, the young man started to elaborate. "My services always please him very much. I believe he's suffered some ill fortune, for he would not shun me without good cause. He knows I am dependent upon his support and encouragement. You see...I'm an aspiring actor."

Aren't we all! "And might I have the name of your benefactor?"

"Victor LaPointe, during the week he works for..."

"The Count Raoul de Chagny," the inspector finished the sentence for him. Without even the slightest hint of the surprise he actually felt, Davier placed his pen on the desk and looked directly into the young man's eyes. Davier firmly believed that there were no coincidences in life, just streams of facts not completely appreciated for their intrinsic value. "Please tell me exactly when you saw Monsieur LaPointe last, and what the two of you said and did."

When the interview with Alex Constantine concluded, Davier located Detective Edwards at a local café where he was taking lunch. He related the curious disappearance of Victor LaPointe to his colleague. The two agreed on a repeat performance of their former visits. Davier would return to the chateau and this time interview the Count and his staff. While Detective Edwards went to the ballet studio and reconnected with the handsome Madame Giry. Perchance her brother had returned from the baths at Lourdes.

After lunch Davier proceeded to the de Chagny estate and was received by the Count in his private library. Raoul was unaware of the inspector's previous visit and his interview with Victor. He thought it most peculiar that no one in the household had mentioned it to him. *Perhaps they thought not to trouble me, but now Victor's gone missing!* He gave the inspector permission to go anywhere on the estate, with the exclusion of the rooms occupied by his wife and son. "But please, feel free to interview anyone you chose. Most of the female servants live in the eastern wing over the kitchens. Small apartments for couples are in that wing, as well. Quarters for the single male servants are in the areas of the basement."

Several hours later the inspector returned to Raoul and met with him alone, this time in his office. Davier informed the Count that the majority of the staff were in conflict over which day they actually saw Victor last. A few believed it to be on the Wednesday before he went missing. Still more placed him at the chateau on Thursday, and the bulk said he was most definitely at work on Friday morning, but only briefly.

"Your chief cook swears he served Victor a light breakfast on Friday. It's clearly in the man's memory because it was most unusual, since the secretary always has a hearty appetite. I was unable to interview three of the servants, a Mr. and Mrs. Sansfosse, they are away for the week visiting relatives in the north, and a certain simpleton named George, who works occasionally tending the hounds." He asked Raoul to check among his papers and see if there was any indication as to what day Victor was last in the office. A careful perusal of the desks produced some evidence of Victor's handwritten entries on Thursday, but there was nothing to indicate LaPointe's presence on Friday. Since all the staff reported that George had not worked on Thursday or Friday of that fateful week, the inspector decided not to speak with him, but said he would like to talk with the Sansfosse's upon their return to the mansion.

Raoul assured the officer that whatever he required would be placed at his disposal, and thanked him for allowing his family the privacy of their quarters and leaving them undisturbed. The inspector advised Raoul that on weekends, his absent secretary sought the pleasures purchasable at The Marching Drum. Raoul was astonished at the information. He had no idea Victor ran toward those tastes and the man had worked for the de Chagny's for over five years!

The inspector thought that perhaps some jealous partner in a liaison had brought harm to Victor. At any rate, the matter would certainly need further investigation. He promised to keep the Count informed should anything definitive surface.

Detective Edwards went to the ballet studio and found a busy Madame Giry entering a carriage to do some shopping. Asking her to delay her outing for just a few minutes, he apologized for troubling her and explained that as a matter of formality he needed to ask her a few more questions. He inquired as to the health of her brother and if the good Monsieur had returned to Paris. Madame informed him that sadly, she had received a letter from Imel saying he felt quite poorly and wished to remain in Lourdes for some time. There he could seek solace in prayer, and comfort from the warmth of the healing springs. The detective offered his sympathies and asked Madame if she knew a man named Victor LaPointe. She replied no. And finally, did she ever have cause to go to the de Chagny estate. He recorded all her negative responses in his little notebook and bidding her good day proceeded straight to The Marching Drum. Where a veritable bed of lies, half-truths, secretive solicitations and misinformation were placed before the detective for his singular mastication. Confused and in desperate need of a good smoke to clear his head, Detective Edwards decided to return to the hotel on the following day in the company of his colleague, Davier. Two minds would be needed just to begin sorting through the confounding complexities of the Pandora's box known as The Marching Drum.

Madame Giry collected herself gracefully after the detective left and went on her shopping trip. When she returned to the house they put their recent plans underway. After fixing black opaque screens on the dormer windows of the third floor, Erik moved for a time into the locked and secluded section of the basement behind the laundry area.

They decided to wait one week before Meg and Erik would go out and locate a body. Then they'd announce the death of Imel Richard Grey and hold a private funeral for him at the cemetery. Formal white cards, bordered in black, would be sent to all her students announcing the temporary close of the studio for a period of mourning due to the death of Madame's beloved brother.

Right on schedule the prowling pair located a body near a warehouse. They brought it to the laundry area of the basement in the dead of night, washed it and dressed it in some of Erik's clothes. The following morning the undertaker went to the second floor and removed the body from a bedroom they'd prepared for this inevitability. At the mortuary, Dr. Abraham DeVille signed the death certificate listing the cause of death as malnutrition and florid consumption. The casket was sealed immediately and marked as highly contagious. When the detectives went to view the body, as a matter of duty to the thoroughness of their case, the undertaker informed them of the risk of contagion. The officers insisted that the casket be opened at once. As soon as the lid was lifted a stench of decay and disease filled the room with such a putrid odor that the two officers, gagging and retching, demanded the casket be closed again and resealed. The face of the corpse was that of an old man, not Victor LaPointe.

The funeral was held at ten o'clock in the morning on a cold day in the beginning of November. The thick, darkened clouds that lay overhead threatened an imminent downpour on the small party of five who entered the cemetery and walked to the graveside of Imel Grey. Christine, Meg and Madame Giry wore long, black wool dresses. Their faces covered with thick black veils attached to tasteful hats. Jean escorted Meg and Christine, and Louisa was on the arm of a tall, aristocratic priest who moved with a fluid, confident stride. The priest wore a black cape with a deep purple collar over a classic black cassock and cincture. His head bore a black biretta with a purple pompom. To commence the service the clergyman placed an elaborately embroidered stole with long yellow fringes of silk around his neck.

Detective Edwards watched the ceremony from a distance; studying the expression of the women and the man he now knew to be Madame Giry's son-in-law. Thirty yards directly behind the detective, the astute eyes of the Daroga monitored every move the officer made. Unaware that he was under surveillance, Edwards took only a cursory note of the priest's rather stately bearing and tranquil, arresting voice, keeping himself vigilantly focused on the reactions of the women.

As the wind picked up and it began to sprinkle the detective opened an umbrella and remained at his post, observing. On the incline below, the members of the funeral party extended their umbrellas as well. When it actually started to rain, the Daroga finally pulled his brimmed hat lower on his head, hunched his shoulders and ignored getting wet. The service became, of necessity, abbreviated. After the concluding prayers, the small group hastened to leave the cemetery, their faces unreadable beneath the umbrellas.

Listening carefully, the detective heard Madame saying to the priest, "Father Raphael, how good of you to come out in all this weather to conduct a service for my dear brother. Imel wanted so little attention in life and only the most modest of funerals." In response the priest took Madame's arm and tenderly placed it on his own as they moved up the walk to the waiting carriage.

Meg, who was just behind them on her husband's arm sobbed, "He was a kind man and we love…loved him so very much."

When they were closer to the unmarked carriage, Madame and the priest lingered on the walk to allow the others to get in first. The driver left the door as Madame summoned him to come to her and receive a gratuity.

At the carriage step, away from the detective's earshot, Jean whispered to his wife, "I didn't care much for the stinky smell. Exactly who did we bury here today?"

He immediately got a stiff elbow in the side, and a hushed and heated response. "A pox marked pauper we found near the entrance to a warehouse. It seems Paris is never at a loss for the destitute lying dead in its poorer districts, they're just not all male and the right height."

As he helped Christine and then his wife up into the carriage, Jean added, "Well it's hard to feign a degree of sadness over this, the pauper's certainly getting a proper grave."

Meg's head appeared from the carriage doorway and she whispered, "Get in here and contemplate not coming to our bed for a while. That should screw your face into a tightness befitting grief." Admiring the fake display of pain Jean promptly presented, she critiqued his acting skills. "Excellent!"

Back at the house they sat in the second floor parlor over sandwiches, pastries and coffee. Listening to the strength of the storm rage outside, they chatted while Erik changed out of his priestly garb and removed his theatrical makeup. He entered the room wearing a white mask and flawlessly pressed black suit and shirt. The Daroga, in some borrowed dry clothes, followed close behind. Placing his shoes by the fireplace Khalil took a seat and the cup of strong Jamaican brew Madame offered him.

"Are the clothes comfortable?" Louisa asked.

Sipping at the liquid the Persian answered, "Yes, since he eats better, the Changeling and I are gratefully almost the same height and build. I believe the detective saw only what we wanted him to see. The Opera's ghost interred, yet again."

Warming his hands near the flames, Erik repeated, "A member of the dearly departed once more. Every time we kill me another layer comes peeling off, like leprous skin consigned to a grave. Maybe that's a good thing. Eventually we'll have no more layers, only the core to bury."

Christine and Meg shot a glance of warning at each other.

Meg protested. "I don't like hearing you say that parts of you are lying in a grave. You've escaped the coffin so many times, don't verbally climb back into one. I think we should salute Imel Grey and thank him." They each picked up a crystal stemmed glass of sherry and toasted, "To Imel Grey!"

"*Bon Voyage*," smirked the Daroga.

Erik blew Meg a kiss, then resting his hand on Christine's shoulder, reached over and acquired a small, diamond cut sandwich from off her plate. Pausing before popping it into his mouth, he added naughtily, "You know I'm not superstitious about referring to myself in a grave. Tombs are calming, restful places…the tragedy of life brought to its final, permanent close."

Christine mused, "I wonder what makes a life more or less tragic. Certainly your being allowed to survive is reward for all of us and not tragedy at all. Don't negate the progress we're making. At least you sleep in a regular bed now, a blessed normal bed!"

Jean asked, "What did you sleep in before?"

Amused, Madame answered without the slightest undertone of gloom. "A coffin, a beautiful black metal coffin with silver handles. The lid is adorned with silver roses."

As Erik settled into a chair beside Jean, Meg's husband playfully smacked him on the back. "*Merde*, how chic is that? So eccentric! A coffin!"

Erik sucked air through his left teeth, making a smug, clicking sound with his tongue. He couldn't resist Jean's approval – a broad smile emerged. "It's still waiting for me in the underground."

Christine pleaded, "The two of you, **stop**!" With a plaintive voice she begged Erik to listen. "Please, for all our sakes, stop joking. We are devoted to you. We love you. Look at me Erik! Die to live…die as many times as it takes!"

Jean leaned puckishly toward Erik, "Guess she means it."

Erik gave her an encouraging smile. "Such a winsome fatalist!" He sighed, "You don't understand, Christine. We kill me all the time."

Christine's nose turned upward. "What do you mean 'we kill you all the time'?"

Attempting to change the subject, Erik's face took on a more somber expression, but he could not remove the twinkle from his eyes. "Would you ladies care to see the certificate stating that I have authority to perform full sacerdotal rites in the city of Paris? The bishop signed it himself. I have the document here in my jacket pocket."

A nonplussed Christine ignored the offer and repeated, "What do you mean 'we kill you all the time'?"

Erik looked at Madame Giry, who nodded consent. He stood and offered his hand to Christine. "Please, come with me. I'll show you."

She followed him to the basement. On the right side was a wide laundry area with concrete sinks, an ironing board and sewing machine. The after smells of detergent and bleach hung in the air. To her left stood a door that he unlocked with a key. They stepped into a stone closet, like an enclosed vestibule, the bare walls of which created a space approximately six feet by six feet. The cool air made Christine shiver. The Phantom took off his jacket and placed it over her shoulders. She slipped her arms into the sleeves, enjoying the strange sensation of wearing his over-sized clothes on her slender frame.

"From this spot we can go in three directions. Today we go to see 'Bad, Bad Erik'." He reached up over her head and the wall behind her rotated on a pivot, allowing for a three-foot entrance into a blackness beyond. He struck a match and entered. Taking his hand as it came back out to her, she stepped inside and he closed the wall behind them. A candelabrum rested on a drawing table. He lit it and then walked around lighting candles in several wall sconces. The illumination allowed her a full view of the rectangular room in which they stood. She walked around slowly, taking in the fantastic sight before her eyes.

The walls were covered with impressionistic life-sized paintings. Here was an extremely thin Erik in a full mask – the specter of the Opera House swinging on theater rigging like a monkey, another showed a man and woman (who he identified as his parents) forcing a little boy to wear a cloth bag over his entire head. The next was of cruel gypsies and sneering people torturing a gaunt adolescent in a cage, then a young man chained to a wall and being whipped, his back full of bloody stripes. As she surveyed the gallery, tears filled her eyes but she commanded herself to study the history of his life. There she stood on the stage of the opera, singing with arms outstretched to Raoul up in his box on the grand tier. Beside it hung a picture of her in her wedding dress and veil on the day she became the Countess de Chagny. The details so exact she could believe the dress was really there in front of her. There was still space on the walls of stone for more portraits before reaching, once again, the drawing table and the way out.

Standing behind her he said, "I haven't painted Victor yet, but I have no doubt that when I am feeling particularly grim, I'll come down here and release his form onto paper or canvas. He shall mock you and place his mouth upon you…and I'll enjoy killing him all over again. These are the paintings that are hanging now, and here are some that are partially destroyed."

She turned and watched him move to a leather trunk. He undid the lock and opened it, then moved away. She walked to the trunk with feet of heavy lead and knelt beside it. Slowly she picked up picture after picture of a screaming, cruel Phantom, performing unspeakable acts of rage. Some of the paintings were torn down the center and she had to hold the two pieces together, others were crumbled and she smoothed them out to view them. Several bore the black marks of an artist trying to destroy his own image. When she had emptied the chest, she reverently placed them back in, stopping at one particularly poignant picture, pierced over and over with the spike of an ice pick. It was of Erik hanging from a rope, struggling desperately to remove the noose from around his own neck. He looked to be about eighteen. Sobbing, she place this picture on the floor. When her tears were drained and there was nothing left but dry gagging murmurs, she bent forward placing her forehead on his. Her head rocked from side to side, as she swallowed the depth of his despair and pushed it down into her gut. She kissed the mouth of the young man turning blue, his eyes rolled upward to a pitiless, vacant heaven.

She sat on the thick, multicolored Persian carpet covering the floor. With her back pressed against the wall she watched him at the drawing table, his hands folded calmly in his lap. Her mouth felt like dry cotton and her eyes burned from crying. "I had no idea. What terrible distortions we have unleashed on you."

Erik's voice was melodious and powerful, its vibration in this small space almost enough to rend the heart, but she was too exhausted and emotionally worn to react. His unwelcome words poured over her head like a stream of artic air. "You've heard of living vicariously through the life of another, well I die vicariously through these pictures…over and over. Each time I create one, or destroy one, I expose another layer of me to the touch of death."

"This works?"

"To a degree and of a fashion, yes."

"They are beautiful and horrible. They scream of torment and madness beyond bearing…wailing inconsolably of spurned affection and vicious rejection. Yet even as they break my heart, I have to tell you they are perfect, and cry of talent unfulfilled."

"Ah yes, the grand dichotomy of life…something instantly and simultaneously, beautiful and ugly. It's strong enough to slam a heart into a standstill, isn't it?" He walked over to the one of her as a bride. Taking his dagger, he started at the top and sliced it completely down the middle. The canvas stayed in place on the wall, obeying the laws of whatever substance held it in place, looking for-all-the-world like it was mocking him. He backed away from it and came to sit beside her on the floor.

Unwilling to acknowledge the truth, she asked, "Where you there in the cathedral that day?"

"Yes, from the choir loft I watched you wed him. Then I came here. Locked myself in this room, got spectacularly drunk and painted that picture of you. I didn't eat for three days. Every time Louisa came to the door I told her to go to hell. She said she would gladly go if I would come out and get cleaned up and eat. I intended to die in here, but she said something that changed me. Her words came through the door like a lightening bolt. I released the pivot and came out."

"What did she say?"

"That after a time Raoul would be like sawdust in your mouth."

"She was right." Christine slipped out of his jacket and unbuttoned the cuff of her left sleeve. With great determination she began to roll it up. The six inch scar on her forearm, just below the antecubital space of her elbow, looked like a silvery pink trophy. She moved it back and forth with her fingers admiring the keloid tissue. "Take your dagger and cut me again."

This time he offered no resistance to her convictions. Once more he burned the blade and cut into her, an inch below the existing scar. He pressed the edges of the slash tightly together with his long, slender fingers – and as before, wrapped the wound in his handkerchief. When he was satisfied she would not bleed he rolled her sleeve down, buttoning the cuff in silence.

In a voice heavy with regret, she said, "Two years without you, two scars."

"I understand," he answered, turning the gold wedding ring on his left little finger with his right hand.

Christine's voice was small and distant. "Sometimes I feel like you and I are on a train speeding into hell. The conductor has abandoned us, the engineer is a demon howling fiendishly as we hurl head long into a burning pit of chaos. I close my eyes in fear and picture your face, your beloved, dear face...and the roaring stops. There is only the sound of your voice in my head and I know peace. I wish I had never left your home beneath the Opera House. I hate being a de Chagny. If only we'd known each other as children and had grown up together."

"Shh," he said. "What will regret buy us?"

He put his graceful fingers into the curls of her hair, rubbing her scalp to console her. Passing his parted lips over her right eyebrow, the smell of her became a taste upon his tongue. Beneath his breath he felt the skin of her face constricting. He inhaled and exhaled over her cheek, taking in only the sense of her that breathing would allow. He brought his lips in front of hers that they might share each other's air. His initial kiss felt as if the sheerest of silk had passed gently across her, tantalizing in that it asked for no response. He was worshipping her with his mouth.

His eyes were closed and she watched this amazing creature undetected. When he deepened the kiss she surrendered to it, allowing it to lift her soul. She drifted upward, to a plane of air containing only clouds and wind – and him. As he withdrew his lips she sighed. Her face still tingled. *How could a man forged in so much pain produce this degree of subtle pleasure? I am his living canvas. He makes himself the paintbrush, tenderly applying the colors that will bring me to accept life's distortions and him.* For a time they sat, simply holding hands.

"I know you are reluctant to wear greasepaint and that Madame Giry worries when you use it. Please tell me why."

Erik rubbed his thighs with his hands. "Years ago I discovered the power of it, too bad being a priest can't last, I rather enjoyed the travesty we committed today. Disguise opened up huge worlds for me. An evil began to possess my mind that I could barely control. I could make myself into anyone and blend in wherever I pleased. There **is** a demon driving the train, Christine, and he's inside me! As you can see from the walls of this room, when he wants to come out and play, we contain him. Unfortunately, when I was younger he often ruled the day. I became so adept at changing my appearance that I moved among people without causing them the slightest bit of alarm. When presented with an opportunity, I could not resist it. I learned to stand right beside others and completely blend in. I heard their secrets, lifted their purses, snatched their jewelry before they had a chance to take note of me. The power of it was pervasive. I increased the circle of my hunting grounds wider and wider around the city. I took bold, imprudent risks. A very strong man caught me removing a lady's earrings and took me by the collar, swearing that he'd haul me into the nearest police station. I managed to wiggle away from him by leaving my jacket in his hands and fled into the sewers. I ran through the waterways and slipped, cracking my skull against a pipe. Dazed and confused I could not reorient myself, and stayed down there for two days trying to find my way back. Louisa thought I'd died out in the streets and was distraught with grief. When I finally returned and understood how upset she'd become, I agreed to only use these tricks when we needed them, and then only with the good Madame present to hold the evil at bay."

"But I've been with you when you're in disguise and she was not there."

"Yes, you are the exception, and I dare say that she would let Meg do the same as well."

"So humanity rejected you, coerced you into hiding behind a mask and then isolated you. Denying itself the genius of your architectural and musical talents by forcing you into solitude."

"People made me an outcast, so I extracted payment."

"For their lack of vision, their lack of compassion?"

"For making their own inadequacies smaller by punishing me for mine, when mine come only in the form of the outer package. They ignored my talents, so Louisa and I shield the package from their sight, create an illusion and charge them for it. I live now to survive and to love those who care for me. The rest of the world, that would crush me under its boot heel if it had the chance, is only the apple I eat."

"You have the right to ask me a question. It's part of our deal, remember?"

He thought for a minute. "When did you first start to love me…no wait, when did my face no longer bother you?"

"I'll answer them both. When I was a little girl growing up in the Opera House and you came to me as the Angel of Music, I loved you. I loved your presence around me and your singing. I don't think I'll ever have the words to adequately describe the healing effect you had on that lost little girl. Your voice compels the mind and the heart to listen, to pick itself up in courage. It's a powerful tool, wielded by a master surgeon, but you know that. When I was seventeen and you kidnapped me," she took his hands and held them lovingly to her chest, "because Raoul's attentions were becoming a threat to our relationship, I was a deeply ambitious and prideful girl. You were forced into revealing yourself to me. Being abducted and tied up in that bizarre subterranean world confused and terrified me. But then you played your organ and the majesty of your voice echoed to the very rafters of heaven. I was enthralled, positive that the angels were weeping at your music. I had to see what was beneath the mask."

He started to take his hands back, but she held them a tighter. Whispering something into his ear changed his entire demeanor. He sat expressionless, waiting.

"You are safe and you can hear this. When I snatched the mask from your face your appearance frightened me, most certainly, but your immediate, intense rage scared me even more. Your voice became the hacking cleaver of a butcher. I was horrified. When your anger weakened and you cried so sorrowfully over what I had done, I felt sorry for you. Yes, pity. Pity and revulsion took the place of fear. I didn't think I could love you as a man." She squeezed his fingers. "I was a stupid…foolish girl. Real love for you came gradually, without my realizing it was happening. As you revealed the man you are inside, I couldn't help but love you…you and your countenance, because it's part of you. Your persuasion is the magnetism of your thoughts and the prowess of your body. When your revelation was complete, your attraction held me fast. I understand now that I will always love you. Every moment together is worth the risk."

She tucked his hands in closer to her chest. "When you handed me back to Raoul you thought you had set me free to have a normal life, but I was already deeply in love with you. I will never love anyone else." She brushed the hair on his forehead back with her fingers. "My love for you is like a tree. When I was little it was a seedling, and when you sent me away with Raoul it was a sapling, but a strong sapling. In the maelstrom of your absence it bent like a bow and touched the ground without breaking. Giving me my freedom placed me in unrelenting torment. Without your presence I came to want death with every breath. I hated myself for lacking the courage to end my own agony!"

Tears were in Christine's eyes again. Her throat began to constrict as she reached into her private spirit to lay the truth before him. She gave herself a moment to recover. When her voice became audible, she continued to speak to the immobile man who sat so calmly beside her. "The tree has grown into a tall grand oak with its roots anchored deep into the earth. It does not bend any more, and if lighting hits it, it bears the scar of the bolt with dignity, holding its branches high, proud to offer itself to its owner. You are the master who owns the tree, Erik, you and you alone." She wiped her eyes and said, "Laudanum is a good drug for those who need it."

Erik's eyelids flickered and he smiled at her. He had heard every word she said, as if she were sitting beside him in a boat on a lake and they were simply commenting about the trees along the shore. He felt whole and complete, deeply loved and accepted. "I wish I could bottle **the peace** of this moment and drink of it at will."

She kissed his bare check and then the mask covering the other. "Let's stand up, I think my legs are numb."

Innocently he asked, "Do you like me better with the mask or without it?"

She rubbed her legs and stomped around the room trying to get the prickly stinging to abate. "I like you both ways. You're the most dynamic, handsome creature I have ever met, but if I'm making love to every inch of your warrior's body, I prefer the mask to be off, thank you." She curtsied but tilted off balance, her circulation still not cooperating.

A single soft knock came from the stone entrance of the room, followed by two quick louder knocks and a fourth soft one. "The good Madame," said the Phantom as he opened the door allowing the light from the little alcove to shine inward.

Madame Giry had changed into a day dress. "Jean and Meg have a carriage outside and will take Christine back to the chateau if she's ready to go." Erik and Christine took Louisa into their arms and hugged her tightly between them. In protest Madame declared, "I'm not a sandwich, you know." They started kissing her forehead and cheeks. Embarrassed but pleased at the affection, she hugged them back. "Come, the turmoil is behind us for a time, let's move on."

They gathered in the ballet studio and stood behind the safety of the curtains. Erik hugged Meg and firmly shook the hands of Jean and the Daroga, thanking them both for all they had done, not just today but over the years, all their unselfish giving and support. They were good friends – indeed more than friends, more than family. Erik proclaimed them a gregarious cabal of schemers knit tightly to each other.

Jean's face gathered amusement, "Thank God I was raised by elderly parents, who in their dotage, taught me to laugh at myself but respect the merits of others, eh?" His next sincere declaration summed up his devotion to the little troupe and his love of their games. He bellowed enthusiastically, *"Viva la mystique!"*

When the Daroga opened the front door to escort the ladies out, he almost stumbled on a pot of lush red geraniums resting on the porch. Picking it up and bringing it back into the entrance, he closed the door and handed the pot to Madame. She read the attached note outloud:

Dear Madame Giry,
We are saddened to learn of the loss of your beloved brother. Please accept our condolences and this small token. If there is anything you will allow us to do, we are at your immediate service.

Respectfully,
Little Kate and Thomas Edwards

Madame handed the pot to the Phantom. "Really, these are for you, dear brother."

Gesturing agreement and renewing their goodbyes, the four who were leaving turned to depart, but Christine paused to whisper into Erik's ear. "Never hesitate to disguise yourself to save your life, or to see me."

"Yes," he replied.

She left to join the others climbing into the carriage out in the street. As the driver pulled away from the house, the rain pounded the cobblestones in wind whipped sheets.

An hour later Erik sat pensively at his desk unable to concentrate on his musical compositions. *Today we buried a stranger. Someone's body bought me time to live in freedom. I don't even know his name. Will I be worthy?* He wondered at the originality of his own thought, something was changing inside him – ticking away in evolutionary degrees. He was still the cold killer, a fast efficient assassin who could ruthlessly end another's life. So where was this bizarre gratitude for the use of a stranger's body belching from? Listening to the storm he watched a brown house spider descend on a silken thread and alight delicately on his desk.

"Where are your babies, little mother?" A morbid, unsettling preoccupation with motherhood ground its way into his thoughts. For years it had not plagued him, but lately it seemed to stalk him even in the blandest of moments. In his memories he could still hear the vehemence of the woman who had given him birth, then whittled away at his self-esteem. One day he had removed his head covering and begged for something. Just a small, tiny thing, but it meant the world to him.

In a fit of shrieking hysteria she'd given her response to his outlandish request. "No! You're a putrid pile of refuse! How can you even ask me? Don't you understand? You will never find a bride. Do you hear me? Never! No woman will accept you as a husband with that horrid face. Put your head back in the sack and go to your room. Leave me alone!"

In tears, the little boy ran from her. How cruel was the world that it would one day refuse him a wife? He pretended he was glad to be banished to the attic of the house, glad to avoid a mother who refused to kiss her only child, or hug him when he begged. He longed to ask his father why he couldn't have a bride. Was he that ugly? He never got the opportunity. His father kept himself occupied at distant construction sites and died too soon to help. In anger, the boy escaped his mother's imprisonment and fled. Stripped of dignity and with no sense of self, all he had with him as he climbed the hills behind her house toward a new existence, was the clothes he wore and the stubborn belief that he had a right to live.

His mother had been correct. Even the golden alchemy of his voice had failed to captivate Christine enough to win her love once she'd seen his face. *Christine.* The lingering scent of her was all over his clothes. He clutched at the slender rays of self-worth she'd poured over him in the basement. *She wants you now old fellow, and she still can't see the truth of who you are. She yearns for a man she refuses to acknowledge is a villainous blackheart!*

He felt the old wounds ripping open as unseen hands vigorously applied the salt. As a child there'd been no male for him to model, no caring father figure whose ways he could adopt, no man from whom he could draw strength and procedure. He felt like a ship burning out of control, adrift at sea. His skin grew cold as he tried to form accusations against uncertainties he could hardly define. His thoughts grew darker as he raged against the injustice of his contorted, meaningless life, but he let the spider live even as his mind screamed out the dreaded words. *Unworthy! Unworthy!*

13 CAGEY THIEVES

A blessed sunny day, unseasonably warm for November, surrounded them. Excited and grateful for the miraculously unpredictable autumn weather, Christine attended to the business at hand. The crowded dock bustled with visitors and businessmen. People hurried past with their coats on their arms, their jackets unbuttoned, grateful for a break from the cold rains. She stood hidden inside a shipping crate on a walkway, and as gentlemen passed she swiftly attempted to lift their purses. The Phantom watched from a crate opposite hers, smirking every time she succeeded. *She is learning to be fast, very fast.* Her hands, or her sword, were only visible for the barest of moments through the flaps on the side of the crate. Occasionally he'd imitate the sound of a trumpet up on the street to announce the arrival of some nobleman. The distraction caused people to turn and loose focus a bit. Seeing no one of importance, they'd resume their trek. Disappointed and unwittingly relieved of their money, the victims proceeded down to the docks with a resigned *'oh well'* absorbing their thoughts. The plan was to play the game to increase her speed and dexterity under genuine pressure, but to play it for only an hour. Too many people in one area with missing purses made him uneasy.

Waiting for their next pigeon he thought back upon the conversation they'd had on the way to the docks. They were riding in a hired carriage, dressed as a young blonde lad and an old man with a full gray beard and glasses, on their way to claim some parcels at the boats. He studied the sunlight touching his palm and saw a thousand colors sparkling on his flesh. *How miraculous is life.* Looking at his young companion, he acknowledged to himself that there was no disguising those bewitching, mischievous eyes, so unmistakably Christine. Before he could censure his own words, they flowed forth from his mouth, "You know this imperfect and solitary piece of creation you see before you will never let you go. You are my obsession."

"That's reassuring. I was worried that you might stop obsessing over me any day now." The fingertips of both her hands started to tap on each other in mid-air, like two little conjoined spiders. She made her voice high-pitched and creaky as the carriage jostled them a bit. "If you manage to wander off, I'll come like a spider and spin a sticky web around you. Besides, I see no imperfections sitting in your seat. Everything looks just as it should be."

She took one of his long slender hands and started to kiss each fingertip. "This one is fine, and this one. Oh, this one has a little smudgy on it...no matter." She licked the substance off. "Jam! Hmm, apricot I think, but I'll have to taste some more and let you know." She opened her mouth wider and placed the whole middle finger of his right hand into it. Slowly she sucked on it and drew it out of her mouth, only to reinsert it again. "Hmm, yes, apricot. Delicious! Want a taste?" She offered the finger to him.

"You are driving me deeper into insanity, if that's possible. Since we don't have a physician at our beak and call, I can only surmise that my mental condition is deteriorating out of sheer and eager lust for you. Do you want to continue to the docks or go back to the house?"

Imitating an innocent young boy she responded in a child-like voice. "Oh yes, Sir. Please, let's go see the boats and all the nobles on the docks. Thanks Sir, you're so good to me."

Pulling on his pant legs to relieve the constriction in his crotch, he explored the ridiculous. "If my brains could be viewed outside my head, doctors would marvel at the contortions you so cruelly put me threw, little minx. But they'd have to examine them quickly because my brains, finding themselves free at last from the confines of my skull, would take off flying, like geese heading south for the winter. Why don't we sit in silence and enjoy each other's presence until we get there? Then we will set things up and let you have some fun."

Barely a minute passed and Christine started to speak again, this time in her normal voice. The Phantom's left eyebrow went up in utter amazement at a woman's ability to chat a man into distraction. She asked, "Tell me how it is that you are such a great lover."

"I had a dedicated teacher."

"Who?" Christine inquired.

He echoed, "Who?"

"Yes, who? We sound like a pair of barn owls."

"You will not judge us?"

"I didn't get the heavenly memo permitting me to judge you."

"We're discussing a book I've read."

"We're discussing a book."

He hesitated for a few seconds. "Madame Giry led me into manhood with the utmost care and patience. Ours is a relationship based on friendship rather than romance. She was only nineteen when her husband died in the service of the army, and I was a thorny miserable teenager. So, I took care of her needs and she took care of mine. She told me that someday I would find a great love of my own, just as she had found with her husband, but I didn't believe her. My adolescent mind thought that no one would ever want this repugnant chewed up face. I owe her more than I can ever repay. Not only has she saved my life multiple times, but she taught me about being a man…a person. She even showed me how to tie a cravat."

"When did you complete your lessons with her?"

"I was twenty-five when she brought a seven-year-old orphan to the Opera House. Part of the wall behind your bed was a screen hiding a passage I built for Louisa. It was the route we took to meet each other at night, no one ever knew of it. When you fell asleep she came and got me. From behind the screen she introduced me to you. 'Erik,' she said, 'this is Christine Daae. Her father just died and she is very sad. Let's try to comfort her.'

"I told Madame that you were an angel. I was smitten from the moment I saw you. As I watched you grow up and learn to be a dancer, my feelings only deepened and widened. You were the one pure, unblemished thing in my life. When you became a teenager I thought my feelings for you would eat me alive, so I started writing you music and felt some release."

"Do you ever miss the Opera House and your old haunts?"

"No, my world isn't focused underground any more. It's focused on you and Michael." He took on a degree of levity, "And the writing of witty little plays for the amusement of the multitudes."

"And who taught you to sword fight?"

"Well, by the way that I hack at it, one could suppose that no one taught me. I've had to fight so many times that the need for total concentration and ingenuity on my feet became reflexive. I learned that reacting swiftly was imperative, and meant the difference between coming out of a fight in one piece or all torn up. But speed doesn't guaranty victory. My goal was always to get the battle ended as quickly as possible, and remain standing on my own two feet, ready to flee. I put what physical strength I possessed to work and discovered that tapping into the anger I felt over my own inadequacies put added force to my strikes. When I was a young teenager in Persia, the Daroga took note of how I fought. He saw that even though I received a considerable beating, I would come out the winner through sheer determination just to live. He told me that my skills were quite poor and that I was winning by the instinct of channeling my energies, which he granted were considerable for one so skinny and so young. So the Daroga had the guards teach me the Punjab lasso, and he paid a French exile to teach me the sword. I showed him slight of hand and on many occasions performed a service resolving political intrigue in the court. When I fled to France and came to live in the caverns below the Opera House, I had to protect myself against the occasional stranger who made his way into the caves. That's when I devised the alarms to let me know if someone was approaching my home. Madame Giry would occasionally watch the ballet students from box number five. I tried to scare her off but she never believed for a moment that I was anything but a human being. Her logic was fascinating. She brought me food and clothes, and became my friend. She encouraged my inventions, and told me that I must take time everyday to practice my fighting skills. In some form or another, I never fail to do so."

"Did the Daroga teach you to twirl your cape during a sword fight?"

"No, I discovered that trick on my own, but it was while I lived in Persia. The blur of black cloth surprises the opponent and puts them off balance. The moving cape provides a distraction and gains a brief element of uncertainty in the opponent. They don't know what height the blade will be at when the spin completes…but I do, and controlling the situation as I return to face them means the preservation of self. Raoul was lucky, just being born a de Chagny made him a powerful man. His rank in society alone granted him the privilege of the best teachers. He learned to sword fight in a manner common to the nobility. So much of what I do is raw and unpolished."

"I disagree. I've seen you both fight and you are the very personification of graceful motion. Why weren't you the victor in the bar fight at The Fish's Mouth back in September?"

"I didn't want to be. I was punishing myself, not in a picture, but by allowing the shit to get kicked out of me."

"Why would you do such a thing?"

"Because I am unbalanced, an unconscionable killer not fit to be Michael's father or your husband. I know my face would give my son nightmares and I don't want him, or me, to endure the experience. Michael will be something I will never be, a count. And you, my love, will never suffer one moment of hunger."

Christine sat thoughtfully for a few moments, "And is there a plan for you to escape again if the *gendarmes* should discover that you're still alive?"

The Phantom did not respond, the carriage halted with a jerk and he looked out the window. "We're here."

The hairs at the back of his neck bristled. His mind returned abruptly from the reverie of their conversation in the brougham to the dock. He carefully studied the crate containing the fledgling thief. A circle of scarlet paper filling the top of the letter "g" in the word *cargaison* (freight) told him that she was fine and still enjoying herself immensely. A familiar voice came down the wooden planks of the slope to the docks. Raoul and his new secretary were headed straight for them.

Raoul was intent on giving precise instructions. "Don't forget to post the notes at the bank tomorrow morning and send a dispatch to the Italians that I have left by boat for England and should attend to them with a personal visit in about fourteen days."

The secretary was busily writing down Raoul's dictates in a notebook, and the Phantom concentrated his thoughts toward Christine. *Do not lift either of their purses, woman.* He saw no movement from the boxes where Christine stood hidden and he refused to employ his talents as a ventriloquist to create any trumpet sounds whatsoever, choosing rather to slow his breath and wait. As Raoul passed the Phantom's hand went to the hilt of his dagger. *Not today, Monsieur, not today. You would be committing a grave mistake to knock at either door.* Raoul got three paces down the walk from them and stopped. His head turned quizzically to the side and he shook it. Unconsciously he had read Madame Giry's name, and the address of the ballet studio, on one of the crates.

The secretary inquired, "What's wrong, your Lordship?" The man sounded like he had a string in his throat and needed to cough to clear it. The Phantom winced – it hurt his ears.

"Nothing, I feel like I've forgotten something." The Count waved his hand beside his head in a gesture for them to move forward to the boats. "Let's keep going."

A few moments later the walkway was deserted and an obscure piece of gray clothing moved from one set of crates to the other. When the Phantom entered Christine's container, she was holding her hand over her mouth trying not to laugh outloud. "Christine, this is not funny!"

"Oh, yes it is. I'm glad I emptied my bladder before we left the house. You have no idea how much I wanted to lift the purse off his pompous ass."

"Christine, he's your husband!"

"No he isn't. I'm looking at my true husband."

They heard workers talking and something bumped their crate – hired delivery men were beginning to move the wooden boxes leaning up against theirs. Silently the Phantom slid a metal bar, locking them inside.

"Shh," he admonished, "these men are here to pick us up and take us back to the house. They're early!"

"Good thing you wrote fragile on the box then, huh?" She had to cross her legs to keep from urinating. Laughter was bubbling to the surface. Alarmed, he sensed her inability to contain it and put his hand over her mouth to stop her. They slid down to the bottom of the box where she gained control over her impetuous desire to giggle by burying her face in his lap.

"Stop it, vixen, afford me some slack!"

"Sorry Sir, but we're not supposed to be in the same box on the way back. You know I can't resist you."

The movers used ropes and pulleys to pick up the crates and put them on a large wagon to deliver them to the address stenciled on their sides. Smacking the crate with the two confederates, the driver in charge declared, "They all have weight, but this one is the really heavy one."

Christine peeled off her false face and her accomplice's glasses. Erik allowed her to take off his wig, and when they were securely roped down onto the mover's vehicle she whispered, "There now, nice and comfy for the ride home? I have a few more questions."

"I'll just bet you do, but consider this fair warning. We are only having a conversation. I am not going to make love to you inside this box."

"What a great idea, I hadn't thought of it, but all right, I'll keep it to words only. Can we snuggle?"

He took her in his arms inside the confined space of the container. She lay on her side, curled up into him, with her lower half in between his legs.

"You are more that just a handful." He yawned. "You exhaust me and I love it."

14 A CONVERSATION IN A BOX

Deviously sensing her mentor to be relaxed and enjoying the adventure, Christine wasted no time engaging her Phantom in discourse. "What was your best day?"

A dubious Erik responded, "You know perfectly well that I can't express myself in words as well as I can in music. You go first this time, minx. What was your greatest day?"

"The first time we made love inside the tomb. You were alive and I had a glimmer of hope that I could have you back in my life. Since then, every time I'm with you becomes my greatest day, because it's one more experience with you."

He hugged his precious cargo a little tighter. "So it has to do with me, not your triumphs at the Opera House? Didn't you enjoy having hundreds of people standing to applaud you?"

Christine agreed. "Oh, at the time it was wonderful, I was delirious, but fame is fleeting. At the chateau I came to understand that you were what truly mattered. What good was honor and acclaim without you? They're nothing, useless...an unsatisfying empty trick. Now you tell me, what was your best day?"

"The day Michael was born," he answered. "When they cleaned him up and handed him to you, the look on your face after all that pain and struggling to bring him into the world. I can't begin to explain it. I was so amazed at the birth of that little boy and at you, so exhausted as you strove to get him here. He was healthy and beautiful, perfect in every tiny detail. I love babies...they make me feel warm inside. I'm just awkward at handling them. I'm so proud of you for bringing our son into this world. You're very brave."

Christine took note of how calmly he spoke. He had not referred to himself in the third person for quite a while, and she took that as a sign that some of his conflicts were lessening. "Yes, that was my bravest day...so far. And Michael is going to grow up a de Chagny and not a D'Angelus, but I won't go there. That can be an argument for another time."

"Smart woman, thank you. We wouldn't want to take on too much too quickly."

Christine rubbed her nose where spirit gum was making it itch. "No, we wouldn't. It's your turn to ask me a question."

Erik thought a moment. "You don't have to answer if you don't want to, but what was your worst day?"

"I don't think I have any that are as black as yours must have been, but the day before I saw you in the street was my worst day. That would be October fourteenth of seventy-three to be exact. After two-and-a-half years of silence, everyday was hell. I suspected that you were still alive but wasn't sure. By that time, your motivations were clear to me. You'd given me to Raoul out of selflessness, because you truly loved me. I loved you too but there was no way to tell you. Full of loathing for my capriciousness, I asked myself how I could have thrown our relationship away so cursively. I found it impossible to forgive myself. Your music was always in my head, my constant companion. I clutched desperately at the memories of it, making sure the sounds didn't grow faint. Your singing lulled me, but every expressive note was torment. Somewhere an almighty edict had been signed without my consent, and there were no appeals. I was not to have you." She grew distant. "Grief and woe were my reward for failing to recognize the season of my visitation. Gradually I walked deeper and deeper into the abyss. The pain became excruciating. I longed for death. I prayed for its gnarled, crooked fingers to twist the life from my greedy heart. The day before I saw you I stopped eating altogether. I knew I'd die eventually. How long can a person go without food?"

Erik asked, "It depends on circumstances. You don't feel like that any more, do you?"

Christine kissed his hand. "No, I have you back and now I understand how much your music sheltered me. It kept me from the affliction that encroached upon my mind."

Erik replied thoughtfully, "Yes, music can be a great healer."

"I want you to describe your worst day."

Erik answered quickly, "Is this a day for robbery or a day for bearing the soul?"

Undaunted, Christine responded, "Aren't we discussing a novel? A book? I want to understand you. I can wait to be enlightened so if it's too painful don't answer. But know this Erik, all your pain is my pain, too. Whatever has been done to you has been done to me as well. We are one entity." She crossed two of her fingers and twisted them back and forth for him to see.

"Will you kiss me?"

She heard the almost child-like shyness in his voice, and got a glimpse of the damaged boy who craved affection even though he held her inside this small space made of pine. She scooted her bottom toward him so she could reach his mouth, and kissed him as best she could while being banged about by the roughness of the road.

He touched the tip of her nose and tried to open 'The Book of Erik' to her. "There have been so many black days in my life. I suppose I would have to line them up by shades of blackness. Certainly your wedding day was not one of them."

Christine's eyes widened in surprise, she would have guessed that to be one of his gloomiest. *He is so complex, there is so much more to learn about him.*

Erik continued, "When I was very young my face revolted my parents. My mother forced me to wear a sack over my head, and my father ordered that I be confined to the house. I ran away when I was nine and attached myself to a band of gypsies, a wandering circus. At one point I had not eaten a meal for three days, and lay beaten in a cage. I committed my first murder and crossed the threshold from freak to criminal. Hearing myself tell of it, I am surprised to realize…it was not my worst day." A single tear spilled from Erik's left eye onto his cheek and he grew silent.

Lying with her knees bent and her head on his chest, Christine turned her face to his and drew circles in the air with her index finger. "Laudanum is a good drug for those who need it." She watched Erik's face grow instantly placid, his tears dried, his breathing was deep and regular. *Asleep and awake,* she thought, *thank you Dr. DeVille.* Outloud she gently directed, "You will not remember these words and you will listen very carefully to me."

"Yes," he answered.

"When we leave this box, you will understand that I do not feel pity for you, only love. You will shed disgrace as if it were a dead skin and leave it here in this coffin. Free of it, you will accept that sharing remembrances with each other increases knowledge and deepens the love we both prize. You want me to know what has happened to you, not because it is grotesque or shameful, but because it is simply part of your life. Reach into your memories and when you awake, tell me of your darkest day. Laudanum is a good drug for those who need it." Christine clicked her fingers together softly and Erik continued without hesitation.

"My darkest day was the first time I was sexually intimate with Madame Giry. I was seventeen and lived in the caves under the Opera House. Struggling to cope with being alone most of the time, I was unprepared for the demands my body made as it bloomed into manhood. Touching myself no longer brought satisfaction and the need to be physically embedded into a woman's pelvis overwhelmed me. My *membre royale* took on a will of its own, and stayed erect most of the time, no longer placated by my hands, it clamored for gratification. I was anxious, stretched tightly like an elastic and thought I would explode. I knew no female would ever have me. My mother repeatedly drilled that truth into my head. In Persia I was an infidel and a freak forbidden to touch women. I decided to go to the streets at night and find a woman, any woman. Somehow I'd hide my face from her and pay her for the experience.

"As I left the underground on the *Rue Scribe* I found the body of a girl who had died during the day. I brought her corpse across the lake to where I was building my home and placed her on the embankment. With her face sunken in and the skin of her arms and legs white and drawn down into her bones, she appeared to have died of starvation. She was dirty, her skirt and bodice were thread bare and torn. I removed her clothes and brought some water to wipe her face. I touched her breasts and opened her legs, admiring her genitals. She was young, maybe fourteen, I couldn't tell. My mind went to an evil place, a place of disrespect and abomination. As I squatted there beside her I thought to have intercourse with the corpse. I was consumed by physical urges I could not control. I tried to masturbate beside her but could not climax. I removed my clothing and decided to lie upon her, thinking naively it couldn't hurt either of us. She didn't smell too badly and rigor had passed, but her skin was cold. I wanted her to be warm. I went to get a blanket and when I returned a rat was chewing at her ear. I hollered loudly and it swam off into the water. I was suddenly filled with a terrible, urgent desire to end my life. I was already a murderer and a thief, and now stood on the verge of committing necrophilia. I was nefarious, loathsome even to myself. This girl would never smile at me or kiss me of her own will. Dead...I was making her my bride. Who was I to disrespect her corpse? Naked I retrieved a rope from the boat and fashioned a noose. I threw it over the unfinished frame of the doorpost.

"I was moving in a fog. Desperately wanting the pain of living to end, I was unaware that Madame Giry had come to stand beside the corner of the house. Her husband had died a month earlier in the army and she was in mourning. Little Meg was but an infant in her arms. What I was planning to do with the body was obvious, it was naked, I was naked, but Louisa's face bore no condemnation at all. She took me inside and brought me to my bathtub. Filling it with soap and water she washed me, gently explaining that I must never be physically intimate with the dead.

Doing so could send my mind into a realm of irretrievable madness. She told me she cared deeply for my welfare and was my friend. If I would allow it, she would be my teacher in these matters.

"'What your body is telling you is the natural course of becoming a man,' she said. 'Women of a gentle, worthy character like clean smelling men. Be friendlier with soap.'

"I actually liked feeling clean, but the stench and dankness of the underground were formidable elements to contend with. When she finished the bath, she brought me to the bed and opened up the world of men and women for me. We were together off and on over the next eight years, depending on our needs."

"What caused the physical relationship to end?"

"It stopped the day I saw you. From the beginning I felt protective and special toward you, the very picture of innocence. I told Louisa that I was smitten and wanted to save myself for you. She suggested that I enter a time of celibacy and use my feelings for you to explore and develop my music. I was never with another woman again until I was with you."

When the deliverymen arrived at the ballet studio with the crates, Madame Giry signed their papers and instructed them to bring the boxes into the carriage house. With her cargo safely secured and the workers departed, she knocked on the one marked 'freight' with her coded knock. Christine and Erik unlatched the side and came forth, stretching and smiling.

"How are her lessons going?" Madame inquired.

"Splendidly," Erik responded. "We almost had a conversation with Raoul. What is for dinner? I'm famished!"

Madame looked in astonishment from Erik to Christine, who shrugged her shoulders and pulled her face up into a comical smile beneath her slightly askew blond wig. "It's true. It took all my control not to saunter out in front of him at the dock. Erik had to clap his hand over my mouth to restrain my laughter. I wanted to call Raoul's name out so badly. Imagine him jarring his brain, trying to discover what universe my voice emanated from. Really, the prod was almost too difficult to resist!"

Madame covered her own lips with a handkerchief, barely suppressing a smile at the imagined antics. Bringing a more serious expression to her face, she touched Christine's forehead as if to mimic checking for a fever. Not sharing the jocularity of the women, Erik steered the newly initiated thief to the exit. "Come, we'll tell her the rest inside."

15 LOOTING THE ATTIC

Sometime during the splendid New Year's Eve celebrations to welcome the year of 1875, a steadfast resolve flowered within Christine. As she watched the brilliant fireworks blossom across the skies of Paris, a buoyant determination filled her soul. If men could display such beauty in the vaults of heaven, surely one young woman could convince a gifted teacher that she should live out her days at his side. Fervently she pledged herself to the quest, vowing that this would be the year she carved the treasure from the mountain, even at the cost of great risk. Winning Erik's invitation to be his wife was the prize she valued above all others. In the safety of her rooms she placed the task before her once more.

To her accounting, only shades of truth dwelt within the walls of the chateau. Life there was a theater production, and she the constantly performing actress. Her real existence consisted of the fleeting hours she spent each week in Erik's blessed company, learning from him, loving him.

What are the blockages? Erik believes his mind too unstable. His face and his past declare him unfit, so he permits only the indulgence of stolen meetings, while another man beds his wife and raises his son. Oh, what is the key? Certainly Dr. DeVille's directions are helping. Erik remains visible and close, he loves Paris, he loves me. But how do we progress further when Erik seems so content?

A way to approach the problem occurred to her as she paced. A silken, viscid web began to weave itself in her mind, and she opened her mouth to speak it to its logical end. "Be Erik, see the thing as he sees it. Perhaps he is not content. Life reinforced the notion he's unworthy and life spewed forth a blasphemous lie!" *Basics, Erik constantly admonishes, 'Remember the basics.'* "If he already wants a life with me, we're impeded because he doesn't trust that wanting can safely lead to having. So what **does** he trust? He trusts music, he trusts illusion, and he likes to live in...subterfuge!"

The answer laid her throat raw with the truth of it. Her heart pounded so hard that she pressed on her bosom to calm it. Falling backwards onto the covers of her bed, she realized how much he truly trusted living in subterfuge. She would join him in a world appearing to be one thing when actually it was entirely another. "A castle's walls crumble to ruin when they are successfully bombarded. Better if an invading army tunnels beneath them and comes up from under the ground. The assailants are inside the protective walls before the owner is aware, and the castle is taken intact."

The pit she would climb into, in order to live a life of deception with Erik, was not as endless as she had supposed; no indeed, it was not! "*Merde benit,*" she announced to the ceiling.

As her heart began to calm, pictures of all the things they would do together played out in her mind. *Independent. Free!* Resolving to control her own damn destiny she stood up and retrieved the box containing her stolen monies. She ran her fingers through the gold and silver, counted the folded notes and decided to hunt for a place to hide it. After tucking the box underneath the bed, she took a taper in a glass chimney and moved into the hall. Blowing out the flame she pocketed the matches. No need to draw attention with a candle, the first promising dawn of 1875 was already breaking. Spots of silver gray light moved across the achromatic colors of the carpet to guide her steps. She traveled quietly to a door identified to her years ago by the housekeeper as one leading to the attic. *Unlocked!* The knob turned freely in her hand and she opened it soundlessly so as not to rouse the sleepers in that section of the house.

The windows of the attic dimly illuminated a flight of stairs going upward. The attic's space was enormous, an open framework of trusses and roof rafters, with roughhewn support beams crossing horizontally overhead. She immediately enjoyed its vast expression. *No pretentiousness at grandeur here, just space.* Light shone into the dusty domain from ornate circular windows strategically placed in the pitch of the roof for decoration. It appeared that at the time of the chateau's construction a singular concession had been made toward economy, the attic had been left as an open area for the storage of the family's paraphernalia. It's walls were simple whitewashed plaster, proclaiming that if future needs dictated, it could be considered as a living space, possibly for the housing of servants.

Without subdivision, the attic seemed to go on forever. Apparently it traversed the entire mansion. Its maze of timberwork reminded her of a troubling night in the Opera House. A tormented, lonely musician had stealthfully followed her and Raoul up the convoluted steps to the roof. There he had hid, listening beside the statue of Apollo's lyre, as she callously planned to run away from the theater without even saying good-bye to him. *Foolish, ghoulish girl! I am the monster, Erik, not you. But you have all my good attentions now, Sir. We will not be separated for long.*

She heard his answer in her head and smiled. *Shh, Christine, focus on reconnaissance.*

Beneath her feet the heavy ceiling joists were covered in a floor of stained planks. Instinctively, she placed the soles of her shoes on the nails in the boards to keep the floor from creaking beneath her steps. As she explored she found boxes and trunks of various sizes, but thought them too obvious a place to stash her recently acquired spoils. *What if the boxes were gathered up by the housekeeper and given to charity?* She came across a cluster of interesting old furniture and a dressmaker's form beside bolts of disintegrating cloth. As she moved around the sewing supplies she found a loose, triangular piece of board cut to fit a corner in the flooring. Lifting it up, the pocket of an angled ceiling brace greeted her. *A perfect place to hide the box!* She decided to continue on and acquaint herself with this new domain.

The entire vaulted dome of the main entrance rose like an enormous upside down bowl into the attic's space. It created an odd rounded wall for her to circumvent. At its back she found a sheltered corner sequestered from sight by a curtain of heavy tapestry. Drawing the curtain aside, she exposed the double doors of a richly carved Spanish oak cabinet. The seven-foot doors opened and closed with two delicately curved brass levers, a metal plate below the right lever contained a hole for a skeleton key. Trying the doors the one on the right responded. Inadvertently left unlocked by its user, the door swung open. Pulling down on a metal bar inside the upper inner edge of the left one, released the second door. Surprised, she found herself before a formidable six-foot safe. Its prestigious red door beautifully bordered with a hand painted golden trellis of winding wisteria and open winged doves. A smaller metal door, ten inches high and eight inches wide, lay flush with the safe's front, just off center. An engraved brass plate affixed to this smaller door read *Bauche de Paris-1860,* and just below the words another keyhole forbid entry. *The mechanism for opening the safe must be in there, under lock and key as well. Whatever Raoul has secured inside this thing he wants it kept close at hand, not stored at the bank. Why else would he hide a safe like this in the attic?*

Carefully she closed the oak doors of the cabinet and covered them with the tapestry. Surveying the area to assure that all was left in good order, she picked up her candle and returned to the stairs leading down to the second floor. No sooner had she re-entered the blue carpeted corridor and shut the door to the attic's staircase, than Raoul rounded the corner.

"Where have you been my darling?"

"Just exploring."

"I want to wish you a happy New Year and escort you to breakfast. I have some free time today. Let's spend it playing with Michael and getting reacquainted, shall we?"

"Certainly."

After they ate and fussed over the baby for a while, Raoul abruptly excused himself and left. Quickly she handed the baby back to the nanny and kicking off her shoes in the hallway, followed the tails of Raoul's coat as they turned the corner up ahead. Swiftly she sprinted to the corner and dropping to her knees, edged her face around it. She saw Raoul do a remarkable, almost predictable thing. He went straight to the attic door, looked from side to side to ascertain no one was watching, and cursed as the knob turned freely in his grasp. *Whatever you've hidden up there you guard it well, Raoul. How eagerly you seek to check on it!* She returned to the nursery so that when he finished his chore he'd find her there.

For the time being, Mondays were spent visiting Dr. DeVille and practicing swordsmanship at the ballet studio. On Fridays, in the private confines of her father's tomb, she rejoiced over her true treasure. When next she entered the darkness of the garret, two strong arms lifted her off the platform. She melded into the clothes surrounding the man who enfolded her and brought her to him with strength and decision. Happily she shed her composed aristocracy and slipped her hands under the lapels of his velvet jacket. *Softness over chiseled muscle, no confusion now, only bliss.* As her feet touched the floor she laughed into his chest. *God, how I love the smell of him!*

His left index finger played with her ear and traveled along her jaw, sending a shiver down her back. "I have a New Year's present for you," he said and lit the candle. He sat down on the stool and withdrew her father's violin from a case that rested on the floor. His graceful fingers placed the instrument beneath his chin and drew the bow across its strings as if he wooed a lover. The well-tuned violin surrendered the depth of its soul to Erik. 'The Resurrection of Lazarus' filled the tiny space, the notes vibrating off the stone and cement in glorious adjuration. She had not heard him play this piece since the winter of 1871, when she had knelt in prayer on the steps outside – a confused teenager still mourning the loss of her gentle father. The Angel of Music, hidden within this very sepulcher, had made the violin soothe her grieving soul. And now the magic of the tune swirled around her once more, like a mesmerizing anesthetic, compelling her to listen, sedating her into a spell from which she wished never to revive. The music swelled upward, like the sound of the surf on the rocks it became her only reality. All else lay enshrouded in a pale, hardly recognizable mist.

When he finished he looked up at her, glitters of umber lights dancing in his expectant eyes. In the glow of the flickering candle he seemed mystical, transcendent, a luminous being from a higher plane. She blinked in disbelief. *Who are you?* In her astonishment the sole accolade that issued through her dry throat seemed barely to suffice. "That was magnificent."

"Wait, I have something else for you." He stood, clearing his throat.

Thinking he was about to sing, she raised her hand to stop him. "What if someone hears your voice?"

"You're worried about the neighbors? They're all dead and if they hear, 'tis with spirits ears. We are completely alone in this part of the graveyard, Christine."

"How do you know that?" And eerie sense of *deja vu* veiled her thoughts. *Have we had this conversation before?*

"There's a funeral later in the east section of the cemetery. It's winter. The only workers willing to work in this cold are over there preparing, and I dare say, my humble efforts will not carry far outside this mausoleum." He cleared his throat again, this time for emphasis. "Do you remember that it is difficult for me to tell you in words how I love you?"

"Yes."

"Well, Madame, please ask me to tell you."

"*Inamorato,* please reveal your heart to me. Tell me of your love that I might rest assured."

His voice rose up from deep within him, its impossible beauty carrying her past care into a paradise of joy. And his words, oh his words – were those of a saint pledging loyalty to the very throne of God. If the angels dared to listen, they would weep in wonder as he spoke.

"I do not love you as a gentle breeze,
Though I would be one if you wished it.
And I love you not as the wind of the tempest,
Though I would be that, too
If you but say it should be so.

No, I love you with the constant air that passes through me.
With every breath I take I love you,
And with each breath I love you more than I did with the last.
I will love you 'til I cease to breathe
And if there is a way beneath the stars,
I shall love you even after that."

It seemed to her that the air in the tomb had vanished. The space between them became a vacuum – absorbing all she was into him. *Lost! I am so lost in you.*

He stood with his arms at his sides. His expression one of near embarrassment, like a schoolboy who'd openly given his heart's pledge before thinking. His dark wavy hair was long and tucked behind his ears. It curled down to just inside his shirt collar. *How endearing that he needs a haircut.* His amber eyes caressed her with their dreams, their sure knowledge of life, their acceptance of her even though she had ripped his heart into slivers of excruciating pain with her repeated rejections at the opera. If she had known of his years of celibate devotion, would it have changed anything inside her? She doubted it. *You are a cruel, witch of a woman, Christine de Chagny, to have wounded this glorious angel like you did. Your rightful desserts are to have him always just outside your grasp. What did he call it? The grand dichotomy of life!*

Erik listened to his own heart beating steadily within his chest and watched in disappointment as her eyes glazed over in private thought. This was not the reaction he had hoped for, she was not in a rapturous state of ecstasy begging him to put his manhood inside her, and he was aching for exactly that. *What is she thinking when she regards me so strangely? She never looked like that as a little girl. Is she sifting the sands of regret through her fingers? What is it she regrets?*

"Tell me a secret," he declared with the voice of a celestial being.

"I have fifty-three little ivory skulls in my bedchamber, one for each grave at the estate. I line them up in correct order and recite their names from memory."

He waved his hand in dismissal of her morbid words. "Cemetery games to fill the times of boredom."

His curling fingers beckoned her to the gable where he stood. As she stepped up to him with her sad expression, he brought his mouth to the curve of skin behind her right earlobe. A spasm of heat spiraled down her back and across her right shoulder, her legs opened like a fissure of earth in a rocking quake.

He breathed into her ear, "I mean the secrets that are in your pretty head right now, and they're not about the little skulls you count, are they?"

Amazing, in four steps and two sentences he had reduced her to a maelstrom of passion welling upward at a dizzying velocity.

He unbuttoned her coat but left it on her shoulders. Spreading it open he eyed the special outfit she'd had the couturier design for this day. A kimono jacket of weightless midnight blue crepe stamped in amber floral devore and tasseled with black iridescent beads, lay atop a simple, long sleeved, tunic dress of a matching shade of blue velvet. Below the mandarin collar, the garment opened at the front with a row of elaborate Chinese knots that traveled from the neck to the floor length hem.

"You are the sublime Nyx, the very personification of night's sumptuous splendors." He carefully, tauntingly undid the first three Chinese closures, exposing her throat and upper chest.

The place was as cold as artic ice but she was so warm in response to him, it could have been the Sahara. Sweat trickled down her spine and into the crack of her buttocks.

"What are you thinking, Christine? Tell me."

He slid his fingers to the back of her neck and rubbed her throat with his thumbs, as if to encourage speech. "Where is your mind, my love?" He placed his ear before her lips and waited, ignoring the zeal mounting within him.

She couldn't force the words out past her vocal cords. Her head was reeling from the sense of him so near. *If I could only stay transfixed in this moment.* She brought her hands to the back of his thighs and pressed him closer. Feeling his hardness, her breath came in little gasps of expectant pleasure. *He wants me. He still wants me.*

Erik turned her gently by the shoulders so that her back rested against the stone. She let the coat slip to the floor. Kissing her throat he deliberately unbuttoned the bodice of her dress down to her waist, surprised to find her completely naked beneath the cloth. His mouth moved slowly across her left collarbone then down to where her breasts began to form in all their promising roundness. Pleased to sense her tensing in arousal, he took a red feather from inside his jacket and stroked her abdomen. Moving slowly, he let the whisper of touch travel upward over her sternum before encircling each breast, each expectant nipple. His persuasions were evocative. "What choice have you but to surrender your secret thoughts to me? And why not surrender them? Open your mind to this lover who waits so patiently to penetrate you and lavish you in seductive pleasures."

Standing against the wall, Christine wrenched the words out, breathlessly addressing the cheek covered by the mask. "Terrified you will leave...full of regret that I am with Raoul and not you. Encased in worry..."

"You think I will leave you?" His hands moved over the lush dress. Languishing at the sides of her breasts, he pressed them upward. "I will never leave you, woman."

Setting her feet further apart she guided his hands down to her hips.

"Lovely dress."

"It's a gift...for you." Placing his fingers in the hollow at the top of her legs, she undulated against his touch. Knowing the movement rubbed the erection inside his trousers, her lips separated in anticipation. "Why must I always be less in control than you, Erik? Why?"

"What does your body want, Christine? Tell me. I will do it."

Rolling her hips against him, "Do you feel these flames? The scarcity of encounters between us fans these flames into a bonfire. I am starving, starving. The mere fact that I have to wait, that I cannot address you any time I please sharpens the hunger."

Wanting to be closer to the resounding chorus of her hip movements he lifted the skirt that restrained sensation. His fingers found her curls and appreciated the wetness waiting beyond. With several tugs he had himself free and pressed his silken head against the spot that pleasured her – stroking, igniting.

Her hands grabbed into the firm muscles of his rump, her hips rising to greet each of his well-placed salutations. "Sweet God, the gates of heaven are in you, Erik, and I failed to see it. I was a raving foolish girl, infatuated with Raoul. I unwittingly let the love of my life slip right through my fingers."

He buried his face into the crux of her neck. He heard her words, but every tiny contained thrust was driving him closer to frenzy. He growled an incoherent phrase into her flesh and could not stop his own rocking. The minstrel tingled and throbbed for her, screamed to reach the pinnacle of home inside her. Barely able to think coherently, he was grateful when she removed her hands from his buttocks and flattened her palms against the wall. She was like a damn drug and he the addict almost out of control, dying to be glutted within her.

Trembling and euphoric, she begged to be released from the uncontrollable exhilaration he was bombarding into her body. "Erik, please," her voice was faint, almost inaudible in the inferno of passion consuming her. "Give me safety. Take me. Take me soon."

"Tell me your thoughts," he choked the words out, voraciously needing her luxurious warmth but wanting her mind, her secrets, even more.

"I…oh God…don't stop, Erik…yes, yes there. Uhh." She inhaled jaggedly. "I am no longer…Ra…oul's…"

Hearing her hesitations he paused, forcing the rhapsody of their human concerto to slow down enough for her to continue.

"No longer Raoul's," she tried to phrase the words in the space he provided but his left hand went to the bare skin at the small of her back, and with his right holding the rigid troubadour, he started the sultry, pounding rhythm at her door again. He was lifting her response to a higher, sharper pitch.

Liquid heat swam in the cauldron of her pelvis. Her mouth came to rest on his – sweet taste of tarragon on his tongue. Strands of scintillating numbness twisted down her legs and up her spine causing little involuntary jerks in her back.

"No longer Raoul's...holy splintered Aphrodite!" Her brain clawed out the sentence, "No longer Raoul's in any way but what you have dictated...I love you, only you...heart's desire, heart's undoing." She pulled his shirt out of his pants and as her hands swirled across the delicious skin of his back she sucked in air. "Perfect male, perfect lover."

Erik pressed himself against her abdomen and chest, constraining her undulations with his own body. His left hand raised her knee up to his hip, and his right fingers, giving no sense of rush or urgency, stroked the opening to her vault. Her breath became less ragged, the clamorous need for air less critical. She reached the plateau with him. Opening her eyes she nuzzled into him. His eyelids were half closed sheltering the amber lights of his eyes from hers. "Erik."

His eyes sprung open.

"I love you."

The upward thrust of his organ into her waiting pelvis sent a shock wave of satisfaction through her being. Lifting her off her feet, he slowly, deliberately let her slid down onto him. Her throat purred an enraptured murmur of gratitude and acceptance. Still inside her he carried her to the bed.

"Happy New Year," she whispered.

"Happy New Year to you," he echoed.

Later, held fast in the security of his possessive arms, she told him about the safe she had discovered in the attic. While she described the smaller rectangular door protecting the mechanism to unlock the safe, he made a study of the nectar of her breasts. Her lips came to rest in a pout. Pressing the issue to get his attention, she finally asked, "What's your advice?"

Drinking a robust kiss he probed her motives, "And why do you want to go into it?"

"To see if it holds anything that might be of useful purpose to our situation."

"I hardly know how to respond to that." He thought about the two silvery pink scars on her arm and her singular, unwavering determination. "I'll have to see it in order to advise you, so prepare for a visit from a dark phantasm tonight. Leave your window unlocked."

"So you don't have to knock? What time?"

"Improper vixen! When the house lights extinguish, when the moonlight is all there is to guide the eye, and the night hunters prowl about searching for carrion." Watching her smile mischievously at the surreal scene he wove for her, he added, "But only to investigate this safe and give you advice, nothing more." His tongue reached for her succulent nipple.

"Let's see if we can make another baby," she proclaimed enthusiastically, rolling herself on top of him.

He pulled her face down to his and tendered an amorous kiss on her lips. Then realizing what she had just uttered, he asked, "Isn't nursing a baby a natural prevention against becoming pregnant?"

Tearfully she leaned down to his ear and told him about the wet nurse. He stroked her hair to console her, and firmly holding her hips positioned her onto him. Letting her conduct the musician in an effort to solace her, and performing every act she immodestly suggested.

That night she leaned on the headboard of her bed, propped up by her pillows. Wearing a nightgown and shawl she watched the drapes in the corner of her room expectantly. As the house clocks sounded midnight, a cloud of gray smoke germinated from the floor upwards. Its wispy tendrils gave birth to the black seductive shape of her lover. Throwing a caped arm out to his side, he graciously bowed low in reverence. Soundlessly striding to the bed he offered his hand, as she reached to light a candle he stopped her.

"Polonaise!" The name of the Polish dance was a soft command. With the music playing in her head, she rose. He spun her in a smooth, wide circle and danced her to the door. Bold, brazen, as if the floor itself belonged to him alone. Opening the door, he leaned out into the hallway. She held her breath in anticipation. When he heard her breathing stop, he turned back to her. Placing his mouth over hers, he sucked the air from her lungs, then blew it back into her. She understood. Easing down the dark corridor, she marveled that he could see from one doorway to the next. As they approached the entrance to the attic she tugged on his cloak. They found it locked. Quickly, he pulled her between him and the door. Placing two thin metal strips in her fingers, he guided her hands, teaching her how to pick the lock. When it released, he taught her how to lock it. Telling her to try it on her own, he simply let his fingers rest on top of hers, considering her motions. As the lock gave way, he whispered, "Like a pro."

He removed a phosphorescent green ball, about the size of a grapefruit, from inside his cloak. As her eyes adjusted to the aberrant light, they moved up the stairs and entered the attic. Like unearthly spirits they moved to the tapestry curtain. There they finally lit a candle and she drew back the drape. He ran his hand across the carved oak doors. "Beautiful craftsmanship." The cabinet's lock was secured as well and he let her pick it as she had done before.

As the doors spread apart she welcomed their release with a muted, "Open Sesame."

Erik studied the lock of the smaller rectangular door for a few seconds then took her hands in his again. "More delicately this time, but add a sharp downward movement at the end to angle the metals upward and disengage the catch." After several attempts the door yielded to them. Once again they went through the process of relocking it and unlocking it, before letting it reveal its contents. The smaller door concealed a recessed box that housed another lever and a combination dial.

"You will have to actually watch Raoul open the safe," he advised smoothly. Surveying the maze of timberwork above them, he pointed to the places where three mirrors should be positioned so she could view

Raoul's hands when he spun the dial's specific combination. Then, like an orangutan, he showed her how to climb up into the rafters and where to place herself, all the while describing in detail the exact angle and diameter of each mirror. After showing her how to come down, he had her review the procedure outloud until she recited it to his satisfaction.

For a while he sat motionless atop one of the chests she had thought to use as a hiding place for her money. Finally, he started swinging his right leg. "It's reasonable to assume that Raoul keeps cash to pay the house staff in there. Possibly other things as well, documents or jewelry. We are paid on Fridays at lunch so he must, of necessity, come to this safe every Friday morning to retrieve funds. Next Friday be up there," he pointed to the specific spot he had chosen in the beams, "ahead of him. This will be dangerous, Christine. I admonish you not to attempt this for a lark. If you decide to spy on him be very quiet. Soundless! Don't try to write down the numbers, or how he turns the dial, until he leaves. You could drop the pencil."

"I'll be very, very careful, even overly cautious, no perfume, no flashy clothes. I promise." She opened her shawl and showed him the cut of her pink silk nightdress. Seductively moving to where he sat, she attempted to draw him up into her arms. "Don't you want a reward for your consultation, *Professeur?*"

"You think you've been afforded an opportunity for another assignation? You've had a full day of adventure and you're not worn out?"

"I'm full of energy and I won't be frowning on wanton rendezvous with you until I'm creaking with arthritis."

Smirking, he folded her arms across her chest. "Minx! I'll see you on Monday. Be prepared to duel!" When he had her safely tucked into her rooms he left as quickly as he'd appeared, without even hugging her. In a disappointed huff she fell back into her pillows.

After breakfast on the following Friday, Christine sequestered herself into position up in the rafters. She deliberately wore browns the exact color of the beams, and practiced memorizing word sequences as she waited. As if called to perform, Raoul appeared right on cue at ten o'clock. He strode confidently to the curtain, never bothering to look up. He drew the keys to unlock the cabinet and the safe's smaller door from a chain in his vest pocket. The mirrors were set to provide her a visual field over his left shoulder. Being left-handed they had surmised correctly that he would stand just a bit to the right and he did.

Four full turns to the left stop at 7,
Three full turns to the right stop at 45,
Two turns to the left stop at 28,
Turn back to 92 and stop.
The 'dog' piece of metal audibly clicks down into the gates.
He pushes the lever down. Louder clicks as bolts retract and voila the door opens.

She paid no attention to the drawers Raoul opened as he worked. Instead she ran the sequence over and over in her head, memorizing it. When Raoul closed the safe's door, he raised the lever to a horizontal position and casually spun the dial. After he left, she wrote everything down on a piece of paper, then quietly lowered herself down to the floor.

She picked the two locks with ease, and then copied Raoul's movements on the dial to perfection. The door to the safe opened, yielding its sheltered contents up to her. Inside, she found a multitude of drawers stacked one on top of the other. The front of each was covered in lush black onyx and adorned with a solid gold pull. Some drawers contained bundles of French money, others bags of loose gems and jewelry, and in one – the title deed to the estate with the seal of Charles the V, the original Dauphin, dated July 12th in the Year of our Lord, 1360. All of this proved very interesting, but it was the drawer situated in the center of the safe that contained the most curious and helpful items. At the front of the drawer lay an antique gold, owl-shaped cigar tip cutter with sparkling ruby eyes. The owl sat atop a card bearing simple, handwritten instructions:

Prepare the cigar and give a glass of the finest liquor to the de Chagny who is being installed under the dictates of progenitor.

Behind the owl she found a blue velvet case containing a faded Jewish prayer shawl and a set of *tefillin*. She recognized the objects from pictures she'd seen at Dr. DeVille's house. *This is most curious. Why are there Jewish items here?* A book written entirely in Hebrew came out next, followed by a red velvet bag embroidered with the Jewish Star of David. Inside this bag she discovered a ten inch hollow gold tube with a fancy filial for a cap. It offered up a roll of parchment, yellow with age and tied with a soft leather cord. She paused to ascertain that there were no noises around her whatsoever. *Quite alone!* With the greatest of care she undid the tie and unrolled the parchment. In a delicate, archaic handwritten script she read:

I, Jacob Benjamin Klein, on this eighteenth day of the gentile's year 1722 take pen to paper to disclose these facts to my heirs, and to our subsequent generations that they might be informed of their heritage, and instructed as to my wishes. Ten years ago, tired of living under the rule of the Ottoman Turks, I left my parents in Palestine and traveled to Egypt to seek a better life in the country of France. I had no letters of reference; only the education my family afforded me in math, accounting and Hebrew. I came here not intending to abandon my religion, but to search out a better life for myself. I reached the port of Marseille by ship. In an effort to keep my meager funds intact for food and lodging, I took menial jobs as I worked my way north to Paris. I availed myself of every opportunity to learn the French language, and passed many a night inside the shelter of a synagogue. Outside of Paris I came across a pair of horses and a carriage with a broken axle. Inside rested a kind nobleman only a little older than myself. When I offered my assistance, he explained that his driver had gone to retrieve a liveryman to repair the axle. Seeing my tired dirty appearance, he invited me to sit with him until his driver returned. He introduced himself as Daniel de Chagny. In broken French I communicated where I had come from and that I sought a new life in Paris. When he learned of my abilities in math, he offered to take me back to his estate where I could show him what I knew of record keeping and accounting. It is under these circumstances that I came to live with my employer and benefactor. He was thirty-five when I met him and had never married. My employment lasted for eight years. In that eighth and final year, Daniel contracted pneumonia and became quite ill with fever, often spitting up blood. The physicians did what they could for him, but his health continued to deteriorate. Grieving over his childless state, and acknowledging that in many ways we physically favored each other, he came upon the idea that I should take his place after he died. Gradually we released the household staff, telling them that the estate would most likely be sold when the Count passed away. We retained only the outside staff that had not seen him in some months. He taught me how to act and carry myself, how to, in all things, give the appearance of a person of high French birth. While he stayed in his bed I began to go to Paris under his name, there to be seen in his carriage and in his box at the theater. I nursed him and cared for him until he passed away. He is buried humbly in the cellars to the south of the older wine vats. His only request was that I admonish my progeny to carry on the traditions of his forebears and leave these lands in de Chagny hands for perpetuity. Therefore, I earnestly charge you. Each generation is to learn of their duty and their responsibility to create an heir to this estate and its holdings. I consider this a sacred part of your birthright, and instruct you to take the heirs in each generation, swear them to silence, and bring them into this covenant. I married the daughter of a young nobleman, Marie de la Croix, she gave me a son and two daughters and we continued the lineage of the House of de Chagny. Blessings upon you for your fidelity to this family commitment, and may the most hateful of curses fall upon you if you chose to betray the wishes of this grand man, the dearest and kindest soul I ever met, Daniel Philippe de Chagny. I solemnly swear to you the truth of these matters. Behold the de Chagny seal below my name.

Jacob Benjamin Klein

Christine carefully rolled the scroll and tucked it into her pocket. Placing the golden tube back in its case, she closed the drawer and secured the safe. Now she understood perfectly why the Count de Chagny kept its contents so close at hand. He needed to assure that this scroll stayed safely under his control. Retreating from the attic, she knew it would be a long time before Raoul intended to bring Michael into this trusted circle of usurpers. She found Justine and told her she was going riding. As she waited for the stablemen to prepare Venus, she cracked her riding whip soundly against her boot, impatient to be off. She took to the woods and rode off the estate straight to the ballet studio. Entering the basement through the carriage house tunnel, she went directly to the third floor, where she entrusted the scroll and the safe's combination to Erik.

16 *LOCKED DOWN*

The middle of February found a frustrated Christine still without a plan for playing the trump card Fate had dealt her. She entered the cemetery deep in thought, her head bowed, the pious mourner trying to decide how to utilize the knowledge of Raoul's heritage to win her freedom. Earlier she had felt curiously ill and wondered if she was coming down with a bout of winter flu. Lightheadedness and a vague feeling of pressure across her forehead lingered even now, but she detected no chill or fever. Nothing would deter her from coming to him at the appointed time. In a few moments she would taste the seraph's kiss and content herself in his arms. She pulled her cloak tighter and quickened her steps. *Must take care of myself and keep my wits sharp.* As she rounded a corner she heard once again the words of the strange being in her prophetic dream. He spoke clearly and without condemnation, *'Even the guardian lost its way for a time.'* Christine's legs became oddly heavy, their weight unfamiliar. She stopped. *Who is this guardian? Could it be me? Madame Giry? No, she never lost her way with regard to Erik, whereas I threw the Angel of Music out like garbage and chose the life of a pompous, titled female.*

Berating herself brought no joy. Only the unspoken satisfaction of acknowledging that she was guilty within the court of her own heart – guilty of heresy against love. A nauseating sensation of dizziness washed over her. Her head stayed stationery but the monuments around her kept moving. Breakfast rolled in her stomach and she leaned over, retching violently. Sensing herself off balance and in danger of toppling over, she reached to steady herself against a headstone, but somehow miscalculated. Her hand flailed in the air. Before she could straighten up another profound volley of nausea blasted vomit out her mouth. Blackness, like the sharp closing of a book, descended on her brain. She fainted on the walkway, thirty feet from her father's mausoleum.

Erik had successfully tunneled from the backside of Monsieur Daae's resting place to the angelic statue of a nearby grave. All that remained to create a functioning alternate entry into the Daae tomb was the mechanism to move the statue. Today he would reveal his work to Christine, and watch with satisfaction as a smile of delight crossed her mouth. He treasured her expressions of surprise and could sustain himself on their effervescence from meeting to meeting. Thinking her held up by some matter at the chateau, he walked the tunnel one more time. He had encased all four sides with sheets of smooth white limestone. No minor feat, but he had no wish for her to travel through moist dirt should it please her to occasionally use this route. Impatient, he pulled out his pocket watch, read the time and flipped it close in disgust. *She's really late. What's keeping her?* He preferred things to move according to schedule. Peeved and restless, he returned to the main floor of the mausoleum. A crumpled mound of dark blue taffeta surrounded by a black woolen cloak lay on the walkway, a breeze ruffling a section of white petticoat like a distress flag. Dread steeled his will. Without a care as to whether or not someone was nearby, he flung the metal doors open and sprinted to her. She was pale, ice cold but breathing, bilious undigested food covered the front of her dress. He lifted her into his arms and carried her to the tomb. Initially, he placed her on her father's sarcophagus, but when she failed to revive he moved her to the slightly warmer air of the upper level.

In the garret he laid her on the bed and rubbed her wrists and palms, calling softly to her. "I need smelling salts!" He thought of the patches of snow outside and went to retrieve some. When he returned he held a small amount to her temples, in a matter of moments her eyes opened.

"Did I faint?"

"Yes. How do you feel?" He placed her hands in his and blew his breath upon them.

"Dizzy, my head is still but the room is spinning. I need to close my eyes." She scrunched her eyelids shut, giving her face the appearance of a dried crab apple.

"What do you think is wrong?" He tried to sound reassuring, but her color was not returning.

"I don't know. I felt sick this morning but came anyway. I can't miss our visits. I would become an absolute shrew toward the house staff."

"You are very pale. Maybe you're not sick…but with child. You did request it."

Christine's eyes opened in alarm. "No, not possible. Michael is still an infant."

"I don't know if we can argue successfully against the case. I remember what you looked like while you carried him and you rather favor the expression."

"Ah. I smell like vomit."

"I'll get some water from below the tomb to clean you."

"We need an apartment with running water. Want to move in together? I'm building up courage to blackmail Raoul."

"Shh, you're not a criminal, and if you are pregnant this might be Raoul's child."

"That's not possible. He's gone on trips most of the time and I watch my cycles like a hawk." Her eyes closed again, she knew he might have spoken the truth. She could be a full six weeks pregnant. The afternoon of New Year's Eve Raoul had claimed his marital rights, and even though she doused herself with vinegar every time Raoul left her, it still might be true. She pushed the despair back down. *Not Raoul's, even if it is a baby, not Raoul's…it must be Erik's.* Her hands clutched at his sleeves, "I love you, with all my being I love you."

He kissed her forehead, "And I you." Fetching some damp rags he returned in a few minutes, as he wiped off her dress she questioned him.

"Would it matter if it were Raoul's?

"No. It would be yours."

"But it's probably your baby."

"Yes. Let's sit quietly until the driver returns to take you back to the chateau."

"Would you leave me? Disappear?" The words were almost incoherent, filled with worry.

"Absolutely not. Be brave sweet Tarragon, be of iron will."

When the time approached for the driver to fetch her, Erik carried a limp Christine to the gate. She had regained nothing of her strength and was too weak to stand erect.

Pulling up on schedule, the driver found his mistress sitting on a low wall surrounding a family plot. She held her head and signaled for the man to come assist her into the carriage, explaining that she felt quite ill. The dizziness was almost incapacitating and the driver, alarmed at her color, bid her lay down on the seat. He placed a pillow under her head and shutting the door of the coach, assured her he would hasten back to the estate. As he climbed up onto the driver's seat to take the reins and speed her home, he thought he saw from the corner of his eye, the briefest of movements beside a mournful statue of a weeping Madonna. A strange sense of foreboding crawled upward from his feet as the sunlight disappeared behind a cloud, casting them into shadow. Off in the distance a dog barked and then whimpered, most likely from the toe of someone's boot silencing it. Checking the horses, he noted they both remained calm and undistracted. He summoned a little fortitude and furtively searched the area of the statue with his eyes, but saw nothing remarkable. Still a sense of dread tightened in his throat. *Cemeteries…homes for maggots and spooks!*

His mistress called to him from inside the vehicle, "Please, let's hurry home." He plopped down and whipped the horses into a gallop.

Lying on the seat with her eyes closed, Christine smiled to herself. She had not spoken. It was not her voice the driver heard, but its perfect imitation.

George, the interim keeper of the hounds, went to the chateau and learned from the kitchen staff that the house was abuzz with incongruous news. The mistress was pregnant again, but quite ill and unable to keep any food down. It seemed that if she attempted to lift her head off her pillows, the bedroom went whirling – causing waves of nausea and vomiting. The Count was abroad on business and a message had been promptly dispatched summoning him home. At the mistress's request a physician had been called from Paris, a Dr. Abraham DeVille. The good doctor had come immediately and for the time being the Countess was confined to her bed. Because of the flurry of activity around Christine's rooms and the general state of consternation in the house, George was unable to unobtrusively enter her chambers and comfort her. He made several offers to be of help, staying as close at hand as he dared, for as long as he dared, but left the chateau in the late evening.

Madame Giry did not hear him return, but at ten o'clock her ceiling shook with several loud thumps, followed by a series of crashing sounds issuing from his apartment. She hurried up the stairs and found his kitchen table turned upside down, its chairs lying on their sides. Several items of porcelain and glass were smashed and lying about the floor. The shards glistened in the light of the gas lamp as she gingerly picked her way through them. He sat at the base of a wall with his back against it. A dent in the plaster above his head and the trail of blood flowing steadily from his forehead, down his face and over the front of his shirt, told her that he had pounded the wall with his own skull. She moistened a couple of clean kitchen towels and tried to apply them. He withdrew, adding mournfully, "Let it bleed!"

Ignoring the order she pressed the cloth to the splayed area. "Stop, just let me put this here. You could not speak with her?"

"*Merde,* Louisa, that stings. She's pregnant and in her bed, ill, probably deathly ill."

"We will find some way to communicate with her. We will. No, don't move my hand." The towel covered his face and he began to wail softly. The dejected sound wrenched at her compassionate heart. She cared so deeply for him, and here he was, yet again a lover in pain, a man denied even the opportunity to assist his mate. Her soul mourned with him.

He yanked her hands away from his face, unattended the blood flowed freely. "What if she dies?"

Tears spilled out of Louisa's eyes. It was unbearable seeing him wounded and open once more. "We must hope and pray for the best for her. She took this path with you willingly, and she is strong! Have faith in her, Erik. You could order the sun to rise on her love for you. Tomorrow I will ask Meg to call upon her at the chateau. Let's see what Meg can learn. Now please, don't move my hands." This time he allowed Louisa to address the bleeding slit of flesh.

The presence of the Baroness Margaret de Castelot-Barbezac was announced to the managing secretary of the de Chagny household at about nine o'clock the following morning. He wasted no time hastening to the main reception area where he found her sitting formally in an armchair. "Good morning, Madame, it is a great honor to receive you. I am the Count de Chagny's secretary, Vincent Fauconnier. May I be of some service to you?"

"Yes, you most assuredly can be of service to me. You can tell me how my good friend, the Countess, is faring. Word has come to me that she is ill. I wish to know what is wrong, and what is being done for her in the absence of her husband."

"Your Ladyship, I am amazed that you know of this so quickly. Our household is in quite a state of confusion. Your friend has indeed taken ill, seriously ill. A physician she trusts implicitly has remained in her personal attendance since yesterday afternoon. However, she is unfortunately in a most agitated state and has been given sedatives to help her rest."

At these words, Meg was on her feet approaching the secretary like a tigress. "You will take me to her at once, Sir!"

The secretary, taken aback by the commanding straight forwardness of the Baroness as she moved on him, stammered a reply, "Yes, Mame." Without a murmur of objection, he hurriedly escorted her up the marbled staircase, and bringing her down the hall to the quarters of the Countess, knocked softly on the door. An elderly gentleman, with wispy curls of white hair floating off his head, and a set of silver spectacles before kind aged eyes, opened it.

The Baroness impatiently pressed the secretary's arm at the elbow. Fauconnier omitted the appropriate apology for interrupting the care of his mistress and proceeded directly to an introduction. "Dr. DeVille, may I present to you the Baroness Margaret de Castelot-Barbezac. She is a dear friend of your patient."

The physician appeared to be in his sixties, stood about five feet four, and was beardless except for a full gray mustache. His eyes squinted as he carefully studied Meg's face. When he bowed and kissed Meg's offered hand the wispy hair on his head billowed out like clouds. His voice was as gentle and soft as his hair appeared to be. "Madame, it is my pleasure to meet you. Please, do come in and greet your friend." He kept her hand and drew her forward. "Thank you Vincent, I will call should we need anything."

Entering the chamber, Meg removed her hat and went to a chair beside the bed. Christine's skin was as white as the sheet. Startled, Meg reached for the hand of her former roommate and its warmth reassured her. "Christine, it's Meg. Can you hear me?"

From a deep, narcotized sleep Christine replied, "Meg, send for The Voice. Tell The Voice to come to Tarragon." With that she drifted back to whatever landscape her dreams presently occupied.

Dr. DeVille stood behind Meg's chair. "She is heavily sedated. Unfortunately, I need to keep her at this level for her to tolerate even small amounts of nourishment and fluids. Your friend will abide very little on her stomach. She has a healthy pregnancy but is having a severe reaction to the baby within her. This condition is rare, but does sometimes happen. She has classic vertigo and will most likely spend the entire pregnancy in bed. Occasionally these symptoms dissipate during the last trimester, but most likely we are looking at a state of near incapacitation for the next seven-and-a-half months, until the birth."

Bright tears filled Meg's eyes while she listened to the doctor. She kissed Christine's fingers and stroked her face, "What can I do for her?"

"Do you know this Voice she asks for? Since I arrived she's requested him."

"Oh yes, he was her music teacher years ago."

"A short visit from him might afford her some comfort. How near is he?"

"He's fifteen miles away. I'll go and bring him here."

Still behind her, DeVille touched her shoulder. His voice was soothing, "No, Madame, there is no immediate urgency to do so, perhaps this evening after the sun has set. I will instruct the butler to bring you both up to us the moment you arrive."

Meg's eyes widened with understanding. "You are most kind, doctor. I will return about six."

"I will have our patient as awake as I can allow."

"Very good." Meg leaned over to kiss Christine's cheek and left the estate for her mother's home.

Meg's carriage returned to the chateau's front courtyard promptly at six. The tall, cloaked gentleman by her side had a black scarf pulled up over his nose and a wide brimmed, black hat pulled low over his forehead. A single butler opened the carriage door and escorted them to the second floor. Christine's chamber door opened before a knock was even placed. When Meg went to introduce the Phantom with a fabricated name, DeVille raised his hand. "Please, I need only to know that he is my patient's good friend." Stepping aside to allow them entrance, he was suddenly affected by the subtle movements of the darkly clad figure who stood gracefully behind the woman in the hall.

The man merely touched the Baroness' arm and without hesitation she halted in her steps, waiting. The visitor lowered his scarf and lifted his face enough for the doctor to perceive a black mask over the upper right quarter of the shrouded face. Two eyes, the likes of which he had never seen before in a human being, studied him steadily. *Amber! Flecks of gold throughout…and he's actively smelling…this is a rare, truly augmented individual.* Not wanting to bow and take his eyes from the extraordinary sight before him, the doctor provided information, "The Countess and I are the only ones in the room."

"You are most kind to receive us." The masculine, baritone voice that spoke to the doctor was intentionally altered, but the attempt to actively mute it could not hide from the doctor's highly trained ears, the beautiful vibrating resonance it contained. Meg's escort touched her arm once again and the Baroness stepped forward. Placing her hand on the doorknob, the doctor went backward into the room so as to watch the stranger move around the woman. The man's feet seemed to slip across the carpet, something like an experienced ice skater moving with expeditious, calculated elegance. The person flowing into the room was one of obvious poise and refinement, each dignified gesture full of pleasant, eloquent symmetry. His every movement spoke of royalty, and DeVille considered that he might be a prince, masquerading as a music teacher.

Meg shut the door and locked it, then tested the lock, twice. In amazement, DeVille tore his eyes from the man to watch her extraordinary precautions. "Come with me, Baroness. With your permission," his head gave a slight bow to the individual Christine called The Voice, "we will excuse ourselves to the Countess' sitting room and warm ourselves by the fire. Please Monsieur, try to be brief." Meg and the doctor left through a side door that they closed behind them. Erik turned quickly to Christine. The flickering lamps in the room created shadows across her face. He removed his hat and cloak and placed them on the foot of the bed. Taking into consideration that some slight color had returned to her features, he moved to her head and kissed her lips. The moment he touched her she opened her eyes, smiled weakly at him and reluctantly dropped her lids again. He leaned in close to his love, savoring her completely unguarded presence, and watched the artery in her neck pulsate with her dear life.

She addressed him by name! "Another baby, Erik. This must be a very special child to warrant this much ado before entering the world. Imagine, forcing me to lay here waiting for its arrival."

His face contorted in pain to see her so ill, he mentally castigated himself for causing her adversity. "Please forgive me, Christine."

"Don't blame yourself. I'm the one who joyfully spread her legs for you."

Surprised at her bluntness, he decided that the drugs must have removed her inhibitions, or was this how she actually thought of him – coming into her between her legs. He had a hundred ways to claim her. He would make it a priority that she understood them all, once she was better.

"This child has made you sick. I have a powder in my pocket that will stop this. When mixed with liquid and ingested it will cause your uterus to clamp down tightly and rid you of the fetus. The cramps will be severe but you will be free of the pregnancy by tomorrow."

She looked at him briefly. Her hazy eyes mirrored shock and her voice grew resolute. "We will not clip this child from my body like a newspaper article. There is a more than better chance that it's yours. It certainly has your petulance, your flare for drama!" She reached for his hand but ended up on his inner thigh, giving it a gentle squeeze. "Stud!"

"Christine, you are forever astonishing me."

"Hmm, good." She smiled dreamily. "You've placed yourself in great jeopardy coming here. Be cautious as you leave. I cannot have you harmed. This vertigo will pass. The doctor says the baby's fine, but there's nothing to be done about the room spinning except wait it out." She drifted off to sleep but returned to him in a minute. "Both the baby and I will survive, and when we do, you should take it as a sign to pay close attention to the words I am about to tell you."

She reached forward. "Put your hands on me to steady the room, I want to keep my eyes open." He took her upper arms and held them firmly while she made an effort to focus on his face. "Sometimes souls are sent into this life together. When they meet, if they're lucky, they are able to recognize each other. We are not humans on a spiritual journey...we are spirits on a human journey. When you met me you said you knew me. You **loved** me. You did the recognizing, it just took me longer. I had to overcome fear, fear of the mysterious and the unknown. But your voice carved a passageway down into my soul and awakened in me the same love you felt. My task is to overcome fear. I love your face because it is yours. Can you love it?" The nausea overwhelmed her and she closed her eyes.

She's drifting again. "Yes, I love it because you love it, despite the whole damn world."

"You are so beautiful to me...inside and out. Your mother didn't understand, superstition probably played a heavy role in her actions. She thought herself punished for some misdeed, or you cursed by some demon's whim. Not true. There is a purpose, a master plan with a specific goal for each of us."

"Shh, Christine, don't exhaust yourself. We will make it through this. You're tough as nails."

"You have the most beautiful golden eyes. Nothing compares to them. They are two suns warming me against the chill of winter. We are not worlds apart you and I, we are one world, two halves of one world. Do you not see it? I am so dizzy."

"Please be still. Rest."

"I don't know when I'll see you again and I have to tell you this, it's too important. Sometimes one word spoken in the right place, at the right time, can awaken a sleeping soul. Who is the sleeper, Erik? You or me? When I went with Raoul I was seduced by position and flirtatiousness, I feared you...you are quite a handful...I was a foolish child, but no longer. With all my soul I love you. Stay in love with me even though I cannot go to the cemetery. Wait for me. Take your dagger to me one more time and cut a hank of my hair. Keep it on you always and be true. Don't forget me, even if I die." She sighed heavily, "But I don't want to die just yet, there is so much I want to do with you."

Unable to fight the narcotic, she fell back to sleep. A ferocious howl wanted to scream its way out of his chest, but he kept his senses sharp and attuned to the task of attending to her. He wanted her to speak, even if she was only rambling. Leaning over he kissed her tenderly. No response. Later he would consider the meaning of all her words. She was what mattered, not him. Rolling her face away, he cut a brown curl of hair from the back of her head and placed it in his pocket. "My love, if you leave this world I will leave it too, so stay around if you have plans for us. I pray the Fates accept this time of trial as a fitting sacrifice."

He fussed over the bedclothes, tucking them in closer in an effort to keep her warm. Wrapping his cloak around him, he thought to retrieve Meg but Christine began to whisper without opening her eyes. In a hushed voice she uttered her last directions to him.

"Seek out good deeds while I am ill and beg the heavens give us length of days that we might truly know each other. Ask them to help us achieve our goals together...as a pair. Beseech them to forgive the wayward guardian for not helping you overcome your burden." He touched her lips and she mouthed the words, "Forgive me."

Four days later, Raoul returned. Dr. DeVille assured him there was nothing he could do but allow her to rest and get through this, the baby was quite healthy. Christine suffered terribly over the rest of the pregnancy. The days dragged by, long difficult hours into the spring and through the summer heat. As her uterus expanded the baby grew very active. "He's romping again," she would tell DeVille, who came to check on her at the end of every day.

"You're convinced it's a boy?"

"Oh, I'm positive. Only a male would want me waiting in state like this."

DeVille chuckled as he took her pulse.

The Count's numerous business trips continued. Whenever he was home he inquired respectfully about her health, but the astute DeVille noticed a remarkable undertone of detachment to his concern. Occasionally the Count presented his wife with a present for the coming addition to their family, but not as frequently as he had with Michael.

Christine didn't care, nor did she feel slighted. She wanted to endure this trial without him. Since she spent her days worrying over Erik, the sight of Raoul leaning over her was almost repugnant. Whenever she was abraded by the nightmarish image of some other woman charming the Phantom, she'd quickly shun the thought, pushing it from her mind. In a small music box on her side table, rested the piece of crystal from the chandelier. She would take it out and hold it, mentally telling the baby about its father. Her vertigo increased and her disposition worsened. Gradually, the only way she could open her eyes and speak at all was to place her hands on the headboard to 'steady herself'. She developed the constant sensation she was falling, even while laying down. The only relief was the anesthesia of a drug-induced sleep.

Meg came to her several times a week and brought her verbal messages from Erik. In turn, Christine would whisper her short replies. From her sickbed she started to weave a story for him, advancing the adventure with each of Meg's visits.

"Begin each chapter by telling him that not a wakeful minute passes that I don't long for his presence." Meg would solemnly promise to pass the message on word-for-word, and Christine's tale unfolded. In a castle not far from here, a young king was attacked by his brother and coerced into abdicating his throne and fleeing the country. The treacherous brother coveted the queen's inheritance and declared she would be his wife. In response the queen clothed herself from head to foot in a long black veil. The only thing of visible color she kept upon her person was a simple circlet of gold resting on her head. Her bizarre attire made her appear strange to the brother, and successfully kept his debasements away from her. With a resolute heart, she flagrantly insulted the illegitimate court by wearing a symbolic lament that she incessantly grieved for the loss of her beloved husband. Most of all, she wished to secret the truth that she was growing greater and greater with child, a beautiful special child. The courtiers believed her insane and locked her in her chambers, bestowing on her the title 'The Black Lady'. While the Black Lady hid beneath her cloth, she composed message after message to her true spouse. The first that reached him read:

No words can convey the true depth of my sorrow. I see with clear vision that what matters most is our love, our blessed, spellbinding love. When I can, I will join you, my husband, my friend. You are my soul.

Ariel George de Chagny was born on the fifteenth day of August 1875. He entered the world in the middle of the night without taxing his mother with too difficult a labor. He was born with a full head of black silky hair and the grayish eyes common to newborns. Perfect in every physical way. When he was washed and handed to his mother she counted every little toe and finger. Spreading kisses on his precious face, she named him 'The Lion of God' because his coming had ruled over all. In the morning she sent a present to her friend the Baroness, a Baccarat paperweight of *millefiori* under a glass dome. The symbol was a message to Erik that they were blessed a thousand times over with another son.

For his part, Erik existed without Christine's visits on a steady diet of memories, and by throwing himself into the work of authoring musical plays. He shaved infrequently and developed a rather gritty, roughish appearance about his person. Whenever Meg entered the house she went directly to the third floor to deliver from memory Christine's narrations. He would sit, wistfully fingering Christine's skull mask, while he listened. No stranger to loneliness he simply weathered the storm by retreating into his own thoughts, and gratifying himself when the need arose. The idea of being in the graces of another woman, if it had occurred to him, would have been repulsive. The day Meg placed the paperweight in his hands he kissed it, and jumping up, effortlessly lifted the bearer of good news off her feet. He joyfully spun a giggling Meg in several wide, graceful circles before placing her back on her feet.

"It **is** a boy," Meg told him. "She named him Ariel. He has silky jet-black hair and rather favors Michael. Congratulations, he's perfect. There's not a blemish on him. The servant who brought me the paperweight says the baby has a set of lungs that can lift the second floor up to the roof! He was born hungry and suckled almost immediately." Erik put his hand to his throat. Overcome with a mixture of simultaneous elation and relief, he could not speak. He studied the paperweight, then looked up with a sudden, terrible question reflected in his eyes. Meg understood. "I can't tell you everything at once! I would need two throats! Christine is well, too. The labor was short and the doctor says the dizziness will subside now that the baby has entered the world."

He kissed Meg's forehead and sat down heavily into an armchair, turning the paperweight over in his hands for he knew its hidden meaning well. The pounding of his heart subsided and he uttered the baby's name for the first time. "Ariel." Meg stood quietly allowing him to bask in the occasion. In a minute he looked questioningly into her face.

"I have one request," she said.

He nodded. "Anything, say it and it's yours."

"Teach me to swordfight, too." His left eyebrow shot up in exclamation.

17 *SPELL OF A WITCH*

Overcoming the vertigo became Christine's highest priority, and it couldn't happen quick enough to suit her. Recovery was on its way, but the dizziness diminished in slow, aggravating stages. She was irritable and short tempered with the staff. When asked if she wanted something to eat or drink she would offer a moody response, and favored hurling something close at hand, like a book or a slipper, into a wall across the room. She dared not throw her dagger, although her fingers itched to let it fly! With her nerves stretched so tightly they were rubber bands about to pull her apart, she wanted to scream, to be up and about, not still confined to this dismal bed! Ah, but when they brought the baby to nurse, her outlook changed completely, she covered Ariel with kisses and frequently asked that Michael be brought into the room with his brother. For a time she had both the bassinette and the toddler's crib in her chambers, demanding that they be left there. Her resolutions regarding Erik, and her gloomy thoughts about her long absence from him, were eased when the babies were with her. One solid look at Ariel told her he was Erik's child, and with the Angel of Music's sons so close, she was surrounded by a large part of him. A part she could touch and hold at will.

An understanding Dr. DeVille listened to the staff's complaints and instructed them to give her plenty of fluids, as much as she would drink, and anything else she might like. He charged them to be patient, "Her mood will improve in short order."

Three weeks to the day of Ariel's birth, she woke up one morning with the dizziness gone. She danced around her room, overjoyed at her freedom from the bed. Little Michael was playing with some blocks in a pool of sunlight on the floor. For the first time in months she knelt down on the carpet beside her son unassisted. Michael looked at his mother and with the innocent smile of a child offered her one of his blocks. She took it. "For me?" Lovingly she cooed the words to her boy and her mouth dropped open. In shock, she sat abruptly on her rump.

Two brilliant, honey-brown eyes with radiant yellow highlights gazed back at her. Michael's long black lashes blinked and he spoke his first words, "Mama funny." He was barely a year old.

We are in big trouble! Not only do you look like your Papa, you're as smart as him. She sent a coded message to Meg via a messenger to have Erik meet her in the woods near the cemetery the following afternoon.

Christine armed herself mentally and prepared to hunt an illusive Phantom. When she arrived he already had logs burning in the firepit he'd built near the pond. His embrace lifted her off her feet and for a while he simply held her, tentatively kissing her face and hair. She appeared healthy. Her eyes were clear and glowing, a genuine smile upon her mouth. He let the caress end when both were ready. Holding her hands he listened while she told him how beautiful the baby was. "He kicks and pushes his arms out even more than Michael, and when he's hungry, *Mon Dieu,* his screams let the whole house know that he is ready to be fed!"

Erik did not reveal his acute disappointment at not being there for the birth, nor did he betray the decisions he had made for their lives. But seeing Ariel through her eyes did nothing to allay the painful ache to hold his new son. He longed to hear this Spartan's cry for food with his own ears.

She knew Erik's tender heart. She was banking that he was full of regret and anger. To test the waters she asked, "Are we going to have another bar fight to celebrate?"

"No," he chuckled pulling at the back of her hair to lift her face up to him. "I cannot begin to tell you how much I missed you. Seven-and-a-half months! I enjoyed your stories about the Black Queen immensely. We owe Meg so much." He turned to the fire and rolled a log over with a heavy stick.

She rubbed the silk of his earlobe between her thumb and index finger. "I've missed you too. Let's sit down awhile."

He brought two blankets from his saddlebags and a bottle of almond liqueur. They toasted the boys and each other. She never asked him to remove the mask when they were in the woods, he would have felt violated and unprotected, and she wanted him relaxed. So she drank again and offered him some more. The liquid cruised down their insides, warming them, undoing the distance paved by time.

His mood was pleasant, almost joyous that the trial of their unwanted separation was over. "When may I worship at your body?" He asked the question casually, as one might inquire after the title of a new play.

Perceptive and gladdened, she understood the underlying heat that prompted his words. "We can plunge into each other in three weeks, but I'll complete you with my mouth right now if you…"

His lips found hers, his kiss soft, totally devoid of insistence. "I'll wait."

The part of him that was male was at times so difficult to comprehend. He had not dismissed her offer, only postponed a pleasure. She would have thought him agonizing to be transported and would have sucked him gladly. *Move on, Christine. Speculate about the male libido later.* "I have a favor to ask of you." He sat waiting expectantly, poking the logs with a stick. "Do you remember telling me in the tomb that you're like a man shot with arrows and poisoned?"

"Yes," he had no idea where she was going with this.

"Well, it's time to clean the wounds so they may heal, and I have a plan. One must always be willing to sacrifice for the plan."

"Shades of Madame Giry's life philosophies are wafting about us." He stopped jabbing the fire to study her eyes.

"I want you to meet Abraham DeVille."

"The doctor? I've already met him. He's your personal physician is he not?"

"I want you to meet him as yours."

"And why would I do that?"

"Because he says we're ready for the next step."

Erik shook his head, thinking that he had not heard her correctly. As he did so a curl of black wavy hair fell forward onto the mask. Certain he had not grasped her meaning, he became defensive, "Christine, I'm not a toy to trifle with, I'm a man and I don't believe I'm ill."

"You are clearly in need of a haircut, and you're right, you're not ill-ill, but we need to go to the next step and I can't do it without DeVille."

"Who is he that we need him to take us anywhere, and what is this next step?"

"I'm not explaining this well so please be patient and listen. You need to hear this." She tried to smooth his wayward curl of hair back into place, but it refused to obey. She stroked his left check. "You are the most incredible creature I have ever met, my unspeakable love. You come and go in my life like an illusion, yet you are very real and worth fighting for. I did something you don't know about. I did it to bring us to a higher level, a plane of understanding where we could live with each other, and I would do it again, a thousand times if it would work." She started to speak faster, fearing that she would have to get the truth out quickly before he bolted. "I have a confession to make. Dr. DeVille taught me how to hypnotize you. I've done it many times since Michael's birth."

Revulsion and anger screeched through his brain. His beautiful, incandescent eyes darkened, and his next words came out like the hiss of a cat, threatened and warning. "Do not play with me, there are limits to what I'm capable of tolerating." His hand went to the ground, pushing him up. He stood in one sleek, feline movement, leaping away from her.

"No, please don't go," her fingers attempted to grab his cloak but obtained nothing. He reached his horse in four strides, mounted in haste and spurred the animal. Leaving her to stew in her own juices before the blaze he had made to keep her warm. Horse and rider dissolved into the trees. Deserted, she picked up a rock and threw it forcefully into the flames, watching the flight of the angry sparks. She hollered in the direction of his exit. "Oh, by the way, Michael is going to have your eyes and he started speaking yesterday. He didn't even bother with one word...he made a sentence! Next year he'll write a dissertation and may need his father's advice." Then weakening she whined, "Are you going to be available?"

Pensive and soundly rebuked, she wanted to throw something else so she grabbed his stick, but hesitated as she took hold of it. This was the last thing he touched in her presence. She began moving some of the logs around, absently enjoying the flames. A bony lime-eaten hand appeared among the ashes, timidly she poked it in disbelief. Her breath came out in little stutters. "Hello, Victor, welcome back." She pulled her knees up to her chest and wrapped her arms around them, lowering her face in resignation.

She stood on the back stoop of the *Rue du Renard* house pounding the door with her fists. Presently, a hurried and out of breathe Madame Giry opened up. "Come in child, I'm so glad to see you. How are you feeling?"

Christine ignored the question regarding her health and demanded, "Where is the coward?"

"He's in the basement, go to him, he's been down there all night." She pressed a key from her pocket into Christine's palm.

"Mama, I've been so stupid! Who was I to think I could change his mind in so underhanded a way?"

The ballet mistress gave her a motherly hug, "You only thought to ease his mind."

"I should never have married Raoul! He's exactly what you said, sawdust in my mouth. I'm an object he owns, no more than his favorite dog or horse."

Madame reassured her, "I know, but becoming the Countess de Chagny is what Erik wanted you to do, was it not? Things are unfolding for a purpose, remember that."

Christine went down the short set of stairs to the basement and entered the stone vestibule Erik had shown her previously. *He said from this point we could go in three directions, that means all three of these walls open up. Which way would he go? I only know the room of the paintings.* She knelt and sat back on her legs in front of the wall leading to 'Bad, Bad Erik'. Making no attempt to restrain the grief in her heart she begged for admittance. Sorrowfully she pleaded until her tears were spent, but not her determination. Believing the hellhound could hear her, she rose up on her knees and placing her palms and fingertips on the stones allowed her conscience to vent.

"Erik, please, don't shut me out like this. I have not betrayed us. I tried to change your noble heart for both our sakes. Please, open the wall. I love you. You and the boys are my life. You believe I tricked you and you're angry. You should give me a chance to explain." Her voice grew hoarse from the effort of trying to speak to him through the stones. "You must be in there, so please listen, my love. You told me once that your own children would run from you in horror, but what if you allowed them to talk to you, as one does to a priest in a confessional, without regard to your features. If they could hear your voice and know your thoughts they would love you, just as I do...and I **have** seen your face! I love it because it's part of you. Erik, come to me, help me to help us both. Erik, are you even there? It's so damp and cold down here, don't leave me kneeling on a wet floor. I'm sorry. Please, find it in your heart to forgive me."

If the apology failed to gain response, she was at a loss as to what to offer next. *Look to the intent, Erik, the intent.* With her forehead pressed against the granite she saw one of the stones at the base of the wall move inward leaving a void in its place. "You are here! Let me come to you!"

She bent over and peered in. *Perhaps there's a lever or a switch in there.* She fumbled in the hole, frantically seeking something mechanical and didn't notice the wall behind her noiselessly sliding open.

Like a snake, an adroit arm encircled her waist. A dexterous hand enclosed her mouth and nose in a cloth saturated with the sickening sweet smell of chloroform. "Oh, this spawn of hell has heard you, witch, and he is in no mood to listen to anymore ranting!" Blackness swallowed her whole.

She awoke to find herself sitting in a chair, her hands and feet shackled to chains attached to a wall at her back. The cell where she was confined held no light of its own, except for that of a slender ribbon coming from beneath a nearby door. She could make out nothing of her surroundings, but stomping her boots told her that the floor was stone. The chair to which she was bound had a cushioned seat and padded arms. *Where is Erik, and why does this place seem oddly familiar?*

"Erik, it stinks and smells musty in here. I get it. Our relationship is in a toilette, so we might as well sit in one. Really poetic!" She sat forward and tried to stretch out her limbs. "If our relationship is in jeopardy, I'm the culprit!" She stopped talking and tried to analyze her situation. "Erik, Victor is back...did you hear me? Victor is back! One of his hands is above ground at the firepit!"

She pulled against the metal cuffs encircling her wrists and ankles, trying to move the chair. It refused to budge, but as the chains rattled she learned the extent of her movement in them. The shackles were lined with felt and not abrasive to her skin. She ordered herself to sit still and breathe in deeply through her nose. The memory of the smell identified her location. *How did he get me in here?* "You've upgraded, last time you had me fastened in this chair I was tied with ropes! When did you add the chains? We're in your house under the opera and this is my own damn bedroom! Is the torture chamber to my left? Erik! Erik? For pity's sake talk to me! I'm not going to cry. I'm not going to beg for freedom. Just let me know that you're close."

Like a fiend summoned from the abyss, his fearsome voice renounced her through the dark. "You **are** an obnoxiously clever girl. All the entrances are sealed...except for two that I never showed to anyone, not even Louisa. No one can find this place any more. To the world it will be as if we ceased to exist. The bowels of the earth imprison us. We are its excrement."

At least he's speaking. Christine amazed herself at the steadiness of her voice, "Good, if you mean to kill us here at least put your arms around me while it happens."

The forlorn sound of water dripping off granite into a larger pool filled the silence. His words were a rasp, "I dare not touch you."

"Because you'd snap my neck you're so angry?" No answer. *What is he thinking?*

"You have trespassed upon my mind, wrongfully invaded my privacy."

Her words were vehement at the insult. "And you did no less to me? You open your throat and the rapture of your voice flows over me, wave after wave, until every inch of my body oscillates with ecstasy at the sound. And now you've stolen me, **again**...and plied me with chloroform, **again**!" She squirmed in the chair and struggled against the chains, listening to their dissonant rattle until she was close to surrender. Finally she whimpered, "I really don't care what you've done to me. You're here and that's all that matters. I'm a crazed addict in need of you, my all-consuming opiate. Without you I'm dead anyway. If we are to die let me crawl to you and die at your side."

"Close your sulfurous mouth, witch!" He spat the words out.

"Scorpion," she flung back at the darkness. "Show yourself."

His response came laden with sarcasm, "Little vexing dragon!"

"Impertinent viper, I said show yourself!"

"Minx."

At the sound of his last epithet she relaxed her shoulders and exhaled slowly. A steady calm came over her. He'd purposefully given her a wedge. "Yes, I am a minx, and you are about to make a grave mistake. My love is a gift I give to you. If you loose me this time, you loose me forever. So consider your actions at this juncture very carefully."

Christine heard the Phantom call to her from far off, as if in some distant corner of the woods. He danced around the sycamores, always just out of view. The wind blew in the leaves. Oh how she loved the sound of it. She wanted to stop and listen, but she heard him insistently calling. Magically her mind flew upward, from the treetops she watched herself running to him, her hair loose behind her, her skin tingling in anticipation. She heard his distinct command, "Open your eyes."

When she opened them she was at the firepit, lying on her side, and Erik was sitting cross-legged in front of her. *How could this be?* She started to move but couldn't. Half-inch black ribbons were tied to her wrists, and looking at her bootless feet, she saw black ribbons there too, over her socks around her ankles.

Erik's face was grim. "I have not hypnotized you since we lived at the Opera House. You are still quite amenable to it, a most willing subject for sublime suggestion. You can only imagine how upsetting it is to learn that you've turned the tables and done it to me, little minx."

"If you want me to apologize again, you're going to wait a long time. I might do it in the next century." She pushed her right fist into the ground and straightened up into a sitting position. There was no need to remove the ribbons – they were adornment, not restraint. "We were never at your underground house?"

"No. I came back after a few minutes and found you with your head on your knees. I surmised that you were thinking of how to reach me. So I hypnotized you from a few feet away and we did the rest together. How did you like it?"

With false bravado she murmured, "I didn't mind. I probably deserved it. Victor's hand is above..."

"I know. I see it. I'll move him to the cemetery, the dearly departed are best served over there."

"Can we leave him here and put him deeper into the pit? I like making toasts over him." They sat by the fire for a few minutes in an unspoken truce before she asked, "Was this our first real argument?"

"Yes, I believe it was and one of us was not even conscious." He laughed and cuffed his knee. "I can't say I enjoyed it. It was more akin to a poker going through my heart than I'd imagined. I'll listen to you now. Forgive me, I'm an insufferable...," her fingers on his lips stopped him.

"Don't say one more damn derogatory word about yourself."

"I am not used to you swearing."

"I'm getting older and meaner. I still want you to speak with Dr. DeVille. I'll go with you if you want."

In exasperation he asked, "Why do you want me to see him, Christine?"

"Before I answer, vow not to hypnotize me ever again."

"All right, and will you do the same?"

"Yes, you have my most solemn pledge."

"Why do you want me to see this fluffy haired man?"

"You draw pictures of your torments, holding the agonies at bay. I cannot draw, so my torments remain undiminished. Promising to never leave Paris didn't gain me a life with you. It only sharpened my longing, and made me keenly aware that I don't live with you. And I want to... every moment of every day. I believe we're playing out a slightly different version of the same scenario we had at the Opera House. Will we have the same tragic end we had before?"

He stood up and started to pace but she continued. "Find a place in your heart to hear this, Erik. I don't want a haunting, I crave possession." He snickered. "Don't cast this opportunity aside. It tortures me that the boys will never know their real father. They won't appreciate what you sacrificed. They won't even understand it! At some point in the future there will be difficult questions to answer. Eventually they're going to ask me who you are. It's presumptuous to think they won't. We'll be lucky if they're not resentful, even hateful, when they learn the truth. You might think I'm wrong, but Michael is developing your eyes...and if Ariel follows suit...well, there you have it. They don't look a damn thing like Raoul de Chagny."

His response was gentle. He was not immune to her sincerity. Even after all these months of absence from each other, the appeal of her spells chiseled away at his will as if he had none. "I'm not an unfeeling rock!"

"Actually you're quite sentimental. What do you think?"

"I've heard this before, except for the part about Michael's eyes. You know how I feel, but at your request, Madame," he bowed with a flourish of his cape, "I will stay put and listen. Yes, my persistent hellcat, my ears are your prisoners, because apparently it doesn't phase you one bit that I'm about to kill us both. Under hypnosis you told me you were quite content to die with me," he raised his arms for dramatic emphasis, "but would I please put my arms around you while it happens."

"I want a lot more than dying together, I want a life. Changing your stubborn mind is no easy feat. You saw what happened a little while ago, and I only gave you a tiny piece of the truth. The dilemma, as I perceive it, is the criteria you've set for yourself...to be acceptable you have to be perfect, unblemished. You believe you're unlovable but somewhere inside there's a vague itchiness. Logic tells you the belief is false. It has to be false because there are people who love you, but how can that be? You search the events of the ugly past and reaffirm the belief that you're unlovable, and I understand, because you have good cause. So I gambled recklessly and had the doctor teach me hypnosis. I tried to change the mind of a genius. One who'd suffered some of the world's worst persecution and survived. The truth is, whether you believe it or not, the depth of the world's rejection of you is the depth of my love...that and more."

"So you toyed with my mind."

"I'm not a great hypnotist, and you were not the most cooperative of subjects, but you were my only subject. I had to try, Erik. I failed before Michael was born, too much excitement. You were less resistive after the baby."

"Define the goal in one clear thought."

"To get you to see yourself as worthy of love so we can be together." He stepped back. "Impossible things can happen! Each time I hypnotized you I told you to feel like it was our first intimate moment...your pulse racing, your mouth dry, a little nervous, so that each time you could experience me accept you over again, completely afresh. I told you how handsome you are, to see yourself as beautiful and desirable...to let your feelings climb higher and view yourself as I view you, virile, mystical. Even my stories about the Black Lady were an effort to help you understand."

"From a sick bed you were trying?"

"From deep in here." She placed both her hands on the middle of her abdomen. "I don't love you as a musical phenomenon or as a marvelous architect. I love you as a person. I want you to be my partner, for us to walk the earth together. A little while ago you told me you're a man, not a toy...that alone is progress. You're not a phantom, either. We are ready for the doctor, you can trust him."

"You are taking a bite out of a bitter onion, there will be tears."

"I just gave birth to Ariel, in life pain is unavoidable. Will you go see Dr. De Ville?"

"Do you know how to keep a woman in suspense?"

"No, how?" She waited for his answer. "How?"

He laughed, a deep throaty laugh that rose from inside him and rang out among the trees like joyous cathedral bells at a wedding. She had succeeded. He consented to go with her the following Monday.

18 *THE GOOD DOCTOR*

Tranquil awareness collected slowly in Erik's brain. He awoke with the dawn and began the ritual of preparation in silence. After drinking a full glass of water, he sat cross-legged on the carpet at the foot of his bed. Wearing only his undergarments he meditated for twenty minutes, and as consciousness rose, he stretched his long arms out to their fullest extent. Inhaling and exhaling deeply, he extended his neck and pulled his face as tightly as he could toward the ceiling. Holding the transcendental position of the plaintive half-cross for three minutes, he allowed the energy flowing from the room to enter his body through the base of his spine. Conscious of the space he occupied, he moved as a liquid. Drawing his legs behind him and lying on his belly, he drew himself into the striking cobra for another three minutes. He ended by relaxing and re-stretching the individual muscles in his arms and legs before coming to his feet. He drew a bath and meticulously chose his cloths and accoutrements for the day, paying attention to the slightest details.

Fall's crisp air surrounded Paris. *A cold winter is coming,* he thought lowering himself into the unheated water, *and where are you taking us, Christine?* The memory of her last words in the woods returned, a siren's voice proclaiming change in staccato fashion from a castle of woodland air. *'See yourself as I see you, my father did send the Angel of Music. We will triumph over these trials, but the solutions may not be simple to execute.'* He immersed his head and gazed upward into the blurry vision of the apartment's increasing daylight. *'Let Abraham smuggle your mind away, Erik, you need to grieve over your losses.'*

His face and upper torso came up out of the water and he addressed the air. "Madame, I am deeply acquainted with grief. Don't live in fairy tales. Frightful wings carry this angel and I restrain my vengeance as best I can. Besides, what's wrong with how we live?" *Everything, if there's a chance we could be happy.* "All right, we'll test the limits and battle Fate itself." He vigorously lathered his feet with soap. "Well toes, what are your thoughts about what she's doing to us? She's trying to trick the trickster isn't she?"

Dr. Abraham DeVille also arose early that morning, and prepared himself by brewing a cup of strong coffee in his kitchen. A widower without children of his own, his greatest loves were his medical practice and his nephew Benjamin. He cared deeply for his patients and frequently offered thanks to God for allowing him to be a physician and a Jew. This morning he repressed an excitement he had not felt in years. If what he had surmised was accurate, he was about to examine one of nature's most extraordinary creations. A mental genius of great physical strength and immense grace, an augmented individual with keenly accurate senses, but one burdened with the face of a monster and hiding from the world. He pictured their meeting in the chateau. The teacher had entered Christine's bedroom with the noble air of an aristocrat, and the doctor had noted the soundlessness of the visitor's stately movements, the distortion around the right eye as it looked out through the mask. The effect of the stranger's presence was charismatic, compelling. Abraham could only guess at the depth of devotion Christine and Meg felt for the man. His curiosity was peeked. The teacher had commanded Meg to halt with only a touch, and at the end of the visit called her away by merely curling his fingers.

Both these women are intelligent and financially independent. Their respect and loyalty must have been earned, not simply surrendered. How did he earn it? Was natural charisma enough?

The doctor gave his sole assistant and secretary the day off, and made certain that his nephew would not be giving music lessons in the house. He wanted to meet this person Christine called The Voice, alone, in an atmosphere where perhaps he could put the man at ease.

The doorbell of DeVille's home rang promptly at nine. Through the lace curtains at the entrance he could see the slender form of Christine standing next to the tall figure of a man in a black hooded cloak. He opened the door and bid them good morning, inviting them inside. The two entered wordlessly, waiting on the Persian carpet that covered the floor of the entrance. "Please step forward into my office. We are quite alone, no one should disturb us."

He ushered them into a pleasant room containing a ponderous desk and deeply cushioned, leather chairs. The walls were adorned with pictures of mountains overlooking fields of wild flowers; wistful clouds reminiscent of the doctor's hair filled their skies. "My patient's give me these so I hang them all. Even though I think they're making a joke at my hair. Aren't they beautiful?" The good doctor chuckled and the Phantom realized the man was quite accustomed to laughing at himself.

"May I take your wraps?" offered the doctor.

Erik lowered his hood. Removing Christine's coat and his own cloak, he handed them to the physician, who placed them on a coat rack by the door that he closed and latched.

"Please Christine, do introduce us."

Christine nodded. "Yes, of course. Doctor DeVille, may I please present to you my teacher and mentor, Erik D'Angelus. Erik, this is Dr. Abraham DeVille."

"E. D'Angelus, the composer and playwright? Indeed Sir, I am most honored to make your acquaintance." His handshake was firm and reassuring, genuinely given. Erik's ungloved hand discerned the softness of the doctor's palm and fingers. The elderly man had not reacted in any way to the black leather mask and Erik could detect no smell of fear.

They stood awkwardly for a moment before the doctor suggested, "Shall we make ourselves comfortable?" He sat Christine in a chair and offered another to his distinguished guest. Instead of sitting behind the thick, well-used desk, he brought a small chair from the sidewall and joined them in a circle. "Please allow me to tell you something of my history. I have been a physician for forty years and have learned to treat people as both spiritual and physical beings. I know you were hesitant to see me. I would be too. I believe that I'm the first doctor you've ever seen, yes?" Erik nodded. "I appreciate your honesty, it's most valuable. If you chose not to answer a question, and that is of course your prerogative, please tell me of your reticence. I will only ask for information that will enhance my ability to help. Everything you say will be kept in the strictest confidence. On that you have my word." Erik remained silent, scrutinizing him. "I need to examine you in the next room and then we can return to this office. Is that acceptable?" Again Erik nodded ascent. "Do you wish for Madame to wait here?" Erik gestured toward Christine with his opened hand. "I understand," the doctor said. "Let's go in there."

As the three stood, Erik froze, knees bent, his hands on the arms of the chair. A full second later a tin garbage can toppled over in the alley behind the house. "Cat," Erik uttered.

Remarkable! Later I must ask him what sensation alerted him initially. They entered a wide, immaculate room with shelves of glass apothecary jars, an examination table and colorful charts displaying various internal organs of the human body. The doctor instructed his new patient to remove his shoes and clothes and started to hand him a dressing gown.

Erik refused. "I will not completely undress. You may study any part of my body you wish. I will remove the clothing from that area and before you move on to the next, I will re-dress with the article that was removed. In this manner we will proceed until you are finished."

"That seems reasonable," DeVille replied. "Please stay where you are and take off your jacket and shirt. The Phantom removed his upper clothing and handed them to Christine, who remained standing to the side. The doctor walked around Erik, and contemplated with a vague uneasiness the multiple scars from a whip, slashed across his patient's muscular chest and back. An eight inch dagger rested in an oiled leather sheath on Erik's right hip. *The angry marks of shackles encircle both his wrists.* "With which hand would you pull the knife?"

"With the left."

"And if the dagger were on the left side?"

"With the right."

"Completely ambidextrous?"

Erik nodded smugly.

The doctor took his stethoscope and listened carefully to Erik's heart and lungs, asking him several times to cough. "Please put your shirt back on and leave it unbuttoned. Take off your shoes and come lay here on the examination table." He patted the white sheet.

Erik put the shirt on as directed and squatted to untie his shoes. "Could I remain standing?"

"Yes, of course, please drop your pants if you are comfortable in doing so. Christine?" She turned her back to the two of them. Erik stepped out of his shoes and handed the dagger around to her. Then he unfastened his belt and unhooked his trousers. Without removing his eyes from DeVille, he hooked his thumbs into the waistbands of his underwear and pants. Letting his lower clothing drop to the floor, he stepped out of the articles like a egret emerging from a pond, and stood before the doctor wearing only his shirt and socks. Another dagger in a sheath was strapped to his right calf. Again DeVille walked around him slowly and saw the scars of the whip on his well-articulated legs and buttocks. *This man has been severely scourged…front and back, but nothing recently.* The doctor suspected that the teacher was skillfully inclined to defend himself from any assault. *There is a branding mark on his right buttock. Someone claimed him as a piece of property!* He touched it gently. Erik did not flinch.

"A gift from a Persian ruler who couldn't quite manage to keep me."

"Please, put your pants on but leave them unfastened. I need to press on your abdomen. It would be a more knowledgeable palpation if you would lie down. It will only be for a moment."

"Lock the door and if you would be so kind, unlock the window. I might feel the need for fresh air." With her back to them, Christine smiled and rocked a little on her feet as she listened to the doctor comply. Erik donned his pants and climbed up on the table.

DeVille warmed his hands by rubbing them together. "I admire the amount of trust you bestow on me, Monsieur. You have a magnificent body. You must exercise a great deal. May I take your socks off and look at your feet?" After the doctor finished examining them, he slipped the socks back on and moved to palpate Erik's abdomen. A pouch with coins and bills in the front of Erik's pants jingled softly. "Money?" he asked.

"Yes," came the laconic response.

On the opposite side DeVille felt another pouch containing small vials. He looked quizzically at Erik, whose expression for the first time appeared to be one of amusement. He offered an explanation without being prompted, "Chinese red smoke."

DeVille smiled. He understood perfectly. "Yes, yes, I know this one. A most effective diversion. When the cap is pushed into the powder and thrown to the floor the red smoke goes upward, startling those nearby and providing you with a few seconds to escape."

"You are enlightened in the finer arts of deception?"

"Not as much as I'd like to be. Magicians are a talented lot, I admire their dexterity. When I was younger I had more time to enjoy their shows." DeVille felt the healthy pulses bounding in each wrist. "You like to wear gloves don't you? To curtail all the sensations your fingers send to your brain?"

Erik smiled, "Yes."

"In the medical profession we refer to someone like you as an augmented individual. Very rare, very special among our species. Your animal instincts are completely intact, even heightened. Let me help you sit up. I want to examine your throat and those remarkable eyes. I've never seen any that would compare to them. What is your descent?"

"Germanic."

DeVille stuck a tongue depressor before Erik's mouth, and the Phantom opened obligingly. "The colors in your irises are amazing, to say the very least."

Before allowing himself the infinite pleasure of inspecting the almost iridescent colors, DeVille checked the sclera of the eyes, the pink tissues of each canthus and the underside of the lids. All were healthy and vibrant. Then, and only then, did he permit himself to focus on his patient's astounding irises. "A person could get lost in your eyes, young D'Angelus, but you probably already know that." Around each clear, black pupil a brief copper colored ring radiated outward into a shiny golden-amber stratum that comprised the majority of the eyes' color. Visible within the amber were tiny specks of milky green jade. The outermost ring of the iris was a thin circle of blue-gray permeated throughout with tiny bright red dots, capillaries carrying a ready supply of blood to the eye. "How is your night vision?"

"Sharp."

"I can imagine. And what color are your eyes in anger or passion?"

Christine spoke quietly, "Bright gold encircled by crimson."

"That seems logical. The capillary beds where the iris is affixed to the sclera are raised. It must be quite extraordinary to behold. Do you feel comfortable removing the mask?" Without ado Erik reached to his face and placed the mask on the examination table.

Surmising that verbalization would intrigue the mind of the genius, DeVille began to speak audibly, as if to an assistant standing beside him taking notes. "Expressive vocalization and taste," he glanced questioningly at Erik who nodded, "remain intact, as are the bony structures of the cranium and mandible. The nature of the affliction appears to be of several types, and is confined to a well-delineated area extending superiorly from the right frontal hairline to the formation of the right upper lip. Its left lateral boundary is the median of the nose, and the right is demarcated by the beginning prominence of the right ear. The tissues of the right outer ear and temple area are healthy. Bilaterally, hearing is heightened.

"The affected area suffers a congenital soft tissue deformity and concurrent nerve anomaly. The right eyeball is of itself intact and functioning normally. However, the muscles and soft tissues surrounding the orbit of the right eye, and those of the right cheek and forehead are totally involved." The doctor placed his hands gently on Erik's two shoulders, "How are you doing?"

"Adequately. I want to hear this, please continue."

"The cartilage and outer tissues of the right nasal passage are absent below the nasal process of the superior maxillary and nasal bones, leaving the right inner nostril exposed. The septum is intact but the mucous membrane of the right nares is dry and lacks secretion. The vibrisoe, or stiff hairs, are missing. It appears that the superior branches, and possibly the medial branches, of the right seventh cranial nerve failed to develop in utero. Since that nerve innervates the muscles to this area, those muscular structures lack tone. They have atrophied and contracted over time, pulling the tissues and skin around them inward, creating a marked hollow around the right eye and below the cheek bone. The resultant exophthalmic effect is furthered by the malformation of the right eyelids and their lack of lashes. These eyelids would undoubtedly suffer occasional spasms with resultant uncontrollable tearing from this eye. Remarkably, the ability to blink remains. The right eyebrow is absent. The lack of nervous stimulation to this area creates an expressionless nature to this side of the face. One is compelled to address the mouth and left eye to determine emotion." He lightly tapped the skin of the right cheek with his index finger. "Sensation to touch is patchy or absent throughout the affected zone."

He gently turned Erik's face by the chin and leaned in, closely studying the abnormality. "Circulation to this part of the face also appears to be hampered. The skin itself is thin, translucent and lacks turgor. The capillary beds are prominent and raised toward the surface. The effect is that of a blue web-like structure similar to a fanned sea coral proceeding from the ear outward, much as one might see in a newborn Homo sapien.

"The final disparity is the formation of at least two dozen raised, irregularly shaped, granular nodules across the right forehead and cheek. The growths appear as small, reddish-blue florets of broccoli. The largest is a half-inch in diameter and the smallest approximately a sixteenth of an inch. The tissues of these nodules are erythematic and fragile." At this point in the examination a profound empathy overcame DeVille and he paused to maintain his composure. He stalled for time by removing his glasses to rub his eyes with his fingers. "These bleed, don't they?"

"Occasionally," Erik answered.

"I can give you a medicinal salve, a mixture of coagulant and astringent. It will help with the bleeding and dry them up a bit. Is it all right to continue?"

"Be my guest." Erik sensed the doctor's compassion but cynically doubted it would last.

DeVille put his spectacles back on and proceeded with the narrative description. "The nodules appear in no particular pattern and are randomly placed within the affected zone. There have been numerous attempts to destroy these nodules. Fibrotic scarring is severe. It is difficult to discern whether duller implements, such as fingernails, or sharper medical tools...perhaps even sandpaper...have been applied to the ailment. I suspect, as a physician, that all three have been employed against the nodules at some point in the past."

Standing in the corner, unseen by the doctor and Erik, large heavy tears of shame and regret began to fall from Christine's eyes. She made no attempt to reach up and wipe them, but remained motionless, quietly holding Erik's jacket and dagger. Hers were the fingernails that dug into his face when they lived at the Opera House. The first time she unmasked him, the horror registered on her face had enraged him. He'd taken her fingers and pressed them to his face. *'Do you feel this? Do you? This is no mask now! This is the flesh of death.'* Her talons had torn into his weakened skin causing blood to flow.

DeVille asked, "May I see the mask?" Erik handed it to him. "Remarkably soft kidskin. How is it held in place?"

"I use theatrical spirit gum or ties. I make the masks to fit my shape exactly."

"So you have created a facial mold? The gum is kept away from the nodules?"

"Yes to both questions."

"There is no current evidence of infection in the nodules, but there has been in the past, hasn't there?"

Erik took the mask and returned it to his face. "Yes, I try to keep them as clean and dry as possible."

"Good. I have not asked you about your sense of smell."

"Your neighbor is cooking a stew for tonight of beef, potatoes, and carrots with rosemary and thyme. Earlier you drank strong coffee, and before that you washed with a glycerin soap that contains eucalyptus oil and a mild medical antiseptic I cannot identify, because I've never smelled it before. Christine's postpartum flow is half the amount is was last week."

Her eyebrows arched in hidden surprise.

"You are an exceptional human being, and I haven't even heard you sing." Before he could stop himself the doctor squeezed Erik's shoulder. "Please finish dressing and I'll meet you in the outer office."

"We'll all go in together, doctor."

"You feel vulnerable and I don't blame you."

Erik finished dressing and taking Christine's elbow they returned to the doctor's office. Before they sat in their respective chairs the doctor had an idea. "My housekeeper has the day off. Why don't we go into the kitchen for refreshments?"

The three went down a hall to a warm yellow room with elongated wooden cabinets and an enormous cast-iron stove. At a polished table with thick curved legs, the doctor placed a variety of pastries and cups of hot coffee before them. While they ate, DeVille became thoughtful, almost reflective before beginning again. "We are comfortable, and in relative good cheer, with the physical exam completed. Aside from the potential danger of infection that your right face presents, you are in excellent physical health. Please, tell me something of your youth."

"From the earliest that I can remember my appearance caused shame to my parents. I do not remember my father well. My mother refused to openly regard my face and insisted I wear a cloth sack over my head. There were cut outs for my eyes, I was not permitted to eat in her presence. Confined to one area of the house, I spent most of my time alone, reading and learning from books. My father was a master mason; his technical materials surrounded me on every wall. I ran away from home before adolescence and stumbled into a gypsy camp. Because of my astonishing face they wanted to display me as a living corpse. At that age I had a fiery, uncontrollable temper and caused some damage in the camp when they tried to place me in an exhibition cage. As punishment they locked me in, and beat me…often. But I stayed by choice, I had figured out how to unfasten the lock the first hour they left me alone. They wanted me to perform, so I charmed them by singing. In return they taught me ventriloquism, magic…slight of hand."

DeVille's voice was sympathetic. "So you suffered rejection and isolation at a very early age, a derision made all the worse in one of such obvious intelligence. A weaker mind would have been crippled into a state of incapacity, left unable to function or suicidal, but you mastered the adversity and lived. How old are you?"

"Thirty-nine."

"Did the gypsies feed and clothe you?"

"Yes. I brought in a lot of money. When they displayed me, I felt somehow gratified by the jeers of their customers and the revulsion I saw on everyone's face. Their terrified expressions turned to wonder as I sang. I both loathed the transformation and reveled in it."

"Negative attention is still attention. What happened to you next?"

"I added feats of magic to my exhibitions and people started tossing larger and larger amounts of money to see what more I could do. As my reputation spread we started traveling to the larger fairs. Accounts of my performances spread to Persia by way of the merchant caravans. A Shah learned about me and asked his chief of police, the Daroga, to bring me to entertain his daughter, the little Sultana. Because I am adept at concealment, the Daroga paid me to perform assassinations for the Shah, which I did. At one point I told them some of my architectural ideas, and the monarch was intrigued. He had me build him a palace riddled with trapdoors and secret passageways. When it was completed, it shone like a jewel. In the sunlight it could be seen for miles. The despot decided to keep the deceptions of his palatial abode safe, by ordering that my workers and I be put to death. The guards amused themselves before my execution by trying to whip my flesh into putty. While they were thus occupied, the Daroga entered, supposedly to enjoy the sport, and slit their collective throats. He helped me to escape and for a time I hid in the walls, trying to heal. The Shah sent the Daroga to search for me. When he failed to recapture the magician for further torture, the Great Light of the Crescent Moon banished him. The Daroga is his cousin and has far reaching connections the Shah fears, so he waved the death sentence to preserve himself. I headed for Paris and my benefactor followed after me. He lives here still. When I arrived I managed to earn money helping to build the Opera House, and later by composing music."

"Fascinating, you show a remarkable ability to adapt and survive. How is it that you came to perfect your musical talents?"

"I am self-taught. I learn quickly and only need to see or hear a thing once." Erik took hold of the doctor's arm and warned him. "I am capable of terrible, monstrous acts."

"No doubt you are." The doctor simply patted the hand that held his arm. "Allow me to tell you something. It is the human condition that each of us is deformed in some way. We all wear masks to hide our aberrations. But at some point in our lives, each of us must face off in a dual with ourselves. The hindrances you must battle have been clearly marked. If chance had not disfigured you, the world would have deemed your face a thing of remarkable beauty. You would have been like the rest of us, who lumber along ignoring our defects, oblivious to their consequences until they cause the most acute suffering to ourselves, or those around us. Only the most unspeakable pain brings us to acknowledge that we may have a deficit, and even then there is no guaranty we will face it until the dual is laid before us and there is no turning back."

Erik withdrew his hand and they grew quiet. The doctor appeared sadly preoccupied with the deviant truths of human existence. He was in no apparent rush to hurry the interview along. Eventually DeVille asked, "What do you do when you feel sad or angry? When you are feeling inadequate?"

"I pour myself into my music, and I have a peculiar practice of repeatedly killing myself and those who have hurt me."

"Please tell me how you accomplish the later."

"I paint pictures of myself and my tormentors. For a time I view the canvases, then I destroy them. I don't know if I am damaging my mind more, but it seems to help."

"You are emotional when you paint them?"

"Yes, emotional and exacting. I strive to make them as accurate as I can."

"How a person copes with rejection and anger matters a great deal. When you feel sad or depressed, try to understand that you are turning anger inward upon yourself. Some people fill themselves up with criticism and self-loathing. Obsessing over their imperfections makes them insecure. They come to believe they are evil and unlovable. The fact that you brought yourself here shows great courage and a willingness to understand. Creating these pictures and destroying them is a way of coping, but if you could rise above the belief that you are a constant victim, you would open a door leading to a stronger mind. One that could negate the necessity of symbolically murdering yourself, or others. Taking control of your reactions, being responsible for them, is the foundation of a less fragmented sense of well-being. See yourself as whole and normal. Christine has tried to assist you with that many times. Then see yourself as deformed and normal. It is an enormous step, especially when we take into consideration what you have endured, but a truly significant one."

Erik violently twisted a cloth napkin in his hands. "I am well acquainted with some form of grief that invades my thoughts at will, despite all my efforts to advance past it."

The doctor's voice became grave and he placed his hand compassionately on top of Erik's. "We Jews know this grief quite well. We grieve over losses we can barely comprehend, but rather than look the other way and forget them, we embrace them. We own them. We are not a well-loved people, let me assure you. We are always prepared to run for our lives should the decree to slaughter us be issued once again. Such tragedy I could tell you of, the milk of human kindness does indeed run thin and polluted."

"It is rancid," replied Erik. Something odd was rising up within Erik's chest. He started to feel a kinship with this man who sat so unpretentiously beside him at a simple kitchen table. DeVille's unwavering kindness, his gentle eyes, and his sad words as he spoke of a suffering that had not hardened him into hatred began to take hold of Erik. This little man seemed to understand him, and was accepting of what he knew. Erik looked at Christine in gratitude. Here was someone he could talk to, a man who could help him quiet despondency, and grow through tribulation. Erik's voice was low, afflicted. "I have succumbed to terrible temptations, and am guilty of murderous crimes."

DeVille did not withdraw his hand. "We are all guilty. Every Yom Kippur the Jew stands before the throne of The Creator and confesses guilt for the crimes committed by all of humanity during the last year. I dare say, I've prayed enough to confess for my own sins and yours, too. It would give me solace to think that my prayers were for the both of us in particular."

"You don't know me."

"I know this, Christine de Chagny is your great and loyal friend, and if you will allow it, I will be your friend as well. A pitiless world cast you off. You retaliated as best you could, and have hidden from its callousness, haven't you? And who could blame you? Your troubles have been odious, yet Christine tells me you have a generous, unselfish heart, a heart like no other on the planet. Perhaps someday you will tell me exactly what she means by that. The mystery of who you are is a part of the power of your defense, yes? I am also told that you have a voice like no other. It would be generous of you to bless me with a song, but not today, Monsieur. We have discussed important matters. Both of us have much to think about. Please return to me, come here on a regular basis. We will learn together."

"What do I owe you, doctor?"

"You owe me nothing. You have paid me with your honesty. I told you when we were introduced that I was honored to meet you. Now I am even more honored, and humbled that you shared so much with me. You are a brave soul, D'Angelus, brave to have survived. There are still decades of years remaining for you to live. The world owes you an apology, but you know you will never receive it. Let's see if we can undo some of the damage the idiots caused."

"Can you call me Erik?"

Christine's face registered surprise.

The doctor's eyes lit up. "Yes, of course, and will you call me Abraham?"

Erik nodded, his head slightly lowered.

"Good. Then with your permission, Erik, I will get the salve I promised you."

19 *HUNTING FEES*

Heralding excitement, the season of autumn brought with it Raoul's favorite pastime on the estate – the hunt of the red deer! With the animals' breeding season completed, and the fawns born in the spring nimble and fast, the very sight of the thundering, majestic herds accelerated his pulse. The hunt from mid-October to the end of November was a time-honored tradition of the de Chagny's. Its amusements served the practical purpose of thinning out the resplendent number of deer flourishing on the lands. The sport of it appealed to Raoul on so many levels. He enjoyed every aspect. This year he was exceptionally pleased as the time of the shooting commenced. He was young and vigorous, in the prime of his life. The babies Christine had given him were delightful, even if Ariel's cries were a bit harrowing and caused a nervous havoc to run through the house.

Only one major draw back had surfaced to mar Raoul's exuberance. Christine's attitude since parturition was one of increasing independence. Every day she seemed a little more determined to do things in her own singular fashion. He granted that the pregnancy had been difficult, but she'd weathered it remarkably well. Her lack of complacency was immensely annoying to him. She'd emerge from her rooms like an armored Cossack, ready to provoke conflict. Their most recent confrontations were intruding upon his preparations for the hunt – a most intolerable situation! He resented having to continually insist that the boys be returned to the nursery and their individual nannies, rather than spend night after night housed in their mother's bedroom. He had never expected Christine to be such a confounding ball of clingy emotionalism and self-reliance. Impatient to pursue his own activities, he decided to placate her for the interim of the hunting season by conceding to one of her demands. He'd allow her to nurse Ariel and deal with his wife's stubbornness later!

With Christine quieted for the moment, Raoul invited three of his closest friends and fellow noblemen to the chateau for the opening hunt. The eldest of the guests, the Count de Benares brought his fourteen-year-old nephew along. The young man had never slain a deer, and his uncle was anxious for the teenager to have his virgin experience. In the gentlemen's retreat just off from the mansion, the party gathered around the bar and over unending glasses of cognac, instructed the neophyte hunter.

The members of the company enjoyed the use of flintlock rifles, rather than bows, and Raoul displayed his proudly. The thirty-three inch barrel gleamed from polish. The maple stock boasted a carved woodland relief affixed with silver inlay. He let the teenager fondle the weapon, while he pointed out its brass patch box and artful trim.

"It's so pleasing to the eye and comfortable to hold," declared the youth.

His uncle explained that the flintlock was so named because the gunlock, which held the priming charge, was ignited by a spark from a piece of flint held between the jaws of the hammer and struck against a metal plate. "See here, the flint creates the spark to ignite the gunpowder and propel the shot. You want to hit the buck just behind, and about a hand's breath above, the base of the foreleg. A shot thusly placed will enter the deer's heart, rendering almost instant death."

"What if I hit the stag, but miss the mark and don't kill it?" asked the nephew.

Raoul answered, "Then your uncle, or my gamekeeper, will perform the *coup de gras*. Remember not to wear perfume and only wash with water tomorrow. Deer ignore most people, but sounds startle them. We shall locate a comfortable blind at the foot of some trees or among some bushes. From there we will remain concealed, with our view unhindered."

One of the other guests added, "In this forested place of seclusion we will wait. Hopefully a buck, or a large doe without a fawn, will come to graze. A deer's sight is hindered when it lowers its head to feed. In this unguarded moment, stealthfully raise your rifle and strike."

Raoul sat back in an over-stuffed leather chair and pointed to the walls, bragging. "What do you think of all these trophies?"

The lad inquired, "Are they your kills? They're astonishing."

"Not all. Some of the eight and twelve pointers are mine...all the sixteen point antlers belong to my brother Philippe. He was a great marksman." Raoul swallowed some alcohol and continued. "My brother taught me to hunt on these grounds. Those were wonderful days of comradery. Philippe was at his ease, more jovial than at any other time. If my shot missed the target he wouldn't criticize or berate me. He'd just whisper that we should move on and hunt in some other spot."

"You miss him don't you?"

"Yes, always."

The boy's uncle steered the conversation away from the maudlin subject of the deceased Philippe. "When a deer's head is up, its hearing and sight are phenomenal. They can bolt away from us in the blink of an eye. If they do, consider your opportunity lost. Let them go."

Raoul explained. "It's difficult to hit a running stag in the trees. Especially since they flee to the areas of heavy cover where the brownish-green coats they're growing for winter make it difficult to fix on them."

"Like pooping in the night on an unfamiliar commode," laughed one of the guests. They started to share their best hunting stories and retired for bed about ten. The five hunters planned to set out early the following morning.

At sunrise the morning sky was overcast. The amassing thick gray clouds threatened a downpour, but hopefully one that would hit later in the day. Despite the potentially ominous skies the men decided to proceed as the younger de Benares was chomping at the bit to attempt his first kill. In the hallway outside the dining room, Christine informed Raoul that she intended to go riding later in the morning and asked what part of the forests his party intended to circuit. Irritated that she planned an excursion on the grounds, Raoul ordered her to remain in the mansion. She assured him she had no intention of staying inside, but would make her ride brief and not inadvertently venture into his hunting area. As soon as Raoul joined his company, Christine leapt to her bedroom to don clothes of deep browns and greens so she could blend in with her planned surroundings. Once prepared, she stationed herself at a small window in a closet – a clandestine sentry, waiting for the group to depart.

The men breakfasted, packed extra munitions and food supplies in their saddlebags, and headed out into the layered vistas of the estate and its forests. As luck would have it they did not spot a single deer over the entire morning and chose to drown their misfortune with a frequent toss of alcohol. They paused at one point to take a small repast and discussed moving further north, deeper into the taller pines. There they had decidedly better fate. Raoul sighted a twelve pointed hart and took aim as it fed upon a wild berry bush. As he started to squeeze the trigger, in the corner of his eye he saw a cloaked individual watching him from the side of a distant oak. He blinked in disbelief. The sinister figure wore the mask of a skull. Raoul hunkered down in the ditch where he'd taken a position and tried reasoning with himself. *The Opera Ghost here on the estate?* Like a jack-in-the-box he moved his head up and down several times, scanning his surroundings, but to no avail. *I am not insane,* he thought with resolution. *He was there!* He crawled on his belly out of the ditch, and as he did so the buck instantly sprung away.

His friends let out aggravated moans of disappointment. Complaining that Raoul had lost them the only animal they'd seen thus far.

Raoul answered with an emphatic, "Shh!"

Chastised, his companions watched the Count continue to crawl forward on his abdomen. With the pockets of his mantled green coat stuffed with supplies, he resembled a well-fed dragon lizard. The deer had vanished, so why was Raoul dragging himself along the ground?

Sensing that the Count was after more illusive prey, perhaps something hidden from their view, they pressed themselves to the earth and formed a cue behind him. Imitating their host's movements to perfection, a human snake of five segments wound its way comically through the grass.

After a few nonproductive minutes, one of the guests whispered, "With our luck he's found a porcupine or a skunk!"

Utterly frustrated by the antics of his mimicking comrades, Raoul stood up abruptly and the others followed suit. The small troupe gathered together, the guests asking if the new game had now fled as well. Raoul smacked the barrel of his flintlock into his hand and explained that he needed to pursue something on his own. Surprised and slightly offended at the directness of their host, they told him fine, by all means hunt without them. They preferred returning to the chateau, where they could get cleaned up and have a few drinks, over crawling on the ground eating dust. As they approached the horses, Joseph de Benares asked Raoul if he would be all right left alone. Raoul answered in the affirmative and asked that they exit loudly from the area, creating a distraction so that he might circle back around his prey. The guests mounted and made a great deal of noise as they rode off, jostling each other and joking that they would rather eat and drink than search for non-existent deer. Tomorrow was another day!

Listening to them gallop away, Raoul renewed his personal hunt. He moved to the north, down wind fifty paces, easing quietly around trees and rocks. He could be patient, so patient. He knew what he saw. For a time he waited behind the hulk of a decaying log, listening to the sounds around him. Occasionally he heard a twig snap and knew his prey had not left. Keeping himself hidden, he took a swallow of bourbon from a flask inside his coat and rechecked his rifle. Then it began, that damnable sound of his distant nightmares, the voice of a madman drunk in rapturous love. Oh, who could forget the sound of Erik singing to Christine through the walls of her dressing room at the Opera House? *I curse your soul, Erik! I spit on it. How could you still be alive?* His skin prickled in sweat. His heart pounded madly. Like the fangs of a cobra sinking into the neck of a rat, the thrill of the imminent kill seized Raoul. *How dare you enter these grounds! Sing your heart out for today you die, ghoul!*

He commenced a careful, soundless attack, moving through the trees toward the place where the ballad emanated. While he approached it seemed to him that the timbre of the voice took on more feminine overtones, as if Erik were capable of evolving sexually, changing gender and pitch the closer Raoul came. He found a large rock and paused for a moment to steel his resolve. Whoever was singing was just on the other side of the boulder. He rounded the rock with his rifle cocked, ready to shoot. There before his eyes stood the back of the Opera Ghost, even taller than he remembered. The black cape rippled in the breeze, the wavy black hair pressed down by two leather straps holding that damnable mask in place. He shook his head in outrage at the blatant insult. The fellow stood at the edge of a peaceful pond, singing to the woods as if he were on a picnic. He watched in disbelief as his nemesis stretched out its right arm. A hand in a perfect black leather glove attached to the sleeve of a brown jacket cast crumbs upon the water.

"Feeding my fish are we? How nice of you, Monsieur!" The singing stopped mid-note and the arm disappeared back beneath the cloak. Raoul was about thirty paces away, but at this distance he had the advantage of a no-miss shot. The Phantom remained perfectly still, his back to Raoul. The Count de Chagny decided that shooting a man from the rear was too easy, definitely unbecoming for a gentleman such as himself. He un-cocked the trigger and laid the gun on the ground, drawing out his blade. Maddeningly, his adversary still had not turned. He crouched slightly and advanced. *Twenty paces.* "Draw your blade and let's have at it! You are trespassing on my property. I want you out of our lives once and for all. You profane this land just by standing on it." The Phantom showed no reaction whatsoever and remained immobile.

"You have no honor! Turn and fight, coward! *En garde!* I demand it! My blade waits to address your stinking flesh, foul creature of the gloom!"

The cause of Raoul's aggravation still had not moved, but a caustic reply was at long last uttered. "What makes you think you'll succeed this time?"

Inflamed into red-hot imprudence, Raoul growled. Running forward he tried to spin his enemy around by the shoulder. His hand grabbed an immovable substance of stone. His own momentum carried him forward. Loosing his balance he stumbled and sunk his boot into the muck at the pond's edge.

His foe was not real! Stunned past coherent thought, Raoul straightened and stared into the jackal face of the Egyptian god of death, Anubis. Anubis, the ancient Guardian of the Dead, the conductor of souls into the west, stared calmly past Raoul to the murky waters of the pond. The black head wore the quarter facemask of the Opera Ghost and a wig. Its eyes were bright yellow slits painted above a long shiny snout. The sharp points of its ears stood alert, as if listening for the wails of mourners announcing the arrival of another customer. The arms were folded across its chest beneath the cape, the length of which touched the very ground. And above the immobile arms, across the well defined muscles of the masculine chest, lay a painted, multi-layered Egyptian necklace of bronze and sapphire blues, reminiscent of the wealth of the pharaohs.

Raoul blinked several times and sheathing his sword in disgust, voiced his own confusion. "What the hell…"

His words choked off in a painful, tight constriction of his throat. Someone was tapping gently on the middle of his back! In horror he realized he'd dropped his vigilance. He spun around, fists up, ready to punch the jaw of his enemy – and there she was. Christine. Dripping wet, in a black wig and cape, her boots a foot deep in the water of the pond. She wore the skeletal mask of Red Death that the Opera Ghost had worn so many years ago at a masquerade. Raoul's brain was stunned at the sight, trying desperately to take in what his eyes were showing him. Nearly paralyzed with fright, and now dismay, he was simply unable to comprehend the vision of his wife's blackened eyes looking at him through the mask of a skeleton. He lowered his arms, mute.

She kept the mask in place. "Surprised, Raoul? Dazzled? Your jealous pride could have killed me," she said lightly.

Several seconds passed before Raoul was able to locate his voice. "What kind of treacherous games are you playing out here, Christine? You just had a baby, for God's sake! How did you make yourself sound like him?"

Christine magnanimously extended her arms out from her sides, and lifting her face to the ceiling of storm clouds above, opened her mouth unleashing the exquisitely beautiful voice that had drawn him to this place of incredible inconsistencies. Wave after wave of despondency issued forth. The sounds of a soul in the wretched pain of unreciprocated love – so ethereal, so distortedly divine, that it brought tears to Raoul's eyes. His heart swelled within his chest. He wanted to tear his shirt, beat his hand against his brow, surrender himself to the aria of destitution and abandonment. He suddenly clapped his hands over his ears. "Enough! Enough!" He screamed for relief.

She shut her mouth, and the sound emitted from the very gates of heaven to torture him came to a blessed end. No doubt of it, somehow she had trained herself to imitate the resonance of his voice perfectly.

Raoul's brain decelerated into a quagmire of murky thoughts. "You come to these woods and play at being the Opera Ghost?"

"This is my time, my space. The Phantom has been dead for four-and-a-half years. They found his body burned and hacked in the tunnels beneath the opera. You are well aware of it. I come here to ease my conscience, and to keep the music he taught me years ago...alive. If you ever enter these woods again, I'll never speak another word to you. And it is for sure that you will not enter my chambers at night, or at any other time of day, for that matter. Make your choice, Raoul. Give me my privacy or drown in vanity over what you think you own."

Raoul's brain seemed to be processing information at the speed of a horse plodding through thick mud. "You come here...to these woods...and play at being the Opera Ghost?" He repeated himself just to reaffirm the words. The fact that he had acted as a fool in her strange scenario started to prick his arrogance. "Your games are of no concern to me, wife. You have my word that your privacy will be guarded and respected at all times."

Christine showed no inclination to remove herself from the water. Beneath her cloak her hand eased from the hilt of her Persian dagger. She studied his conflicted face, and in a flat, emotionless tone offered gratitude. "Thank you for letting me have my life, and for allowing me the opportunity to expiate my soul for the sin of leaving a talented teacher, and a friend, to die alone in the bowels of the earth." She held out a hollow reed to him. "This is what I used to breathe and speak through when I was under the water."

He hadn't heard her sound so desolate in years. He pictured her face beneath the mask as one of utter sadness, and thought to make amends by once again bestowing upon her an outrageous gift. "I give you these woods to the north of the mansion, Christine. They are yours to do with as you please. Let them be your personal playground. Here, take my hand and let me help you out of the pond. You have my word you will not be disturbed again. Come back to the house with me and get cleaned up. We'll play with the boys and visit with our company."

She did not accept his offer, her eyes piercing and cold from behind the skull.

"You look so strange in that mask. It sends chills through me."

"The boys are fine. They are being cared for by the nannies you hired. I told the staff to permanently move them, and their little beds, back into the nursery, as you requested. This is my time, Raoul. I need to stay out here for a while. I want to sing and pray."

"All right, I can certainly understand why you don't want to sing like that at the house. The staff would be at wit's end to perform their duties. They would no doubt find themselves captivated and unable to move. But you will return for dinner, won't you? Remember we have guests."

"I will be at dinner and in a dress."

Raoul shrugged his shoulders trying to conceal his stupefied state. He left the pond rattled, in need of time to sort this out. Christine listened to his horse's hooves grow fainter, then when she could no longer hear anything but the wind, she allowed herself as impish grin. She had not taken her eyes off the foreboding god Anubis. The wind swirled through the trees around her, the distant singing of an angelic chorus gathered on a far off hill. The downpour would start soon. She gave a sharp whistle. A bright eyed, well-groomed German Shepherd pranced out from the trees. She gestured for the animal to lay down. It obeyed immediately. Hunkering on the shore, it rested its head on its front paws, silently awaiting her next command. Had Raoul touched her it would have attacked.

The time of magic was upon her. She spread her arms out again, letting the sound of the oncoming storm secure enchantment. Breathing in deeply through her nose, the smell of dead leaves and tree sap filled her nostrils. She drank in the sensation of her heavy wet clothes and hair, the skin on her body tensed with a a thousand delicious points of ice. The stimuli her nerves were sending to her brain was powerful. She let herself experience every miniscule message her body delivered. This was true, animalistic feeling. Vibrant life.

"Behold, Anubis, a budding warrior stands before you. Take note of me because I defend your name with honor. Bless me and strengthen me, for the battle has begun."

She disengaged her boots from the sludge of the pond and approached the statue. On tiptoe she reached up and kissed the tip of its shiny black nose. Then reaching around beneath the cloak she opened a simple latch. The front of Anubis swung open like the lid of a sarcophagus-closet. "Deliver up my treasured Pharaoh, Anubis. Release him once more to the living."

Red Death stepped out of his tomb of resin and plaster.

"Hello, my lover," she modulated her words for gravity. "Welcome back from the dead."

He enfolded her in his arms, feeling the wet coolness of her face with his. "That was definitely interesting. I was waiting for him to blow a hole in the back of Anubis or try to run him threw with his sword. He's ever the polite nobleman to prefer the frontal assault."

"A character trait I hope we will always be able to rely on. Let's get me out of these clothes."

"Hmm," he responded, running his finger down her neck to her breasts. I'll light the fire in the pit. You'll be warm and in dry clothes in no time at all."

"That's not the fire I had in mind. It's been six weeks since the birth, and Abraham said it's all right to resume intimate relations with my husband. When I corrected him and said 'my **first** husband', the good doctor asked, 'Whatever do you mean?'" Biting her lower lip her fingers moved to his pants and discovered another god standing erect.

On the same turbulent afternoon that Raoul enjoyed his unexpected hunting trip with Anubis, Madame Giry had a visit from another kind of hunter. A Detective Thomas Edwards to be exact. He came to the ballet studio late in the afternoon with urgent business to discuss. There seemed to be no immediate way to put the man off. Left without recourse, she took him into her office and invited him to take a seat.

After they were settled, she offered him a drink, which he refused. "No thank you, Madame. Please forgive my bluntness, but I'm having a most unusual week thus far. I'd like to discuss with you some of the peculiar facts I have uncovered."

Madame Giry, sitting with her forearms on her desk and her hands folded together, could discern just a tinge of excitement in the officer's voice. That tinge concerned her greatly.

"You may, or may not be aware, that twelve months ago the secretary of Count Raoul de Chagny, a man named Victor LaPointe, disappeared from sight one weekend and has not been heard from since. At the time, my partner and I made extensive inquiries at the de Chagny estate and at a local hotel called The Marching Drum, an establishment where Monsieur LaPointe liked to spend his weekends."

Madame Giry shifted her weight in her chair and pulled at her bodice in an effort to be more comfortable. A movement that did not go unnoticed by the detective. "The police were made aware that LaPointe had gone missing by his male lover, a young man named Alexander Constantine. Do you know Alex Constantine?"

"No," was Madame Giry's singular reply. A carved wooden rose at the upper corner of the door frame rotated, alerting her to the fact that Erik had returned to the house and now stood in the outer perimeter of her office. "No, I have never made the young man's acquaintance."

"I see. Well, when we concluded our investigations at The Marching Drum, we instructed Monsieur Constantine to contact us should he come across the slightest bit of information that might be helpful in locating Victor LaPointe. In the beginning of this week, Constantine did indeed come forward with some most interesting news. Apparently he has known of it for some time. That he didn't bring it to our attention sooner is most irritating, for it is an important clue."

"And what information has he given you?"

"Sometime last March, or April, a very peculiar woman paid a visit to The Marching Drum. The individual was exceptionally tall and wore a thick black dress that flowed to the floor. Since her face was hidden behind an opaque black veil, she appeared to be in devout mourning. The visitor wanted to know if Victor LaPointe had any family and was directed by the desk clerk to the room of Alexander Constantine. Monsieur Constantine was most intrigued by the person's appearance. It seemed her mysterious appeal was in no small measure enhanced by her unwillingness to reveal her features. Despite her very feminine, almost mythical aura, Constantine was convinced that he was in the company of a male. Perhaps he didn't tell us about his unexpected guest because he hoped the stranger would return to him. At any rate, the trans-dresser, if it was a man, displayed obvious homosexual tendencies. Constantine told his visitor, for a fee I might add, that Victor had a little girl out of wedlock. A six-year-old named Grace DesJardins, who was in the care of friends at a nearby house. Although Victor did not see the little girl very often, he was in the habit of giving her caregivers money every couple of weeks to defray the costs of dressing and feeding the child.

"It is my opinion, that the girl's predicament is most tragic. Her mother passed away when the child was a toddler. Since there appears to be no extended family on either parent's side, her care fell to Victor.

However, his interests in her development do not appear to have gone much past that of financially providing a place for her to grow up."

"Monsieur Edwards, I'm not sure how any of this, has anything to do with me."

"Yes, well I'm getting to that. Please accept my apologies, yet again, for being so forward with this information, but I am obliged to hunt down leads wherever they take me. I have gone to meet this little girl and her caregivers, two sisters, Emily and Denise Rupae. The women used to work in a nearby bar, but it seems that since last April they've had no need to work. The sum of one hundred francs comes to them every week, by courier. The funds are sealed in an envelope with no return address, and lay inside a note advising that the monies are to be used explicitly for the care and rearing of Grace DesJardins. I'm telling you this history to provide you with needed information. This sum is double the amount these two women received from Victor LaPointe. I myself stood waiting where the sisters reside and intercepted the courier to question him. I gave the francs to the ladies, but kept the envelope and the note it contained. You can imagine my surprise when I discovered that this courier picks up these envelopes every week from the same manager at the Paris branch of the *Banque de France*. This particular manager was willing to inform me, after no small amount of persuasion, that the funds are drawn against an account held by a lawyer named Pierre Toussaint. Monsieur Toussaint will not tell me on whose authority the money is sent, or who, if anyone, reimburses him for it.

"One could imagine me at about the end of my inquiry, having run out of possible avenues to explore. But I was a most curious child, Madame. As a little boy, I took apart every gadget that I could get my hands on, just to see how it worked. Even if I couldn't get it back together in working order, at least I understood its dimensions and physiology. These preoccupations satisfied me to no end."

With that the detective sighed, as if in happy remembrance. "I cannot begin to describe how much satisfaction those intriguing mechanical dissections gave me. But I digress. I am investigating a missing person, not a murder. I decided not to compell Monsieur Toussaint to divulge his client's name. Perhaps, he is representing himself. For all I know, Victor LaPointe is in the Alps, engrossed in a new lover who has swept him off his feet. Alienating important people here in the city is foolish. Especially people who may one day be of great service to me. A police officer needs to keep his associations open. So instead, I took myself to the *Chambre des Notaires,* where my worthy associate and I began to peruse the ponderous volumes of deeds and titles recorded there. Expending a great deal of effort in an attempt to procure a list of clients Toussaint serves. We had some success I might add. You can imagine my intense interest, when I discovered that Toussaint facilitated the purchase of this house for you."

"Yes, Monsieur Pierre Toussaint is one of my attorneys and has been of sound service to me in the past. I still don't understand what this has to do with me."

"Well, if nothing else, it affords me an opportunity to visit privately with you once more, but I would truly like to discuss the circumstances surrounding this little girl. Unfortunately, she is not benefiting from this financial windfall. If anything, her care is the most deplorable I have ever witnessed. The sisters squander the money on alcohol, drinking themselves into stupor while the child starves. In the past seven months the little girl has not received so much as a new dress or a decent pair of shoes. I doubt she has the protection of a decent winter coat. She never leaves the house. Because Victor has not paid a recent visit to these women, they do not feel themselves accountable. They are, if I may be so bold as to say so, women of ill repute, prostitutes, albeit retired for the moment. Since I do not have a corpse that would allow me to declare Victor LaPointe dead, I cannot have the child decreed an orphan and placed in a reputable orphanage."

"I see, so you have come to verify that I am a client of Toussaint's and to...ask for my advice about this child?"

The detective nodded. *My guts tell me that all these little cogs and wheels somehow fit together nicely, and that you, dear lady, are involved up to your pretty nose...but occasionally my guts are wrong, so I'm willing to tread lightly for the time being.*

"Please allow me to think on this for a while and get back to you with my thoughts. It is admirable that you are considering the welfare of this young girl at all, there are so many waifs about our streets."

"Thank you, Madame. I will appreciate any suggestions you may offer. How are you doing since the death of your brother?"

"I miss him terribly at times, but I know that I shall see him again. I'm sure of it."

"Indeed, we shall all meet in the hereafter. Do you think you could show me the third floor of this house now that he is gone?"

With that, Erik took off like a bat from a cave. Flying up the ladder to the third floor, he planned to remove the black screens from the windows and pick up anything fresh, such as a piece of fruit or a wayward biscuit. He yanked down the pictures of Christine and threw her mannequin into the passageway behind the Japanese screen with a hasty apology.

"Sorry, my sweet."

Madame Giry smoothed back the hair on her head with both hands, even though everything was quite in place and she looked immaculate. "Of course, by all means, let me take you up there." As they headed to the doorway she hesitated. "Would you still like to go to dinner together, Thomas?"

The detective had not anticipated her acceptance of an offer made so long ago. He turned the brim of his hat round in his hands. A placid and composed Madame Giry observed the maneuver. *Now I know what you do when you're caught off guard, detective.*

"Why, Louisa, may I call you, Louisa? I would be most delighted to take you out to dinner. Please, name the restaurant and the night. I am at your complete disposal."

If only you were disposable. You sniff around like a persistent hound. She smiled discreetly at the officer and replied, "Then let's go out tonight, there's a new restaurant in the Italian quarter, *Il Scalino Su*. I've heard wonderful things about it from the other parents. Shall we pick up Kate and take her out with us?"

"Madame, I would be delighted! What a treat to have the three of us together for an entire evening." He bent over and taking her hand kissed it twice.

She proceeded to lead him upstairs to the third floor by way of the front staircase, pausing to turn on every gas lamp. *See how kind I am detective? I wouldn't want you to stumble, and look, I'm taking you by the front, since you've already nosed around the back.* On the uppermost landing she fumbled in her pocket for a key. Sighing dramatically as she opened the door, "Oh Imel, I do miss you."

The Phantom dissipated into an alcove with a decorative urn. *Go ahead, detective, snoop 'til your heart is content. We can always meet again later.*

Detective Edwards entered the efficiency apartment and stood near the doorway while Madame Giry lit two small lamps, one by the closest chair and the other at the side of the bed. He took note of the bed's neatness, the modest furnishings, and an empty glass candy dish on a small table. The sink in the kitchen was dry, the cabinets closed. He walked into the *salle de bains,* no personal items were on the counter or sink. "Have you ever thought of renting this space?"

"No, Monsieur. I still come here from time to time and remember the conversations I had with my brother. He was such a joy to talk to." She sat herself in the chair near the lamp and brushed imaginary lint from her skirt, straightening her shoulders and twisting her hips slightly in an appearance of adjusting her position. Edwards' eyes were fascinated at the delicate display of femininity, but he remained on target.

"Do you ever come up here at night?" She licked the tip of a finger and touched the corner of her mouth as if to remove a persistent crumb. *Damn, focus man!*

So you watch the windows at night do you? "No, Monsieur, I don't think I've come to this apartment at night since the funeral. Usually in the evenings I'm quite tired. I find myself enjoying the luxury of bed earlier and earlier."

She bent over to regard the tips of her shoes and provided him with a tantalizing view of her upper chest. As she reached down to wipe a polished leather toe, a gold chain bracelet moved from under her sleeve to her visible wrist. The glint of it distracted the detective once more. He openly admired the slender hand and fingers – imagined them touching him. Straightening, she sighed as if bored and played with the clasp.

The detective took the subtle prompt. "Shall we get your coat and fetch Kate for an evening's meal at *Il Scalino Su?*" He offered Madame his hand and assisted her up, watching her move reverently to the lamps as if she were in a shrine. On the landing she gazed back sadly into the room. Then solemnly locked the door with her key, testing the knob to make sure it was secure.

As they descended Edwards pictured her across the table in shimmering candle light. He reached to touch her hand and politely accepted her invitation to experience the luxury of her bed. *What do your breasts look like? Are they as well defined as I imagine them to be? Pull it together, Edwards, you're out on reconnaissance! Where is the money coming from for Grace DesJardins?*

In the apartment, Erik pulled Christine's mannequin from the space where he had tossed it. Bowing deeply, he chivalrously dusted her dress and explained the need for stashing her so unceremoniously into the dark.

20 EXCESSIVE DEBTS

Entertained and well-fed after three days of tracking deer during the day and feasting at night, Raoul's hunting partners left the estate on Sunday. In the end, each had slain a buck. Even the nephew of Joseph de Benares lost his preverbal virginity, by bringing down a twelve pointed male.

"What a kill," his uncle had proclaimed as they cut open the hart and initiated the young man by smearing arterial blood upon his cheeks and forehead. "We'll get the head to a taxidermist and have it mounted in your father's halls!"

The teenager had stood there grinning as the gamekeeper field dressed the animal. Raoul stomped around with the others, boasting over the boy's prowess, but secretly he was growing anxious to see them depart. The scene of Christine singing gloriously to Anubis kept playing over and over in his head. Certain that he had stumbled upon much more than just a game to sate her conscience, he chastised himself for not investigating the statue more thoroughly, and for giving his word to honor her privacy around the isolated pond. A mental argument raged within him. *I am the Lord of this estate and have every right to know what diversions occupy my wife. Philippe would never have put up with this. Examining the situation closely would have been an imperative for him!* With these thoughts plaguing his brain he sent his guests on their merry way and strode out to the stables. There he retrieved his horse and hurriedly rode off to uncover whatever facts lay hidden in the woods.

He scoured the areas where they hunted Thursday, but was unable to locate the pond and the rock. He had been steadily sipping bourbon that morning, and acknowledged that perhaps he'd inadvertently led his guests to another site entirely. He knew behemoth stones were situated around the family cemetery, but found it difficult to believe he'd directed the party to a place of reverence. He circled back toward the chateau and approached the rocky area from the east. By being thorough he eventually discovered the tranquil pond, a bare quarter mile from the graves of his ancestors. Jumping down from the horse, he walked to the water's edge, amazed at how addled the alcohol had made him. He looked to the hills surrounding him and the imperial wind-blown rocks. *Sound could easily bounce around in here.*

Off to the side he found a firepit, banked by a circle of smaller stones. The wood and ash it contained had been doused with water. Disturbed, he walked around pounding his fist into his hand. For a time he stood brooding in front of a pine tree with strange marks cut into its bark. They ranged in height from his chest to his waist. *How very odd! Why would she savagely slash at a tree as if to punish it?* He decided to carefully survey the ground for tracks. He was a hunter after all. To his chagrin there were none. No imprints gave evidence of his former presence, and Christine's boots should have left deep marks in the mud at the water's edge after she extricated herself from the silt of the pond's floor. It was still October. The ground was hard, not frozen. He thought back, there'd been no precipitation since he'd found her in this bizarre scenario. Now that he was cold sober, he was sure someone had deliberately removed the tracks!

At the waters edge he turned round and round, scanning the trees, searching, probing. *Probing for what?* The truth seemed close, frustrating, just out of reach. Like someone waving a flag through a dense fog right in front of him. In a sudden brittle revelation he spun around toward the rock. "Where the hell is Anubis? That thing was much too heavy for her to move by herself!" He jumped on his horse, barreling back to the mansion.

Christine had not seen Raoul leave that morning. In fact, she'd not spoken to him since dinner when he'd abruptly pulled away from the table and gone into his office, shutting the door behind him. A definite sign he wanted privacy. His abandoned friends had retreated to the hunting lodge, and she'd assumed he joined them later. She wondered what could have enticed him back to work on the last evening of his friends' visit, and went to see if he labored at his desk even on Sunday mornings.

Everything in the office appeared to be in good order, but Raoul was absent. The chairs were tucked into place, quills rested alongside black inkpots, and tidy stack of papers and journals awaited entries. In the middle of the secretary's desk, two ledgers bound in leather and entitled Accounts Receivable and Accounts Payable lay side by side. She opened them both and scanned the numbers. Then taking a piece of paper began making notes with a feather pen. Something seemed amiss. Expenditures appeared to far exceed income. Common sense dictated that this was a precarious financial situation. She rechecked current entries. Deposits from procured bank loans were recorded, but she could tell that these infusions were not enough to prevent the business from operating at a loss. Disquieted she moved to Raoul's desk. There she uncovered a box of neatly written letters from clients demanding the return of down payments for ships never received, and bills from suppliers stating their payments were in arrears. Her hands began to shake as she read the explicitly threatening language in the letters. She returned to the secretary's area searching for the accounts describing the management of the estate itself. She had just begun to grasp that the estate was operating in the black, but barely so, when Raoul appeared in the doorway.

"I am surprised to find you in here, Christine. Paper work never interested you before." Raoul's eyes looked haggard, his face and clothes dusty as he trod heavily into the room.

"Don't insult my intelligence. I came in here searching for you. Did you say good-bye to your guests this morning?"

With an air of authority he strode to the desk where she sat. As he leaned on his fingertips, his hands looked like two spiders landing on the blotter. Straight legged, he bent at the waist toward her. "Yes, then I went for a ride. Where is that damn statue of Anubis you put over by the pond?"

She lifted her nose in defiance. "You told me you wouldn't go back there. You gave me your word! How could you?" She raised her hands up pleadingly and sweetened her voice. "Before we discuss my activities... and your lack of honor, I want to talk about the shipbuilding business."

Raoul threw his scarf into a chair, his coat and jacket followed. Furious, he unbuttoned his vest and yanked at his cravat. He needed air! "You want to discuss finances, Christine? Shouldn't you be tending to the boys?"

"The boys are napping. They'll be waking soon, and I'll be there to nurse Ariel while the nannies feed Michael lunch." She picked up the Accounts Receivable journal reverently, placing her right hand on top of it, as if to take an oath on a bible. "It appears that we're having monetary difficulties."

Raoul's glare was frosty. He jerked his head to the side, mulling over his wife's stubbornness. He walked back and forth in royal aggravation before roughly pulling his chair out from his desk. Blowing out his breath in frustration, he sat down heavily. *Women!* Pushing the hair on his forehead back with his fingers, he grunted, "Where's Anubis?"

"Returned to the Opera House the day after you found me there. I paid movers to take him. Shall I retrieve my receipt? My games are trivial pursuits, the fancies of a mind with too much time on its hands. I want to understand what's going on with our finances. Are we in debt?"

"Why are there no tracks on the ground?"

"It rained after you left the pond and the next day there was a brisk wind. They put the statue on a four-wheeled cart. Did you check closer to the access road?"

"No."

"There! See, problem solved. No mystery at all. Now, as to our finances, are we in trouble?"

"We'll be fine. We've just hit some rough patches. It happens in business. I may have to discuss curbing shopping and entertaining expenditures with you, but I need to review matters more carefully before I make any requests. There's nothing to worry about yet."

"Because you've taken out bank loans?"

He shot a look of disbelief at her. "Did you read everything? Yes, because of bank loans. Shouldn't you go to the children? It's close to twelve. I'll come up in a little while and visit with them."

"I want to help. Let me help, Raoul. Tell me about these figures and what they all mean. I can be of use to you. I'm sure there are dozens of ways to cut expenses. I could even run the estate. That would allow you and Vincent to focus more on the shipbuilding."

"Well, that's a generous offer, Countess de Chagny, and I will consider it. Now run along upstairs and see to the boys. Wait, I've changed my mind. I'll come up with you and play with Michael while you…oh, just cover your breast while you feed Ariel." With that they stood up and went to the boys together.

The following day, Christine arrived at the house on *Rue du Renard* about eleven. She went to Madame Giry and gave her a joyful hug.

"Why so happy this morning, child?"

"Mama, the dim semblance of a happy future is forming on the horizon. Do you see its beginnings? I do! Yesterday, I made a most enlightening discovery at the chateau!"

Madame winked and touched the tip of her nose for good luck. She kissed Christine's forehead and pressed the key to the third floor into her hand. "He's in the basement writing music. I'll go tell him you're here."

Christine let herself into Erik's apartment, smiling in contentment when she spied the upper bedclothes turned down neatly to the foot of the bed. *I see, perhaps he wants an engagement in the sheets before swordsmanship.* Striving for patience, she folded her arms across her chest and went to the front window, confident that no one could see her through the darkened screens. Looking down into the street, she watched a number of people entering and exiting the house directly across from them. While she studied the activity, Erik entered quietly through the Japanese screen and slipped up behind her.

"Hello, my darling," her voice quivered slightly as his arms wrapped around the front of her in greeting. Tenderly he pressed his lips into the base of her neck. She felt his heart beating against her back. Surely he must feel hers. "What's going on across the street?"

He kissed her earlobe. "I think they're moving and putting the house up for sale." He placed his hands over hers and passing them over her breasts, whispered, "Goddess, make me alive again." Instead of unlacing her bodice, she turned around within his arms and brought her lips to his. His fingers moved to the back of her head, pressing her face even closer. He wanted to be lost in the opium of this mouth, but the cry of a hawk screamed in his head once more, and he broke the kiss before its dreamy spell laid siege to his brain. Holding her out from him, he asked, "What's happened?"

She could not resist a teasing smile and rested her hand on the right side of his face below the mask. "Why are you all in black today?"

"Dark clothes for distressing music downstairs," he replied. "I'm composing a piece about Agamemnon removing Briseis from Achilles."

"Hmm, how appropriate," she mused. "What do you want first, maestro, me or my news?"

"I want to know what's in that precious head of yours."

"Raoul is in debt, a lot of debt. If I correctly interpreted what I read yesterday, things cannot continue. There is a strong indication he's plunging us into bankruptcy."

"I'm sorry to hear that. Let's sit at the table. What did you see?"

Christine recounted what transpired in Raoul's office on the previous morning. "He is in a weakened state and pliable," she offered. "We could make a plan."

"Take care not to push him too hard. Don't make the mistake of thinking he's a little lamb. A man backed into a corner can be a dangerous animal."

"I knew you'd say something like that, I just knew it!"

"He doesn't know you have the scroll does he?" She shook her head. "You should return it to its pouch before he discovers it's missing. I made a copy of the words. I'll go get the original."

She placed her hand on his arm to arrest him. "No, please don't. It's powerful leverage. I want you to keep it here. I **should** go back to the safe, but to inventory the contents of the drawers."

"Yes, very wise. The contents of the safe would indicate the seriousness of the financial situation. You must be very careful entering that attic, Christine. Take rigorous precautions that no one, absolutely no one, sees you."

While she listened, her fingers pulled absent-mindedly at the black silk fabric of Erik's sleeve. Her hazel eyes were watery, translucent with longing as she studied the cleft in his chin.

He recognized the unmasked desire swimming in her eyes, the eagerness in the contour of her mouth. Her obvious plea ignited his loins, like a match to tinder – and simultaneously corroded his mind with fear. How long could this affair last? In what unwelcome minute would she recover from this fire and loathe all she'd embraced so eagerly these last months? And once his demonic face became hideous reality, under what guise would she mount an exit? Perhaps there'd be a gradual slippage, a transition from lush passion to polite distance. Or maybe she'd just refuse to come to him, tossing the physical pauper away like garbage. His insides twisted violently, rotating between awe of her and jagged despair. *Draw back before she's depleted – burned out. Why suffer the discordant echo of her steps as she retreats!*

His head pounded with the incessant beating of a drum. He fermented with love for her. *Don't flee from me…stay, stay close, my love. You are life itself, hope incarnate. Will you leave…how could you not? Until that unhappy hour, what unspeakable joy is mine, what stabbing pain! You are safe beneath me, woman! I won't hinder your departure. There will be no gnashing of teeth, no pleading, no nasty whining that I've changed for you, evolved enough to walk this dark, uncertain trail to the sound of this infernal drum, because every touch is…*

"Pleasure." His speech was thick, deliberately restrained. "You are raw, undiluted pleasure, Christine. We don't have a lot of time. I have an appointment with Dr. DeVille at three. Talking to him is helping. I haven't felt the urge to draw a picture in weeks."

She needed no illumination, no enlightenment. The madness raged behind his eyes again, robbing him of happiness, filling him with grief. He walked the edge of some fragile cliff, despondent, counting himself alone. Since New Year's, she'd put herself in his shoes many times. She'd come to comprehend a little of what the demon tearing at his insides felt like. They had no need to travel to hell – it walked with them. She refused to calm him with opiates, and faithfully honored her promise not to hypnotize him. Instead, she'd pull him from the precipice gently, with her body, ministering to him with the healing power of sex. The invitation was there already, written in the folded quilt and sheet upon his bed. She unbuttoned the top of his shirt, spreading the cloth to expose a tiny space of flesh. Touching the curls on his chest invitingly.

He was certainly acting like he had all the time in the world. Rekindling him would take a moment. It wasn't until his lips set into the mildest of his sulky pouts, that she realized she was already having an effect on his concentration.

"Good, that's so good." Her fingers pulled insistently at the hair on his chest. "Abraham can help us. He is such a gentle soul. He's seen tragedy in his own life. Did you know that?" She looked directly into his golden eyes and saw the rings of blood on the outside of each iris pulsating. "The ancient wise ones wrote that when arousal occurs the mind waxes thin, speech evaporates until the act of heat is completed." With her hands beneath his elbows she guided him to his feet, continuing as she walked him backwards toward the bed. "To not satisfy that heat is cruel, and to deny its expression in the face of Aphrodite's blessing…is unforgivable. Every instance of rejected opportunity is recorded in the ancient annals of time for the gods' consideration."

"Shh." Achilles hushed Briseis with the kiss of his mouth.

Later that afternoon, Christine made her way to Raoul's safe in the chateau's attic. The mansion was peaceful with the servants resting, and Erik's babies asleep. She was told the Count had gone to the *Banque de France*. When she opened the safe she found every tray, every velvet bag empty. Only the scroll's golden tube and the owl shaped cigar cutter were still in place. But the money and all the jewels, even the archaic deed to the property, were gone. *He must be leveraged to the hilt,* she thought. *Erik makes money and frugally doesn't spend it. Raoul can't seem to hang on to it.* She carefully closed everything and went to her rooms to think.

Raoul returned around three o'clock and she hurried to the office to speak with him. Both men stood as she entered. Without looking at Vincent she asked him to please give her a few minutes of privacy with her husband. The secretary happily complied. Exiting promptly, he said he would take tea in the kitchen and wait to be summoned.

Raoul chastised her. "This isn't a good time, Christine. What do you want?"

"How is business going today? I can sense it's not good, so you might as well discuss it with me."

Raoul threw his arms up and leaned his butt against the front of his desk. "Talking to you about our situation can't make matters any worse, can it?" His predicaments came forth in a reluctant, foggy manner. "Today I was unable to procure any more loans against the estate. The truth is we are mortgaged to the bank's allowable limits. I've tapped out our reserves as well. I lost two ships in storms at sea. I have a third, a smaller vessel half finished. We need to carry the payments on the current loans and get this next vessel completed. A buyer who knows the quality of our work is already sending salutations. He's very interested. If we can manage this financial hump and get this ship sold, I can see an end to this difficult period."

"Two vessels were lost at sea?"

He breathed in deeply and exhaled through his nose, she remembered Erik's warning about the cornered animal. "Yes, in April I sailed the two together to Italy." He sat in his chair and tossed a quill onto some papers. "They were both lost in the same foul, spring storm before they could be delivered and accepted by their purchasers. The deposits made on the two ships had to be returned. There was no insurance, so they were a total loss. You didn't hear about it because of your illness."

No wonder he's been reticent to declare the situation to me. Pride. Christine came over to him and placed her hands consolingly on his shoulders. "Thank you for your honesty, Raoul. I understand that you were trying to spare me from worry. Let me talk to Jean and Meg and see what we can come up with."

Raoul rested his forehead in his right hand, secretly grateful that someone else would be thinking about his problem, and perhaps rescue him from his mistakes – like Philippe did when he was a child. "I'm so embarrassed. I don't want the family and my other associates to know that I cannot absorb these losses anymore. If Jean and Meg cannot help, come to me at once and tell me."

While Christine was having her conversation with Raoul, Erik sat in DeVille's office deeply engrossed in a description of everyday life among the Romani gypsies as they moved around Europe. He explained in some detail the process of traveling from place to place, and dealing with the local authorities to obtain the necessary permits. One would think that the caravans spent the bulk of their energies erecting tents and performing various attractions, but that was only a small part of the drama playing out in the carts and wagons as they journeyed about. The majority of the Romanies' work addressed everyday survival needs and maintaining their culture. They taught him to make his first leather masks, and to display himself only for a price. Once he demonstrated his ability to bring in a substantial income, Erik went from captured freak to a position of respect within the community. Since his intelligence and ingenuity proved him worthy, the leaders often took him into negotiations with the townspeople. He became a valued asset to their clan. When the Daroga arrived unexpectedly at their campfires, trying to convince them to part with their magician, there was a great reluctance to do so. In the end, the Shah's free flowing money greased the wheels of resistance and allowed him to leave for Persia.

Dr. DeVille was fascinated. "What an amazing existence. It never occurred to me that the gypsies and itinerants must deal with practical matters on such a profound scale. You were a part of their cohesive group yet you chose to leave. Why?"

"I'd learned all I could from them, and the thought of a new frontier appealed to me. I have but one true home, my own head."

"Which you have learned to guard and keep safe." Erik opened his hand in ascent. "Let us talk a little about this home. Shall we do some serious work for you?"

Erik swept his elegant hand sideways. "Yes, of course doctor."

"Perhaps our discussions are allowing you some relief. You said you have not felt the need to recreate anger or despair in a painting for several weeks."

"Correct."

"Excellent! If you think about your life this afternoon, what would you say is the strongest emotion underlying your experiences?"

Erik reached up and removed his mask, laying it on a little table beside the coffee and pastries. He had not made this great concession since his initial examination. From his seat, DeVille leaned his body closer to show appreciation and acceptance.

"Unrelenting loneliness."

"Can you elaborate for me? Try to define it."

"This feeling of loneliness saturates me. I am imprisoned behind this face. Even my jailor doesn't want to see me. I hate the world for its rejection. I hate that it condemned me to abiding loneliness, and I detest myself for being the flailing son of emotional desolation. I would rather have the whip than the rejection of someone I care about. This kind of loneliness makes the whole world seem like a forsaken, windswept graveyard. My only companions are my own screams. That's as it should be I suppose. I deserve no less." Erik sipped his coffee and returned the cup to the table before he continued. His eyes grew distant and strangely surreal. "And why not? Graveyards are for the dead and my face is dead...dead and rotting on my skull, like my insides used to be. When I was younger I took my decrepit spirit and buried my existence in the caves beneath the Opera House. No pulse, no feeling of life...except..."

The doctor urged him to continue. "Except...?"

"Except for the music from the theater. The music fed my soul and saved me. I constructed a massive organ, played my compositions to the water rats and lived. From the catwalks above the stage I watched an innocent girl and fell deeply in love. When others were around she was dull, lifeless. But when she thought no one was in the auditorium, she sang with every fiber of her being, pouring out grief over the loss of her father to the point of physical exhaustion. In her bed she would cry for a death she was too weak to create for herself. Her anguish, her articulate loneliness, slashed my heart sharper than the bite of any whip I'd ever felt. So I started to talk to her through the walls. I let her believe I was the Angel of Music, rather than a love starved rarity."

"So you heard what no one else was hearing?"

"Yes, and she heard me too. When I sang, she'd beg me not to stop. Our souls touched through music."

"So loneliness can teach a person how to perceive its character within the heart of another?"

"I never thought of loneliness as a teacher before. Yes, it taught me to recognize it within her."

"And does this lonely woman still live?"

Erik suppressed a snicker. "Oh, yes, she still lives and my heart refuses to love another."

"You are not with her?"

Erik's tone was so cold – it could have chilled the bright sun of summer. "No, I'm a monstrosity. She deserves better. Others would shun her for associating with me. I can't have her suffering."

"Even monsters deserve mates, Erik." A few quiet moments passed before DeVille spoke again. "Would you let me hypnotize you so that we can try to identify the more specific blockages that stand in the way of your well-being? Perhaps we can dissolve them. I promise to be careful of your mind, and leave you only at peace with whatever information we may uncover."

Erik's muscles grew tense, he was uneasy and reluctant to comply with Abraham's request. For Christine's sake he forced himself to be helped. "I believe I am your patient, doctor, please proceed."

"Normally I would ask you to remove your shoes and loosen your lovely burgundy cravat, to make yourself more comfortable. But you have already paid me the great honor of removing your mask, so please do whatever you like to be at ease."

The stately romantic, with the jet-black hair and the face of rubble, withdrew a flask from inside his jacket. He offered it to the doctor, who graciously refused, then took a long drink of bourbon. After returning the container to his pocket, he thought for a moment. Removing a slender dagger from a scabbard underneath his arm, he placed it on the table between the fancy porcelain cups, and loosened his tie.

A nonplused Deville sounded more like a Jewish mother than a doctor. "Keeping a razor sharp knife twelve inches from your fingers helps you to relax?"

Erik did not respond. DeVille asked him to close his eyes and picture them walking together into the alley behind the house. As the backdoor yielded to Erik's grasp, they heard the shriek of a hawk and the two flew as birds from the doorway. They traveled over the city with the pleasant wind in their faces, the rampant blue of the sky all about them. For a while they soared and tumbled, only to recover and fly higher into the sunlight. The doctor asked him to find a street for them to land, that they might rest for a bit. They drifted down to a cobblestone lane just as twilight brought the mists off the river to envelop them.

Dr. DeVille shook his coat like a bird settling down, and thanked him for the respite. He told Erik that he liked this place very much. It was quiet and serene.

Erik cautioned, "Serenity can be deceiving."

The doctor agreed and elaborated on the thought. "We are prepared to venture far out of our way to guaranty we are not subjected to the impassioned control of our emotions. Past events are past, here we are not the victims of events beyond our control. We are the captains of our own ships."

"Ships, our own ships," was all that Erik said.

"Erik, I am your loving guardian. Do you trust me to protect you?"

"Yes."

"We are free right now, are we not?"

"Yes."

"Who is the jailor who would not visit you?" Erik moved uneasily in his chair, his left eyebrow drawing down into a deep frown. The doctor took him further into hypnosis and Erik relaxed. In his mind he took the doctor's hand and the doctor smiled at him. "Now Erik, call the jailor forth to us."

"As you wish, there they are."

"They, Erik, who are **they**?"

"The jailors of my heart. They are vicious and have rejected me."

"Yes, I see them. They are across the street. We are safe. Can you tell me who they are?"

"My father, my mother, Christine and Raoul, and behind Raoul stands..."

"Stands who, Erik?"

"Raoul's brother, Philippe. He is a ghost, as are my parents."

"I see. Those three are dead and no longer walk the earth, yes?"

"Yes."

"Can we excuse those three for the moment? We can talk to them later."

"All right, they've left us."

"Erik, nothing we say or do here in this street can hurt us. As a matter of fact, this place is under my personal protection. Here we can have a game of make believe, and the game will only make us feel good about ourselves. Do you understand?"

"Yes, make believe."

"Christine was a jailor?"

"My heart's jailor and the jailor proved to be most cruel. The jailor rejected me after years of teaching her, so I tricked her and put her in prison with me. But my face and my temper frightened her. I weakened and set her free."

"She does not reject you anymore, Erik. See she is walking toward us with a tray. I can't see what's on the tray, can you?"

"Yes, I can see it."

"What's on the tray, Erik?"

"A jewelry box containing her love. Next to the box are my two sons." DeVille's eyes grew wide in surprise. *Of course, they are his children! Michael looks just like him. How did I not see that?* Abraham was obliged to think for a few moments and reshuffle his perceptions.

"Does Christine want you to have what's on the tray?"

"Yes, very much. She is smiling but she is sad. She does not want to be with Raoul. She was my bride before she was his and I gave her to him. I set her free."

"Why Raoul?"

"She cared for him deeply and he could give her a normal life."

"I see. Please take the tray from her Erik, and don't forget to thank her. Make the jewelry box small enough to place inside your pocket and hand the boys, one to her and one to me, all right?"

"It's done."

"Now, what shall we say to Raoul?"

"En garde, monsieur!"

"So we raise our sword and challenge him. This is our adversary. This is the person who blocks our happiness and Christine's. What happens next? What do we do?"

"We wait for Raoul's death blow to end me."

"And Raoul **does not** deliver it. You are not dead, Erik, you are alive. They leave us, Erik. Christine is with the boys in her house and Raoul left in another direction. You and I can come back to the office and be together. We have done very well. Yes, we have. You will remember everything we saw and did together, and we will discuss this without reservation. There are no reprisals, no repercussions for anything that happened in the past. All is well, and as you open your eyes to me, you feel calm and are at peace. We are friends. We enjoy each other's confidence and company. *Oui?*"

"*Oui.*"

"At the sound of three open your eyes and wake, Erik, one-two-three."

Erik's eyes opened. The doctor sat exactly where he had been before they took their trip. A sad smile crossed Abraham's mouth, and his eyebrows were drawn together in a frown. *Now there's an incongruous mix, a smile and a frown situated together. Why didn't he let Raoul end me? I am prepared to die.*

"Erik, for some reason you will not defend yourself against Raoul. We need to talk about that a bit, but not today. I want to think some on these relationships and what they mean. Is that all right?"

"Have I lost a friend?"

DeVille chose not to stand up and place himself in a position of power looking down at Erik. Instead, he moved the legs of his chair nearer so that he could lower his voice for emphasis. "You have not lost my friendship. We are fast, you and I." He touched his patient's hand. "Now I understand something of what Christine means when she says you are the most generous soul she has ever met. I will at all times respect your wishes about these relationships. Soon we will need to talk about what they mean to you…and to her."

Erik did not respond. He bent forward in his chair and resting his elbows on his thighs, clasped his hands together, pensively regarding the floor. "It's difficult to picture myself as a father. I don't even know the correct way to hold a baby."

"Holding a baby is a thing easily learned, giving to another in unselfish love is quite difficult. You have already mastered that better than anyone, myself included, could ever teach you."

Erik searched DeVille's eyes and read nothing but sincerity there. He felt a kinship with this little white haired man in the spectacles.

DeVille saw the softness overtake Erik's face and the water that sprang briefly in his eyes then disappeared. "I will not withdraw my friendship from you, Erik. I make this solemn promise to you – only death shall part us. We will analyze these matters slowly, cautiously, so as not to injure your noble heart. We shall cause the least amount of pain possible to everyone involved."

"You don't know me."

"Give a man a chance to learn. I might surprise you. You are constantly surprising me!" He gave a playful pat to Erik's knee. "I am certain of at least one interesting fact. You promised to sing for me this afternoon, and I am most anxious to finally hear you. Come let's go to my piano in the parlor. I'm holding you to your word. Do you know the range of your voice?"

"To be honest, I do not. Every change in pitch or intonation I attempt seems attainable."

"You may well be the personification of verbal enchantment walking among us! The timbre in your natural voice is, and of itself, most pleasing. I enjoy listening to it very much. What piece have you chosen, dear boy?"

"I prepared a surprise for you, Abraham, the initial service for *Yom Kippur.* You are going to hear *Kol Nidre* in a fashion befitting the reticent soul, halted mid-journey by the sudden, sure knowledge of the radiant existence of God. Apprehension turned to wonder, then laid bare to love. I have researched the meaning of this prayer. The Jews are quite an interesting people."

An hour later, Abraham DeVille sat in his parlor and liberated a grief he'd held inside for forty years. Blessed at last with the courage to rip open the doors of self-censure, he mourned for a loss that had changed his entire life. He wept with the abandon of an innocent child, without resistance. Rivers of heartache welled up from within him, washing, healing – fracturing their containment and surrendering him to pure, cleansing emotion. As the physician's frail body shook in the spasms of grief, an unquestioning Erik compassionately held his new friend.

In a corner of the room, an unseen angel went to its knees in reverence and admiration. This had become sacred ground. With Abraham's release, the die was cast at last.

21 *EMANCIPATING GRACE*

Havoc seemed to be on vacation in Erik's mind. He felt none of the destructive effects waged by self-doubt; in truth, he was almost jovial. Creative ideas flashed in his head like pictures, and he hastened to jot down notes and outlines on paper to capture them. Barely given time to reap the benefits of Dr. DeVille's treatment, Erik was summoned to Louisa's kitchen table the following morning for a serious discussion. After ten minutes of mental tug-of-war he needed a break and raised his hand for intermission. He stretched out his arms and rubbed his temples to ease his head, which actually hurt from their topic of conversation. To achieve a further moment's interlude, he cracked his knuckles – playfully distracting her.

Unhinged, Madame Giry rolled her eyes and pleaded, "Please, don't do that!"

"Life was easier in the caves beneath the Opera House."

"This is a new day, a new life…without caves."

"I guess if I could kidnap Christine, I could steal a little girl, but where would we put her?"

"Thomas says…"

"It's 'Thomas' these days?"

"Erik! Detective Edwards says the situation is deteriorating badly at the Rupae's and he needs to remove her as quickly as possible. We would only have her for a short while, probably a couple of weeks."

"What if she turns out to be a spitfire, Louisa? Have you scrubbed and polished that possibility until you're satisfied?"

"I've worked with little girls my whole life, I think I can handle one six year old. I'll keep her close to me. You move up and down the house through the passageways. She won't even know you're here."

"What about the money that keeps going to those women for her care?"

"I'll tell the detective to meet the courier and send him back to the bank. The bank will notify Toussaint, who will notify his client, and so on and so forth. We'll let that part play out naturally."

Erik looked at her sympathetically. "You are a sucker for castoffs, you know that?" He slapped the table with his open hand. "But thank God you are!"

"You know, I ask very little of you."

"All right, tell Edwards when he picks up Kate to bring Grace here until he can stumble upon where she rightfully belongs."

"Move one of the smaller beds into my room and place it beside mine."

"Consider it done, Madame! Your wish is my command!"

That afternoon, Raoul and Christine received the Baron and Baroness de Castelot-Barbezac into the office at the chateau. After greetings were exchanged, Christine indicated to Vincent that they should leave, and the two excused themselves. Christine said she wanted to go to the family cemetery and leave flowers at Philippe's grave. Vincent in turn, announced he'd go to the library and set about composing the rough drafts for letters of payment. When they left, Raoul asked if he could call for refreshments. Meg and Jean graciously declined.

Jean spoke first, "We are prepared to meet you at the bank tomorrow and transfer funds into your account. What sum do you need initially, and what will you require on a monthly basis to help you ride through this?"

Raoul wrote some numbers on a piece of paper and slid it across the desk to them. "I will not forget this. You're saving my business, and will have my loyal friendship for life. I swear it. Also, I promise to keep you constantly apprised of the financial situation as it evolves."

Neither Jean nor Meg showed any reaction to the amounts they read on the paper before them. Meg simply stated, "You should have asked sooner."

Humorless, Raoul responded, "I had no desire to tie myself financially to Christine's friends, or to make myself a burden. This is only for a short period, six to twelve months at the most. We'll work very hard to become solvent."

Jean spoke next, "It's a little late for so much pride isn't it? Besides, you should trust the discretion of those who truly hold your best interests at heart, Raoul."

"You're right, I am very grateful. This is not easy for me, thank you for not being repulsed by my words."

Sensing that his sincerity was transient, Meg interjected, "Your benefactor wishes to help carry the loans for you to prevent foreclosures of any kind."

Jean explained further, "We are not your benefactor, we're only the agents. Your benefactor wishes you to know that you are most welcomed."

Meg asked, "Do you want to know the identity of your true benefactor?" Raoul did not answer, only studied her face, perhaps to read there the name of the generous person bailing him out of difficulty. Meg weighed the risks and elected to press glue onto his overbearing expression. "Do you believe that to love a thing can trap you into the service of others?"

Raoul responded, "I do not understand your meaning."

Meg elaborated in a condescending tone. "Well, a priest may ardently love the doctrines of the church, or a rabbi the teachings of the holy books, but to embrace their positions as leaders in their communities, they have to accept their congregants and their congregants' foibles, as part of the package."

"Oh, I see, and what does this have to do with me?" Raoul asked pensively.

Jean taunted him. "Your benefactor finds himself in a similar position. Loving a thing and having to take care of the trappings that come attached to it."

Raoul bristled and shoved his chair back from his desk, warning them, "Be careful not to push me too far."

Jean's eyes smiled at Meg, mentally handing the prod back to her. "Have we gone too far, Raoul? Have we? Actually, we think we haven't carried this quite far enough. You have no idea of the great generosity and unselfishness that lies beyond this gift. You should only hope to match even the smallest measure of it."

"Indeed, well that would be a high aspiration to set for myself, wouldn't it?" Raoul was puzzled and suspected that either their mysterious allusions were a joke, or they were making fun of him. At any rate, his arrogance would not let him proceed further into the subject without trying to be the aggressor. "If my benefactor has not the stomach to bring me these funds face to face, then I have not the inclination to confront him either. Perhaps we should end here. I need to retire. This is a damn humiliating experience for me."

Jean and Meg rose. Looking down at the Count, Jean reached across the desk and offered no apologies for pushing Raoul's aristocratic buttons. "We'll meet you at the *Banque de France* in the morning. Will you be rested by ten o'clock?"

Insulted, but with his anger successfully repressed, Raoul stood as well and shook Jean's hand. "Thank you, and who will be listed on the documents as the lender?"

Meg's reply was curt. "We will be listed as the agents for an anonymous source, known to us alone."

When the Baron and Baroness were settled in their carriage and headed off the estate, Jean took his wife's delicate lace-gloved fingers and brought them to his lips. "How did I ever get so lucky as to have one as beautiful and as loyal as you, to grace my side as a partner."

Meg blushed deeply. "Let's just hope these risks pay off." She leaned over and snuggled next to her husband as the driver picked up the pace.

At the de Chagny cemetery, Christine sat on a stone bench considering the location of the graves. Surrounded by the grandeur of the mature trees she prayed for guidance and a resolution to her schemes. She reached down, running her hand across the tops of the wild grass surrounding her, willing her cares to leave for a while. "Take them from me, angels, they seem impressively heavy right now."

The incandescent, luminous pear-shape of her dream appeared before her at eye level. Once again its substance elongated and the same glittering celestial figure floated above the ground.

"Am I awake or asleep?"

"Which do you prefer?" asked the gentle being without opening its mouth.

"Let's pretend I'm asleep."

The golden apparition with the almond eyes and ear length curls inclined its head, almost playfully. "And so you are."

"Who are you?"

"Menachem, the Comforter. I was created when the first form of grief was experienced on this planet."

"That must have been some time ago, we're a sorrowful place."

"Eons, by creatures totally dissimilar from those here at the present."

"I've noticed that your comfort comes packaged in an alarming box of vexation. To what do I owe the honor of your presence?"

"You just called me. All things suffer, Christine – the animals, humans, even God."

"God?"

"The Source suffers because it desires the love of every breathing individual. That longing is the cause of all the worlds. The tension of that suffering brings the very universe into reality and sustains it. The rise and fall of nature's cycles, the birth and death of everything in the sublime organism of the cosmos, was created by the attributes of ultimate love. Even the stones cry out in the glory of it."

"How are they crying out? I don't hear them."

"They're not solid and still, as you believe them to be. They move constantly and sing continually. It's quite beautiful."

Christine reached into her pocket and pulled out a piece of white granite about the size of a small lemon. She carried it upon her person at all times, for it was the stone she'd retrieved from the ground at the boathouse when she told Erik she was pregnant with Michael. "Can I feel what you are describing?" A pleasant tingling sensation filled the palm and fingers of the hand she wrapped around the stone. She regarded Menachem with cheerful gratitude. "Everything is doing this?"

"Yes, everything. You are attuned to the character of it when you listen to the wind, as you often do. We have seen your struggles with The Voice and wish to give you a gift. Will you accept it?"

"There you go again, offering something without me completely comprehending the consequences. All right, I accept."

Menachem moved a hand through the air between them. The sound of laughter filled her ears, a sweet magnetic laughter, a soul truly at peace and happy. The eloquence was unmistakably Erik's. "He will succeed, Christine. This is monumental. His soul will have surmounted a tremendous hurdle. He will love himself exactly as he is, and when he does he will write his greatest piece of music. It will praise God for the creation of life."

"Who is he?"

"The Voice is the outward expression of pure love. It is the fruit of praise born totally of free will."

"Why did he submit to this torturous process?"

"Most of humanity detests itself to some degree, and it was created in love. He fused himself into this curse. He could have taken any other but he chose this one, with its humiliations and shattering rejections. He chose to master self-loathing and return to God the reflection of the love he was created in."

"What should I do next, Menachem? I need guidance."

"Stay strong. Hatred is about to compress you tightly. Remind The Voice that a name is only a form of address."

"A name is only a form of address," she repeated. "When should I tell him?"

A flock of migratory ducks flew overhead and Christine looked to the sky.

Menachem was gone. Instinctively she knew she'd never see him again, but his answer came on the wind. "You will know."

The exotic smell of lilies surrounded her. She walked back to the chateau comforted, but no closer to the answers than before she found the scroll. Reluctantly she acknowledged that events were now transpiring well beyond whatever control she could exert.

At the ballet studio the front door ringer made a melodious chime to summon the mistress of the house, and Madame Giry hastened to answer it. She opened the door with a broad flourish and a smile. There stood Detective Edwards with a little girl in a dirty brown dress and a tattered plaid wool coat. Her shoes were too small and too tight for her growing feet. The backs of the pumps had been pushed inward and flattened so that her heels, in mismatched socks, extended out past the leather. A waif in a pair of self manufactured clogs. The child held the detective's hand and kept her head bowed low, her chin touching her chest. Despite the cold she had nothing on her head of blonde hair and wore no gloves.

Louisa bent her knees to bring her face to the level of the little girl's, but was still required to address only the top of her head. "Hello, Grace, I am Madame Giry, welcome to my home. Would you like to come upstairs and see where I live?"

Grace did not respond, so the detective answered, "She's a little shy. Come on, Grace, let's go see where Madame lives." The three walked upstairs, and as they entered the apartment the smell of cinnamon *Madelines* filled the air.

Grace's pale, little face finally lifted upwards when Madame said, "I just took the *Madelines* from the oven, but I have no one to help me eat them. Maybe you could help me, Grace."

The timid child stole a glance at the person speaking to her. Her first impression of Madame Giry was that she was being offered cakes by an angel with a long blonde braid encircling her head, like a halo. She tried to hide her dirty clothes by bringing her arms up over her chest and shuffling her feet behind her. Her ears and fingers were frigid, blue with cold, but the kitchen was warm and smelled so good.

Madame watched her closely and tried to interpret the signals she was giving. "Grace, come stand with me by the stove. I'm a bit chilled and want to warm up before we eat the *Madelines*." Grace left the detective and moved to Madame's skirt. They went to the oven together and Madame put out her hands, warming her fingers. Grace stayed close to Madame's legs and put her hands out too. "Detective Edwards, can you pour us some cider? It's there on the table. We'll be ready for sweets in a minute, I think."

The detective had been watching Madame with the young girl and thought he had made a good choice for them both. When they sat down to eat their snack, Madame told them that afterwards she would show Grace where she was going to sleep, and that tomorrow she would take her shopping for some pretty new clothes. Grace still had not spoken. Her little eyes seemed dull and alarmingly distant as she ate the creamy *petite* cakes. A concerned Madame considered what activities might best help this frail guest acclimate to her new surroundings. *Dear child, what have they done to you, what have they done?*

When the detective prepared to leave, he took Madame's right hand into both of his and thanked her sincerely for her kindness and hospitality. He told her he would go directly to the bank in the morning and tell them that the courier needed to bring the envelopes with Grace's funds to this house until notified differently. Madame deemed it ironic and humorous that the monies were now coming full circle. After the detective left, she took Grace to her bed and cuddled her, deciding not to give her a bath right away, but rather to tell her a story about an Angel of Music that sometimes visits little children and sings to them to help them fall asleep.

22 FOOLISH BETRAYAL

Erik held the practical belief that every day on the calendar could not be exceptional. The myriad of daily occupations demanding one's attention in order to just live, naturally dictated that the mundane be addressed and cared for most of the time. Nevertheless, the events of the following day proved to be such remarkable turning points, such precise pivotal juxtapositions of Fate, that they earned the accolade 'extraordinary'. He remembered their bitterness, and their sanguine sweetness, all the rest of his life.

Madame Giry, who had been slowly paring down the size of her classes through attrition, sent word to her remaining students that sessions for the rest of the week were canceled due to urgent personal business. Classes would resume on the following Tuesday. She and Grace were up early for bathing and primping before proceeding to the dressmakers and the cobblers.

As the doors of the *Banque de France* opened for business, Detective Edwards went inside the prestigious establishment to explain that the funds designated for Grace DesJardins should be sent to the address where she currently resided under the care of Madame Giry. He presented his appropriately doctored documents, proving to them that Grace was now under his direct supervision. The bank's managers promptly sent a courier to the offices of Monsieur Pierre Toussaint. The latter hastened to the financial institution to personally instruct its officers regarding his anonymous client's wishes in light of these new circumstances.

Meg, Jean and Raoul met at ten o'clock outside the *Banque de France* and entered into the richly marbled, gilt-edged lobby together. Jean was immediately handed a sealed envelope from Monsieur Toussaint's assistant, letting him know that as agreed, Toussaint was on the premises should he be needed. Jean slipped the letter into his pocket, explaining to his wife and Raoul, "I am told that the account is already set up and only needs for us to address the paper work." They proceeded to the desk of a manager in the new accounts department.

Erik also rose early and after dressing himself as an affluent businessman, with an appropriately applied new face and beard, picked up Dr. DeVille. These two planned to present themselves at the Opera House as potential patrons and get a tour of the opera's structure. During the tour they intended to slip away and in the labyrinth beneath the opera's cellars, hold a session in the Phantom's former domicile. Only Christine was at home, practicing her harpsichord music and awaiting the arrival of Benjamin DeVille for a lesson.

All their strategies seemed to be unfolding as each of them had anticipated, but Fate is a wily bandit, ever prepared to ensnare the most well thought out plans and rob them of good fortune. About twelve o'clock, a middle-aged man with a graying mustache arrived at the front door of the ballet studio. He had the driver of the carriage deposit his suitcase and trunk on the porch, took his fedora hat into his hand, dusted off his jacket and rang the bell. No one responded. After several rings he walked around to the back of the house, but could find no obvious indication that anyone was about. Puzzled that all seemed closed and locked during business hours, he returned to the front and sat down on his trunk, where he contemplated his next move. Despite his dignified demeanor, he could not help but laugh at the predicament he found himself in. He had hoped to surprise Louisa, but it appeared that the surprise was on him. Chagrined, he folded his arms across his chest and thoughtfully stroked his mustache.

The neighbors across the street noticed the gentleman sitting on the ballet studio's porch and went over to inquire if he needed Madame Giry. Relieved to be addressing actual people, he asked if they knew her whereabouts. Regrettably, they did not, but invited him into their home. Apologizing profusely for its topsy-turvy state, they explained that they were in the process of moving. From their parlor he could watch the ballet studio's front door, and at least be out of the bleak November weather. They were certain that Madame Giry would return soon. The stranger gladly accepted their gracious offer and introduced himself as Imel Grey.

When Christine finished her lesson with Benjamin, they took some coffee and chatted in the salon for a while. They laughed when she remarked that she'd been studying with him for two years, except of course, for the period of her 'internment' with Ariel. Benjamin told her that she played quite well; he was delighted to teach such a diligent student. She gave him a present, two tickets to Friday's performance of 'Tristan and Isolde' at the Opera House, and he thanked her. After he left she mentally resolved to save some money by postponing further lessons. *I'll speak with Raoul and write Benjamin a letter in the morning.*

She went upstairs and was with the boys when Raoul returned to the chateau. In spite of the fact that he had been given a financial reprieve, he seemed irritable and asked to speak with her alone. Since they were just down the hall from her quarters he insisted on ushering her into her own rooms, ignoring her protests that they should talk in private downstairs. Here he could have his way with her, and she could offer little resistance.

Walking over to the front windows, where the afternoon sunlight was best, Christine started to pull two chairs forward. With her back to him she inquired, "How did everything go at the bank?"

"It went well, no inconveniences whatsoever. We don't have any payments for six months, which is really most generous, actually too generous." She went to sit down and he stepped forward. Putting his hands on her shoulders, he forced her to turn toward him. He searched her eyes carefully, and although he felt her muscles tensing, he noted that she openly returned his gaze without attempting to shield herself from scrutiny.

Christine marveled that the touch of two men who both loved her could be so decidedly different. Raoul held her like he owned her. She was a possession he could physically handle whenever he wanted, an adornment to proudly display in public, but she believed that in his heart he worshiped her. Erik's touch was also firm but he enticed and cajoled, coaxing patiently until she responded to him. Erik's forbearance fueled her desires, provocatively driving her instincts until she churned with hunger, craving ecstasy with their bodies joined together. Erik was the artist and Raoul the well outfitted hunter. *Only experience could have shown me the truth of this.*

Raoul watched her eyes glass over in thoughts far removed from him. Annoyed, he shook her a little. "Christine, what was really happening in the woods with that statue of Anubis? How did you get him out of there? There are no impressions from a cart or footprints around the pond, no indications that anyone was there at all. Not even my footprints from when I found you singing to it." He felt her become completely rigid and he tightened his hold.

She saw jealousy and anger dance in his eyes and tried to rotate away from him. "Raoul, let me sit down. Why did you go back there? You promised you wouldn't. The statue is gone, that's all that matters, isn't it?"

"Do you still love me, Christine? Because if you do, you'd understand why that's not all that matters. Were you alone out there?" He insisted she answer by pressing his thumbs into her shoulders.

The pain was instantaneous. "You're hurting me! You are my husband and I respect you. Let me sit down, please. I want to talk to you about Benjamin."

He released his grip and she went again to sit. In a wellspring of rage, he roughly pulled her arms and kept her standing. "You haven't answered me. Tell me the truth. Who do you really love, Christine?"

Her face grew red with anger. Raoul ached for the return of his compliant, depressed little wife – this one looked like she wanted to spit in his face! Her jaw tightened, forcing her words out in a hiss, "I said you're hurting me!"

"Not as much as you're hurting me. Were you alone out there? Give me a straight forward answer for God's sake!"

"All right, I love..."

"Stop! Don't say the name! I don't want to hear it!" He shuddered involuntarily, his mind screaming a warning that he was about to hear his greatest fear spoken outloud.

In the terror of suspecting she might say 'Erik' he suddenly let go of her. Christine had been pulling so hard to gain her release that she was caught off guard. Her own body weight threw her to the floor. Her bottom missed the seat of the chair behind her, but her head did not. A loud crack issued forth into the room as the decorative wood and her skull made contact.

Raoul seemed not to care. "You've gone too far. This is more than a man can take! I thought I could put up with all this, but I can't." She came to her feet and his hand reached forward like a claw ready to tear into her, but he froze for a second and then retracted it. "You have broken me in two, Christine. You're a harlot! I don't want to know who it is that has your heart. I'd have to kill him." He started to walk back and forth, his hands knotting and re-knotting into tight fists.

She sat down quietly in one of the chairs and rubbed the back of her head, thinking to let him rage on until he was calm again. Before she'd hit the floor, she was about to wickedly declare that she loved him, but he'd stopped her. *Maybe it's best to just stay silent.*

His face was contorted and set. His chest heaved dramatically, giving the appearance that he would explode if he didn't submit to the anger laying siege to his brain. "No, let's not speak the demon's name. That odious, murderous name! It belongs in the grave, so let it reside in hellish silence for the time being."

The ranting paused and he came to a stop in front of her. She hardly recognized the menacing individual towering over her head. With his teeth clenched and his broad shoulders hunched, he'd spread his fingers apart like fiendish talons and looked like a vulture. *You're the demon, Raoul. Go! Leave!* She tried not to cower. "You need to focus on your finances right now. I'm sorry if my games caused you pain, I'll be more careful not to intrude upon your hunting."

Her flippant talk of intrusion blistered him. "It's been four-and-a-half years since I took you from that Opera House. In all that time I never heard you sing to me like you sang in those woods…to a statue. A statue of death! Your voice was mesmerizing, angelic. I was enthralled by its richness. You sounded exactly like him, only feminine, yet masculine too." He put his hands to his temples. "Oh my God, I'm becoming irrational. The only person who could have possibly brought Christine Daae to sing in adoration to Anubis is gone, dead, decomposing in unhallowed ground."

His bitter denunciation halted for a second as an idea dawned in his brain. "You've created a substitute for him, haven't you? It's the only way you'd ever let someone other than me touch you. I know it."

Fear started inching up inside her. She pushed it back down into her gut, realizing that she might not be able to control his fury. How did he know someone else had touched her? This abusive deluge wasn't going to play itself out and defuse as she had hoped. "Raoul, you are being truly absurd. Really, you're working yourself up over nothing."

He sarcastically whined her own words back at her, "Raoul, you're being absurd, truly absurd!" Growling something incoherent, he stepped forward and jerked her back to her feet. "You cheap little prostitute! You're a damn, filthy liar!" With his right hand he slapped her face so hard the impact flung her back into the chair. Hair pins flew off her head in every direction, letting her brown curls tumble in disarray. Reeling from the blow, her hand went to comfort the stinging skin. Hot tears spilled uncontrolled over her cheeks. In her entire life she had never been struck like that. Stunned by the fierceness of the slap, she had no reaction but tears.

Raoul spun on the ball of his foot, the back of his arms swinging behind him, casting her off as he stormed from the room. "Don't move! Stay right there, Christine. I'll be right back."

In a few minutes he returned with a decanter of American bourbon and a crystal glass. Acknowledging the red handprint on her face with a dispassionate lift of the container, he sat down on the edge of the bed. He filled the glass with liquor, drained the contents, and refilled the glass again before he spoke. "The cat is out of the bag, Christine! So let's see. Is it little Benjamin DeVille? No, I think not. He adores music but he's too oriented toward family. He'd love to have children, but he'd want to raise them for himself. Family does seem to mean something to those Jews. So who is it, and where does my precious little strumpet meet with her lover?" His tone was barbarous, demeaning. "Here, Christine, do you two fornicate here?" His arm gestured across her bed. "No, not here, that's a bit too bold. Justine might see and come tell me."

He rotated the glass back and forth in his hand studying the hue of the alcohol before taking another hard swallow. His next words were as effective as another slap across her face. "He doesn't want you to be with him, does he? And you're wondering how I could possibly know that. Curious as hell to learn how I came by that information without a personal consultation with the Grand High Lord of Perdition. I know he doesn't want you because in two years he hasn't ventured to the front door to claim you! Whoever beds you, should have made you his when you became pregnant with Michael, but he didn't...and I understand why." The whiskey warmed him. It seemed to Raoul that he was thinking rather clearly. "God, it's good to have the truth out in the open, isn't it?" He kissed the side of the crystal, raised it in a salute and finished off the second glass of whiskey.

"You don't understand anything, Raoul. I want to take the boys and go to Meg's until you calm down."

"My contemptuous slut, whose own lover doesn't want her, you're not going anywhere, not ever again. It's time you learned submission. You're going to do exactly what I require of you, any time and every time that I tell you to do it." He spread out his arms for emphasis and pronounced each word distinctly. "School is in, Christine, and I am the head master! Michael and Ariel are staying here with me. Those boys are my heirs, the key to continuing the de Chagny line."

Christine's cheek still smarted from his blow. His words about Erik not coming to claim her chilled her veins like icy poison. She understood the pit Erik was attempting to claw his way out of to have a life with her, the sacrifice he was undertaking by laying his soul bare to Abraham. Hatred for Raoul's hubris shot through her like an army waging war. Her better judgment told her to keep her mouth shut, but the thought that Raoul would imprison her in this chateau away from Erik forever, caused her next words to spew forth with more anger than she'd ever known.

"The de Chagny line, the de Chagny line! Yes, let's talk about that line. They are not your sons, Raoul. Do you hear me? Not your sons! Someone better than you has been inside me. I have betrayed you with another!"

With all his strength he threw his empty glass at her head, it broke into a singing spray of tiny crystal shards on the wall behind her. In a flash he was up and took her by the throat, lifting her off her feet, pressing her into the wall where the glass had just shattered. Her face took on a bluish tint, but she heard his next words quite clearly. "Betrayal! You think you can teach me about betrayal. You whore!"

With primitive certainty she knew that he was about to kill her. Her last spoken words on this earth would be the unsatisfying revenge of her confessed adultery. In her mind she whispered good-bye to Michael and Ariel. *Have a good life my babies. Grow tall.* She started to loose consciousness.

Raoul studied her cyanosis with the calculated control of a skilled hunter. His fingers loosened their hold on her carotid arteries allowing blood to return to her brain, but he continued to keep her pinned. He let her slender body slide slowly down the wall until her feet rested on the floor. When he felt her stand on her own weight, even though her eyes were closed, he knew she was conscious and able to hear him. He breathed his next words into her right ear like a non-penitent teenager dragged to the confessional by his mother.

"I know the boys are not my biological heirs!"

One of his hands squeezed her shoulder tightly while the other still held her throat. She pictured her dagger in the bedside drawer but knew that Raoul was too strong for her to break free. Erik's words played in her head. *Don't push him! He's not the lamb you think he is.* She resolved to survive this, if it were possible, by yielding to whatever was about to come. She was thinking of ways to sneak away from him later, but the significance of the next words he carefully placed into her ear shocked her brain into stillness.

"When I was thirteen, I contracted German measles. I was very ill for over a month. In the fever, my testicles became swollen and terribly painful. The physicians told Philippe that in all likelihood I had lost the ability to father children of my own. You see...a bout of German measles can cause sterility in an adolescent boy, particularly if he's unfortunate enough to be as sick as I was. Oh, the swelling recedes and the boy can maintain an erection, but his ejaculate is lifeless. When you didn't become pregnant in the first two years of our marriage, I knew the doctors' prediction was true. Especially since I couldn't get enough of you, even in that near stuporous state of yours. No, it wasn't for a lack of healthy enthusiasm on my part. I tried to tell you before our marriage, and I wanted to tell you after the wedding, but I could never muster the courage. I thought you would believe me wicked for letting you think we could have a family. In your dismal depression I berated myself almost daily, and then you miraculously started to become happy again. When you told me you were pregnant I knew you'd taken a lover. I waited for you to leave with the man. I even took extra trips out of the country to give you ample opportunity, but you didn't go! So I asked myself what could possibly be the reason you didn't leave. A woman's calculations must have told you I wasn't the father."

He put his knee between her legs forcing them to separate, and then brought his other knee in to join the first. Letting go of her shoulder, he grabbed at her skirt, pushing the folds up to her waist. "Either you didn't know the father, which I doubted, or the father didn't want you." He pinched the crotch of her underwear and ripped it.

She opened her eyes and stared out into her bedroom. The winter sun had set. They stood in rapidly advancing darkness. Raoul's hair appeared silver, not blonde, in the corner of her vision, and the smell of liquor nauseated her. He pushed his fingers into her. Her eyes went big and round, and he suddenly pulled his hand away.

"Madame, your heart may be saying no, but your body is saying something else entirely." Still holding her throat he started to unfasten his trousers. She tried to move one of her legs back in between his to make it difficult for him. "Oh no, what is this? My little tramp still has more fight in her? I like that, yes I do." He released her throat completely and stepped to the side of her to avoid her legs as she began to thrash. Taking her by the hair, he hauled her toward the bed. She let out a scream and tried to pry his hands off. Turning slightly, he punched her in the face. As her knees turned to liquid, he threw her like a doll onto the bed. With her back on the mattress her strength returned, she kicked viciously at him and missed. In a panic she tried to scoot backwards to the other side of the bed and get away.

Feeding on her fear, he tore angrily at her bodice and like an animal bit her on the upper part of her breast. She reached to scratch his eyes, but he took both her hands and savagely pulled her arms above her head. Holding her wrists with his left hand, he punched her solidly in the chest. With the stab of the blow, air rushed from her lungs. The next inhalation was too painful to attempt. She stopped struggling. He bit her, equally as hard, on the other breast. "These are mine, you know. Given to me by our wedding vows, and by default from your cowardly paramour because he won't show his face to protect you."

Something snapped. She became passive, a stone. The eyes she turned to the bedroom window were emotionless and dead – dead like her father. Her tears dried on her cheeks.

He finished with her and got off. Removing the rest of his clothes, he sat naked in one of the chairs drinking bourbon straight from the decanter. He felt no shame over what he had done. Instead, he congratulated himself for finally speaking the truth, rationalizing that she deserved this treatment. After all she'd certainly earned it! It was good to have her finally put in her place. He'd raise those two beautiful boys and make sure her lover never got anywhere near her again. *I am the head of this house and I control the situations within it.* Patiently he waited for his sexual prowess to return, he would take her again and continue to do so for as long as he liked.

Impervious to her state, he eyed her as she rolled to her side and hesitantly pulled herself into a sitting position. He sneered as she carefully covered herself with her torn clothing. Since he had no desire to hear her conjure up any objection to his new demands, he decided to dictate more rules. He pointed his long index finger at her. "You will never leave this chateau. Consider yourself confined. You will let me have you anytime I wish it, and you'll do any sexual thing I capriciously demand. Out of the kindness of my heart, I'm going to tell you why you're going to submit to this. Because if you don't, I'll go down whatever snake hole this man who has fornicated with you hides in. I'll expose him as an adulterer and then I'll kill him. And if by some curse out of hell, it turns out to be your precious ghost... Well let's just say he has a great deal to loose, doesn't he! So the boys are mine, and you are mine, exclusively."

He took his relaxed sentinel in his hands and openly started to fondle himself, pleased that it responded by growing long and hard again. Christine studied him and hugged her knees to her chest. When she went to speak her voice was hoarse from the chokehold he'd placed on her.

"Don't you think it's strange, Raoul, that in relationships we often end up loving what we initially hated, and hate what we impetuously loved?"

"You're talking nonsense." He admired his erection and stood up with his side toward her to display his fine achievement.

The genuine disdain on her face, the defiant way she tightened her arms around her bent legs, maddened him. The last shred of his patience evaporated. He stomped the few feet to the bed, but this time it was her turn to deliver the verbal slap. "Sit down, Raoul. I have Jacob Klein's scroll." He stopped abruptly, like a toy soldier in need of being rewound to move its arms and legs. "I know your family's history and if I take the parchment to the authorities you'll forfeit your lands and your title."

Disbelief flash flooded into anger. *How had she gotten into the safe?* He yanked her by the hair. Ignoring her screams, he punched her in the jaw. She fell back onto the bed dazed, her lip bleeding where his crested ring had just sliced it. "Give me the scroll, Christine, or I'll really hurt you! You have no idea how much pain I can inflict! My family built this place!"

"I don't care if you loose everything, Raoul!"

He pounced on her as she tried to leap from the bed, and sat on her lower abdomen. Safe from the legs she kicked unsuccessfully into the air behind him. Holding her wrists down onto the mattress, he hollered, "You're a part of this, too! You married me at the altar before God Himself."

"Then I take it back! I take it all back. Do you hear me? I'm not yours! I don't want you!"

"Give me the scroll, Christine!"

"No, I hate you!"

The servants heard the more vocal parts of the heated argument going on between their employers, but because of the thickness of the walls and doors no one was sure of the content of the disagreement. The entire house grew tense and still as the servants whispered hushed sentences to each other, trying to define for themselves what duties to perform. The cooks did not bring the evening meal into the butler's pantry, although the table in the dining room was set and ready for use. For a time, the butlers waited in the kitchen with the cooks and the rest of the staff. The two nannies took their supper to the nursery and kept the boys close together. Around seven o'clock, everyone still congregating in the kitchen, agreed that should they be needed, they could be readily summoned. So they retreated to their quarters and closed their doors, hoping for the storm to pass and all to return to normal.

At eight o'clock, Christine regained consciousness and opened her right eye. The left was swollen shut. She lay flat on her bed with Raoul passed out on his stomach beside her. His arm lay possessively across her chest, with his hand resting on her throat. She marshaled what courage she could, steeling herself for what had to be done. Dizzy but not disoriented, she gently slid herself out from beneath his arm. Ignoring the grinding pain in her head, she got to the bathroom. Carefully she washed the blood off her face, and surveyed the slit in her lip, the black eye, and the other bruises she saw looking back at her. Pulling her hair back, she fastened it with some combs, and dressed in her riding clothes inside her closet. She hurried to the attic as quickly as her aching head would allow. After retrieving the money she had hidden there, she quietly proceeded to the nursery and found the nannies dozing in rocking chairs, holding her babies.

Horrified at her swollen battered face, the women wanted to get compresses for her, but she silenced them both and threw some things in a basket for the boys. She told one of the women to call for a carriage to be brought around to the back of the house. Christine and the other nanny crept downstairs, carrying the two sleeping boys through the kitchen. As she waited by the kitchen door, she remembered the signal she was supposed to use to alert Erik, should she need to urgently leave the house. But nothing, not even Erik, could entice her to re-enter her room and risk waking Raoul, just to put a candelabrum in the bedroom window. That plan was formed before she had two children in her charge. *Perhaps its better this way, I'll just go.* When the carriage came up she hugged the nannies, and the driver helped her to get settled inside with the boys. They left the mansion at a sedate walk, trying to be as soundless as possible. One of Christine's hands was on the two boys asleep on the seat, the other clutched the dagger tucked into the sash around her waist. If Raoul chased after her on horseback, he'd come away with a nasty scar. She was an odd mixture of defiance and regret as they entered the public road on their way to the Castelot-Barbezac estate.

Earlier, when Madame Giry returned from shopping with Grace, she stepped from her carriage to find a large trunk and a suitcase on her front porch. She managed to maneuver around the items, despite the child tucked into her skirts. Opening the front door, she instructed the driver to put her packages inside the foyer. Holding on to the clinging child, Louisa went directly to the trunk and turned over its tags. She stood straight up with a start when she read the carefully written words:

Imel Grey, Boston, Massachusetts,
USA to Paris, France.

Frantically her eyes searched from doorway to doorway up and down the street. Emerging from the house across the road, and coming straight toward her, was a man with deeply speckled gray hair, her mother's deep blue eyes and a broad grin of relief on his face. Her chest sank.

The newcomer marched up the flagstone steps and gave her a bear hug. "Louisa!"

"Imel! My goodness! Imel! How many years has it been?"

"Thirty years, Louisa, thirty. You were ten when I left for America, and you know something? You haven't changed a bit! You're still that cute little girl, just taller, and who is this precious little one folded inside your clothes?"

A flattered but flustered Madame Giry responded, "Imel, let's step inside out of the breeze. This is Grace DesJardins."

Imel reached down and took the child's hand. "*Enchante*, Mademoiselle." He placed a little kiss upon her mitten, but Grace quickly withdrew her hand and hid her face in Madame's skirt.

"She's shy, Imel. She just arrived yesterday to stay with me for a while. We've been out shopping and having great fun. Haven't we, Grace?" Grace only burrowed deeper into the clothes of her hostess. "Can you stay with us for a visit, Imel? We have so much to catch up on. There are some pressing matters I need to explain to you. I live on the second floor and there is an unoccupied bedroom we'll set up for you."

"Louisa, that is most gracious of you. I'm sure we have many stories to share with each other. Let me cross the street and see if one of the boys at your neighbor's will help me bring up the trunk. The suitcase I can handle by myself."

As the Phantom returned to the house, he was exceptionally pleased that his little excursion with Dr. DeVille had gone so well. The good doctor now understood just about all there was to know of Erik's life in Paris, including the murders he'd committed and the accidental death of Raoul's elder brother, Philippe. Sitting together in the parlor area of the subterranean house, like two henchmen, Erik had described the bizarre, seesaw relationship he'd had with Christine in the recesses of the theater, how his face and emotional intensities had frightened her. In early '71, when he overheard her agree to elope with Raoul, he abducted her and coerced her into agreeing to be his bride. Without disclosing his reasons for changing his mind, he simply told DeVille that he'd recanted and freed the girl to be with her suitor. He stayed for a few more weeks in the caverns and after faking his death, moved to the house he and Louisa had prepared as an escape.

He had no direct contact with Christine until the fall of '73, when she had miraculously confessed that she wanted him. Leaving no room for pathos, Erik explained to DeVille that he was subject to almost uncontrollable bouts of temper and depression. To safeguard Christine's welfare, he had insisted she remain a de Chagny. And although these bouts had become somewhat easier to manage, he was still quite capable of murder, if he, or someone he loved, were threatened.

DeVille had absorbed all this information like a sea sponge. He had reminded Erik that some people go through life without ever experiencing the love of a true heart. Apparently there was an entire ensemble that cared so much for the Phantom they were willing to risk everything to assist him. Erik had asked the doctor to list them and DeVille happily complied. "Madame Giry, Christine, the Daroga (who I have yet to meet), Meg and Jean. Each of them loves you and can be counted on as a most loyal friend, Erik. And there is still another that I did not mention."

"Who, doctor?"

"Why me, of course! Dear boy...me!"

Erik came up the back alley after checking the street, as was his custom, and noted suspiciously that every light on Louisa's floor was lit and all her drapes were open. He was certain that something was amiss. He entered the carriage house cautiously, concealed by a cloud of gray smoke, and stealthfully gained access to the trapdoor in the floor at the back. Once inside, he traversed the tunnel into the basement of the house, entered the passageway leading to the upper levels and climbed immediately to the second floor. He paused to remove his cloak and made himself comfortable inside the wall between Louisa's kitchen and her living room. Through a peephole in the wood of a picture frame he saw four people at her kitchen table: Louisa, the Daroga, little Grace (who still hadn't uttered a word that he had heard of), and a stranger with a kind, jovial smile. Something about the stranger's eyes and mouth, his manner of speaking without hand gestures seemed familiar, and then he heard Louisa call him Imel. *Imel? Imel! Holy fireballs from Zeus' butt...Imel!* The Phantom used his ventriloquist skills to make the sound of something crashing in the living room.

A startled Imel exclaimed, "Good God, what on earth is that?"

The Daroga leaned back in his chair and shot a knowing glance at Louisa, who was already on her feet. "It's probably my vase. Sometimes it topples over if it's too close to the edge of the table. Khalil, please pour some more coffee for all of us while I check on things."

In the parlor Louisa looked at the Japanese screen and pointed her index finger toward the ceiling. Then she spread all ten fingers out, meaning that she would meet him on the third floor at ten pm.

Later, when Madame entered his apartment she found Erik sitting in a chair with his hands across his abdomen, relaxed and contemplative. She wondered how he could be so placid when her own stomach flipped around in wretched knots. "How was your day?"

"Mine was excellent. I grow fonder and fonder of Dr. DeVille. He's an honorable and interesting man, very accepting of my circumstances. He understands almost all of our history."

"All?"

"Well he doesn't know much about Persia yet, and we've not discussed my parents to any great length. How was your shopping?" Before she could answer, Erik came to his feet and taking Louisa into his arms attempted to dance a few steps with her to some glorious music in his head.

Displeased at his flagrant lack of worry, she pulled at the sleeves of his jacket. "Stop being so gallant. You know very well we have urgent issues to discuss."

"Yes, but I love your dancing, Louisa, always have. You are like a..."

"Delicate willow. Thank you." She stepped out of his arms and curtsied.

He bowed to her. "That may well be the shortest dance I've ever had!" He mimed offering his hand to an imaginary partner and danced a circle around Madame. Then gracefully letting go of even the invisible, he stayed in one spot, turning in a slow, seductive circle as he swung his arms above his head, clicking his fingers. Louisa watched in amazement as a sultry gypsy danced to a romantic, inaudible guitar. His head tipped elegantly forward and a lustrous lock of black hair fell onto the mask. For a moment his entire body tensed and trembled in expressive delight before his head and lissome arms curved backward like branches in a wind. With his back arched and his limber chest lifted toward the ceiling; his hips began to undulate in a dramatic portrayal of passion. From behind him, his hands, with the fingers open and pointed to the floor, moved in circles at the wrists to his outer thighs. Once there, the fingers spiraled downward in sensuous circles, rubbing and caressing. With his elbows bent and the heels of his boots clicking together, he spun around twice, ending with a look of torrid heat. He broke the mood and smiled at her like a boy.

In spite of her frayed nerves, she clapped. "Incredible! I could smell the campfire. Taste the smoke. The guitars were..."

"Latin and vulgar," he tapped his temple, "...and all in my head. The dance is one I watched the carnival gypsies do at their fire camps when I was a child. Did you like it?"

"Oh, yes. You do it magnificently. You could easily make money teaching it. We just have a few minor household problems to take care of before you sign up any students."

"All right, let's pluck this next recontre off the field of battle, and bite it before it bites us. Who is the man downstairs with features so similar to yours?"

"My brother, Imel Grey."

Even this shocking news failed to mar Erik's serenity and he teased her. "That's remarkable. You have a brother, and one with graying hair. I've never known you to keep secrets from me. Where have you been hiding him all these years? Not in a carnival, I hope."

She was in no mood for banter. "How can you be so insufferably calm at a time like this? I really have a half-brother, I just never mentioned him. When I was a little girl he left my parents' home and went to America. He's been in Boston where he indentured himself to a printer. At the end of his apprenticeship he purchased his own printing press and worked as a publisher outside of Boston, in some place called Dorchester. He's a very pleasant fellow, Erik."

"From what I saw, he seems most amiable, but how's he going to feel when he finds out we buried him?"

"I have no idea. None! And I'm open for suggestions. There's no need to sing to Grace tonight. She's exhausted from our shopping and is sound asleep on my bed. The Daroga is entertaining Imel with stories about Persia, so we have time to make a plan."

"Do you need help to move Grace to her own bed?"

"No, I'll just leave her where she is and climb in beside her later. I've decided to let her tell me how to care for her. Right now she's a docile lamb and wants to be cuddled. She still hasn't spoken a word. God only knows what she's been put through."

"It seems we have an abundance of challenges before us. How delightful."

The two sat down in the cushioned chairs to draw out each other's thoughts, just as they had done so many times before. Louisa was about to explain that Imel knew nothing of the current housing situation, when the loud thumping of someone pounding at the front door and simultaneously churning the front door ringer was heard throughout the house. Erik and Louisa leapt to their feet as if their home had suddenly come under attack by the military. Straining to see out the windows, all they could garner was the edge of the front porch and a single horse tethered to their gate. The rider was hidden by the porch's alcove.

A worried Louisa predicted, "This cannot be good."

"Take the Daroga with you to the front door, Louisa. I'll get into the passageway."

23 ODE TO THE MISSING

A harried messenger handed Madame an envelope sealed with the crest of the Baron de Castelot-Barbezac. She and the Daroga went back into the foyer to read its contents while the young man waited beneath the stone arch for further instructions. The cryptic note inside was in Meg's hurried handwriting.

Mama,
Urgent that Jean and I leave immediately with Christine and the boys. Will be in touch with you in a couple of days.
All affection - Meg

Madame Giry went to the messenger and asked, "Do you have any idea where your mistress has gone?"

"No, Madame. I do know that the party left the estate in the common carriage, not one with the Baron's crests."

"Who was in the party?"

"I am not sure, Madame. I was aroused from sleep and ordered by the Baroness herself to bring you this communication." Madame Giry thanked him for coming out so late at night and passed him a franc. As she watched the servant untie his horse and prepare to mount, she said softly to the Daroga. "Get Erik, something is very wrong."

"Which passageway is he in?"

She latched the door and without turning her head pointed to the darkness on the stairs. Khalil's eyes found Erik already in his cloak standing in the shadows above them. The maestro's open hand came silently into the light and Louisa passed him the note.

Erik read Meg's disturbing words. "I'll go straight to the estate and inquire after the direction of their carriage. With any luck I'll be right behind them."

The Daroga stepped forward. "I'll go with you. My driver is waiting down the street with my carriage. Meg's servants are already ruffled, a masked man asking questions in the middle of the night may disquiet them even more." The Phantom nodded.

Madame climbed the stairs with the Daroga close at her heels to fetch his cloak. Louisa's addressed Erik over her shoulder, "Wait, I'll get some money, just in case you need to grease a few wheels."

Ten minutes later the pair disappeared out the back. From a second floor window Imel saw the two figures slip through the metal gate and vanish like vapors into the night. His sister came to his side and whispered to the darkness, "God speed."

Seeing her pensive expression, Imel put his arm around her shoulder. "Can you tell me what's going go, Louisa? Who is the man who left with the Daroga?"

Madame Giry sighed deeply and raised her hands in modest surrender. "I need to take you into my confidence and reveal my most guarded secret. I do not know what has happened this night, but it cannot be good. Without your support we may loose all that we hold most dear."

Her tone evoked a brother's protective feelings. "You have my word, Louisa. I'll keep your secret in strictest trust, and assist you in any way I can."

"The second man is you…and the police think him to be in his grave."

His eyebrows arched in surprise. "You don't say. That's extraordinary." Louisa's expression was one of anguish. He took her two hands in his, rubbing them to encourage her. "I came here hoping to get to know you, and I find myself involved in a most intriguing plot! The gentleman's moving pretty good for someone who's busy decomposing." Like two conspirators, they peered out the window. The night was clear and a half moon shone brightly in the sky. In a low voice Imel remarked, "No doubt it would be better for them if a thick fog would roll in."

"If this is going to be your attitude, dear brother, then I hope we'll not be separated again. Let's check on Grace and then I'll tell you what I've concealed with my ballet career since I was sixteen."

Imel and Louisa waited through the night, expecting any minute to receive some bit of news. At nine in the morning the following telegraph arrived at the house:

> BELIEVE RAOUL PRECIPITANT - STOP - PROCEEDING TO PERROS-GUIREC - STOP - INN OF THE SETTING SUN - STOP - DAROGA

Three afternoons later the Daroga and the Phantom returned from Brittany to the house on *Rue du Renard*. After they entered the basement area through the carriage house tunnel, Khalil went immediately to Louisa and brought her down to Erik. The two men were disheveled and unshaven. They wore the same clothes they'd been in when they departed.

Erik explained that they'd taken great precautions to enter the house unobserved. At their arrival, they'd discovered two men watching the ballet studio from the bottom of the street, and a peevish Detective Edwards observing the two men from a position just across the boulevard. Madame explained that the two were most likely private detectives hired by Raoul. Everyday they had come to the front door inquiring if she'd heard from Meg or Jean. She'd refused to answer them, and was unaware that Detective Edwards was also on active surveillance. She wasn't sure if adding Edwards to the pot made them safer, or put them more at risk.

Surrounded by the security of the basement's granite walls, Erik and the Daroga related the events of the last three days. Thinking that Christine would direct her group to Brittany, where she'd spent her early childhood, they'd searched there but to no avail. The coastal region was near deserted except for the locals, November being an uninviting time of year for vacationing tourists. If a group of people had arrived unexpectedly in the area and requested a house or an apartment to rent, they would have been relatively easy to locate. Erik's face was forlorn as the Daroga listed all the places where they'd made inquiry.

Madame Giry didn't hesitate to express her concern. "You both need food, rest and a bath. Imel is with Grace on the second floor. You can go to the third. Take the stairs. I'll bring a meal to you."

They agreed and a haggard Daroga added, "We need to sit and think. Obviously, Raoul hasn't found our elusive quarry, the continued presence of the detectives outside is proof positive of that."

Erik removed his mask to rub his face and inquired, "How are Grace and Imel?"

"You will be pleasantly surprised at Imel. I have taken him into our trust. Grace, on the other hand, finally spoke and then only to whimper that she misses the Angel of Music. She wants to know how to find him because she's been praying and he doesn't come."

Erik managed a very weary smile. "Ah, the missing. Louisa, will you please send an invitation to Dr. DeVille to join us for dinner?"

"Yes, I'll send Imel and have him return with the doctor if he's available. What are you thinking?"

"That I need Abraham's keen mind to help sort this out."

Two hours later, while Grace and Imel ate dinner on the second floor, Louisa sat with the Daroga, Erik and DeVille at the third floor kitchen table. The chicken and vegetable stew was most satisfying, but conversation was in short supply. They ate in silence, engrossed in their own considerations. Erik, though near exhaustion, was being driven by a well contained, but fanatical need to find Christine and the others. Every moment that passed was an agony eating away at restraint. They knew nothing more than the contents of the note received three long nights ago. What had transpired to motivate those they cherished so much to flee from Paris in such disarray? Whatever the cause, the desire to choke the life out of Raoul smoldered within him. His near psychotic stress and distraught imaginings could be read in the deepened crow's feet of his left eye and the set line of his rigid mouth.

The signs of rampant inner conflict had not escaped the nurturing eyes of his doctor. DeVille could only guess at the depth of Erik's wired mental state. When he observed that Erik could no longer force food into his mouth and gave up trying by setting his fork on his plate, DeVille took the opportunity to break into his friend's aloofness. "Let's not continue to look inward for solutions to this dilemma. We'll be more productive if we pool our thoughts and try to analyze what has happened. Certainly something terrible motivated Meg and Jean to take Christine and the three children and go into hiding. What would have prevented them from contacting you?"

Madame Giry responded with certainty, "Danger, grave danger, to them, to us."

The doctor reiterated, "So they are trying to protect you, and themselves from harm."

Erik stated simply, and out of great fatigue, "We must find them."

Abraham rubbed his chin thoughtfully. "Despite the toll of these last few discouraging days, we need to amass what we do know and place it before us for examination."

Erik spoke moodily, "I thought I knew her better than she knew herself. I was wrong. I cannot feel her presence anywhere around me. I am sure she has left Paris and this is a very big world."

The Daroga sighed. "Trying to find people who don't want to be found is damn perplexing. I'm exasperated and at wit's end. We need a dose of blessed magic."

Abraham continued to verbally turn over the problem. "Maybe we can use what the two of you just said. Erik, you admit you're wrong to think you know her so well, and the Daroga assumes that they do not want to be found." Abraham rubbed his fingertips on the tablecloth, continuing to reflect.

Madame Giry added, "Men think women are without logic and therefore unfathomable. Our illogical nature makes us too complex for you to comprehend, but basically women only want security and appreciation."

The doctor elaborated on her words to reason further. "That is not so difficult to understand. They want everyone safe and in one piece. Now, what has Christine ever said she will do in return for the appreciation of her affections and friendship?"

Erik said gravely, "She told me that when we were apart, during the first two years of her marriage, her heart turned to stone. Everywhere she sat became a tomb because she was dying. She promised me she would never separate us by leaving Paris." He stood up suddenly. "I may know where they are." He ran to the door, yanking his cloak off the rack.

The others yelled out in unison, "WHERE?" And they scampered to keep up with him.

Like a racehorse at the start line, he opened the door and bolted down the back stairs. Hollering as he rounded the newel post, "They may be somewhere near the cemetery, probably trying to decide what to do about Raoul while they wait in secret avoiding an all out war."

The moment this possibility occurred to Erik he began calculating the amount of time it would take to traverse the distance to the cemetery at a full gallop. At the basement vestibule the Daroga caught up with him. Madame Giry shouted from the stairs, "Wait, Erik. Wait!"

The two men paused and turned as she and DeVille caught up to them. She placed her hands on Erik's upper arms and looked into his eyes. "I love you, please for all our sakes be careful, and if you ever heard me say anything before, let what I am about to tell you stay fixed in your mind." He studied her face obediently. "Let her do the talking, whatever she says, whatever she wants, let Christine dictate it and support her." He turned to go and she pulled at his jacket's sleeve. "Promise me."

He kissed her cheek, and resting her chin between his right index finger and thumb, he told her, "Always and forever will I listen to your voice of reason. Your insightfulness has saved my life more than once and I know it well."

"Good hunting!" she said.

The Phantom and the Daroga stepped into the space that opened in front of them as the wall moved on a well-oiled pivot. They disappeared discussing how they would evade the prying eyes of the three detectives and expeditiously obtain fresh mounts to continue the search on horseback.

Amazed at the movement of the stones and the swiftness with which the two vanished into concealment, Dr. DeVille clicked his fingers and said to Louisa, "Most interesting, they're gone before the eye can blink twice. He really understands the dynamics of swift, secretive exits, doesn't he?" He ran his fingers across the stones but could not begin to conceive how Erik accomplished the feat he had just witnessed.

Madame Giry smiled proudly. "He is our genius, Monsieur. His mind is on a plane up here." She waved her hand over her head. "Please, come back upstairs. I'll introduce you to Grace and Imel."

Erik and Khalil investigated every house near the front gate of the cemetery, but not one of the rustic French dwellings yielded the vision of Jean's common carriage. A mile down the road they began to discuss how far they should proceed before mentally drawing a perimeter in which to contain the initial search. The Phantom suggested they check several small cottages and tool sheds near the back gates, and work their way around to the main road before widening their scope. He told Khalil the dwellings were usually occupied by caretakers, or their hired laborers, and were separated from the actual walls of the graveyard by a densely wooded hill. Within ten minutes they reached the posterior of the graveyard and tethered their horses, continuing on foot through the woods that concealed the cottages from the cemetery. They located the dwellings without difficulty, only one had lights on inside. A reconnoiter of the adjacent buildings gave them the location of a communal barn. Jean's common carriage and two horses were housed there. Right alongside a meticulously cared for hearse, the funeral carts used to haul dirt and the additional horses employed by the caretakers to pull them. No one was about; only the cottage with the candles lit inside was occupied.

"Very clever, don't you think?" whispered the Daroga. "I wonder who thought of hiding so close to the cemetery?"

They peered in the side window of the cottage's front room and discovered it contained a tiny kitchen and a small table beside a sitting area. Together they sighed with relief as they saw Meg and Christine sitting in rocking chairs. Each woman had an embroidery hoop in her lap, and her head bent forward apparently dozing. Jean and his driver were nowhere in sight. Despite the relief they felt at finding the ladies, they exercised patience and signaled to each other to head around the back. There they came across the windows of two darkened bedrooms. In hushed words, the Daroga reminded Erik that steady nerves and patience were needed now. Carefully they scanned the outside to ascertain they were alone.

The Daroga asked, "Where is Jean? Surely he didn't drive the carriage here himself."

"We'll probably locate him soon. When we go in we must be careful not to frighten them."

Erik lifted a dagger from a sheath on his hip and slid it between the sill and the window of the bedroom on the left, easing the frame upward. "I'll go in here. You take the other room. We'll meet back outside in a minute." He slipped silently into the room and found two cots. One contained the easy breathing of a sleeping toddler and an infant. The other was empty and must be where Christine slept. He realized that Jean and Claude were probably asleep in the room beside this one.

He admired his tender little boys and a tremendous sadness filled his soul. He had only seen them from a distance last September, and had never even touched Ariel. He put his fingers in front of their faces and felt each of them breathe upon his skin. *God, they are so beautiful, two rosy-cheeked cherubs.* Both boys had long, delicate fingers. Michael's hair was pitch-black like his. *How is it that I never think to ask Christine about them when I see her? Pain, too much pain!*

The Daroga came soundlessly into the room through the window and whispered to Erik. "I found Jean and his boy next door. I woke Jean up. He'll meet us outside in a few minutes. He says that one of his servants came here yesterday and told him Raoul went to Jean's estate. De Chagny was agitated and brandishing his Winchester rifle, threatening to kill Jean if he didn't come out and tell him where Christine was hiding. The servants informed Raoul that their employers were not at home. Everyone's been hoping that Raoul's temper would calm down soon. Apparently there is more Jean wants to tell us. And by-the-way, he's very glad we're here." The Phantom listened closely to the Daroga but kept watching the babies, his head thoughtfully leaning to one side. "Erik, did you hear me? We need to go talk with Jean."

The Phantom nodded and pointed to the boys asleep on the cot. The probing eyes of the Daroga dropped downward. "They're magnificent. Just look at your boys! Have you ever been this close to them?"

"Not really."

"Don't live so long as a specter hiding in the mists that you forget to be a man, Erik." Khalil squeezed the Phantom's shoulder with his hand. "I give you permission to have a life, give yourself permission, as well."

"I need to speak with Christine before I talk with Jean."

"Take whatever time you need. We'll wait outside." The Daroga exited through the window.

The Phantom went to the door and cracked it open. Christine was closest, with her face turned away from him and covered by her long hair. His lovesick brain pumped adrenalin into his veins. The desire to touch her was almost beyond control, but he steeled himself and prepared to awaken her in degrees.

In her dream she heard him playing her father's violin from inside the underground house. She floated in the moist air across the lake, swirling lazily in the tune. Mixed within the rich, haunting melody, he called softly to her. His flawless voice a ballad of its own, drifting through the song of the violin. "Christine, come to me. Come to the Angel of Music, Christine, come to me. Come!" Her eyes fluttered open and she realized it was only an ecstasy in her mind. She brushed the hair back from her face and looked to her bedroom door, noting that it had come open.

In the dim light of the flickering candles, the sight of her face twisted his hopeful expectation into a vicious, gnawing anger. Her left orbit was swollen and tearing, she could hardly open the eye. The left cheek and jaw were mottled with purple bruises – her eyebrow and lip sliced but scabbed. She would be scarred!

As she took a candle from the table, he retreated deeper into the room, standing mute at the head of the boys' cot. When she reached the door she smelled the Persian musk. Pinching out the candle's flame, she stepped inside, remaining in the doorway. He stretched out his arms, his fingers pleading in silence. *Come to me!*

The candles in the room behind her cast an almost iridescent glow into his yellow eyes, easily identifying where he stood in the dark. She closed the door behind her and did not move forward. She knew that even in the poor amount of moonlight shining through the window, his piercing eyes could see her every detail. He lowered his arms, leaning against the wall in the anguished realization that he still had not touched her. A gaping chasm marked the space between their souls. Wordlessly she unbuttoned the simple white peasant's shirt she wore, and allowed it to fall over the belt at her trim waist. She undid a strip of linen wrapped around her chest and stood before him bare breasted. Her face and chest were deeply bruised where she had been pummeled, there were two distinct and purulent sets of bite marks in her flesh.

He bit his left index finger to keep from howling in rage. His right arm reared back to pound his fist into the wall, but she put her finger to her lips to gesture silence. "Shh."

"On my oath, you shall never suffer this again!" His words were cold, pregnant with the promise of malicious cruelty.

Christine's voice was even, without the slightest quiver. "'Never' is such an enormous word for only five letters, don't you think?"

"Evil's gruesome clutch has found you, punished you because of me. This beating was mine to take, not yours. A bitter poison has invaded our coupling."

"Why? Because I've become repulsive to you?"

"No, you are the most beautiful creature ever created, but how can you forgive me for not being there to defend you? For three days I have been wild to find you. Finally you stand before me and still remain outside my arms." His voice became angry. "I should have taken you from your father's tomb the first time we met there...refused to let you part from me, but I let fear manipulate my perspectives. I denied us both!"

Christine sighed impatiently. "I'm so tired of being afraid. Every shadow has been my enemy, a place for Raoul to pounce from and harm us." She wrapped the linen round her chest and brought the shirt back over her shoulders, buttoning it.

"You don't have to worry about that anymore. I will protect you. I would like to kill him very slowly, but before I do we have to move you. He has detectives sniffing all over Paris and it's only a matter of time until their bribes uncover the scent that leads them here. I found you through the memory of a promise."

"Do you still wonder why I love you, Erik? Do the reasons still remain a mystery to you? Or perhaps you're still busy doubting if I love you at all. I'm only asking because all of this," she gestured toward their children and herself, "is going to be difficult to protect if you don't trust that there's real love for you here."

"I owe you an apology. My liberties put you in danger. I eagerly pursued you, refusing to contain my hunger, when I should have foreseen these events and stayed away. Forgive my amorous persistence, I've loved you so selfishly."

"Have you been wretched these last three days?"

"Yes, wretched. Miserable. What do you want me to do, Christine?" Madame Giry's advice echoed in his head.

"Stop apologizing for loving me! I have a perfect understanding of what it feels like to be wretched and in love. We are drawn together, you and I. Would you apologize to your fingers for their desire to play an instrument, or to your brain for creating the music which flows from it so naturally? I want every piece of you you're willing to share. You chose me," she rested her hand over her heart. "There are thousands of women in Paris and you chose me – and I chose you! I chose you three nights ago, and I choose you again tonight for I want no other. I am tired of being denied, Erik. If hell barred the way to you I was willing to travel through it."

"Was?"

"I'm so fatigued. We should congratulate me for putting words and phrases together. I spit up blood for a whole day and fear has robbed me of sleep. Raoul knows I have Jacob Klein's scroll. He also knows the boys are not his. He's always known, from the moment I told him I was pregnant he's known. He's sterile and can't father children of his own. His ruinous pride blocked him from telling me." Her voice weakened dramatically and he expected her to start sobbing, but her resilience was remarkable. She continued. "I think I have finally thought of a way to leave him with all of us safe and alive."

"What do you want me to do?"

"You will have to hide a little longer. Raoul still believes you to be dead. He thinks I play a game with my lover, pretending he's a substitute for you. If I can get Raoul to promise to leave me alone and let me have my own house away from the estate, then eventually I can procure an honorable divorce."

"What house do you want?"

"The one across the street from you."

His mind began to fly. *It could work, a tunnel under the street.* "What about the boys? Babies need to be with their mother don't they? Maybe I could learn to be a father."

"Yes, you could. Raoul can adopt babies with someone else for a partner. Think about it, our relationship would have the time and the room it needs to grow, to mature. You could come to trust in the love I feel for you."

Erik regarded her with great pride. "How strong you are for both of us. Please wife, let me touch you."

At last she came into his arms. He held her gingerly. From the way she split her inhalations, he was certain several ribs on her right side were cracked. "My love, there may yet be hope for this man, if even now you do not spurn me."

She rested her forehead onto his chest. "I wish this ordeal I created for us was already over. I was impatient. Against your advice I pushed him. I opened Pandora's box and told him the truth."

He rocked her gently back and forth. "He already knew the truth, Christine. You told me he's sterile."

The Daroga lifted up the window, his voice urgent as he tapped the sill with his fingers. "I hate to interrupt this but Raoul just pulled up in a carriage with two male servants and a driver."

Christine waved to the Daroga. "I feel emotionless inside, like I'm dead and somehow still able to move. It took all my strength to leave the chateau with the boys. I want all of this hiding to end."

"Then end it shall. I'll fight Raoul for you tonight."

"No, please wait, let me try talking to him first. Maybe I can wrest my freedom from him. Meg, Jean and I have pistols in our clothes if things should get out of hand. Stay close, if things don't go well for me, take the boys and run. If he agrees to my plan, I'll return to you when he leaves."

She kissed him with her sore, puffy lips. "I don't want another murder, I just want you. Let me try."

The Phantom dropped out the back window and Christine stepped into the little sitting area, shutting the door behind her. Meg was already awake with her hand on the pistol beneath her embroidery. Christine took her gun from her skirt pocket and aimed it toward the door. She whispered to Meg, "Erik and the Daroga are out back." A second later Raoul stormed through the door with two men pressing behind him.

"Christine!" he shouted and came to a standstill. Raoul's hair was uncombed, his loosened cravat pulled off to one side, and his gaunt face said alcohol had replaced food as of late.

Not the prim and proper gentleman now, she thought. She aimed the gun straight at his chest and in a stern, sharp voice commanded, "Halt where you stand, Sir!"

Raoul remained in the doorway, looking without remorse at the bruises spread across her left face and her frightfully swollen eyelid. He noted her set stance and the way her hands did not tremble as she held the pistol.

"Christine, I'm so relieved to see you." He turned and bowed slightly to Meg who stayed seated. "Meg, you seem quite well. Enjoying your excursion?" He started to step forward into the room when he saw the muzzle flash out of the corner of his eye and heard the loud crack of the gun as it fired. The sound of the bullet as it whizzed past his head and landed in the wall beside the window, returned him to a standstill.

He put his hands up at shoulder height and turned again to Meg. A stream of smoke trailed upward from the pistol in her hand, she still had not stood up. Deftly, she drew a second gun from beneath her sewing and dropped the one with the spent shot in her lap. "She said halt!"

"And I have," answered Raoul.

"Send the men back to the carriage and tell them to go down the road," ordered Christine.

Raoul kept his hands in the air and told the men standing behind him, "Do as she says." The servants murmured suspiciously and retreated to the carriage. They waived to the driver and went with the vehicle to the front of the barn, about sixty feet away.

Erik, Khalil and Jean stood beneath the trees enveloped in blackness. When the gunshot rang out they started to rush forward, ready to aid the women.

The Daroga spread his arms out. "Hold! Look! One of them must have fired a warning shot at Raoul." They could see the men moving the carriage to a distance. "Let's move to the front window on the opposite side. You two listen while I keep my eyes on the three with the carriage."

Bent over, they crept to a window near the stove. Jean peered in. "Raoul has taken a seat in a chair right by the door. Both girls have pistols trained on him. It's under control for the moment." He brought his head back down and the Phantom quickly glanced into the room. Erik slid his dagger between the window and the sill so they could hear the conversation inside.

"We'll rush him if we need to," Jean whispered.

"I don't like this. Let's just kill him," the Phantom responded. "I can sneak up behind him with the Punjab lasso."

The Daroga kept watching the servants from the corner of the house. "Wait now. Louisa said to give heed to Christine's wishes and you told us she wants to make him an offer. If the confrontation goes awry, we'll create a distraction and draw Raoul away from them. Better that he's on the outside with us, than in there with them."

Jean reached inside his cloak and produced a pouch. "Here," he said and handed a white mask like Erik's to the Daroga. "Put this on." Jean took the elastic of a second mask and drew it over his own face. The Phantom eyed him incredulously and Jean managed a gregarious smile. "What? You think you're the only one who can have a little fun?" The Phantom shook his head in disbelief.

The Daroga donned his mask. "Excellent, these will be of use. Do you have a gun on you? We've only got our daggers and swords."

"Nice rescue," said Jean. "Yes, I have a pistol, and I have more masks, too. Claude and I play with them."

Jean handed a black facemask that covered from the nose to the hairline to the Daroga and offered another to the Phantom.

Erik gestured refusal, "No thanks, I have my own. Do you have anything else in your bag of tricks?"

"No, that's it."

"Then Jean, by all means let's listen to what they're saying. You watch."

Jean straightened into a half crouch position and brought his two eyes up over the lowest edge of the window's glass pane.

"Be careful not to fog up the window with your breath!"

"Got it."

24 *RETALIATION*

Raoul sat impatiently in the wooden chair, suppressing a bilious rage. For the moment, he'd summoned up enough self-restraint not to throttle the two women, but he detested having to obey their petty whims and sit with his arms elevated in the air. This awkward position made him feel like a silly buzzard, plucked from flight and restrained from alighting on a carcass. Scuffing his boot heel back and forth over the rough floorboards, he plotted his next strategy. "I'm surprised to find you supporting the flight of a runaway wife, Meg. Where is your husband? Why isn't he in here with his gun cocked and aimed at me?"

"Tell us what you want Raoul or I'll aim for your head," Meg announced defiantly.

Ignoring Meg's edict he baited his wife. "Christine, you've been most difficult to locate. My detectives have been busy making inquiries for three days."

Christine walked sideways to the empty rocking chair and sat down. "What do you want?"

"Can I put my hands down?"

Meg issued a directive. "Place your hands on your knees."

"I had no idea you two women were so strong minded." He put his hands on his thighs and toned down his sarcasm. "How could I have so misread your capabilities?"

Meg retorted, "You only see what you want to see, Raoul. Answer her question."

"I want my wife and my two sons to come home with me. I want the rightful return of my property."

Christine spoke again, "This is my home."

"This place is your home, Christine? You reside on the backside of a cemetery without servants? Do you wash your own floors and cook? I doubt it. How do you propose to support yourself?"

"I'll make you a deal Raoul, buy me a better home and I'll let you have my friendship."

"Buy you a better home? Where? What home other than mine could you possibly want? You have an entire estate to play on."

"I want the house across the street from Madame Giry's, and I want to live there with my boys, legally separated from you. Buy that house and sign the deed over to me. Guarantee in writing that you will never touch me again, or bring harm to anyone in Meg's family."

Raoul clucked his tongue. "My wife has so many terms. Let me ask you again, just in case you didn't hear me. How will you support yourself?"

"I'll teach. I'll bake. I don't want anything from you but the separation agreement and the house."

"Oh, I see." His foot tapped in aggravation. "Regardless of what you think you can accomplish on your own, Christine, I want my children and I'm going to take them."

Meg enjoyed her next robust declaration immensely. "They're not your children, Raoul!"

Thinking to take her by the throat he started to rise, but the second he moved Meg brought the barrel of the gun upward. With her hands steady, she pointed it straight at his head. He hesitated, remembering the flash of the gun's muzzle. *She's more than ready to fire, probably missed deliberately last time!* He placed his butt back on the seat.

Meg continued, "I know about the boys and I know about the scroll, as well. You're not a bad man, Raoul, just a truly spoiled one. One who doesn't act on his noblest inclinations. I think you should stay still, and listen like a good schoolboy to Christine."

Raoul could barely contain his anger. "Dearest Meg, perhaps you can tell me why the reprobate who fathered these boys, isn't here providing for them? He's not a very good person, is he?"

"He is a good person, a prince with a generous soul. Perhaps the greatest soul I've ever known, but with a dash of eccentricity for flavor."

"Eccentricity or insanity? Is it Erik?"

Christine leaned forward in her chair, her words emphatic. "No, it is not! The Daroga and I buried Erik, and his broken heart, near the well in the underground. You know that we did. We buried him with the gold wedding band he gave me. You can go check the caverns and read the police reports for yourself if you like."

Raoul shifted back into the chair, folding his arms across his chest. *Are you lying? Would you tell me if he was alive?* "Can I ever have your heart again, Christine?"

"I told you, you could have my friendship!"

She seems sincere. "Your friendship is a thing to be most prized, Madame. Do you promise to give it, if I buy this house and submit the agreement you want?" *If she's dead you can always take another wife.*

"Yes." Christine was afraid of Raoul, but pitied him as well. She was the adulteress. Her immorality had brought all of them to this microcosm of time that threatened to explode about their heads. *No, don't think negative, be strong. You knew I wanted Erik and you married me knowing yourself to be sterile.*

"You have a bargain and what about my family's scroll?"

"You keep your word and I will return it to you, intact. You can correspond with me at Meg and Jean's estate."

"You'll go there if I promise to leave you alone?"

"Yes. Let me know when I can safely move into the house."

The trio listening at the window decided that since Christine had obtained her wishes from Raoul it was time to draw him out of the house, away from the women and children. The Daroga instructed Jean, "Remember, our goal is to double back here to the house and be in one piece."

"If you hear crying or howling, any kind of noise that's not these idiots, I'll be about twenty to thirty feet to the right of the sound," added the Phantom.

"Or the left," said the Daroga.

Jean asked, "Well which is it, the left or the right?"

The Daroga adjusted his mask a little. "Depends on the direction you're facing when he makes the sounds."

"We'll send you in first, Jean. That will place you in front of me. I'll try to stay to your right, which will put me to your left if you look back toward those trees."

"Right," said the Daroga.

Jean made a face. "I don't get it. I'll just go in and take my cues from the both of you. Thank God there's no snow, we won't leave any tracks."

The Phantom thought for a moment. "Actually, tracks would be helpful. They'd never know there were three of us if we stepped in each other's footprints. Nevertheless, you've given me a grand idea about misdirection. Let's go in together. I'll position Jean. Daroga, you and I will draw them into circles. I have an artist's charcoal in my pocket. That can add to the confusion."

"I don't get that either," said Jean.

"You will," said the Phantom. "The idea is that we'll be the hunted for a while, then we'll play turn around and do the hunting ourselves." The three crept back into the woods and went north of the house. At one point the Phantom stepped out from the shelter of the trees into full view, threw a stone to attract the attention of the servants – and waved.

"A masked man, a masked man is behind the house," they started shouting. Before the women could react Raoul charged out the front door and ran to his men. Rallying to the challenge of an invader, the group hastily grabbed their rifles from the carriage and sprinted into the woods with the driver hollering, "He can't out-run all four of us!"

The pursuers reached the north gate and helped each other over the wall. Raoul landed on the cemetery side first. "Come on, come on, hurry up," he shouted.

When the four were once again standing together, they turned and took in the view before them. In the achromatic moonlight the gravestones looked bleak and foreboding. There was absolutely no sound, not even a breeze. The cemetery appeared deserted and strangely hostile, as if its residents preferred their rest left undisturbed.

Bewildered and more than a little afraid, the youngest asked, "Why are we going in here? This is hallowed ground."

Unmoved by malevolent superstition, Raoul instructed them to advance in a horizontal line with their guns at the ready. "Have courage, we're after a ghost masquerading as a man." He meant to be ironic but the mockery went unappreciated by his servants, who eyed each other nervously. "We'll move in an unwavering line and flush him south."

The oldest servant asked, "Why south, your Lordship?"

"There are no gates on the south side of the cemetery, we can corner him there."

They crept forward slowly, eyes darting to the left and right as they weaved around the smaller tombstones. At the first mausoleum they came to, Raoul signaled for the two servants to pass it on the left, while he and the driver went to the right. Raoul had not obtained its front when he heard the two servants on the other side calling frantically.

"Come look at this, your Lordship. Quick!" On their side of the stone structure was a large black arrow pointing to the front of the mausoleum with the word *SOUTH* clearly printed above it.

"Our visitor is quite helpful," the youngest servant said cockily.

Raoul's response was abrupt. "You fool, he's playing with us! This isn't working. We need to spread out more. Fan out, damn it, and keep flushing him south." They separated again into two prongs, unaware that as they moved forward Jean and the Daroga had already maneuvered around behind them, and were watching from only ten yards away.

Raoul's party came into a wealthier section of the cemetery where large statues adorned many of the mausoleums and crypts.

The younger servant, fascinated by a particularly fearsome effigy of Death in a long robe with a sickle, tripped on a stone grave-cover and discharged his weapon. The sound echoed like the blast of a cannon ball among the tombs, deafening the troop. The bullet flew past Raoul's head missing him completely, but blew off the nose of a tall, marble angel with a head of long curls. The angel was placed beside a set of stairs going down to a crypt. In its hand it held an unlit lantern, incongruously guiding the way to the underworld without a light.

Raoul spun around angrily, "Damn it, that's twice in one night I've been shot at! Rein in your enthusiasm, Alfred. Take care to aim at true targets!"

"Sorry, Sir, won't happen again. I need to reload." Raoul ducked behind a structure and continued on.

Suddenly, the driver, a scrawny fellow named Fredrick, bellowed out, "He's over here, boys! I just saw his masked face peer out from around a statue! Hurry, he's hiding over here!"

The older servant, Simon, shouted back, "No, you're wrong! I can see him! He just popped up behind a tombstone. This way!"

Raoul growled, "Idiots!" He could not see his men so he started in the direction of Simon's voice. He paused when his eyes caught some writing on the back of a monument. *SHOULD THE MASTER OF LIES,* there was an arrow beneath the words pointing to the next monument, where the end of the message read: *BE COVERED IN FLIES?*

What the hell? The cemetery was silent for the moment and Raoul scanned the area closely, searching for the prankster. *Nothing!* Cautiously he moved toward where he believed Simon to be but found the area vacant. He turned slowly in a full circle with his rifle at chest height, finger on the trigger, ready to shoot. As he turned he studied each object carefully and his eyes came to rest on another note written on the side of a different mausoleum. *THIS WAY TO THE NAME OF A WIFE BEATER.* An arrow pointed to the right where his eyes had just passed! Raoul squinted to improve his vision and brought his gaze to the next mausoleum where these words greeted him: *RAOUL WAS HERE!*

With all his strength he screamed out at the top of his lungs, "Where are you boys? Answer me this minute! Where are you?"

All three came at a run, colliding into his sides, nearly toppling him over in the dark. Disgusted he pushed them off. "This visitor is no ordinary man. He knows me," seethed Raoul. "Would you like to tell me how we pursue him and he has time to write us notes?" In his agitation he slapped Fredrick soundly across the face. Alfred and Simon shied back, out of his reach.

"We'll get him, your Lordship."

"Yes, we will."

Fredrick resentfully rubbed his cheek, inwardly hoping their prey would escape. "It seems our ghost has a sense of humor!"

Raoul spat, "Let's hope he chokes on it, because he won't be laughing when I get my hands on him. Simon, you and Alfred go right. Fredrick, you're with me. Steady on, men, this one's clever." They broke into two groups again and began to duck and weave around the headstones and burial urns, still believing they were moving south.

In a few minutes the pair of servants grew tired. With false bravado, Simon told Alfred to sit while he walked a circle around them to make sure their 'little rabbit' was not in the immediate vicinity. He handed Alfred a flask and told the lad to have a drink. "Save me some, I'll be right back."

While Alfred gratefully drank the liquor he read the inscription on the grave-cover where he sat. It was for a young boy who had died at the age of seven: *OUR BELOVED SON, WE SHALL MISS YOU.*

"Oh my God, that's awful," he moaned. "I wonder what he passed of?" Soft, soulful crying started to come from the grave. Alfred catapulted to his feet. Freaked, his skin crawled in waves, as the hairs on his arms stood on end. Something cold tried to grab his ankle and he pulled his leg away madly, too frightened to scream. He lost his balance and fell backward, the flask hurling out of his grasp. The metal clanged forlornly as it hit against stone somewhere. As he laid in a disjointed heap, with his eyes to the stars in the clear sky above, the eerie sound of the weeping little boy re-commenced.

"Alfred, Alfred, stay here and play me." Terrorized, he fainted – his urinary bladder releasing its warm contents into his pants.

His partner, Simon, crouched down behind a tombstone about forty yards away, listening intently. He'd heard the sound of metal bouncing on stone, he was sure of it. Simon pulled his jacket tighter around him and clutched his gun to his chest. He exhaled and saw his breath. Tugging at his cap, he cursed. *Damn-it to hell, it's getting colder!* The chilling, plaintive howl of a distant wolf reached his ears. *Merde! There are dogs in here! The rogue's got dogs with him...I don't like dogs.* He stood and fired his rifle into the air. When the sound wave receded, he cried out to the night, "There are dogs in here, Count. Dogs! Maybe they're the caretakers? They got dogs don't they?"

A shivering Alfred came up behind Simon and touched his shoulder. Simon was so startled, he leapt forward two feet off the ground – turning as he landed, ready to punch his attacker with the stock of his weapon. "Holy hell, boy! You scared the britches off me!" Relief caused a shudder to pass over him. "You can see I'm not wearing britches anymore now, can't you!"

"Sorry, Simon, but you're the one barking like a dog! I swear I just heard the ghost of a little boy crying over there. I'm freezing. I think I wet myself."

Raoul and Fredrick reached the two servants. Raoul's voice dripped with contempt. "Well, here are the four of us together again! I've missed you, Simon. Have you missed me?" Raoul smacked him soundly on the side of the head. "Start thinking clearly, man, and shut up! You are all excellent morons. Caretakers don't take care of graves at night!"

"Yes, Sir. Yes, Sir," the three mumbled.

"Now fan out again and keep flushing him south."

"Pardon me, your Lordship," said Alfred, "but I'm wet."

"Do you want us to stop and fan you dry, Alfred?" Raoul voice was rancorous.

To get the subject off Alfred, Simon asked, "I've become a bit confused, Sir. Which way do you suppose is south?"

Raoul could not believe the incompetence of the men he had brought with him. "South, Simon, hasn't moved. It's that way," and he pointed north. "Now let's get this ghoul before he decides to leave for an early breakfast!"

Raoul and Fredrick moved to the left and began a guerrilla style advancement, hurrying from one shadowed area to the next, dodging what slivers of light there were between the structures as if they were the enemy. Fredrick dropped back from Raoul to mock his employer. "Keep flushing him south. Keep flushing him south. I'd like to flush you, Count, right into the Seine!" Up ahead, Raoul turned a corner and dipped from sight. Fredrick broke out in a run, trying to catch up and didn't see the Phantom's foot placed in his path. He thought he tripped on the walkway as he went sprawling into the air. He landed flat on his prominent nose with a crunch. An excruciating finger of pain shot through his brain, he came up on his hands and knees, certain he'd fractured the bone. Involuntary tears sprang from the eyes he clenched shut. He groaned, too hurt to even swear. As he did, he choked on the taste of warm blood, flowing freely from his nostrils over his lips.

Strong hands came firmly into Fredrick's armpits from behind, helping him stagger to his feet. He felt a handkerchief being placed over his nasal passages and a beautiful, angelic voice spoke into his ear. "Good, keep your eyes closed and press here, real hard. You have a bloody nose, my friend, but you'll be all right." Fredrick gripped his injury tightly as unidentified hands eased him into a sitting position; then gently pushed his head back so that his chin lifted to the sky. The aesthetic instructions continued, "Rest against this. Don't get up until the bleeding stops and you can open your eyes."

"Who are you?"

"I'm the phantasm you've been chasing for the last thirty minutes." A muffled laugh, similar to the sound of water gurgling into a pond, echoed in Fredrick's ears and a chill of icy fear whipped down his spine. He stretched his free hand into the air in front of him, groping, but acquired nothing.

Raoul entered a common area encircled with mausoleums and statuary, one of which was the angel with the head of curls whose nose had been blown off earlier by Alfred's accidental shot. With genuine disdain, he recognized the guardian. He'd conducted a search that circled back on itself, almost to where they'd started. Totally frustrated, he flung his rifle over his head, swearing an unintelligible curse at the Angel of Misdirection. He blinked then stepped closer to the statue. A brand new candle burned in his lantern and someone had smashed the upper right quarter of the angel's face. Raoul thought its resemblance to the Opera Ghost remarkable and deliberate. He sat down, studying the confounding angel and commanded his brain to draw up a new plan.

Not too far from Raoul's uncanny statue, Jean and the Daroga hid behind a scalloped alcove containing a life size statue of the Virgin Mary. They were whispering to each other that the cemetery had grown much too quiet, when the Phantom appeared out of nowhere right beside them. In a hushed but exaggerated politeness, the Daroga asked, "And where have you been?"

"On top of a mausoleum."

"So how's this going to end? It's coming on midnight and something's amiss here, we have daggers and one pistol between us, while they have rifles."

"I'll remember that for next time," Erik responded as he lifted his mask and wiped his face with a handkerchief he slipped from the Daroga's pocket.

"Are we cut off?" Jean inquired.

"Not if we can get to Gustave Daae's grave."

Jean replied skeptically, "You want us to pay respect to Christine's father? He can't help us, Erik."

The Phantom punched his comrade's arm playfully. "No, I don't want to pay my respects. We could actually escape through the waterways beneath it, but I still have a few tricks up my sleeve. I don't want to turn tail and run just yet, do you?"

Jean straightened his collar. "No, absolutely not. I'm up for running around the cemetery with bullets flying about for at least another hour or so."

The Daroga added, "Well, I don't know if I am. This has been a rough week of hide-and-go seek for these aging bones. What's their status right now?"

The Phantom wiped his left palm with his right hand, creating a clean imaginary slate. "The driver is here at my pinky, we're here at mid-palm with Raoul sitting forty yards behind us at my wrist. The two servants are just on the other side of that family chapel over there," he pointed to the building and then to the tip of his thumb. "They're having a discussion about whether or not they're still moving south. They want to suggest to Raoul that it's time to go home because they're badly spooked from crawling around this place, but they don't have the courage to ask him. Thus, we have sort of an imperfect triangle with us in the middle."

Jean was baffled. "How do you know all this?"

"I spoke with the driver when he broke his nose, don't ask. I ease-dropped on the two servants, and I can smell Raoul from here. He's up wind and hasn't moved, so he's probably still sitting, contemplating how much the angel looks like his nemesis."

The Daroga yawned. "Erik, do you remember what I said about not being a specter and having a life?"

"Daroga, that was only a little while ago, how could I possibly forget? I need to think."

"Well I take it back, please be a specter and let's send these boys home. I need my bed."

"Got it. It's time to play the 'Man of Illusions Game' and put them in the center of the triangle, and us at its points. Change into the black masks." The trio huddled together as the Phantom explained the final act of the play.

Raoul sat holding his head in his hands when a stone landed at his feet. Looking to where it must have been thrown from, he spotted more writing on the wall of a rather ornate crypt. "Sure, why not? You write but you don't visit." His rifle rested in his lap. He picked it up and checked it. "Everybody's gotten off a shot tonight, except for poor Raoul, and it's finally his turn." He stood up and leisurely stretched his back and legs, then walked to the writing. *FOLLOW THE ARROWS AND YOU WILL SEE*...a series of small arrows followed, *THAT EVERYONE HATES YOU INCLUDING*...a final arrow went to the corner of the structure and he cautiously stepped to it, rifle cocked and raised.

"Me!" Erik let Raoul have one very astonished look at his face as he rounded the corner. "You should never have hurt her. Coward!" The Phantom blew a blue powder off his palm, forming a luminescent cloud of dust around Raoul's head. Raoul backed up a few steps, blinking and rubbing his eyes. He inhaled to speak, but the vision of a red devil laughing despicably danced before him. He fired his rifle at the fiend but a troop of smaller subordinate demons flew in to protect their leader. The assistants pulled at his trousers and started poking his legs with stinging little pitchforks. He managed to kick them off as an army of extraordinarily large fire ants marched over him in full attack. His flesh burned and itched terribly. Vainly he struggled to wipe one limb free, when another would call for his immediate attention. The Phantom stood calmly watching Raoul hallucinate and counted quietly in his head. When he reached the number fifty-three he stopped and said, "Hello Raoul, this is Erik. Are you having a nice time?"

Raoul went down on his knees and began clawing at the ground. "Erik, are you in there? Erik, answer me!" The Phantom left him pleading with the dirt.

Simon, Alfred and Fredrick stayed in position when they heard the shot, waiting for an indication of what was to follow. Somewhere close by, a melancholy singing commenced. The dark, nocturnal voice was mystical and macabre. The vibrato it contained unthinkably delightful. Its baleful nuances seemed to come and go, calling to them, drawing them. Left without a will of their own, they had no choice but to abandon the asylum of their stations and seek the source of the powerful melody.

Gladly they came to the crypt issuing the inexplicably gratifying voice, but instead of discovering the source of the melody, they were embarrassed to find their Count – digging at the ground with his bare fingers.

The singing stopped and a tall fantastic creature in a black cape and black face mask appeared on top of a tomb thirty yards in front of them, to their left his twin appeared and to their right, a third. The capes on the apparitions bellowed out in a late, nighttime breeze and despite the fact that none of their mouths moved, Raoul's men distinctly heard, "Take your master home, he is ill."

They were momentarily paralyzed with horror. The nefarious being had morphed into three!

Fredrick shouted from beneath a badly swollen nose, through equally edematous lips, "Fire boys, fire." As the shots split the air in discordant volleys, the spirits stretched their garments out wide and dropped from sight. Each de Chagny employee raced to the spot where a specter had stood and each found nothing of substance, nothing at all! Fredrick waved his gun for them to return to Raoul. They helped the Count to his feet and Fredrick reassured him, "It's us boss, we're going home. I think I hit mine, he's gone."

Simon and Alfred added that they had hit their targets as well, but Raoul only sniveled, trying vainly to pick apart something invisible floating in the air before his chest. Alfred suggested, "Let's get him to the maids." They started moving toward the north gate, with the pale half-moon close to the horizon in the sky above them.

The trio of ghosts waited unnoticed among the trees for the hunters to pass by, and then followed them out to make certain the de Chagny group left the premises.

Jean said, "What a delicious moment when you blew that powder into Raoul's face. What was it?"

"A substance called *Phantastica*. It's pulverized mushrooms and herbs in powdered sugar. The iridescence is added for effect. When breathed in it causes a severe, but temporary madness. He'll be fine in a day or so."

The Daroga added dryly, "Most resourceful. I'm glad you thought of it. You didn't happen to blow a powder on Christine to make her love you, did you? Because how she feels about you seems to defy all reasonable logic."

"I'd make a mint selling such a thing if I had it. Men everywhere would want some."

Jean spoke up, "I'd purchase a whole barrel full and fling it all over Meg."

The three chuckled. They had reached the edge of the trees near the house and watched Raoul's men put him in their carriage and leave.

Inside the house, they were greeted by relieved hugs and kisses. Jean proudly showed off a bullet hole in his cape, producing the desired effect within Meg, who thought him so brave and cunning. He winked at Erik as she embraced him. Christine and Meg wanted to hear all the details of the chase through the cemetery but Erik held up his hand. "On the way to the estate we'll tell you everything. Daroga, if you would be so kind as to get Jean's carriage and bring it here for us. I would like to give these three a near-Eastern present." The Daroga nodded, and Erik invited the fugitives to each take a chair.

He stood behind Christine and asked her to close her eyes. As Jean and Meg watched, he took an ampule from inside his cape and broke it above Christine's head allowing an essence to fall into her hair. She was immediately enfolded in the sweet scent of field grass and leaned her head back to enjoy it. The Phantom massaged her temples and her neck, telling her softly what a capable, good person she was, how much he loved her in all things and without question. When he finished he told her to rest for a few minutes and moved to Meg. Over her he broke an ampule containing the delicate smell of lilies, which lingered and soothed. He rubbed Meg's palms and forearms, telling her that bravery and courage like hers were unsurpassed in the annals of history. He pledged his undying friendship, and vowed to stand with her all his life.

He went to Jean, who anxiously awaited his treatment. He had never seen a ritual such as this before and was most intrigued to feel its effect.

As the Daroga re-entered the room, Erik placed a leaf of tarragon in Jean's mouth. Over Jean's head he broke a small, bulbous glass containing the essence of cinnamon. He massaged Jean's shoulders and scalp, lauding the fervent loyalty and trust Jean gave so freely to their troupe. He called Jean 'The Achilles of France', and told him how honored he was to be counted among those Jean called friends.

When the gift was complete, the three fugitives opened their eyes, feeling refreshed and invigorated despite the tension and emotional trauma of their recent days. They gathered up the sleeping children and what few belongings they had with them, and left the cemetery in Jean's carriage with Erik and Khalil's horses tied to the back. The Phantom drove while Jean and the Daroga sat inside the brougham and recounted their adventure among the tombs. Erik smiled as he listened to their embellishments, and the gales of enthusiastic laughter that followed each description. At one point he even found himself laughing and stomping his foot. They parted company on the road outside Jean's estate, and once attaining the pleasantness of their clean individual beds, they each slept through the day and did not rise until the evening.

In the morning a young police officer handed Detective Edwards a report claiming vandalism at the cemetery. The detective went reluctantly to investigate. He didn't relish the idea of viewing the handiwork of teenagers out for sport, but the officer told him there might be some interesting stuff to see at a graveyard. Since the private investigators had quit their surveillance of Madame Giry's last evening, he felt he could move on to other matters. Thomas climbed around the graves and read the notes, studied the angel with the peculiarly smashed face, and found traces of the blue powder. He tasted the later and thought it curiously odd. *Whoever did this is intelligent, out for recompense, and possesses an astute knowledge of chemistry.*

Edwards located the head caretaker and interviewed the man in front of the workers' cottages. He listened attentively as the fellow told him that his cousin, who was employed at the Castelot-Barbezac estate as a groomsman, rented a cottage for an indefinite period of time. He had been well paid to let a small party stay there. Two women, three children and a man comprised the company. One of the women was badly bruised and looked to have been in a fearsome fight. When the detective asked if he had heard their names, the caretaker told him the man was called Jean and the two women were Meg and Christine. He was never given a last name, but believed them to be well educated, as they had a nice way with words and refined manners. The renters were no trouble but had already left. When the detective entered the cottage, he smelled a pleasant combination of aromas. He walked around and felt the stove; it hadn't been used in hours. All was neat and in order. He counted the number of cots and the number of chairs and then went to the stable area and spoke with the man caring for the animals. He could add nothing further to the mystery except that the renters had stored a carriage and two horses with them. The carriage bore no insignias but was definitely upper class, fine leather seats, oaks trims, and plush velvet curtains.

The detective stood outside the humble group of houses with his hands in his coat pockets, and decided to light up a pipe. As he inhaled on the stem, enjoying the taste of the tobacco smoke, he played with the names in his head. *Jean, Christine, Meg, and 'Raoul' on the wall in the cemetery…Meg and Jean…Jean and Margaret de Castelot-Barbezac? Yes. Christine and Raoul…Raoul and Christine de Chagny, de Chagny! He remembered the funeral of Imel Grey. And what do all these people have in common? Madame Louisa Giry!* He held his pipe thoughtfully as a flood of ideas and connections streamed into his mind. The sudden vision of the two men watching the ballet studio, day and night, jarred his brain with a profoundly accurate realization. He was willing to bet that the woman who had been beaten to a pulp was Christine de Chagny. Genuinely irritated, he knocked the tobacco from the pipe's bowl with the heel of his shoe, then hurried back to the police station to make further inquires.

25 *THE ABDUCTION RECALLED*

The aggrieved and reluctant Count de Chagny proved to himself he could be a man of his word, and purchased the house on Rue du Renard for Christine. His solicitor brought the keys to her, but not the deed. By way of explanation she was told that the transfer of land needed time to be officially recorded. The advocate assured her that the house was available for her immediate occupancy. She could proceed to move in and decorate at her discretion, as her husband was giving her carte blanche with the home. With a degree of condescension, the solicitor told her that the Count was also willing to give her a weekly allowance of a thousand francs. He handed her an envelope containing a considerably larger sum of money as an initial present, explaining that Raoul's generosity would allow her to establish herself. In return for this subsidy, her husband requested that she keep the matters at hand in complete privacy, and that she not involve others in the circle of trust she had already extended to her current hosts. Christine asked for the letter with Raoul's pledge of safety for her and Meg's family during the separation. The advocate was not in possession of such a declaration, but promised that he would make inquiry as to its status. He informed her that her magnanimous husband wished to reunite with his wife, and had purchased the house in good faith, believing she would earnestly consider reconciliation.

Meg and Christine paid a prompt visit to Monsieur Toussaint at his offices. The lawyer agreed to compose a letter to Raoul requesting that all future communications to his wife come through him, and in writing. Christine wore a demure black dress and a black hat with an almost opaque veil drawn down below her chin. She lifted the veil and let Toussaint view her face before lowering it back into place. From behind his desk, Toussaint, a kind and sensitive man who prided himself on the honor with which he represented his clients, told her that to represent her properly he needed to be quite blunt. She asked that he continue. "Madame, I assure you that I will work diligently on your behalf, but there should be no further verbal agreements between you and your husband. We should seek a formal written statement outlining the specific terms of this separation, the amount of the weekly stipend, and the manner in which he may visit the children. Nothing less is acceptable if we are to provide for your safety and care."

Christine agreed. Toussaint told her that since the Count now owned the property and had extended the keys to her, she was indeed free to move into the dwelling. He counseled her to practice extreme caution and not provoke Raoul. "Change the locks and have new keys made at once, Countess. Try not to be alone in the house until the terms are more formalized."

The two ladies proceeded to the house for their first tour. Christine's hand trembled as she unlocked the front door. They peered into a pleasant entranceway, the back of which revealed a staircase with a banister leading up to the second floor.

"Go on, go in," urged Meg. "It's yours. The skies forecast sunshine, but it could rain at any moment and we'd be stuck in the downpour!"

Christine smiled at Meg's prodding and entered. The house was somewhat smaller than the ballet studio but had the same general architecture. To their right was a formal parlor with a set of French doors leading into a dining room. From the parlor's windows they had a full view of Madame Giry's. Meg squeezed Christine's hand encouragingly as they looked to the dormer windows in the roof across the street. On further examination, they found a most adequate kitchen situated at the back of the house, directly behind the entry and staircase. They located the laundry area and the larder in the basement. The backyard was small but held ample space for the addition of a conservatory with tall glass windows and wicker furniture. Meg laughed, spreading out her arms in a sweeping prediction, "With some plants and a few touches, what a fine place it will be to relax in the spring and summer."

Christine felt herself unwinding and began to enjoy the adventure. To the left of the front entrance was a less formal sitting room with a splendid gray stone fireplace for gatherings. A hallway leading off this family room produced a smaller room used by the former mistress as a sewing area. The room just across the hall appeared to have been utilized by her husband as an office. At the end of the hallway, they found a large game room that occupied the entire north end of the first floor. Its windows encompassed views of the back yard and the Boulevard of Ships. On the front side of the house it looked directly at the corner occupied by Madame Giry's office.

Christine's eyes lit up. "This will be my bedroom!"

Meg quickly surveyed the distance to her mother's official domain and teased her friend. "Well then, we'd better be about the business of buying you a bed and some linens!" The ladies linked arms in solidarity and toured the second floor. There they uncovered bedrooms, one of which would make an excellent playroom for the boys. The third floor was an unfinished attic area used for storage. All in all, the house suited Christine and her needs very well. Hugging her shoulders she permitted herself a tiny, buoyant flip of hope.

Meg winked at her and asked, "Shall we go across the street and visit Mama?"

Erik's initial contribution to her home was to haul Anubis out of the carriage house and place him against an inside wall in Christine's future bedroom. The statue would become a door leading to a tunnel traveling under the street to one of the Erik's secluded basement rooms. Erik and the Daroga commenced digging at once, planning to formulate their own set of building codes as they worked.

With the men industriously occupied, Madame Giry, Meg and Christine sat down excitedly to make their own plans.

"Curtains first," declared Meg, mischievously elbowing Christine, "and a bed, Mama! Where shall we hunt for a bed?"

Christine blushed a rosy shade of pink and cheerfully added, "Yes, where?"

Little Grace was quite taken with the ladies' animation and started to ask questions about the unfolding plans, wanting very much to be involved in setting up the home. Grace had become a precious part of their clan. She called Madame Giry 'Mama', and everyone referred to Imel as 'Cousin Richard'. Imel said he rather liked the appellation, confessing that it sounded irreverently grand to him. Grace threw an occasional temper tantrum, but Louisa and Imel had become adept at soothing her. In one regard they were especially blessed, Grace unabashedly loved music. No one ever had to direct her twice to begin a lesson. Every morning after breakfast she eagerly climbed up on the piano's bench and started picking out notes with Louisa. Her head bobbing happily between the sheets of music and the magical keys where she sought to place her fingers.

Sometimes, when she was an exceptionally good girl, the Angel of Music sang to her at night before she slept. Those visits were always considered extremely special. She was very bright and quickly made the association between temper tantrums and no songs from the angel. For her birthday on December third, they decided to give Grace a ring with a small ruby, something that would remind her how much they all cared for her. The child loved the ring and spent all day admiring its brilliance under different lights. When she worried that she'd grow out of it, they assured her it could be sized so that it would always fit her as she grew. She seemed pleased with their answer and gradually bestowed more trust upon her new caregivers. She never discussed her life with the Rupae sisters. Whatever had happened to her while she was under their supervision she kept locked away in her mind, safely obliterated from her current life.

On one particularly stressful winter day, when she had not been allowed on a shopping trip for furniture, but had remained good natured and accepting anyway, the Angel of Music came to sing to her while she tossed restlessly in her bed. When she finally fell asleep he emerged from the wall and sat beside her. Grace's nostrils flared defiantly with every inhalation. He recognized a superior determination to succeed, housed in a small body of energy. His head leaned to the side. Something struck him as odd about the way she balled her hands into tight little fists, even in sleep. From some dark space within, Erik instinctually knew she had already been violated. The realization saddened him. *Your secret is safe with me, child.* He passed his hand in the air over her head. *Stay strong, struggle with what has befallen you, but overcome it. Someday you will find a man to love you, so strive to love yourself as well.* He stopped and listened to his thoughts for Grace, reverberate back to him in the canyon of his mind.

In the second week of December, when the painters finished her bedroom walls and her new bed was about to be delivered, Christine had a nightmare as she slept at Meg and Jean's estate. She planned to move herself into the house as soon as possible and bring the boys when their rooms were prepared, but the stress of these transitions was taking its inevitable toll. In her dream she climbed up a long winding staircase to visit the Angel of Music. When she arrived at the top she found a shower running. She gently drew back an orange curtain to greet him, and a hideous stranger with a mocking laugh, turned to face her. His entire head was a nearly skinless yellow skull. He had no nose at all, only a black upside-down heart shaped hole to breathe through. She tried to retreat, but he grasped her wrist, screeching at her through clattering, diseased teeth. "Don't be frightened because I have no nose, Christine! You saw my face in the underground. You know it's a cellulose appliance I put on and take off as I please. Here, you can hold it while I clean it." He dropped the odious thing into her palm, and reached for a ridiculously over-sized brush with steel bristles. He was going to scrub the dried mucous off it right in her hand! Disgusted, she threw the detestable object at him and ran screaming down a narrow hall. She awoke scolding herself for her truly shameful lack of resolve and went to the kitchen to make a cup of hot chocolate.

That same night a worried Madame Giry also experienced a frightening nightmare, one that left her drenched in sweat. Early in the morning she hurried to the third floor to tell Erik about her malevolent, foreboding dream.

In an effort to calm her, he remarked, "Now you're having dreams too? Wait, let me guess. An angel blossomed out of a golden pear and told you I was fighting a battle against a thorny, self-loathing dragon." He didn't want to alarm Louisa by admitting that he too was experiencing an irritating sense of impending violence.

He was elated to have Christine move in across the street, but had misgivings that their relationship could evolve as harmoniously as she wished. Suffering from feelings of inadequacy, he worried almost constantly about her safety. How could he protect her from Raoul's vengeful anger, and his own unpredictable nature? Raoul wasn't a dog; he wouldn't just lie down and lick his wounds in consolation. Erik knew he would have to deal with him, but on what terms and in what arena? It irked him that he couldn't shake these needling premonitions, and the apprehension that he would prove inept as a husband and father. More than anything, he longed, just for once, to experience real joy and a hopeful outlook. He cursed the evil fears that invaded his mind like a marauding army of Saracens, but was at a loss as to how to combat them.

Louisa's answer pulled him from his gloomy thoughts. "No, there was nothing about angels in my dream. There was, however, a raging fire and your little boys were in it! We need to take heed to this, Erik. It may be a warning."

He passed her a cup of coffee. "When will the water be turned on across the street?"

Louisa's dream was quickly placed on the back burner, as a horse and moving van pulled up outside Christine's house announcing the arrival of some new furniture.

"I'll go down to them, they're early," Louisa said.

All that Christine had purchased so far was a Louise Philippe bed and several comfortable chairs. Other items were being considered, but she wanted to get the walls freshened with paint and wallpaper before adding more furnishings. Under Louisa's instructions, the movers started placing the items from their vehicle into Christine's new bedroom. As the deliverymen worked, the painters arrived, followed closely by a carriage containing Meg and Christine. Thus the hustle of the new day began, with Erik and the Daroga plowing their way under the street, and the women busy with their continued planning.

Towards mid-day, Doctor DeVille appeared at Christine's front door with a pleasant, reassuring smile and a Japanese Sago Palm in a pot. "They say these make wonderful house plants," he announced. "They're easy to grow. I haven't killed mine."

"Thank you, Abraham, please come in. I'm afraid the only chairs I own are in my bedroom. Let me go get them," a nearly mended Christine offered.

The doctor added quickly, "Wait, we can sit in there. I know you're all extremely busy, but what I want to discuss with you may be of value. Please allow me to speak with you and the maestro privately. Perhaps the painters could break early for lunch."

Madame Giry took the plant from the doctor's arms to place it in the kitchen, and a winsome Meg chimed in, "Christine, do you trust me to pick out a kitchen table and chairs?"

"Yes, of course. It will be a relief to make one less decision. I love your tastes. Surprise me."

Meg winked and taking Grace's hand, shouted, "Mama, can Grace come with me?"

Madame Giry reappeared and took one look at Grace's longing face. "Oh, go. Have a good time, just promise you won't leave Meg's side! I'll stay busy across the street and prepare some food. Doctor, please stay and eat with us, stay for dinner as well. We'll fill you in on all the latest developments. They're so unbelievably wonderful! I'll pull our boy out of the dirt and send him to you."

DeVille inquired, "Erik is in the dirt? Where?"

"I'll let him tell you," Christine offered with a most intriguing grin. She introduced the painters to the doctor and then sent them on their break. DeVille took a tour of the house with her and when they entered her bedroom the life-size statue of Anubis caught his full attention.

"A ruse," came Christine's captivating reply.

"A stratagem," corrected a dirty Erik from the doorway. He held a tray of teacups with a pot sent over by Louisa. "I apologize for my appearance. I left my project and hurried over when Louisa told me you were here. The Daroga and I are tunneling."

DeVille clasped Erik's hand. "Fascinating. I've been worried about you, but I can see you are keeping yourself quite occupied. Is this what I think it is?" He pointed to Anubis.

"A door," answered Erik.

"Figuratively and actually...yes?"

"Yes." Erik sat on the wood floor and Christine and the doctor settled into the chairs.

DeVille wasted no time getting to the point. "I've been doing some research and I believe you have adequate grounds on which to annul your marriage to Raoul. If he believed himself to be sterile before he wed you and failed to inform you, he married you under false pretense. Apparently, both the state and the church agree with me. I've learned that the Catholic Church is especially adamant on a sanctified marriage being the only proper conveyance for the birthing of children. In fact, according to them, the sole purpose of marital intercourse is to produce children!"

Christine's response to Abraham's happy report bordered on sadness, "Raoul wants a reconciliation. I haven't decided how to respond to that repulsive request, much less pursue an annulment."

The doctor counseled her like a protective father. "You respond through your lawyer. Let him deal with Raoul de Chagny. Has Raoul apologized or shown any kind of remorse for the assault?"

"No, but I pushed him past the edge of reason. This is my fault."

"Christine, Raoul beating you black and blue is Raoul's fault, not yours. He is solely responsible for his actions. Don't mollify them. This transition is exciting and stressful for both you…and Erik. A sound relationship, like a sound home, is built on a foundation of understanding. Can we take a little time here? I want you to consider providing me with more information. I'm at an impasse now and want to assist you. I believe it is possible for the two of you to have the emotional and physical security you so desire." The doctor turned to Erik, "Help me to fully comprehend why she calls you the world's greatest soul, Erik, and under what set of circumstances does she refer to you as her first husband?"

Christine sighed deeply and sat back in her chair, musing softly. "The answer to those two questions lies in the answer to this one. How does a talented genius with a face considered ugly by the world, get a seventeen year old girl he's ruefully abducted – to actually love him? He forms a plan, Dr. DeVille, he forms a plan and he weaves it like a tapestry. Tempting the soul to fix upon its pleasures by drawing in the intricate colors and patterns that will please the eye, and he does this with the patience and persistence of a master craftsman."

Erik lowered his head in shame. He knew there were other ways to win a woman's heart, but at the time he'd been sick with love for her, and spurred into recklessness by Raoul's unwelcomed courtship. Listening to her verbalize the abduction of four years ago would mean experiencing it from her perspective. It would be agony to know her perceptions. He'd frightened her terribly. *What will be gained if I leave? Nothing. According to Abraham, acknowledging my actions will improve the dereliction of my mind. In the end, won't I understand her just that much better?*

Abraham asked him, "You agree to hear her account of this event?"

Erik's eyes were disconsolate and sober. "If she will tell it, I will listen."

Abraham looked with compassion at Christine. "Please, give me these pieces to the puzzle."

Christine drifted away for a few moments, traveling mentally to the memory of those unpleasant times. "The home he built for himself in the caverns, lies between two massive rectangular foundation walls that support the structure above, and keep the waters of the subterranean lake contained. It smells of mold and decay down there, but less so inside the house, where the heat of the candles and the fireplace tend to keep the wetness at bay. The walls are of uneven stone, the rocks jut out in peculiar places. I awake in a haze, the stench of chloroform in my throat, strange shadow-shapes form and move across the rocks in the shimmering light of the flames. As the candles burn down, it chills my blood, for without the movements of these odd shadow creatures, I realize I will be in the pitch-black. So I cherish even the scariest light, no matter how disorienting. Occasionally, muffled, almost imperceptible sounds come across the black waters of the lake. I cannot begin to fathom their meaning...they leave too quickly and bring no consolation. For the most part, there is total silence, and in that despondent, forlorn absence of sound my terrified mind wanders freely and knows no peace. I am alone.

"This eerie, isolated place where I am held prisoner contains a bizarre mixture of furniture. My captor sleeps in his own room, in a coffin, to remind him of his own unavoidable death, while I am placed in a bedroom with a normal bed. There is a sitting room of Louis Philippe furniture and a sad collection of faded silk flowers. To the side, up some steps of stone, a landing contains a massive black and gold organ. When the misanthrope pounds at the instrument the stones vibrate unmercifully."

Through some clever device, she had allowed her mind to stand distinctly in two worlds, the past and the present. Her face was the color of wax, her voice somber and contained, as if she moved through the rear of a dimly lit church to attend a funeral. "You know, doctor, his music entreats and commands. It tears the heart and withers hope, and if he sings," she gasped and drew back in her chair, her shoulders sagging. "Well...if he sings, there is nothing to do but surrender and let his voice take you wherever he wishes...because he is the master and capable of accomplishing whatever pleases him."

She rubbed her upper arms as if she were in a draft. Erik got up and wrapped a shawl around her shoulders, then stood at a distance with his arms folded, listening.

"My teacher, my Angel of Music has become my jailor! He avows love for me, but what kind of love disquiets and terrorizes? I am enamored by Raoul and want to run away from Paris with the *Vicomte*. When Erik abducts me from the stage during my performance and carries me to this home of horrors, I am angrier than I have ever been in my life. When he returns and bursts through the door, like a madman on a wild rampage, I insult his hair and his choice of attire, I curse his birth...then turn right around and almost incoherently beg for freedom, knowing full well he will never grant it. He churns around the parlor, whining bitterly that I have given him no alternative but to steal me. Leaving with Raoul would be an odious mistake, my love is not meant for the spoiled prince-ling! It is Erik's prize, Erik's alone! We are two irrational human beings, emotion ruling every word, every desperate gesture.

"When he leaves to check the caverns, I succumb to hopelessness. In an effort to destroy myself, I strike my head repeatedly against a jagged wall. Dazed, I crumble to the floor and there I sit, bleeding all over my captor's Persian carpet, waiting like a child for his assistance. 'What foolishness have you attempted?' he asks as he helps me to my feet. His sniveling words are so insincere. He ties me with rope to a chair, telling me it's for my own safety. Oh, how I hate him! I dread the loathsome, icy touch of his fingers on my person, his foul, despicable breath! During those first hours of my captivity, my kidnapper is agitated and anxious. He comes and goes from the house to the upper levels of the world many times. He watches intently, fearing that those from above will attempt a rescue and stumble upon the access to his house. He checks on me regularly, ranting and blistering about Raoul, then storms out on yet another slavish scouting trip.

"On his last deranged expedition, the Daroga and Raoul actually make it past him, but they fall through a stone passageway right into Erik's chamber of mirrors! My crazed imprisoner is delighted when he discovers that he now has two additional victims to torture. With gruesome intent he heats the chamber, and in a frenzied speech pleads with me to marry him. His will is strong. The men are broiling inside Erik's invention and he has not an ounce of compassion for them. He bullies me into believing that he will roast them alive if I don't consent to be his living bride. The only way to win their freedom is to agree to Erik's coercion.

"He shows me a box on the mantle. It contains two intricate bronze levers. One is a scorpion and the other, a grasshopper. If I turn the grasshopper something horrible will happen. The four of us, and everyone in the theater above, will be destroyed as barrels of gunpowder beneath the floor explode. He says there is enough to level the block! But if I turn the scorpion, all will be saved…except that I have sealed my fate, and given my word that I will become his bride! Back and forth…my mind whips between the two choices. Marriage to Erik or death to scores of people! What can I do but acknowledge the worth of the souls he has trapped and condemned so maliciously? I turn the scorpion, expecting to witness the instantaneous release of the Daroga and Raoul from the torture chamber, but there is to be no end to the torment Erik is willing to administer. We have entered the sovereign presence of Satan's own son, and he stands immobile, catatonic, staring at me in nerve rattling silence. The unmasked portion of his face is blank. What fearful, dreaded emotions lay hidden from me behind those sulfurous eyes? His arms hang limp at his sides, his hands are idle! We are about to perish and he does nothing!

"Moments of excruciating terror slip past. Are they dead? No. Now I hear the sound of water filling the container of mirrors next door. Relieved from the heat, the Daroga and Raoul shout in thanksgiving. While Erik and I stand outside their cell, looking at each other like two idiots consigned to hell. He is perfectly erect, the tallest, darkest, most menacing soul I have ever seen. The water inside the chamber keeps rising and rising, apparently reaching a level where it threatens to drown its two victims. The Daroga starts pleading with Erik to turn off the tap…turn the scorpion so the water will recede.

"The situation is beyond belief. First he will roast them, now he will drown them, these men whose only crime is that of trying to release me from imprisonment! I have to secure their freedom, so I step up close to Erik. Taking one of his arms, I place it around my waist. He moves like a mannequin, holding whatever position I stick him in. I take his other arm and place it around me as well, tearfully vowing that I wed him on the spot, he is my husband...always and forever! Then I place my mouth on his and kiss the Dealer of Death as fully, and as deeply, as I can muster."

Her mind left them for a moment, gradually the color heightened in her cheeks. Abraham and Erik watched, marveling at her strength of character. She casually removed the shawl from her shoulders and laid it on the arm of the chair, using the action to firmly plant herself in the present. Somehow she had remembered that she was not living the past, only recalling it – made stronger in the distance afforded by time, she allowed the separation to empower her.

"When I broke the kiss, to which I might add he barely responded, I took his hands in mine and placed them over my heart. I begged him to listen to me. I swore again that I was his wife. I told him I did not wish two corpses for a wedding present, and those words seemed at last to return his mind to me! He twisted the scorpion and the water drained back out into the lake. We drew Khalil and Raoul unconscious from the chamber. When the Daroga regained thought Erik took him above ground to his brougham. On his shoulder he carried a still unconscious Raoul to a cell in a dungeon used by the Communards. He told me that Raoul needed care and a chance to regain his strength before he could free him.

"I expected Erik to deviously take his rights as a husband without delay, and prepared myself to cooperate, but he did not. Swirling around, he left me standing in the parlor and went to play his organ. The song was of no particular emotion just something soft and charming. I went to his side, asking what it was. He calmly told me that it was a German lullaby. I sat on some floor cushions beside his bench, confused, disheartened... in shock. I let the melody soothe my soul and I began to cry. When he asked what my tears were for, I told him I was grieving for the loss of the career I had hoped to achieve, the life I had planned with Raoul, and the end of my innocence which was about to be taken from me.

"He stopped the music and took my hand, helping me to my feet. Gently he escorted me to the couch and sat me down. He wet a cloth and came back to me, tenderly wiping my face and brushing the hair away from my forehead. He told me that he would not touch me intimately unless I wanted him to, that he loved me and would always love me, that he only wanted for us to be together that I might appreciate the depth of the feelings he held for me. He asked if there was anything that I wanted from him." At this point, Christine paused to chuckle. "I told him to please do something about the strong smell of decay about his person. I might add that he has only smelled of musk and tasted of tarragon, since then."

Christine leaned over and drank some tea before continuing her soliloquy. "I was exhausted and asked to sleep. I have no idea how long I slept; time is irrelevant in the underground. I awoke to the smell of food cooking and dressed quickly, emerging from my bedroom to find Erik placing breakfast on the table. He held out a chair for me and beckoned me to sit. Something about his attitude had changed. He seemed the courteous host, not the cruel monster, not the simpering animal that alternated between whimpering and demanding I love him. I liked this man. He was calm and elegant. Erik has always had a way of summoning me to him that is most intriguing. He raises his hand and rolls his fingers backwards, one by one, starting with the pinky and ending with a grasping motion, bringing his hand toward his chest. He used that gesture to call me silently to him that morning and I came.

"I have never been able to read his mind, but on many occasions he has read mine. He told me I was ravenous and needed to eat, and indeed I was. As I sat there stuffing eggs and pork down my throat he spoke to me in a kind, mild tone. He explained that I had come of age and needed a man, a mate, and that he was going to be that man. He told me he wanted an opportunity to show me something of his nature, his true nature, and asked that I be patient while he did so. He pointed to a little wooden box turned upside down on the tabletop between us. He said that the box represented us, and the topsy-turvy world we presently found ourselves in. He gave me his word that he would take good care of Raoul and instructed me to never speak Raoul's name outloud to him during this preliminary period of our relationship. He asked, that should I ever honestly find myself attracted to him, I go instantly to the little box, turn it right side up and read its contents. And then he swore to me, that if I did not want him as a man by the end of two weeks, he would free me. All he desired was this one chance to be accepted as a loving husband."

At this point Christine began to cry. Tears spilled over her eyelids and onto her dress. Initially, she made no attempt to wipe them. Erik came and knelt in front of her, his own tears streaming from beneath his work mask and down his dirty chin, leaving trails of wet grime. He handed her a clean handkerchief, kissing her palm profusely as she took it. She passed her left hand through his hair as she blew her nose with her right. Witnessing this sudden explosion of tender emotion between the two of them, Dr. DeVille asked if she wished to stop. She shook her head no, and kissed the top of Erik's head where it rested like a puppy in her lap.

She pushed his shoulders up and he turned himself around, resting his back against her knees. No longer afraid that he could not protect her, he would, no matter what the cost. Damn the entire world, he would lay down his life for her in an instant. All she needed to do was flinch as if she were in discomfort.

Christine began again to speak. "This is a great man who sits before you doctor, a generous, sweet soul…one that I hated with all my being, one that I teased and tormented, and one that I love now more than my own life. You see, I stood up from that breakfast table, screamed like a banshee and flung off his mask. Spitting at him, I raked my nails across the distorted side of his face. Blood spilled down upon his shirt and tears poured out his eyes as I called him every foul name I could think of. And he sat there, never raising a hand to me, never trying to stop me. I ran to my bedroom and slammed the door shut. There was silence on the other side. No music, no singing…just silence."

The next few sentences she spoke sadly into the air above their heads. "Erik and I have shared such explicit joy and so much laughter, surely heaven must have learned of it from the ancient books of wisdom. Why on earth place the pain of such a stumbling block of revulsion and loathing between us?" She lowered her head and looked directly into Abraham's kind, consoling eyes. "It isn't heaven that calls the players forth to act, is it? We're not in a divine game. No, it's our own natures, and the depth of our own characters that put us to the test." She passed her hand again through Erik's hair.

"When I came out from my room I found him sitting in a chair beside his coffin, reading a book. He acted as if nothing had happened and smiled at me when I approached. He wore the mask again and had on a comfortable wool jacket with a shirt unbuttoned at the collar, no tie. He seemed to be a man relaxing at home. When I started to apologize for hurting him, he rose and touched his finger to my lips to silence me. He said he was reading The Iliad, for the hundredth time, and asked if I would like to have him explain the story up to this point. We went into the parlor, but instead of just relating the tale's events to me," here Christine paused to suppress a chuckle, "he acted them out. Swords plunged into warriors, chariots ran wild, heroes were victorious then died. Hearts were given away in willful love. His animated portrayal was beautiful. I sat on the sidelines spellbound. In my mind I could see everything he described. When he brought me up to the point where he was in the book, he shut it with a crisp clap and announced in a prestigious voice, 'To be continued'. We went to the organ and he played while I sang. No stress, no demanding! He never insisted on his marital rights, never took them by force. We spent our days like that...filled with his colorful entertainments and the ecstasy of his music. He showed me his magic and his art of ventriloquism. He unrolled blueprints before me and explained the structures he'd built: palaces, secret passageways, stairs that come and go, doors and mirrors that turn and revolve back upon themselves. I was amazed at his wealth of talent and his skills.

"Then one day, after about a week," she rested her hand on Erik's shoulder in question, and he nodded affirmatively, "as we sat together on the couch, I asked him to take my hand and hold it. He did as I requested, but he didn't just hold it."

Erik got up and sat on the edge of her bed. He took her hand and began to demonstrate her words as she spoke them.

"He started to rub my palm with his thumbs, and massaged each finger from the base to the tip. Then he took my other hand and did the same with it. When he finished, he placed my hands in my lap. I was so relaxed. He stood up and lifted my feet to the couch, allowing me to lie down. I placed my hand over my eyes and told him that what he had done felt lovely. He asked if he could give me a present of smell, and I told him yes, please. I heard the tiny crunch of glass breaking, and all around my head was the delicate, sweet smell of field grass. I asked him what was next for I wanted more of this luscious feeling. He went to the end of the couch and put my feet in his lap, and started to rub them as he had my hands. With my permission he slid my stockings off so his hands could be directly on my skin. I have no idea how long he massaged my feet because I fell asleep. When I awoke, he was still holding them, waiting patiently. We ate dinner and each of us went to our individual beds to sleep. Everyday for three days I asked that he perform this ritual on me again. Each time he complied and slowly, slowly I began to feel more than relaxation. I began to feel arousal."

Erik stopped rubbing her and studied her face intently.

"On the third day, I took his hands and moved them further up my legs, he massaged where I directed. I unfastened my dress and rolled to my stomach, telling him to rub more of me. His delicious fingers worked over my back, my arms, my neck. When I turned to face him he was calm, totally in control, and not distant. I could see he was involved but restrained. I deliberately placed his hands upon my bare breasts and inched further up the couch until my head lay over the arm of it. With my chin extended and my face safely hidden from him, he carefully rubbed them until my entire body tingled. I told him to kiss me and he placed his mouth on my abdomen, so delicately that I thought I was being brushed with a feather. I could not bear the thought that he would not proceed lower, or do anything further, without my prompting him. I jumped from the couch and ran, half out of my dress, to the table. Turning the little box right side up, I found inside a small roll of parchment held by a black ribbon. In a curious, slurred handwriting of red ink it simply declared:

You may have me.

"The strength of those four precious words brought a young woman, held in secret beneath the ground, to his side. I placed the scroll in his hand and curled his fingers around it with my own. I heard the roaring of the sea in my ears, and for the first time in my life I knew where I truly belonged...beneath his wondrous hands. We went into my bedroom where we spent most of the next four days."

She covered her mouth with her hand and laughed. "Oh, we'd come out occasionally to eat but as we brushed against each other in the kitchen the attraction was magnetic. We'd start to kiss and touch, and end up returning to the bedroom to make love again. Those blissful days are a blur. I remember never seeming to have enough of him. He did everything I asked and more. He brought me through waves of pleasure, the intense peaks of which reached higher and higher. I gave myself to him completely and bound my love to him forever. He was *allegro, adagio,* whatever I desired, for as long as I wanted. Never would I have believed that a person could feel what I was experiencing. Not only did my mind exalt at his singing, but now his very touch brought on a dizzying exhilaration. There was no part of my body that he did not caress and kiss, nor I of him. I became lost in my addiction for him, a slave to the cravings I felt. He would leave to tend to Raoul and I could barely wait for his return. My mind lay dull to any other thoughts as my body waited for its lover to come back – hungry, so hungry to feel him move over me again. We opened some kind of door inside me, a floodgate into womanhood that I wished never to shut. Over and over he would pulsate through me. He became more than my mate, he was an extension of my very being, a part of me, the whole of me. Together we became one living thing, feeling only the other, tasting only the taste of the one held in our arms. We would sleep and wake only to roll like a ship on the waves again, I the capstan gladly bound with his ropes and lost...so lost in rapture that I longed to be swallowed whole inside him. Then on the fifth day of our intimacy he took me to his own bathtub and bathed me, washing me carefully, his hands lingering on my body in the bath water as if to memorize every curve, every hollow beneath his touch."

Christine surveyed her palm, and continued speaking resolutely to it alone, as if she had dismissed the two men in the room from her mind, and now addressed only her own body. "He dried me and tenderly dressed me in new clothes, new shoes. When I went to kiss him, he kissed me back. His lips were soft and lingering, clinging to my mouth as if unwilling to separate. I thought we were going out somewhere together. He took me in his boat to the *Rue Scribe* side of the lake, where Raoul was standing, waiting. I could see Raoul as we came to the water's edge, but he could not see us. I climbed lightheartedly up onto the little wooden dock and walked for a ways toward him. I wanted to tell him how happy I was married to Erik. That he shouldn't worry about me, for I wasn't his true love as he had thought, I was Erik's. I turned to make sure that Erik was behind me, but the boat had already retreated into the blackness.

"Too late I realized he was freeing me. I ran along the bank screaming for him to come back, pleading for him to retrieve me. Raoul heard my cries, stumbled into the darkness until he found me and pulled me, like a dog, after him. I resisted and tried to free myself from his grip but he hauled me behind him, ignoring my pleas. He yanked me through the wrought iron gate and it slammed shut. I wanted back inside but the gate self-locks. As I shook its bars, calling tearfully for Erik, Raoul wrenched me clear and hurried me up the street. Raoul checked us into a hotel and tried to reason with me, but I refused to speak, waiting for a chance to spring away."

Christine lowered her hand. "Three weeks later a notice appeared in the classified section of the paper stating, 'Erik is dead'. Raoul showed it to me and explained that Erik had told him to watch for it. He said that his body would be by the artesian well below the fifth cellar. I could go and say good-bye to it if I wanted. We went to the Daroga's house and Khalil escorted me to the lake. The body was wrapped in bandages exactly where Raoul said it would be. We buried it in a crevice in the wall and covered it over with rocks. The Daroga told me to leave my little gold band with it, and I did. He said I was free now to marry another. A month later, Raoul and I were wed in the cathedral. Shortly after that, the papers reported that the police had found a charred, quartered body in the tunnels under the Opera House. They declared the reign of the Opera Ghost at its ignominious end. That someone seeking vengeance had meted out an appropriate judgment upon the Phantom. I was supposed to believe that the body we had buried, and the one that was found hacked and burned were the same, but in every private moment I reached out for Erik and I could feel him still alive. I tried to live but felt empty…emotionless. Where was the Thief of Thieves who had plundered my heart and my woman's body? Gone, evaporated. Time started to crawl by. It took forever for an hour to pass, and then an aching eternity for the next to end. Desolate without him I surrendered to grief and began to die, slowly, in tortuous…miniscule amounts."

Erik took her hand in his again and sighed deeply. He spoke in a solemn, rhythmic tone. "My life has always been about hiding and surviving. I learned to be an expert engineer of secret passages and trapdoors. Always prepared with a way out, a way to escape and flee to freedom. I never wanted anything like I wanted Christine. When she turned the scorpion I was in shock, I couldn't believe her bravery! Oh, I knew she did it to save Raoul and the Daroga. I like to think I would not have killed them. I knew to the second how much time it would take to end their lives in the chamber, but I was near delirium with lovesickness. I don't honestly know if I could have let them out on my own. I was consumed with despair and wanted her, or a quick death to end the misery that was eating me alive. When she agreed to be my wife there was no trapdoor to flee through. I was numb…standing there looking at my wife!

"My mind told me to seize the opportunity, to show her who I was, that if given the chance I could be magnanimous, gracious and intelligent. On the couch, when she finally gave me her hand, I saw the door opening. She just didn't know how to walk through it, so I showed her. It was easy to practice restraint because she was walking straight toward me." He tapped his breast. "When she surrendered her body I showed her things that please and delight the human flesh. Then I responded to her will, whatever she wanted, and as many times as she desired it be performed. I defined my love for her by performing the acts that satisfied her. I gave in to her will...her will, not mine, and a strange thing happened. I watched her bloom and open up her body to me, accepting me completely. She actually craved me – me! My compulsion to have her for myself changed into something else. It evolved into a different form of love, a deeper love I was unprepared to experience. I listened to the Daroga, who berated me for stealing her, and started to believe that I had no right to her. I had stolen her, tricked her. And because I had come to love her, truly love her, I released her to have a normal marriage, a place of wealth and position. I thought I could live on the memory of those two weeks with her, so I re-entered celibacy. I experienced our time together in my mind – the rhythm of her body moving against me, the feel of her in my arms, her laugh, her manner of speaking. Each time I relived those days I yearned to see her. She was so close, still in Paris. I succumbed to her overpowering appeal. I would wait for a glimpse of her out on the street as she shopped, or as she went in to view a play. I tried to breathe the air that was just in her lungs, so I walked right behind her, taking in her scent but forbidding myself a touch. I told myself to back off, that I had released her with my contrived death, I was not worthy of her passion."

"Because you felt you couldn't keep up with her?" DeVille asked.

"No, because I believed I didn't deserve the guileless lust that she so willingly poured over me. I had to keep her free. I had tricked her into thinking I was the Angel of Music. I had abducted a pure soul and opened it to the world of sensuosity. I had no idea she loved me, too. She never told me and I never assumed it to be so."

DeVille rubbed his chin. "As I see it, her abduction delayed Raoul, and gave you a single shot at obtaining the impossible. You considered yourself unacceptable as a perspective beau, so you courted her through the walls of the theater. Even if you had some concept of normal courtship, I don't believe she would have permitted you the opportunity. Is that not so, Christine?"

She brightened, "You are correct! That is the precise truth of it. I was much too smug and priggish to have allowed it. You did the right thing, Erik! We've just been slow getting to where we should have been all along, because the obstacles were so great. Oh, thank you, Doctor. I see the truth of it for the first time!"

"Slow down. I want to ask you both if you want to say anything to each other at this point." Christine and Erik stood, taking each other by the wrists, tears springing into their eyes. Abraham thought Erik was going to apologize and suggested, "Perhaps I should step out," but neither of them paid any attention to their white haired physician.

Christine asked incredulously, "You walked right behind me?"

Erik leaned forward, "Many times, you are my wife."

She shook his arms, "And did you ever smell Raoul on me?"

"No! Never!"

"What does that tell you, Erik? Think!" She brought his hands to her chest.

"That even when you thought I might be dead, you couldn't get him off you fast enough."

"You have my heart, you always will. I love you! I love you! I should have escaped from Raoul and returned to you through the theater."

Erik responded, "I should have told you what was going on in my head, I just didn't know how to say it."

"It doesn't matter. It's in the past. The important thing is that you couldn't stay away from me. You had to have babies with me, even if only to end my depression!"

Even Abraham's eyes glassed over in tears. His head was actually bobbing with excitement as he announced, "Really, the two of you are married, married in the most ancient sense of the word. Yours is the queerest tale I've ever heard, and I've heard quite a few, but you are definitely married!" He took his empty teacup and placed it on the floor. "Marriage takes courage, so be brave. Erik, let every inch of dirt you move as you crawl to her under the street, remind you to never set her free again. She doesn't want to be free of you! Always remember that perfection doesn't make you worthy of love, it's an unreasonable criteria for none of us are perfect. It is your capacity to love that has made you loveable. Christine, he doesn't take for granted that you love him. He barely allows himself to accept the notion. You are going to have to tell him...and show him, every day. Now Erik, smash this under your foot, as a sign that what the two of you have done together, cannot be undone."

Erik did as he was told. The couple grabbed the doctor and hugged him to them.

"Blessings, children! *Mazel Tov*! You should only know health and happiness. Let nothing separate the two of you. Stay always together."

"And what about Raoul?" asked Erik.

"He should take another wife," Christine declared merrily.

Abraham added, "Yes, he should. He cannot have yours, Erik!"

26 *HEAT FROM THE DRAGON*

In the hectic weeks that followed, the two struggling lovers, now for the first time together in proximity and intent, cherished the promise the coming New Year held out to them. Everyone agreed that while Christine prepared her home, Christmas would be celebrated at Madame Giry's. Erik and the Daroga worked earnestly on building the tunnel. Initially they broke through the basement wall in Erik's room of paintings, worked downward to a level beneath the basement and across the street, shoring the walls with lumber as they proceeded. Once they attained Christine's basement they reached Anubis by constructing a simple wooden staircase that they concealed inside a temporary wall covered in paneling. They planned to enclose the area in brick at a later point in time. Everyday, workers appeared at the house to remove old wallpaper and paint, unaware of the labors going on in the basement.

Christine decided to live with a minimal amount of furniture until the walls and floors were finished. She purchased an armoire and the pieces necessary to create a sitting area in her bedroom. She chose muted greens and oranges for the entranceway and instructed the workers to proceed to the family room and the kitchen next. Every morning flowers, notes, boxes of candies and an assortment of presents arrived by messenger from Raoul. All of which she returned unopened, but she kept an accurate list of the dates and times of the deliveries, and gave them on a weekly basis to Monsieur Toussaint. The good Monsieur contacted Raoul's attorneys who repeatedly responded that they would keep their client in check. With the monotony of a mill grinding wheat into flour, they offered up a profusion of apologies and inane excuses why the deed was not signed over to Christine, and why she did not, as of yet, have a written agreement defining her separation.

Every rejected endearment stuck in Raoul's craw like a barb. A steady flow of alcohol did nothing to improve his humor. His temperament at the estate became foul and abusive. On a whim he would pick up some piece of crystal or porcelain and fling it as far he could. The aggravated head housekeeper ordered the comely Justine to follow him discreetly and clean up every mess. Secretly the woman hoped Raul would eye the maid and satisfy himself. But if Raoul did manage to spot the girl trailing after him, his anger boiled over furiously. The sight of Justine only made him think about his wife. He'd stomp around the mansion calling out that Christine was the most stubborn woman he had ever met, and hurl some other fragile object. When venting and alcohol refused to calm him, he called for his driver and ordered that he be carried to *Rue du Renard*. He'd sit in his brougham, stewing in his rage and spying. He saw Madame Giry cross the street, along with Meg, and a little girl he did not recognize, two elderly gentlemen, one with wispy white hair and the other with a pleasant, portly middle – but no one he could consider to be Christine's lover.

Raoul was not aware that on the corner directly across the Boulevard of Ships sat Detective Edwards in a coupe watching him through binoculars.

It irked Edwards that Louisa's house was once again being scrutinized. *How odd that the Count de Chagny sits in his carriage right out in the open! He certainly has a set on him.* The detective took pride in the notion that no one had discovered his presence, when actually, everyone but Raoul was cognizant of the detective's ongoing surveillance.

Looking out from one of the screens on the third floor, an un-amused Erik told the Daroga and Imel, "They hang out in the street like they're waiting for the arrival of the Pope. I could choke them both."

Wiping his face with a towel a jocular Daroga suggested, "Instead of choking them, let's join them. I'd love to mess with Raoul. He's probably like a skyrocket ready to explode while he sits in his coach fuming like a child. What a party we could have!"

Imel playfully entered in, "I could take a tray out and offer them both a drink."

"Hemlock," shot Erik.

"Look," said the Daroga. On the sidewalk below an authoritative Detective Edwards was marching straight toward Raoul's carriage. "Wouldn't you like to be a fly on that hat right now?"

Edwards rapped soundly on the carriage door and an impatient Raoul pulled the curtain aside. "What!"

The detective calmly bid the aggravated Count good evening and introduced himself. "Do you wish to report that your wife is missing?"

"No!"

"Well, do you wish to report that she's in danger?"

"No! Why are you asking?"

"You do seem to be spending a great deal of time vigilantly watching her house. I'm just curious. One could imagine, without too much difficulty, that you are protecting your wife, or perhaps hoping for a chance to sneak a glance of her."

Raoul's fist slammed against the inside of the carriage door. "I'm just admiring the house – and it is my house!"

"For hours on end, Sir?"

"Yes, I really like it a lot! If I wanted to protect my wife, I'd hire guards, and if I wished to see her I'd walk in the front door."

The Daroga elbowed Erik, "Raoul really looks pissed! Allah be praised, I love this!"

Once they breached Christine's basement, Erik spent his nights in her bed, where he could satisfy her lusts and be there to protect her. It concerned him greatly that she had not received the deed or the separation agreement. That night they lay together, discussing the latest item she'd sent back to Raoul, a large box from a local pottery. Erik patiently told her, "Perhaps you push too hard. Do you know he sits across the street sometimes and watches this house for hours?"

"I didn't know he sits out there. How far away is he?"

"A house or two down the block. I want to suffocate him with his own smugness."

Christine rolled over into his arms and slipped a slender, silken leg between his. "He'll tire of it eventually and move on. I don't want him to seek hope where there is none...my passions are for you alone. Long live the Angel of Music and may his nights be steeped in love!"

"Behold, a woman whose spine is straighter than a sword, a woman to be prized."

The following night Christine sat at her vanity in her riding pants and shirt. She was tired and not sure if she had the energy to draw a bath. She and Meg had spent the day making lists of items needed to stock the kitchen, and then gone into the attic to appraise it for useable space. Thinking about the rows of jellies that would one day be stacked on the attic's shelves, she picked up her brush and started on her hair. Behind her reflection she saw Raoul step into her room from the hallway. Outraged, she slammed the hairbrush down so hard she cracked the heavy piece of glass covering the top of the vanity.

Raoul ignored her display of temper. He was completely taken by the vision of Anubis in the corner. "What the hell is this? Is this the same fellow that was in the woods? I believe it is!" He walked over to it and without the cape around it, easily saw the latch. He opened the Shepherd of the Dead and found an empty sarcophagus. Closing the lid he looked around its sides. It appeared to be bolted and sealed tightly against the wall. Unbeknown to him, the entire statue, with its lid latched, moved on tiny wheels and cleverly pivoted away from the wall, revealing the stairs going downward to the tunnel. Raoul had only opened the cover and not discovered the triggering mechanism to the door. He stepped back frowning. "Rather ominous don't you think to have the Harbor Master of Death so close?"

"Raoul, get out!"

"This is my house, Christine." He grabbed her arm and on a capricious impulse threw her inside Anubis, holding it shut by leaning against it with his back. When she failed to make the rancorous protests he gleefully anticipated, he feared she lacked air, so he threw up his arms in frustration and opened the box. Christine waited patiently inside, her hands defiantly on her hips. He flung her into a chair and menacingly pulled a rope from his jacket pocket, threatening to tie her up. "Shall I restrain you in cords like he did?"

"You're no expert at restraint, Raoul. You're acting like a clown. Get out!"

Inflamed by her insult, he yelled, "You're driving me insane! You will not read my letters but you take my money. You return my gifts and are brazen enough to live in my house. I see no lover coming here, Christine. Who is he? Who replaced me, damn it! I know it's not Erik. Tell me it's not Erik! He's a bony freak of nature that doesn't deserve your heart the way I do! Why can't I have your heart? Look at your hand – you still flaunt my ring. How can I lose hope when you still wear the diamonds I gave you? You scorn your vows too easily, Madame!" He twisted the rope round his hands and pulled it taut like a garrote.

Ignoring the threat, Christine straightened her back and took hold of the chair's arms. *I can't give you my heart, because Erik's walking around with it.* "I'm sorry Raoul, I will not tell you who sired the boys. You can take my body and abuse it, but your physical strength and your threats will not win my heart. My heart is gone. It was gone a long time ago." She looked to the floor, the memory of the painful separation from Erik astonishingly sharp in her mind. Her voice became earnest and sad. "I don't think I realized how dead I actually felt inside. All I can offer you is my friendship, and coming here to accost me has put even that in jeopardy. You can have your ring."

"You're friendship means a great deal to me but I miss my wife! You are still my wife, you know. I'm tired of waiting out in the street to confront this devotee of yours. I believe I'll wait for him in here."

"I'm sorry I hurt you so much, Raoul, but if you're going to wait for him in here, you're going to have a long wait."

"Come home with me, we'll talk about this there. I'll not leave without you, so you really have no choice. Wake up, Christine! He still hasn't come to claim you. He doesn't want you, he'll never want you like I do. He's probably tired of playing 'Erik' for you. What can he give you that I cannot? Does he have an estate, money, and servants to wait on you? No, I doubt that he does. He would have used his influence before this, if he had any."

Knowing Raoul to be a potentially vicious man, Christine took care to speak in the past tense. "Erik gave me a kind of wealth you cannot comprehend, a wealth of soul."

"Are you saying you love his memory more than God?"

"He was a gift from God. Please Raoul, try to understand, being with him and then suddenly being without him, was more than I could cope with. I didn't take a lover for money or position, and certainly not for sex. I had those things with you. I wanted him to convey Erik's sincerity. Even the silent recreated moments of Erik's blessed presence touched upon my needs. My paramour helped me re-experience the past, helped me regain a taste of what I'd lost."

"Your words could anger a saint, they're certainly stoking **my** rage." Raoul twirled the rope in his hands. "What makes you think I want to hear any of this? I can be sincere. I'm being sincerely calm right now, and I've just heard you say you'd swoon and invite me to your bed if I'd just put on a goddamn mask!" Her continued rejection of him was unreasonable, provoking. He couldn't bear it. She'd called him a clown and he was no one's buffoon! Toxic juices began to percolate within him, eroding better judgment. Fervently his ego demanded her retribution. *Wrap the rope around her neck. Still those acidic, empty lips. Enjoy the cyanotic shade of blue she'll become!*

He savored the picture playing out in his mind. "Tell me where the scroll is, Christine."

After the Daroga and Imel said good night, Erik stayed a little longer on the third floor, putting the finishing touches on the second act of a musical play he was composing. During the day he'd had a few excellent ideas and wanted to get them down on paper. He stood up and extinguished the candle, deciding to look in on Louisa before crossing over beneath the street. The tunnel needed esthetics but was more than functional. He checked the street and found Raoul's carriage still stationed down the block. *Damn, he's persistent! Go home Raoul, let it go.*

Across the street, Raoul mocked her. "Not feeling up for further discussion, Christine?" He came around behind her on nimble legs. As she went to stand, trying to keep him in her visual field, he grabbed her by her long hair, forcing her to sit. The gun clicked in her ear as he cocked it. "You know, I absolutely hate the idea that you have this place. You'll bring the boys here as soon as you have it ready and whoever fathered them can come for a visit." He tied her arms to the chair.

"Raoul, don't do this!"

With a cursory wink he slipped a scarf from her vanity across her mouth and gagged her. "Shut up, Christine, if you won't tell me where the scroll is I'll burn the house down with you in it. I own it. I can destroy it. The scroll is probably in here somewhere. You'll be gone and unable to show it to anyone, and I'll have the boys. If this man happens to step forward with my family's history, I'll denounce him as your lover and the law will stand behind me." In haste, Christine stood with the chair attached to her, so he lashed both it and her to the bedpost. "You didn't think I could commit murder, did you? Surprise, I'm reveling in it! No blindfold for you, *Cherie,* I want you to watch all this foolishness come down around you."

Raoul un-cocked his gun and flew to the bedroom doorway. He ceremoniously waved good-bye before going into the family room where the painters had left cans of paint and thinners next to their drop cloths and brushes. He pried open several cans with the claw of a hammer and started throwing the oil based paint as high on the walls as possible. Some of the liquid splashed back down on him but he didn't care. When he finished with the paint he reached for the turpentine and doused the walls with all there was of it. He hollered to Christine, thinking to needle her. "I think I've uncovered a real talent, decorating seems to be one of my fortes." Because he was bellowing in the other room he didn't hear the wheels underneath Anubis move smoothly out from the wall.

Erik smelled the fumes before he opened the door. He entered quietly with his dagger drawn and looked with momentary dismay at Christine in the chair. *Still Alive!* Propping Anubis open with her hairbrush, he went quickly to cut her bonds. She pointed to the other room and he nodded. He handed her his candle and put her into the opening, whispering that she should go straight across the street. She pulled at him gesturing for him to leave with her but he shook his head, shutting Anubis behind her.

In the next room, a cavalier Raoul took out a cigar and a small box of matches. He stepped carelessly forward to light up his wall of art. The moment he struck the match several events happened almost simultaneously. The air directly in front of him belched into a blinding ball of blue-orange flame that ignited both him and the wall. Instantly set on fire, his eyelashes and eyebrows were seared off in a heartbeat. His hair went ablaze. Smacking the flames on his face with his hands, he howled in pain – then spun in confusion as the greedy flames consumed his clothes, roasting his skin.

The fire on the wall fed hungrily on the accelerant and quickly burned through the dry lathe and plaster, eating its way upward to the second floor. In seconds, the fire licked the ceiling over Raoul's head and broke through what would have been Michael's room above. The family sitting room was rapidly became engulfed. When Erik rounded the corner, a heavy acrid smoke was replacing the breathable air space, Raoul was staggering backwards resembling a human torch. Like a panther prowling close to the ground, Erik crawled on his belly to Raoul. Beneath the gathering level of smoke he went for his rival's knees, hitting them squarely from behind. Raoul hit the floor with a resounding thud, and Erik managed to roll him tightly in a painter's cloth, suffocating the flames.

Detective Edwards ran frantically from his carriage to Christine's front porch when he saw the flames gathering inside, but found the door locked and unforgiving to the repeated shove of his shoulder. He hurried to Raoul's sleeping driver and yelled out the location of the nearest fire station, then scurried round to the back where the windows were lower, thinking that perhaps he could break one and get inside from there. As he turned the corner the Phantom came through the front door, setting a still cocooned Raoul down from his shoulder onto the sidewalk just as the driver pulled up. "This is for Philippe," Erik whispered into Raoul's ear as the driver climbed down. "Get him to Dr. DeVille's on Summit Street." They lifted him into the carriage. "Hurry now, go on!" Barely had the driver placed the reigns in his hands when Erik smacked the rump of one of the horses, sending them off at a gallop.

Like a cat unleashed and free to save its young, the Phantom turned and sprang back inside. Finding the front room completely involved, he realized the seriousness of the fire's aggression and skirted around through the kitchen to get back to Anubis and the tunnel, unaware that the flames were already escalating through the attic and would soon involve the roof.

The Detective saw a man's shape run past the kitchen window, but could not swear the man was Raoul. He went to break the window with his elbow but the glass cracked on its own, before he could deliver the blow. A second later, the heated expanding air within the dwelling exploded outward, shattering all the windows and blowing the Detective off his feet with its pent-up force. He landed on his bottom fifteen feet into the back yard, and watched in horror as the intense flames leapt out toward him. Unable to shuffle backwards, he laid flat, barely escaping the fury's evil touch. A couple of blocks away, two *gendarmes* saw the brief fireball balloon upward into the sky, then settle downward. One of them ran to the fire station and the other to the street of the blaze.

Inside the tunnel Erik knocked down the temporary buttresses he and the Daroga had just installed, collapsing the tunnel close to Christine's house, then dashed toward Madame Giry's basement. He smelled the briefest whiff of Christine's perfume and knew she had passed safely through the passageway. Louisa was waiting for him as he surfaced on the other side. His irritated throat barely let him rasp out the words, "Your dream was true, it warned us."

He stunk of pungent smoke. With his mask and face streaked with black soot he bent over coughing up trails of black glue. Louisa helped him through the opening in the wall by propping the entrance with her body, and hauling him forward by his jacket's padded shoulders. "Thank goodness, the babies are not in there," she proclaimed.

Still coughing, he managed to choke out a question. "Christine?"

"In the street trying to get the fire hydrant opened."

Erik cleared the basement and sprinted full tilt through the ballet studio. The Palladian windows showed him the tragic scene of the house across the street, florid flames and smoke billowed from every opening. A fire wagon had already arrived. The firemen were off the vehicle priming their hose and taking positions to drench the house next to Christine's to protect it, as hers was obviously unsalvageable. He reached the porch just in time to see two *gendarmes* dragging Christine up the street, arresting her for tampering with a fire hydrant. Before he could vault over the steps and come to her aid, a huge volley of flames split the roof in two. The heat of this final, major evulsion drove the startled firemen back. People in the gathering crowd of onlookers let out a unified scream. Looking up, Erik could have sworn he saw the fire take the shape of a dragon's head. He froze in amazement.

Madame Giry reached his side. "Wait, don't expose your existence to them. We'll go to Toussaint and get her released. Get some money."

From one of the upstairs windows an excited Grace asked Cousin Richard if he saw the dragon. "He lifted his fiery head over Christine's house! Did you see it?" Imel braced himself on the windowsill but kept staring at the roof. Indeed, he had seen the beast and doubted if he would ever forget the unbelievable sight.

Having regained his ability to function and something of his hearing, Edwards came around the corner of the burning house and took in the drama playing out across the street. He saw Madame Giry standing next to a black-faced man, but the sight of two policemen putting a struggling woman, with wild hair and wearing pants, into a police wagon caught his attention. When he glanced back at the ballet studio the front door was closed, both Madame and the dark man were gone. His eyes traveled to the upstairs windows where another man with his mouth agape was beside little Grace. *Interesting, quite a crowd over there tonight.*

The police were pushing Christine into the wagon and she was resisting, straining to look at her house. "Let me go you imbeciles, there may be people in there!" she shrieked.

"What made you think you could tamper with the fire hydrant?"

She shoved her hands into the barrel-shaped chest of one of the policeman. "I read in the newspaper that they were installing more of them in our neighborhood. One does have to occupy one's mind somehow!"

"That does it! Get in wench!" They took her under the arms and the knees, lifted her up and tossed her into the wagon on her butt. One of them accidentally tore open the shoulder of her shirtsleeve. They laughed as they slammed the door shut. Listening to her kick at it with her shoes, they engaged the locks.

Edwards noted that the *gendarmes* had the flailing woman safely confined and went to speak to the fire captain, who had just arrived on site. He informed the captain that the fire may have been deliberately set, and wanted to know the officer's thoughts on the matter once they could get inside and investigate. Absorbed in thought the detective stepped up to the crowd of spectators, gesturing for them to move further back. *She managed to flee from you at the cemetery, so you torched this house, didn't you Raoul!*

The police wagon with Christine banging at it from the inside, pulled away as the detective rang Madame Giry's front door bell. She and Erik had already departed out the rear and were headed to Monsieur Toussaint's. Imel hurried down the stairs with little Grace beside him. The door opened and each serious faced man closely studied the other.

Edwards broke the gaze first and looked to Grace. "Hello, Grace, are you all right?"

The child nodded her head vigorously. "Is Christine safe? Her house is on fire."

"She's safe, honey. Don't worry," Edwards answered.

Grace's eyes grew big. "Her house, she's lost her whole house!" she wailed. As Imel reached down to her, she threw herself into his arms. He picked her up, patting her back as she buried her sobs into his shoulder.

The detective had a questioning look in his eye. "Excuse me, I'm Detective Thomas Edwards and you are?"

"Madame Giry's cousin, Richard, just arrived from America. I'm staying with her for a while and helping to take care of this little one."

"Christine's lost her house," murmured Grace despondently. Imel tried to soothe her by stroking her blonde curls.

From the street, the fire chief called to the detective and Edwards turned to go. "Nice to meet you, Richard. Please tell Madame that I was asking for her."

At the police station a resolved and quieter Christine was taken to the booking area where she was presented to a pale, somber officer with a curled mustache. From behind an enormously thick journal the *gendarme* asked for her name and address, informing her that she was under arrest for maliciously tampering with a public facility, namely a fire hydrant. She pulled her torn shirtsleeve up to cover her shoulder and told the man in slow, precise words that it was her house that was on fire – she was only trying to put water on the flames.

The booking officer appeared disinterested. "Madame, you shoved a policeman and we are not to be trifled with. If your house was burning, we offer our sympathies. You should have allowed the public servants to do their jobs and remained uninvolved. We will get to the bottom of all this in the morning." Christine judged it better not to call the man an imbecile and bit her tongue to keep silent. They escorted her to a small cell near the booking desk and locked her up.

After being apprised of the situation, Monsieur Toussaint hastened with his clients to the police station. Madame Giry and Erik waited outside in a carriage, while the lawyer went within and inquired as to the whereabouts of the young woman brought in from the scene of a fire. He was told that 'her highness' had not been arraigned before a magistrate yet, but would appear before one in the morning. The lawyer slipped a fat envelope across the desk to the jailor, telling him that it contained a good deal more than any fine his client might be assessed. He explained that she was a woman of position – discretion would not only be appreciated, it would be well rewarded. The policeman released Christine to her lawyer and redid the booking entry to show that one 'Christine de Charme' had been detained and released due to lack of evidence. A defective ink pen unfortunately spilled its contents over her address, completely blotting it out.

When Christine entered the carriage outside the police station she found the glad arms of Erik and Madame Giry waiting for her. They were greatly relieved to have her back in one piece and unharmed. Gently, Erik told her how much they had underestimated the danger Raoul posed for the house was a complete loss. He took her hands and holding them firmly, described what happened in the family room after she left. "Surely, he is badly hurt, Christine. We should find him."

Toussaint adamantly agreed and they went directly to Dr. DeVille's. Finding no one at home, they took to the public road and headed for the de Chagny estate. As the dawn of December sixteenth broke, the carriage and its occupants once again waited outside while Christine was within. In a few minutes, she returned to anxiously report that Raoul and the doctor were both there. Raoul was seriously burned. She would stay and send them a message as soon as she understood the extent of his injuries – assuring them that the doctor felt she was in no danger. "Raoul can barely move and Abraham says he urgently needs my help." They kissed her and returned to *Rue du Renard* to sort out the catastrophe of her home.

27 *RAOUL'S INCANTATION*

No amount of self-inflicted castigation helped to ease Edwards' conscience on the morning after the fire. A brisk wind swept across *Rue du Renard,* forcing the detective to tighten his coat despite the appearance of a bright sun. *A day of cold unfeeling light,* he conceded. He stood penitently, watching the burned out shell of Christine's house, as he waited for the fire chief and his assistants to come out of the blackened ruin. The last of the smoke had finally dissipated, now all that was left of a life-almost-started was this ruble, with its scarred bearing walls and chimneys to mutely accuse him. Edwards held fast to his suspicion that Raoul deliberately set the fire, and reckoned in true guilt that he had provoked the Count into igniting the blaze. He certainly knew Raoul's volatile personality. Why hadn't he practiced forbearance? He chastised himself for prodding the man with questions meant to incite him; but it grated against the detective's ethics that de Chagny had beat his wife so severely she was almost unrecognizable. He already knew Christine was safe and that she was the woman taken to the police station and then released. Actually, who could blame her for trying, albeit without success, to get some water on those unrelenting flames? *Just as well,* he thought, *she could have been badly hurt re-entering the house, and what in the world was she planning to use for a hose?*

The fire chief emerged and walked directly to Thomas. "It was intentionally lit. A large amount of accelerant, probably paint and thinners, was thrown on the wall in the front sitting room nowhere near the fireplace. The chimney's flue is clear."

"I'll talk to the painters when they arrive. Have your men hold them. I need to go into the house across the street and have a talk with the owner. Did you find anything else?"

"There are no bodies, least none we've found so far. Heard you took quite a tumble in the backyard at the blowout. How's your derriere?"

"Damn sore, thank you. I saw a man running through the kitchen, maybe a neighbor, he might have made it out through a window. We should inquire if there's anyone in the neighborhood with injuries."

"Shameful waste, if you ask me, old home like this one being lost, heard it was recently purchased."

"Yes, by the de Chagny's. Thanks, I'll be over there for a bit," he pointed his thumb at the ballet studio.

Madame Giry let the detective in when he rang and escorted him into her office. "Cold day, detective, can I get you something warm to drink?"

"Yes, please."

"I'll be right back." Louisa went to the second floor where she set a full pot of coffee and some cups on a tray. She decided not to wake Erik; he was exhausted and might need to be fully alert in the next few hours. She'd been unable to force sleep upon herself. Her mind was too agitated. She wanted to be awake when word came from Christine. Richard and Grace were wrapping presents at the kitchen table and labeling them – ribbons, glue and paper lay all about. She kissed both their heads and returned to the studio with the coffee and some orange biscuits.

The detective stood up as she entered. "Smells good. Here let me take that from you." He placed the tray on her desk. "Quite a mess across the street, Louisa. I'm aware of your close relationship with the Countess de Chagny. This is tragic."

"You have no idea how tragic, Thomas."

Her use of his first name pleased him. Occasionally she allowed him to escort her to dinner at a restaurant, but she always kept their interactions on such a formal basis. She was a hard nut to crack, very secretive about her life. "I, of course, need to investigate all possible factors leading to the blaze and its containment, before filing my reports. Do you know if anyone was caught in the fire?"

"Christine was with her husband, Raoul, but they both got out."

So he did go inside and I missed it. Merde. The detective cleared his throat. "Do you know where Christine is this morning?"

"Yes, she is at the de Chagny estate, tending to Raoul. He was injured in the fire."

"Was he badly hurt?"

"I don't know. We're waiting to hear from her."

We? "Just before Christine's house became an inferno I saw a man run through her kitchen. I couldn't see him well enough to identify him. A little later there were two men over here."

"You probably saw Raoul running from the fire. The two men over here are my cousin, Richard, and a Persian friend of mine. In his own country, the Persian was a police chief and still goes by the title of Daroga. His name is Khalil Salim."

"Can you describe them to me?"

"Of course, the Daroga is tall and dark skinned, my cousin is shorter and graying, he wears spectacles. Richard is upstairs with Grace wrapping presents. Would you like to meet him?"

This Daroga must be the man I saw standing next to her. A friend? "I spoke briefly with him last night, but an introduction from you would serve my investigation more adequately. Perhaps we could go to them in a few minutes." The detective reached into his jacket pocket and fingered a little box inside a velvet pouch. "Louisa, may I speak to you privately and not as a policeman?"

"Of course, please do, Thomas."

"You're a very good person, a kind, loyal soul...but you're a woman of very few words. You say so little that I am often compelled to interpret what you're not saying, and your graceful actions say volumes. I know you've been helping Christine to get settled across the street, and I am truly sorry for her loss. Sorrier than you might think because I verbally goaded Raoul while he stewed outside in his carriage. You see…I know he beat her savagely in early November. He's a flashy patrician with a cruel temper. Unfortunately, there are a lot of very spoiled, amoral men in the world. I've no doubt that you'll be here for her, if she chooses to rebuild her home. You've a generous spirit in you, Louisa. You took in little Grace, and trying to help her ease into a normal environment cannot be easy."

Louisa savored the sweet deceptions accomplished by his last assumption. The success of their live performances was like pylons of sugar on her tongue. *Please define 'normal environment', detective. I don't think this house quite fits the dictionary's description.* She chose to keep the subject on Grace. "I don't know if I should send her to a parochial school, or teach her here in more private surroundings. I'm leaning toward doing it myself, perhaps with Richard's help. He seems most willing. Grace apparently knows how to swear proficiently. When she's upset she uses her outrageous speech to acquit her anger and control the situation. I don't want her alienating, and perhaps bullying, other students. She needs friends, not subjects."

"We knew there would be issues with her."

"Yes, issues." *Ah, but none so disastrous that our Angel can't surmount them.*

"Does the money still come regularly for her care?" Madame Giry looked at him in silence, and after a few seconds nodded her head. "There, you see, you just did it again, this saying of very little with very few words. You have a great deal to hide I think."

Madame Giry was tired, but not so tired that she couldn't spar with this imp across the desk from her.

She opened her mouth but Thomas pushed on. "Please wait, let me continue. I don't care what you have to hide. I really don't. You see, my heart has disappeared down a manhole and only you can retrieve it." Louisa's back straightened, her eyes grew wide and she pulled her hands across the top of her desk closer to her person. *She's retreating man, speak up fast!* "Yes, it's true, I have genuine feelings for you, Louisa."

Madame Giry concealed her contempt and softened her face. "Is this a policeman's technique to trick me because you think I have something to hide from you? I assure you, Monsieur, I...."

The detective raised his hand. "Don't, Louisa, this is no trick, and I know you have much to hide. Furthermore, I believe you do it out of necessity, and that you use everything in your power for the good of the people you care about. I'm going to help you. I just need some direction...when it's appropriate. I'll ask, or you can guide me if you like."

"And why would you offer such a thing?"

"Because I love you. I love you and I hope to be a part of your family someday. Give me time to prove my worth to you." He reached into his pocket and pulled out the pouch. "I have something for you...a present." He slid the gift across the desk toward her, watching her movements and expressions closely.

Madame was caught off guard, petrified that the pouch contained a box with an engagement ring. *This is not a proposal! Don't alienate him, Louisa. Be careful, so careful.* She concentrated on the detective's eyes and realized that she should have seen this coming, his entire face held nothing but affection and hope. She slid the box out of its velvet enclosure. It was black leather with gold trim, and appeared expensive. She offered a reserved smile to him and lifted the lid. The box held a rectangular gold broach. At its center was an intricate red enameled rose, adorned with a delicate ribbon of embedded marcasites around its long stem. *Eternal love!*

The detective made a mental note to buy her flowers later, "Merry Christmas, Louisa."

A somber Christine climbed a back staircase at the chateau with another tray of clean bandages. *It seems so odd to be here after all these weeks. How quickly my will has carried me onward, yet here I am back again with all the same statues and pictures, in all the same places!*

The house servants were busy in the kitchen boiling rags and hanging them to dry. They had been genuinely glad to see her. She'd received their discrete smiles and inquiries with all the graciousness she could marshal. "So good to have you back, Mame. How is the Count doing?"

"Not well," she would reply, "but don't give up hope."

The entire household was focused on Raoul's condition. Every one of them knew the seriousness of his extensive burns. All morning he'd been drifting in and out of consciousness. She couldn't begin to imagine the intensity of his pain. DeVille kept him swaddled in ointments and bandages but a sticky, serous liquid seeped continuously from Raoul's wounds. It took about two hours for the drainage to soak through the dressings – then they'd change them as gently as they could. Abraham was grave. In the hall he'd explained that Raoul was loosing a tremendous amount of vital fluid through his burns. "We must be extremely vigilant and keep him drinking. Force him to swallow water, juice...whatever he will take. If we cannot give him what his body needs, he will die. If by some grace he survives these initial hours, he is still in mortal danger from rampant infection. The loss of so much skin is catastrophic. Without his skin to protect him, purulence is a certainty."

Abraham knew from Raoul, that he had kindled the fire and tried to burn Christine in it. To the good doctor it was a non-issue; he continued to attend the Count without judgment. His only concern was the welfare of his conflagrated patient. DeVille was in a self-proclaimed battle against death, and in Raoul's case, he gave up a little more ground to the Reaper with every passing minute. The Count's head, chest and arms were the worst areas. The injured man could hear and speak, but could not see because his eyes had been burned shut. When Christine arrived, Raoul told her how relieved he was to know she was still alive. He had been distraught thinking they would find her body in the ashes and debris.

"Christine, I nearly killed you and you've still come to nurse me. Forgive me, please forgive me. Someone helped me out of the fire, who was it?"

DeVille told him, "Had it not been for that someone, Monsieur, you would be dead right now."

Raoul asked, "How much time do I have?"

"You must keep drinking, constantly sip at the fluids, we will help you. If we cannot keep up with the amount your burns are leaking, I fear you may not survive this tragedy."

"Can we fix your house, Christine?"

"Don't worry about the house. Here Raoul, drink," and she held a glass to the opening in the bandages where his burned lips were covered in unguent. When he slipped back into unconsciousness she sat beside him, with Dr. DeVille in a chair nearby. Two hours later he awoke and they rolled him to his side, propping him with pillows. The sheets beneath him were saturated, and his bandages as well, but they opted to let him sleep if he could manage it.

He slept for only another fifteen minutes, and when she offered him something more to drink he refused. "I want to talk to you both. Listen carefully, because I'm speaking from the depths of my soul to you." She placed her hand on his foot and gave it a squeeze, Abraham brought his chair closer and told Raoul they could both hear him. Through clenched teeth Raoul continued, "I know I don't have much time. I can sense I'm dying. It was Erik in the house last night, wasn't it? He's the one who saved me."

Christine whispered the answer. "Yes, Raoul, it was Erik and he could have let you die."

"Erik fathered the boys, didn't he?"

What's the point in denying it any longer? "All my trips to him have been fraught with hellish fear, my darkest secret, my greatest joy. I took the way gladly, for in loving him I am restored to life. The boys are his gifts."

"I want him to come here to the estate and be me. Dismiss half the household servants today, and half tomorrow. Start with Justine and the upstairs staff. You and the doctor can tend to me as I die. I'll try to hang on."

"Raoul, what are you saying?" In disbelief she brought her ear close to his lips.

"You loved me once and I turned it into hate. I'm going to give this to you. I can have peace in all this torment if you'll let me give this to you.

You know the truth about the de Chagny's. Explain it to Abraham. You know it can be done. Go to Erik, bring him here to me."

"Raoul, I don't think he'll come. He saved your life but he doesn't want to see you."

"Give me something to drink, and then get pen and paper. Write my words to take to him. Use the de Chagny seal on my desk to close it. Later you can burn the letter or keep it with the scroll in the safe."

Dr. DeVille was standing at Raoul's head. "You must hurry and do as he says, Christine. I cannot leave him, but I will write a note as well. Bring Erik to us quickly if this is to happen!"

When the carriage with the de Chagny crest pulled up to the house on *Rue du Renard* the sun was already low in the sky. Christine allowed herself one singular, disheartening glance at her house. *Total carnage!* She took the steps two at a time and turned the ringer. Erik and the Daroga were already on their feet on the third floor looking down the front stairwell as Madame opened the door.

"Is he dead?" Louisa asked.

"Quickly, we must go upstairs." They hurried to Erik, who swept Christine into his arms, kissing her in relief. Although she had bathed and changed her clothes, the smell of smoke still permeated her, as it did all of them.

"You're exhausted, Christine. How is Raoul?"

"He's charred from his head to his waist, his arms, the front of his thighs. His eyes are burned shut, and his eyebrows gone. If he survived, he would be badly scarred for the rest of his life, but he is not going to live. He is dying, even as we speak he deteriorates and I cannot stay. We are pressed for time."

"Why did you leave him and come here?" asked Madame Giry.

Christine fell into a chair and undid the clasp of her cloak, pulling the garment away from her throat. Actually, she was past fatigue, her brain broached on numb. "I don't know how to diplomatically say this, so I'll just say it. Please, listen closely. You always like to make a plan, and a back up plan should the initial one fail, but we don't have time to think about possible flaws right now. We need to act if we are going to act at all." She engaged Erik's eyes. "Raoul wants me to bring you back to the chateau, so that after he dies you will take his place and become him. Exactly as it happened with Jacob Klein, you will be the new Count de Chagny."

"Raoul knows I live?"

"He has guessed at it for a long time. This afternoon he asked me if you were the boys' father and I told him the truth. Erik, he is not truly a de Chagny, and your name isn't really D'Angelus…and I can barely wrap my mind around all this…but think of it, you would be my legal husband and father to your own sons!"

Erik clenched his fists. "Christine, don't ask me to trade away what little sense of myself I possess. Wouldn't it be better to sell the estate and keep the money? Together we'll pay off the debts. We could go somewhere, or stay here and make a life together. Why gamble our future with this outrageous charade?"

"We've always been playing a game of some sort. He wants to give you his title, his position…the lands you admire so much would be yours. You wouldn't come to me through a tunnel, you'd walk right up to me any time you choose. No more saying goodbye in an hour. Do you remember how luxurious it felt to spend an entire night together across the street? I don't know about you, but a tension, an actual tightness in my shoulders miraculously disappeared. As Raoul, you need never fear being caught by the police. Free, Erik, we'd be free, but it is for you to decide. I have a letter from Raoul and one from Dr. DeVille." She reached into a small satchel strapped across her chest. "Here, I had to write it for him, but he instructed me to close it with his seal. He's already started to dismiss the household servants."

Erik looked at Madame Giry and to his chagrin she smiled. He broke the seal on Raoul's letter and read:

Good Monsieur,
My body is failing, but I assure you, my mind is sharp. What does a man write as he dies? I know full well, that I have been undone by my own hand. I also know that

you have read the scroll of my ancestor and therefore understand the pretense that brought me to my rank. Before I take leave of this world I want to thank you. You may find that bizarre, but it is a sincere gratitude I extend, not only for saving my life last night, but also for the past events that transpired between us. Erik, I am grateful to your loyal heart. When you left Christine with me in the caverns, you gave me a life with her. It was the greatest gift I have ever received. I believe you unselfishly gave away your own happiness for the sake of hers. Only a genuine love could have motivated your actions. Over the first two years of our marriage I watched her spirit whither. Without you the merriment left her eyes, her ambitions ceased, even her posture changed. When her enthusiasm suddenly revived, I knew in my soul you had to be the cause. It was obvious to me that you wanted her to remain as my wife. I thank you again for the moments of joy I shared with her, they are all to your credit, not mine. You lived in shadows while I paraded her out in the world, but she never belonged to me! At some inner level that she forbade me to touch, she always remained yours. I instructed my servants to afford her all privacy wherever she wanted to go, and I looked the other way because you had her heart. What a paradox, even though she bears my name she has remained loyal to you throughout. And now I am dying. I offer you my lands, my title with its prestige, along with my carelessly obtained debts. I offer you a chance to be her legitimate husband, the Count, and father to your own children. Think of it, Erik, they will only know you as a de Chagny. Ask Christine what she would prefer, and seize the day, Monsieur. The worst will be my sisters, become a recluse, as if you weren't one already, and keep them away from you. If you don't want to build ships, retire from the profession. I was not much good at it anyway. I implore you to accept this gift from me. Let the last of your life be the best. You will not die alone in some ignominious cavern but as a noble Frenchman!

I am no longer your rival,
Raoul de Chagny

Erik wanted to tear the letter to shreds. "Raoul tried to kill you! He needs to meet with me face to face and say this."

"He cannot come here, Erik, he's dying. You're going to have to go to him. He's making this offer the only way he can. Please, read Dr. DeVille's note. I cannot stay for long.

Dear Erik,
We both know that false prophets cause nothing but turmoil, they are nearly useless additions to humanity. But this offer of a different future is no false prediction, coming in the guise of comfort - only to increase malady. The proposal is authentic, and I attest to the dire state of Raoul's condition as he makes it. Erik, consider carefully that the deathblow Raoul dealt was to himself and not to you. I believe he would have untied Christine and freed her before the fire reached her. Is this life something you might want? If it is, then we must act quickly. Once Raoul dies we will not have much time to make the transition. We can deal with the logistical problems together as they arise. If you come here, my friend, I will help you cross the thresholds. You can always try it. He is gravely ill and as his substitute you might die at any time you choose. If you decide to come, tell yourself you will be a worthy person to carry his title.

Your devoted friend,
Abraham DeVille

Erik handed both letters to Madame Giry, who read them quietly to herself and passed them to the Daroga. With his face nearly unreadable, Erik studied Christine. "All I want to do is love and protect you. What do you want?"

"I want to be with you, anywhere. Raoul's proposal assures the boys' titles and gives a grand house to us. As Abraham said, if you don't like it, Raoul can always die again later. We'll bury you as many times as it takes for you to live. If you want to try this, you will only have to act out the part a small amount of the time. A name is only a form of address. You'll be a Lord, not a man hiding in the shadows."

"I'll still be hiding, just right in the open under everyone's nose. This is…"

"Doable," Madame Giry finished. "With a little ingenuity this is doable."

He stared at her in disbelief. "Louisa! I cannot leave you. You are as dear to me as breath."

"And I feel the same! We'll work out the problems later. You should go there. Take the Daroga with you."

Christine interjected, "Raoul cannot hurt you. Even if he ordered a servant to harm you, DeVille and I would tell them he was hallucinating."

Erik looked squarely at Christine. "He beat you to a pulp and tried to burn you in your own home. Make no mistake, it is I who would harm him."

"He has paid a dear price for his folly, Erik, not only will he die soon, he is in a tremendous amount of pain!"

The air seemed thick with expectation. Erik held out his hand and curled his fingers for her to come to him. Wordlessly she rose, her cape slipping from her shoulders and remaining on the chair. Before her, she saw no miscreation, no masked ghoul capable of malevolence. Her lover beckoned, the man whose body pleasured her, the maestro – his every touch a work of art. Reverently she moved to him until he stopped her with his outstretched hand.

His fingertips brushed across her upper chest, moved to her upper arm and then her back. He walked a circle of intent around her, holding her at arms length, constantly making contact with her clothes. The Phantom's eyes stayed fixed upon the changing aspects of her head, and she remained motionless as he spoke – a priestess being prepared by the high priest.

"You know this is dangerous?"

"Yes."

He deliberately took his time and commenced a second circle, his fingers gliding over her at the exact same level as before. A tingling sensation rippled down her arms. The saliva glands in the back of her throat constricted tightly.

The rich velvet of his voice swept over her. Once again there was nothing but him. "You will stay by my side? Go anywhere I deem we should be?"

In wonder, Louisa and Khalil witnessed the ceremony going on between the two lovers. They listened intently to their words, marveling at how still she remained.

"Yes," Christine said solemnly.

"The authorities could put us to death for perpetrating this crime."

"Yes."

"Do you love me, Christine?"

"Yes."

"Describe what you claim to feel."

"I would rather be hacked in two than be without you anymore. Let me have one last kiss and then the peace of death, rather than suffer miserable years separated from you. You challenge me, because you believe that something this intense will burn out one day. It must, because you are not worthy...but you are worthy!"

Exalted, Erik heard her attack his deepest fear. He opened the gate within him, allowing her to sting the worry with a blade dipped in the lethal venom of a spider. *Yes, let it die!* He brought it forth for her to pierce again. *How does she know the measure of it so accurately?*

"Nothing will end my feelings for you, Bright One. What is inside me for you only grows in intensity. It is the sun itself and lights the way to truth."

He stopped in front of her, humbled by her words, secretly overjoyed. "Then I am yours, Black Queen. Command me as you will...but do you honestly expect me to just walk right in the front door of the mansion with Raoul at home?"

"Yes, exactly, boldly claim whatever is Raoul's. Consider yourself the Lord of the Manor. If anyone asks, we'll tell them Raoul sent for you, which he did."

28 *IMPERSONATING THE DEAD*

A pair of distinctively tall, cloaked and hooded men, their faces shrouded with black scarves, assisted Christine to exit the carriage in front of the chateau. The two were armed to the teeth and more than ready for a confrontation. Christine had insisted that such defenses were unnecessary, but the Phantom had felt particularly ruthless and cynical as he and the Daroga prepared. He walked the steps of the marbled staircase in a normal manner, but every inch of him wanted to hug his back to the wall and slide up sideways, so he could defend himself from both a frontal and a rear attack. Having the Daroga beside him was a boon, but even Khalil had sweat breaking out upon his brow. They expected the men of the household to be on the alert to defend their injured master. They met no one – their carriage driver had opened the front door. Making their way quickly to Raoul's bedchamber door, Christine knocked firmly on the polished wood. A very somber Dr. DeVille greeted them as the three stepped inside.

The Phantom moved to Raoul's bed and surveyed his enemy with vacant eyes. He saw the extensive bandages and the brown ring of serous stain on the pillow behind him. A ghastly smell of burned flesh, rot, and strong medicinal ointments issued from Raoul and hung in the air of the room. The defiled man made a low moaning sound, and the Phantom knew he was clenching his teeth down hard in an effort not to scream. He questioned DeVille, "Have you given him laudanum?"

"Of course, yes, every time he drinks."

"And hypnotism?"

"I cannot break past the excruciating pain to achieve a hypnotic state."

"Where may I touch the flesh?"

"His lower legs and the back of his thighs are not involved."

"May I?"

"Erik please, go ahead."

The Phantom relaxed his neck and shoulders. Absorbed in his own thoughts, he moved to a coat rack and hung up his cloak and sword. He closed his eyes – then turned toward Raoul. Expanding his chest several times, he entered another realm, one of different purpose. Focusing on Raoul, he issued a directive. "Lock the door, no one enters or leaves." The others obeyed and stood in the middle of the room, observing. The Phantom sat in the chair directly to Raoul's right, and altering his voice began to speak to the sufferer words whispered in so hushed a fashion that the others could not make them out, but Christine could hear the lilt of it. He sounded like another man, a different man, but someone familiar.

Raoul spoke audibly, "Philippe?"

The Phantom made a low buzzing vibration come from his throat and raised his voice to a level they could all hear. "Come to me, Raoul. Come to me. Do you feel my presence, brother? Come to me!"

Raoul struggled to speak through the oceans of intense pain that smothered his brain. "Philippe, it is so good to hear your voice. I've missed you."

"Listen carefully, Raoul. I'm here because you are in great distress. Listen to my voice, only my voice, it's just past the pain. You will find me in my voice. Can you see me?"

"Yes, Philippe, I see you. Please stay with me, I'm hurt." The Phantom leaned forward and slipped both his hands, palm upward, between the sheets and under Raoul's right thigh. Raoul's voice was weak and sleepy, "Refreshing, so cool."

"The pain is easing, Raoul. It's moving into the back of your thigh, and as it moves away from you it's getting smaller and smaller. It's floating out of you, out through my hands. There goes more of it. I'm ordering the pain to leave and it's submitting to me."

"Thank you, Philippe, it's leaving." Raoul took a deep breath, expanding his chest without splinting himself to stop it. Christine stepped forward, fearing that he was breathing his last. The Phantom shook his head emphatically, warning her not to approach. The Daroga took her upper arm and restrained her from moving closer.

"Raoul is not yet at his end, Erik is only making it more tolerable," the Daroga counseled in a whisper. She stepped back and removed her cloak, finding a chair she sat down exasperated.

The Phantom's voice was still that of Raoul's brother as he continued to soothe him. "As I take my hands away, the pain will end as I go. Ready, Raoul?"

"Don't go, stay and wait with me."

"Wait?"

"I'm waiting for Erik."

"He's here, Raoul. Let me end the pain and then you can talk to Erik. Ready?"

"All right."

The Phantom slid his hands out from beneath Raoul. Again he made the low buzzing vibrato into Raoul's ear. Then he told him to fall from the sky on his back, a deep, deep fall into a comfortable place of peace and happiness. He asked Raoul where they were, and Raoul told him that they were on the deck of a ship about to cast off for Italy. "Is Erik still here?"

"Yes, I am here," Erik spoke in his natural voice. "How are you feeling?"

"All right, this is a grand day. Where is Philippe? I don't want to loose him."

"I'm here," the Phantom answered in Philippe's voice.

"I want to introduce you to the Opera Ghost, Philippe. He's come at last. Thank you for coming, Erik."

"Why did you want me here, Raoul?"

"Let me repay the debt I owe you. Give me that bit of peace, Erik. Take my title and raise your boys – be Christine's husband."

"Rest, Raoul, please rest. At last you are comfortable. Philippe and I will stay right beside you. We can talk in a little while, but for now, sleep, and wake feeling calm, free of torment." Raoul's chest rose and fell in an easy rhythm. The Phantom watched his breathing for a few moments and then stood up. They agreed that he and the Daroga would stay with the patient, while the doctor and Christine also tried to rest. They would exchange places in the early morning hours before dawn. The doctor showed them what needed to be done, and retired to the room next door, leaving explicit instructions to call him immediately should anything change. Christine wanted to stay and work alongside them, but they insisted she sleep for a while. What could she do that they could not? In the end, she agreed and went to lie down in her bedroom.

The night passed quietly. Around three in the morning a winter rain started that turned to sleet, making the roads slick and treacherous. The two men kept the fire going in Raoul's bedchamber and stood watch over him. Every hour, Erik went to him and told him to stay on the ship and have a good time exploring around with Philippe...and to keep drinking liquids. The early dawn broke to find Raoul gratifyingly free of pain, but no stronger for their efforts. DeVille and Christine met with them in the next room to discuss the day's plan. They expected a visit from the police at some point. Erik suggested that the dismissal of the house servants proceed after the inspectors left.

DeVille doubted that Raoul would last through the day, and the Daroga added thoughtfully, "Let's hope he can hold on. It would be good for the authorities to see him injured, but still alive."

As predicted, officers Edwards and Davier were at the mansion about eleven and asked to see the Count. Christine ushered them into his room as if they were entering the sacristy of a venerated saint. They were aghast at the severity of his condition and asked how he could have been burned so badly. Christine brought the officers to the downstairs reception area and told them she had not seen the fire start. She and Raoul had been looking at the paints and discussing colors. When she went for refreshments, he may have lit a cigar and caught himself on fire. An unthinkable, tragic accident must have occurred when she was out of the room. Certainly Raoul was paying dearly for his lack of caution around the volatile liquids. Edwards was skeptical, but agreed that Raoul was suffering for his lack of care. The detective doubted that Christine had doused her husband with a flammable substance and set him on fire. He would have fought her off and she appeared to be completely unharmed. Davier asked if Raoul was expected to survive. Christine explained that all was in God's hands, the future rested with Him alone.

After the officers left, Christine sent a note to Madame Giry, explaining that they needed her help and asking her to come. Christine dismissed the rest of the house staff and Raoul's secretary in the afternoon. By evening everyone had departed. That left in their employ, only those who worked outside and lived in small cottages on the grounds. Christine explained to everyone that it was the Count's wish to have them leave and seek other employment. Only the head footman, Raoul's personal valet and the chief cook asked to speak personally with the Count. Christine promptly took them to his room. Raoul assured them that his incapacity would bring difficult financial times upon the estate. Letters of recommendation would be written for them by the Countess. He wished them Godspeed, and reiterated that as he recuperated he wanted to be cared for by his doctor and the few people closest to him.

About midnight, Erik sat in a chair next to Raoul and dozed off. In his mind, he and Christine were picnicking by the sea. He thought this odd since he hadn't actually enjoyed the shore in decades. His sweet companion offered him a section of roasted pumpkin sprinkled with nutmeg, then pleasantly insisted he eat an entire, stringy, uncooked chicken. He was trying to politely excuse himself from the meal, when without warning she began to move like an automated mannequin. On her feet, she gazed past the churning waves and pointed. He followed the direction of her arm and saw a huge galleon of a ghost ship with its sails and upper decks on fire. It seemed perfectly normal that an obviously decrepit, three-masted warship would be floating by all aflame.

He looked up at Christine and to his amazement she spoke in Raoul's voice. "This isn't going to hurt," the he-she said. She took his wrist and he rose to his feet. With a dagger she made a cut down the length of his forearm to the base of his thumb. Offering no resistance whatsoever, he watched as blood, thick like molasses, poured with aching slowness from the wound. As every heavy droplet hit the white sand, it gave birth to a dozen brilliant orange poppies. The flowers were springing up all around their feet. "There," said the feminine Raoul, "isn't that nice?"

"Erik, are you there?" Instantly, he awoke from his dream knowing the real Raoul had called him.

"Yes, right here." Erik's voice was tender. The ruthless cynic had vacated the premises, for who could remain cruel in the face of this much suffering? He had seen all of Raoul's injuries during the changing of the bandages. The charred tissues were like gray mushy pudding. If the man lived, his nose would slough off, and the skin of his head and hands would be hideous, gouged ravines of scar tissue. Erik doubted if he would ever see again. Madame Giry sat in a comfortable chair nearby, alert the moment Raoul spoke. She poured apple cider from a pitcher into a glass and handed it to Erik for Raoul. He could only coax Raoul to take a sip. Despite their efforts to keep him in clean bandages, a fermenting infection was rapidly taking hold. Raoul had become feverish, but his thoughts were still lucid.

Erik slid his hands back under Raoul's thigh. "Your fingers are so cool." Raoul didn't flinch in disgust, he had resigned himself to the fact that his demise was imminent. "Thank you for helping me to die in peace. The worst will be my sisters, keep them away from you. I have no advice for how you should look in public. Perhaps the mask would be appropriate. It's up to you." One could almost sense a smile beneath the strips of cloth. "Who could believe we would sit side by side without desperately trying to kill each other." Erik lifted Raoul's head, and he took a few more sips when Erik told him it contained laudanum. "You've had my life in your hands on a number of occasions, and each time you chose to give it back to me."

"Are you in pain? Do you need anything?"

"I need you to answer two questions before the Reaper claims me. Where did you and Christine meet? Please, I want to know."

"Where would one meet a ghost, but in a tomb?"

"How strange…was it her father's? Yes, of course it was. I myself have never entered the mausoleum. I had no need to, but it makes sense, a private place where she could see you, and you are no ghost, Erik. Thank you for telling me. I needed to know."

"How can I repay you for what you're giving me?"

"It's enough that you will raise the boys de Chagny's. I have not failed my ancestor's wishes, consider me repaid." Raoul took several swallows and coughed a little. Madame Giry helped Erik sit him up. Erik supported him as she turned the pillows. The Daroga entered quietly and nodded. He had completed his rounds; all the doors were locked and secured. Erik lowered Raoul's chest and head back into the pillows.

"I'm like a wounded deer being gutted while it's still alive. I have a fever don't I?"

"Yes," Erik replied. "Rest and conserve your strength."

"Please answer my second question. Appease me, Erik. I need to know. How did Philippe die?"

"Your brother sought you in the caverns the night I stole Christine. He was sure you ventured down there alone to rescue her, and he came to aid you. He must have slipped on a stone and hit his head. He drowned in the lake. When I found his body, I took it to the side near the *Rue Scribe*, and laid him on the embankment so that others would find it and give him a proper burial."

"Is that the truth, Erik, swear on Christine's life that it's the truth."

"I swear it. Your brother did not fall at my hand."

"I believe you. He died because of me."

The hours stretched on and Raoul's infection continued to devour him. Before sunrise he became stuporous, and towards nine drifted into a coma. When he could no longer drink the end came swiftly. They were all in the room as he breathed his last. Christine shuddered and asked if he was gone. Erik raised his hand. "Shh, you can feel him, he's in the room around us." Erik closed his eyes and everyone watched in amazement, as the air in front of his face seemed to consolidate and move in a clear, but perceptible ripple. Erik appeared to be listening to something. He opened his arms and uttered a single word, "Always." The air stopped moving.

They buried Raoul in secret that night, in a shallow grave in the cellar. They turned Raoul's mattress, changed the sheets and bandaged Erik. The plan was, if Erik could tolerate it, to keep him wrapped in dressings for over a month, and then gradually decrease the amount of bandages over the next month. Erik complained that the pace seemed too slow, but DeVille assured him it would indeed be a miraculous recovery from such a burn. Erik argued that no one had seen the extent of Raoul's injuries beneath the dressings except for the five apostates! In the morning, Abraham went home, but continued to make evening visits to the mansion to discuss with everyone possible solutions to some of the enormous perplexities before them.

The process of turning Erik into Raoul proved problematic on multiple levels, some they'd anticipated – others totally unforeseen. They asked Erik what would help him remain calm for the process, and feel the least fragmented. Initially he requested two things. First, that he say very little outloud. His voice being damaged as a result of the fire seemed logical, and the scarcity of speech would afford him time in his own head to find his way into this new role. Second, they needed to solve the issue of where Christine would sleep, because lying alone in Raoul's chambers seemed intolerable to him.

"Where do you want me to sleep?" Christine asked in anxious hope. "Here in your room?"

The Pharaoh's mummy nodded vehemently, tapping the bed.

Doctor Deville made a suggestion. "Move in, Christine, so that you can nurse him back to health."

Blushing she responded, "He'll need care for years no doubt."

"I'm sure of it," the Daroga let out a chuckle under his breath.

Madame Giry cautioned her. "Spend as much time as you can telling Erik about Raoul's life, but only to a point, respect his tolerance to hear the information you present."

The mummy crossed his arms over his chest. "When I'm well, you're not going to expect me to go out and kill deer are you? I'm a musician, not a hunter."

The doctor interjected quickly, "And you won't give it up, it is your soul. I shall order that you play music to restore the movement of your hands and fingers. Wear gloves around other people. Disastrous events often cause patients to reconstruct their lives, so let us discover a hidden talent lying dormant within you. Devise a way to bring that enormous black and gold organ here. Do it before you employ new house servants, that way Erik can spend time putting it together and restoring its tone. I want to caution you about his bandages. Change them every day and stain them with diluted tea before you take them outside to burn them. Make sure the staff working around the barns, sees you doing this chore from time to time. Let a little meat or fish spoil and occasionally burn it with the dressings to add a putrid smell. Don't be in a rush to hire household staff. Focus on getting Raoul better, then on your finances."

Madame Giry added in a satisfied tone, "Excellent! There, I told you this was doable!"

Christine kissed the top of the mummy's head. "I'll be happy to remain a de Chagny after all!"

Madame Giry closed the ballet studio, probably for good, and explained to Imel that she was needed for some time on the de Chagny estate. Imel suggested that he move there with her until everyone figured out where they wanted to make a permanent residence. It took Madame Giry and the Daroga two weeks to move the organ from the underground house to the chateau. They brought the instrument in pieces following Erik's directions, while Imel and Christine cleared an area in the cellars where Erik particularly liked the acoustics. They gave Grace the prestigious job of 'supervising' their work and exploring the house. She quickly took up daily residence in the library, where she enjoyed the books, and in the southern salon where she played Christine's harpsichord.

With Grace safely distracted, Erik worked under lock and key in the cellars, reconstructing the organ – a labor of love. While he restored the instrument, Christine composed letters to Raoul's business associates and his two sisters, explaining that he had suffered severe burns in an accidental fire, but was already over the perilous initial phase, and well on the road to recovery. They took care to politely inform his siblings that nothing was needed except for the time to heal, and promised to keep them apprised of Raoul's progress. A visit in a few months would be most welcome. Flowers, baskets of fruit, get well wishes and prayer cards announcing masses to be said at the cathedral for Raoul's recovery, started arriving as soon as the sisters were notified. Erik and Christine worded their thank you notes carefully, so as not to encourage premature visits from the two.

After the organ was assembled, Erik took to vibrating the floors of the mansion's first level with the enormous range of its voice. Little Grace searched diligently for the best spot to listen to the injured Count exercise his hands, and settled in an alcove in the hallway outside the kitchen. There she would sit with a number of her dolls, entertained for hours by the music coming from below. Imel suggested she take a composition book and try to pick out what notes she thought were being played.

In a month they hired a cook and a single nanny for both boys. Before the arrival of the two servants, Erik took to remaining full time in his chambers, safely concealed behind a locked door. Meg and Jean brought Michael and Ariel back to the chateau, and promptly took them to Raoul's bedroom. They had expected Michael to cry at the strange appearance of a mummy, but amazingly the toddler wanted to finger the bandages around his father's face, and play with the lips he found embedded there. He giggled merrily at the tongue that periodically flew out at him, trying unsuccessfully to catch it with his fingers. For the first time, Erik held Ariel and they taught him how to feed the baby a bottle. As bodily functions took over, the new Count firmly announced that he was not ready for changing diapers and tried to hand the baby to Christine, telling her to have the nanny do her job! As she scooped Ariel from his arms, he asked her to please bring the baby back as soon as he was cleaned. Meg winked at Christine. They were well on their way to bonding father to son.

The following week they hired an upstairs, and a downstairs maid, then a utility man to assist with inside jobs and drive their carriage when needed. Madame Giry rose honorably to the mundane tasks of running the household, organizing assignments the way a head housekeeper would do. Many of the rooms were unnecessary for their current purposes, so she closed them off, telling the staff to focus on the areas occupied by the family.

Everyday, Christine and Erik studied their financial situation, and discussed how to climb out of the hole of debt Raoul had left them in. After they had an accurate grasp of their monetary predicament, the task of becoming solvent seemed overwhelming. For relief, they'd turn to an ironically lighter discussion, that of creating a world of illusion for them to have a tolerable life together. Erik thought it ridiculous that they couldn't surmount the myriad of issues facing them. He suggested that they define their goals and proceed from there, as if they were starting afresh.

Christine piled the accounting journals in a stack on the floor, and cleared all the objects off a table they'd set beside Erik's bed. Taking clean paper and pen she announced, "All right, let's name the goals." She raised a delicate finger for each. "Get out of debt, raise the boys, not be discovered, and at all costs remain together. Any others?" Erik shook his head. He loved watching her take command. She wrote a singular goal on the top of four separate papers. Then they commenced to outline what they thought might be the specific solutions.

"Start with the debt page," Erik requested. "I could forgive the repayment of the monies Raoul owes me."

Christine advised against it. "I don't think we should do that, we should appear to be in the process of repaying the loan. It establishes appropriate accountability. Let's make payments until the loan is paid off. Channeling the money back to ourselves should be easy, we'll instruct Toussaint."

Erik was impressed with her deviousness. "I can see that I'll have to keep a vigilant eye on you! Apparently you and Louisa are cut from the same bolt of cloth. She keeps money coming to her for Grace." She cackled like an old witch and squeezed his bandaged hand. They thought it better to create a little more operating capital by selling off some of the de Chagny properties, starting with the land on *Rue du Renard*.

Erik carefully drove a finger beneath the bandages on his neck and scratched. "You know, my major frustration is not this plague of dressings I'm forced to wear, it's my total lack of knowledge about building ships. I don't know a damn thing about making a vessel sea worthy, much less managing to squeeze a profit from the business."

Christine tried to soothe him by helping scratch the itch with the round end of a hairpin. She offered to personally put talcum powder on all the right places the next time they changed the cloths. "Raoul didn't know how to make much of a profit from it either."

"I'm very lucky to have you, my goddess." Erik asked for books, manuscripts, detailed drawings, anything that might be of use to him. She brought everything she could find, and he began pouring over them. They ended up commandeering an even larger table for his room.

A few days later, when she arrived at the bedchamber with his lunch tray, she turned the key in the lock and found Erik throwing his dagger into a painting on the wall. He stepped forward, pulled it out, and returned to position to throw it again. He had put on trousers, socks and shoes, a brown woolen vest over his bandages and a bright red cravat. His head, chest and arms remained hidden from view. When she collected herself from the comical site, she asked, "Do you want to sit outside for a while? I think we could start to take you outdoors. It would help in your healing process to move you around, and the new staff could finally get a view of you. I'm sure they're most curious."

Erik let the dagger fly out of his hand again. It landed soundly into a bunch of painted grapes. "That sounds good. Check my bandages and make sure I'm covered, woman."

Christine set his lunch on the table and he sat down to eat. "You're an amazing person, Erik. The more I know you, the more I love you. I used to hate this place. I loathed everything in it. Now I can't wait for each day to begin because you're here." She started tightening the dressings and tying up loose ends. "At least both your eyes can show through now, you can see the outside world. We'll put a warm coat around you and a hat over your head. Remember to keep your eyes shielded from the staff."

Erik turned in his chair and tugged at her waist. "Raoul is a fortunate man."

"People liked Raoul. They liked doing amusing things with him, but people love you, Erik. They love you so much they put their own lives at risk for you. Do you love us in return? Do you love me?"

"Hmm, mummy love woman," he grunted.

She laughed. "I'm serious. How do you love me, Erik?"

"I think it's time you completely stopped calling me Erik. Come up with some pet name for me, I'm ready for it. And I love you with the positive P-L-Y words."

"The ply words, you love me with the ply words?"

"*Oui.*" He nuzzled her abdomen with his forehead then looked up at her. "Looser here please." He pointed to the strips over his nose. "Yes, the positive P-L-Y words are: powerfully, possessively, passionately, phenomenally, and any other P-L-Y words I can come up with. Those four are the first ones in my head at the moment."

"You caught me again. Here finish your lunch while we discuss your nickname. I'll be happy to have an alternate way of addressing you. You're definitely not the old Raoul."

"How about Crispy, or Toasty? Maybe, My Adorable Charred Thing?"

While he ate, she considered other more acceptable terms of endearment. She didn't speak until he put the last bite of roasted potato in his mouth. "I like Angel, or My Angel. I'll only call you Raoul in more formal circumstances."

He gazed at the ceiling – waving his fork and chewing. "I like that. I almost died and could have been one. You used to summon the Angel of Music. Yes, it fits. Try it out."

"Do you want dessert, Angel?"

He sang the answer, using the fork to direct the tune. "I do if it's you."

She laughed again. "Come on, we'll take a break and sit you in the afternoon sun for fifteen minutes." Together they made their way down the stairs and out to the patios. The first floor maid was so thrilled to see her employer, that she scurried off to get the others. The cook brought out a tray of coffee and puffed pastries, called *palmiers,* and waited near the other servants while Christine introduced them to their employer.

"Angel, this is Marie, Antoinette, Blanche and Joseph, our new house staff. Ladies, and gentleman," she nodded to Joseph, "may I present the Count."

The servants hovered expectantly. Christine was not prepared for what happened next but kept her composure. Erik lifted his head to a point where the brim of his hat just shielded the color of his eyes from their sight, and in a hesitant, perfect rendition of Raoul's whispered voice said, "I am so pleased to meet you. Thank you for the excellent services you render to us, my recuperation is hastened by all that you do."

The women swooned over his gracious praises, and Joseph bowed deeply. When he straightened he spoke for the group. "We are honored to be at your service, Sir. Anything you need, just holler, we'll promptly tend to it. You have my word. We're thrilled to see you getting better."

"Your faithfulness is deeply appreciated, Joseph." Erik extended his hand and Joseph gingerly accepted the feeble, trembling handshake the nobleman offered.

"We'll be about our chores now, Sir. Please excuse us." He bowed again and shooed the women back inside.

The head of the house stretched out his legs and breathed in the air, then deliberately rolled his shoulders – as if trying to get comfortable. "I've been thinking about my opera, Christine, my 'Don Juan Triumphant'.

It is the best musical piece I ever composed, and I could sell it under my pen name. It should bring in a tidy sum."

"You would do that?"

"Oh yes, it's hidden in the house by the lake. When I'm better, let's go retrieve it. I'll tell Louisa, I know she would love to hear it played again. You see, I'm keenly aware of the love my friends have for me, that love you spoke about upstairs."

The French doors opened behind them and DeVille stepped out. "Good, this is good. You are out in the sun for a bit." The doctor sat down. "Excellent, coffee and *palmiers!* How is it being a husband and a father, my friend?"

"Not as difficult as being a damn shipbuilder! The profession appears to be more of an art than a science. Choose a master builder and a foreman with a team of workers. Decide if you're building a brigantine, a barkentine or a fast schooner. Outline the project and draw up the plans. Create a quarter-scale model for depth measuring and perspective. Select the heartiest of timbers available, and the choices are vast: spruce, pine, birch, beech, oak if you're extravagant. Lay the keel and frame-out the elegant outline of the ship's hull. The timbers sprout forth from the keel like the skeletal ribs of an unfortunate beached whale!"

He formed their shape with his bandaged hands by bringing the base of his palms together and spreading his gauzed fingers apart. "Piece together a smooth, hydrodynamic hull, fit the decks, and raise the masts, making sure to pack the boards with rock salt to prevent rot as you go. There's a whole debate over iron bolts versus oak pins called treenails, and who really knows for sure? I know, I don't!" He lowered his head in resignation. "Supply the rigging...miles of line, blocks, chains and sails. And always keep in mind that the more space there is for cargo, and the less offered to the crew, the greater the profit margin from any venture undertaken by the buyer! It's an aggravating puzzle to unravel, and there's so much more to tell, because I'm of the opinion that the ship should be purchased in the harbor it's birthed in, not sailed to the harbor of the buyer and then sold. So, how do we make a vessel so appealing that the demand for it causes a client to swoop-in, and pluck it up at the first available opportunity? I'm working on that perplexity in the back of my mind even now!"

Christine hugged herself with glee. Obviously there were no limits for him, no limits at all.

"My, you've learned a lot...and you're quite feisty about it too. That's excellent! You will need your spirits rallied, for it would be absolutely criminal of us not to pile more onto your plate."

"I have plenty to masticate on, thank you!"

"Have you given him the news, Christine?" DeVille popped a pastry into his mouth and poured more coffee for the three of them.

"No, Abraham, I was waiting for you."

"What news?" Erik scratched at his bandaged forehead. "What spell has the witch and the warlock conjured today?"

Amused at his colorful symbolism the doctor swallowed some coffee. "Have you given any thought to how many children you might want?"

"No, I have not. It's up to Christine." Erik offered the *palmiers* to her. "How many do you want, goddess?"

"Pastries or babies?"

"Very funny."

"One *palmiers* please, and I would like to populate the planet with the beautiful children you produce. How many are you willing to give me?"

Erik thoughtfully considered the brown winter lawn that led down to the boathouse beyond, and remembered an evening when he stood over there, listening to the news that his child was coming into the world. What a night that had been for him, exhilarated, lonely, questioning, wanting to hold her and brutally restraining himself. "Could the next one be a girl, do you think?"

Christine spread her hands over her abdomen. "I believe it is a girl. I feel totally different than I did with either of the other two." Erik reached over and brought her fingers to his bandaged lips.

Delighted at Erik's reaction, DeVille asked, "What's for dinner? I brought some wonderful liniment with me. We can tell the really snoopy people that this is the reason Raoul's skin has stayed so supple.

Say that you rub it on him every day, Christine. Starting next week gradually apply fewer bandages exposing more skin. Start with his neck and hands. Erik, don't forget to wear the gloves around the staff for a couple of months."

Christine took the bottle the doctor held out. "I believe we're having lamb, and to heck with just saying 'I rub it on him', I will rub it on him...everyday!"

"Absolutely," Erik kicked his leg out from under the chair, scuffing his heel back and forth, using one of Raoul's mannerisms. Then with a flare that was all Erik, he brought his shoe down smartly and smacked his hand onto the top his knee in a show of enthusiasm.

29 *DOUR SISTERS*

Late in February, DeVille agreed to set a grateful Erik free of the vile bandages. Before Erik could walk around the mansion wearing only his blessed mask, they needed to decide what to do about his full head of wavy black hair. Raoul had been a sandy blonde, and would have been hairless and grossly scarred had he survived. Madame Giry and Christine favored a wig. Erik offered to let them pour acid over his head and remove his hair permanently.

Abraham adamantly vetoed any further mutilation. "Nature has done quite enough, thank you."

They compromised with a temporary solution and waxed most of Erik's hair away, leaving small clumps here and there that they altered with peroxide. A stoic Erik managed to weather the entire, arduous ordeal, informing them at its conclusion that he had a new respect for women who employed the practice to divest themselves of unwanted hair.

Even with the mask on, Erik thought he rather favored a derelict from a freak show, or a mad scientist about to perform unspeakable experiments. "I'm definitely nefarious looking, don't you think?" They decided to bring Grace to him and study her reaction. Grace knew Raoul only in his dressings, and had stayed at a respectful distance on the rare occasions that he'd left his room for a period of sunlight. The Angel of Music had found her here on the estate, and told her to be well behaved and kind to the Count, since he had suffered so terribly.

The little girl was most agreeable to being brought to meet their injured host. Madame Giry explained that all his bandages had been removed, and he wanted to know if even badly scarred he could still have friends. Grace went fearlessly down the hall holding Madame's hand, and waited politely in the entrance to be invited in once the door was opened.

"Please, come in child and meet Raoul," invited Dr. DeVille.

Grace tiptoed in with tiny, quiet steps and investigated the interior. Her eyes circled the room, and came to rest on a man in a mask with wizened clumps of hair about his head. He sat in a big leather chair and smiled at her. "Would you like to come closer, Grace? I won't hurt you, and I'm feeling much better now that the bandages are off." He extended a white, cloth gloved hand to her.

She stepped forward timidly and found the courage to ask, "Do the burns hurt?"

"No, all the pain is gone. How do you think I look?"

"You look like a guest at a masquerade party. It's not so bad."

"Do you like what I have left of my hair?"

"No." She replied honestly. "It's scary."

"Should I wear a wig?"

"Yes."

"What color hair would you like best, Grace?"

"Black. When Cousin Richard reads stories to me all my favorite heroes have black hair."

"Then for you I shall wear a black wig. You're so kind to help me, Grace. Would you like to walk me out and show me what you know of the house? Don't you find the colorful pictures and the elegant statues, lovely? Let's go guess who they all are."

"Will you play the organ some more?"

"Yes, I will. I'll even show **you** how to play it. Do you like it here, Grace?" Erik gently took the child's hand, the two strolled out together like a pair of old friends. Madame Giry shrugged her shoulders at Christine, who had put her hand over her mouth to keep herself from laughing hysterically.

After DeVille shut the door, an amazed Louisa declared, "So we'll get him a black wig until his own hair grows back. Then he can tell everyone his own hair is a wig! Who could have foreseen this?"

The staff watched curiously as the Count and Grace walked around together. Grace told Erik her favorite room, besides her own of course, was the southern salon. "It's Christine's favorite room, too. Do you favor it?" Erik assured her that he did indeed like it. It was most inviting.

Christine suggested to the cook that they serve a festive meal that night to celebrate; beef, perhaps, or a pork roast with wine. Marie spent a great deal of care over the preparation. The dining-room table was immaculately set, the stemware and china polished to a sparkle, the silver candelabrums agleam below their wax tapers.

The Count thought the dinner delightfully prepared, but ate only modestly. Every time Marie offered to fill his wine glass, he politely refused, placing his long fingers over the crystal, and saying he preferred the coffee. After the meal, a disconcerted cook, who had taken great pains to select the most appropriate vintage to accompany her culinary creations, made inquiry of her mistress. "Why didn't he enjoy the wine? He used to, there's a whole cellar full of those bottles."

Christine patiently explained that the Count was inebriated when the fire started. "He feels that if he'd had his wits about him, none of this damage would have happened. I doubt that he will ever drink again. We'll have to wait and see. Your veal chops with apple brandy sauce, and your chocolate mousse were delicious, Marie, absolute perfection. You did a wonderful job. He ate your food, didn't he?"

That explanation placated her for a short while, but all the servants were equally perplexed about the Count's strange occupation of hiding in the cellar and playing his organ. "He's definitely a loner," Antoinette told Blanche at lunch. "His Lordship likes to spend long hours with only himself for company."

"Hush now," Marie counseled, stringing green beans for a winter soup. "The mistress says he's been through a terrible ordeal, it's a miracle he lived to tell about it. Let's give him time to adjust to being out in the world again. Just take a gander at his poor noggin!"

"Thank God he took to wearing a wig," Blanche added pumping a cherry tart into her mouth. "I could hardly bear to look at him when they took those dressings off his head for the last time! The sight gave me a swift case of the vapors."

Antoinette shuddered. "Gave me the creeps as well. Looked like Death itself prowling about in a mask…come to fetch us to Hades for a roasting. But Lord above, the music he does play! I declare by Saint Sebastian that he's gifted from heaven! Must have studied for years in a conservatory somewhere."

Cook blessed herself with the sign of the cross. "I hope he never stops, God bless him. I open all the doors to the wine cellar when he plays, hoping to get every scrap of music to float upstairs. Maybe he'll play the harpsichord in the salon when his sisters come for lunch on Sunday."

Indeed, it was true. Every several days, Raoul's two sisters relentlessly sent requests to see their brother. Since Christine's notes and reassurances no longer seemed to appease them, Erik conceded that to put off a visit any longer would probably goad the two females into initiating a formal investigation into their brother's health. Perhaps, if they could demonstrate Raoul's lucidity and his capacity to function, the siblings could be successfully 'kept at bay' as Raoul had suggested. Erik practiced Raoul's movements in his room. He already had Raoul's voice down to near perfection. He chose clothes of deep blues and reds, colors Raoul favored, and since Raoul was a little larger than him across the chest and shoulders, the jacket sagged nicely, giving the appearance he had lost a bit of weight recuperating. Erik chose to wear his mask but not the wig, permitting the sisters a partial view of his deformed head. Shielding his eyes from them would be another matter. Christine suggested that they eat in the formal dining room with all the curtains drawn – the darker the better to execute their charade. The staff had grown accustomed to Erik's lovely amber eyes as Raoul's, but the sisters would not be fooled by a change in eye color from a fire, no matter how hot the blaze! Louisa suggested that she take Grace and Imel to spend the day with Meg and Jean, lessening the complexities of conversation during the luncheon. Since they knew the sisters to be prompt, DeVille planned to create a distraction by making an appearance a few minutes after them.

The sisters arrived, decorated in elaborate silks and feathers, exactly at noon. Christine and Joseph escorted them into the southern salon for a brief visit before the meal. Lucille Michelle de Chagny-Rouseau and Jacqueline Antonia de Chagny-Laurent, both Countesses in their own right, were refined, cultured women. Lucille was the older and more outspoken. Jacqueline had grown up a bit shy, because of a pronounced strabismus in her left eye, but could be a gregarious conversationalist after a few glasses of wine. Erik had only seen them from a distance at the baptisms, but his photographic memory and Christine's coaching had prepared him for the inquisition.

He rested on a chaise with a blanket over his knees, the early afternoon light coming through two windows directly behind him. This position placed his face in advantageous shadow and strategically illuminated theirs. They were appropriately shocked and grieved at what they could see of his condition. When they entered, he began to rise but the sisters flung their hands about, protectively insisting that he remain seated. Their surprising arm movements reminded Erik of four catfish flopping frantically in the bottom of a boat. He maintained his composure and in a clear rendition of Raoul's voice, thanked them and asked them to be patient, explaining that he was still regaining strength – fatigue might compel him to excuse himself at any moment! He sincerely hoped he would not have to retire from their company to his rooms. Lucille asked if there was anything they could do to make him more comfortable, and Raoul responded that keeping their first visit as short as possible would be a great help. The sensitive egos of both sisters were instantly pricked. The exact response Erik wanted.

Christine had described in detail how much Raoul relished tormenting his sisters in peculiar, small ways. They had doted and coddled him when he was a boy, refusing to let him grow up until Philippe interceded, finally separating Raoul from their care. When the sisters whined and pleaded for the return of their charge, an enraged Philippe let loose his temper at them. "For God's sake, pull your tits from his mouth and let the whelp become a man!" Insults and arguments had flown back and forth for a whole day in the chateau, but Philippe had won. The next day, he signed his little brother onto the crew of a ship bound for Italy and Greece, ensuring that the spoiled ten-year-old would experience something other than the soft touch of women.

With great dignity, Joseph ushered Dr. DeVille into the room, taking the sisters attention away from their brother's callousness. The doctor bowed deeply. "Ladies, I am enchanted to meet you both. I have heard so many wonderful things about you. How was your ride over here? Surely, you must be pleased to see your brother in this degree of health after such a devastating accident. Christine, I'm famished, what is for lunch?"

"The cook has prepared a baked sole in a white wine sauce with baby peas, and for dessert, crème caramel."

"Sounds wonderful, Joseph tells me they are ready to serve us. Ladies, shall we proceed to the dining room?" Before the sisters could protest that they had only just arrived, DeVille swept them up, and taking both by the arm escorted them out into the hall.

Christine winked at Erik and helped him up, whispering into his ear, "He's a maestro in his own right!"

"God love his wispy head!" Down the corridor Erik delivered a reserved imitation of Raoul's swagger. During the entire meal he offered up an excellent example of a Count not yet totally on his feet, taking small bites of food, sipping sedately at his coffee, and saying very little. At one point the current status of the estate was under discussion. Raoul assured Luce and Jacky (using their brother's pet names for them) that his ships would be built again, possibly they'd restart in the summer. Until then the farmlands and the lake would provide adequately for their needs. Raoul made it through the greater part of the meal and when dessert was served, a cautious DeVille insisted he be allowed to take his patient upstairs, leaving the sisters to converse with Christine.

"My dear," asked Jacqueline, "how do you survive with so few servants? The lack of help you're suffering under is almost barbaric."

"We're doing fine. Raoul is much less embarrassed with fewer eyes studying his condition. He has taken to wearing a wig occasionally. Black hair for now, like the Norse princes of old, it's difficult to go out with his head in this shape."

"It's absolutely monstrous. He looks like a ghoul escaped from an asylum!" declared Lucille.

"Luce, that's awful! At least he's alive and still here with us," but after a few seconds of reflection Jacky concurred. "He does resemble a depraved maniac, doesn't he!" She started a timid giggle and her sister silenced her with a disapproving glare. Embarrassed, Jacqueline coughed into her embroidered handkerchief. "Pardon me," she offered.

Christine took the awkward moment to furnish the women with an invitation to see their little nephews, but Lucille asked if they could be excused as well. She was feeling rather tired herself. They had Joseph summon their driver from the kitchen, where he'd taken lunch with the household servants, and departed without the slightest mention of a return visit. Christine joined Erik and Abraham in Raoul's sitting room, where they complimented each other on the successful completion of their mission.

Erik asked, "Do you think they'll go to the police?"

"Absolutely!" Christine snapped her fingers in satisfaction. She was correct.

The following morning Lucille and Jacqueline entered the police station, and were promptly escorted by the officer in reception to Andre Davier's desk. After Davier seated the ladies, and formal introductions were made, he inquired as to the subject of their complaint. When he heard the general nature of their report, he stopped them from proceeding, asking if he could also bring his partner over to listen to them. The two noblewomen were delighted and welcomed the added attention to their grievance. Officers Davier and Edwards sat in rapt fascination as the dyed ostrich feathers secured to the bonnets atop the ladies' heads bobbed and fluttered with each vehement sentence they uttered.

Lucille began the heated dissertation. "Our brother is the Count Raoul de Chagny, and we want to report that an imposter has taken our brother's rightful place on our parents' estate! We want the usurper removed, arrested, and prosecuted at once."

Jacqueline quickly joined the denunciation. "The imposter is a monster with dreadful hair and a mask over the upper right part of his face. He thought he could fool us, but he didn't. We knew the instant we walked into the room he was a fraud!"

"Wasn't your brother extensively burned in a fire last December? We saw him ourselves and were aghast at the extent of his injuries. It's a true phenomenon that the man survived," responded Davier.

Lucille retorted, "This man is definitely not our brother. He does a remarkable imitation of our brother's movements and gestures, but he doesn't look a thing like him."

"Did he sound like your brother?" asked Edwards.

"Oh yes," answered Jacqueline, "but he barely teased us at all. Raoul loves to tease us into total frustration, and his wife served a totally inadequate meal, only three simple courses and then dessert!"

Lucille added, "The first thing he did was make it perfectly clear that he didn't want us staying too long, very unsociable, and this man eats like a rare bird. Raoul always gulped down his food like a famished wolf. This counterfeit is too dainty and dignified, he is not our Raoul."

"How did his wife act toward him?" inquired Davier.

"She calls him 'Angel'. How vile and disgusting is that? Such familiarities right in front of us!"

"And how did he address the two of you?"

Jacqueline's head flew up. "He called us 'Luce and Jacky'. Those are our nicknames! But Christine served me custard and she knows I hate it! I don't think she wants us to visit our brother again."

Davier raised his eyebrows whimsically at Edwards, and inadvertently chastised Jacqueline with his next remark. "We thought you said he isn't your brother."

An amused Edwards added to the insult. "Well, ladies, this does seem a bit odd. A man undergoes a near-death fricassee that puts his business at a standstill, barely serves you an adequate number of courses when you visit his house, and doesn't tease you enough to suit you. Sounds like a charlatan to me."

"Don't be an imbecile, detective, there's more." Lucille's stare could have covered hot tea with frost.

"Yes," questioned Edwards, "what else?"

"On the way home our driver told us that the few meager house servants still left in Raoul's employment report that he plays a massive organ in the cellars like a gifted god. He's Artemis' brother, Apollo, reincarnated! Raoul never played an instrument in his life! He would have loved to, mind you, but our older brother, Philippe, wanted him to learn the shipbuilding business, and pursue more masculine hobbies... like slaying innocent deer." She twisted up her face.

"Disgusting sport!" added Jacqueline emphatically. "Blood and guts everywhere, dreary stuffed heads with sightless eyes hanging on the walls!"

As the condemning diatribe concluded Edwards sounded almost contrite. "My apologies for sounding flippant. We shall go to the estate this very week, and make a through inquiry into the matter. We will then report back to you with our findings. Will that be acceptable?"

"Oh yes," Jacqueline responded. "Please, let us know when you're coming. We'll have a meal prepared that will melt your palate with pleasure. Your mouth will tingle for a week remembering it!"

Lucille sincerely regretted boosting Jacqueline's nerves before coming to the police station this morning. Right after breakfast she'd plied several glasses of champagne into both of them for added courage. Now she'd have to get her babbling, socialite sister out of here before she ordered lunch for everyone and shamefully served it without a waiter.

That afternoon, Erik napped in Raoul's bed on the bliss of a newly delivered mattress. He'd spent the entire morning going over their plans for dealing with Lucille and Jacqueline, and wanted to give his brain a rest. They anticipated a visit from the police within the next few days, and he hoped to have their next communication with the sisters delivered by the very officers the women had employed to unveil the deception.

In his reverie, he saw a luminous Christine float straight through the wall to the foot of his bed. Playfully she rubbed his toes through the blankets. A breeze drifted through a window, blowing a lace curtain out toward the room, a ship's bell clanged warily in the dense fog outside. He sighed in resignation and spoke to her figure. "Nothing compares to the smell of the sea, the sharp taste of salt that hits the tongue. Think we will ever cross the oceans together and see the vast countries beyond?"

Her image ignored his proposal of adventure, and instead of answering pulled harder at his toes to rouse him. "Wake up, Angel. I have something to tell you."

Erik's eyes flew open. *I must be tired – I was deeper into sleep than I wanted to be.* Her sad expression, the way she still held onto his toes, as if wishing to stay connected to him, and the glassy tears she tried to restrain, told him something terrible had happened. He moved his feet away from her and sat up. "What's wrong?"

"A messenger from Benjamin DeVille is downstairs. Abraham died peacefully in his sleep last night." The tears won the battle and started to overflow onto her face. "Jews are usually buried within twenty-four hours of their deaths, his funeral is tomorrow at nine o'clock in the Jewish cemetery. The messenger says it's a private service, but Benjamin is asking us to attend. Should I tell him we cannot go? You haven't been seen in public yet."

For a few moments Christine thought Erik had not understood her. He sat so still, so devoid of feeling, staring blankly at her face. In his lifetime he had experienced many a dreary news report, and been immersed in the finality of death more times than he cared to recount. But nothing had ever touched him so deeply, or made him feel as vulnerable, as the prattle that just left the lips he loved most in the world. "The messenger is wrong. Abraham is not dead!"

"Erik, he's gone...he's..."

"Where is his body? He is not dead! Stop saying that he is." A tremendous shudder raked through Erik, as if he stood feverish in a chilling wind. He reached solemnly for his wig and went to the bathroom.

"Do you want to go downstairs?" choked a weeping Christine. She didn't know whether to follow him, or try to reason with him from where she stood. She wanted the news to be a lie as much as he did!

He placed his cloak over his arm and beckoned for her. "Come." They went to the marbled entrance where Benjamin's messenger stood holding his hat, waiting for their response. Christine thanked him for bringing them the news but Erik stiffly directed, "Take me to Abraham DeVille."

"His body lies in his house. Members of the *Chevra Kaddisha,* the Jewish burial society, are tending to him, preparing him for burial."

"Then we go there." He turned and kissed Christine's cheek. She watched mutely as he marched out the front door.

Erik entered Abraham's home, a place where he'd come to find acceptance and a degree of peace, with a terrorizing detachment rising within him. His mind bitterly exhorted him to turn and go back to the estate. *He's an old man. What do you care? He died, so what?* Erik silenced the disabling demon with a back handed smack across its impudent face. He entered the parlor across the hall from Abraham's office and found Benjamin sitting on a sofa with two elderly ladies on either side. Benjamin was in a black suit and wore a black yarmulke upon his head. The left side of his jacket's collar had been ripped free from the lapel and the jacket's shoulder. Like a wind torn sail it pointed haphazardly toward his left chest. Around his left upper arm he wore a band of black cloth bearing a Star of David embroidered in gray metallic threads.

He stood up and gratefully shook Erik's hand. "How good of you to come." Erik reached over and hugged him, hard – it was all too true. Benjamin had met both Erik and Raoul many times, and knew from Abraham the details of the parody Erik was attempting to act out. "These ladies are from the synagogue. Their husbands are upstairs with my uncle."

"May I please see him, Benjamin?"

"Of course, please excuse us." Benjamin bowed briefly to the women and led Erik up the stairs. He knocked softly on the door of his uncle's bedroom and walked in. Abraham's modest bed had been moved out from the wall, permitting anyone who needed access, the ability to walk completely around it. Twelve inch white candles burned atop tall brass pillars placed at the foot and the head of the bed. Two aged gentlemen sat on chairs up against the wall, reciting a continuous flow of Hebrew. Benjamin explained their presence. "These men are from the burial society, they are reading the psalms for my uncle. Offering praise as substitutes for him, reminding God that he was such a good man, that even after death his prayers continue. Gentlemen, would you please give us a few minutes privacy?" The elderly Jews nodded and left the room discretely. Benjamin waited by the door as Erik approached the body lying in repose.

Abraham had been washed and scented with perfumed oils. His hair was combed, his eyelids closed. Someone had dressed him in a plain, white linen garment, and placed a black yarmulke on his wispy white hair. Around his shoulders they'd wrapped a prayer shawl with wide black stripes. The front of the *tallit* was drawn across his chest, its ritualistic macramé entwined in Abraham's soft fingers, as if he had momentarily paused during his prayers to rest his eyes.

"May I touch him?" Erik asked.

"We are not allowed to touch the dead, but please, go ahead. I know my uncle loved you as a son, and that you cared for him, too."

Erik brushed the old man's pale cheek with his fingertips. *Cold, so very cold!* He knelt beside the bed, resting his forehead on the edge of the *tallit*. From this position of reverence, quiet tears began to flow. *Oh Papa, what is God that He would give you to me only to rip you away? What am I to be without your guidance? How cruel is heaven to dispense love and hope, then dispassionately remove its succor. Oh God, how I hate you and your ignoble throne of glory! You abate the pressure of a boil only to rack the body with a consuming cancer. Papa...Papa, did I ever tell you that I love you? Let me say it. Please God, give me the strength to say these simple words, and somehow let Abraham hear them.*

"I love you, Abraham DeVille. You are my friend, my true father throughout eternity, past all care, past pain. I love you."

Erik felt Benjamin's gentle hand upon his shoulders. "The men are here to place him in his coffin. We need to stand and bear witness to Abraham's worth upon this earth. He is a soul we were blessed to know." They watched with their backs pressed to the wall, as a plain coffin of pinewood was brought into the room and Abraham's body lifted, amidst the ascending praise of the Hebrew psalms, and placed into the box. Benjamin moved forward and kissed the corded knots, the *tzitzit*, held in his uncle fingers. "*Baruch Dayan Emet,* blessed is God the righteous judge," said Benjamin in a coarse whisper.

As the men nailed the lid to the coffin and moved the candleholders to their new positions at the casket's ends, Erik waited in anguish and despair. Each crack of the hammer onto the head of a nail shattered into his soul the despondent cry of abandonment. When they were finished, Erik offered his own prayer, "Oh wretched, mournful day. I wish your dawn had never come."

Benjamin led the way back downstairs. In the front hall, Erik invited him to the chateau for the night.

"No, thank you. I shall stay here. Can you come early in the morning? It would help with my own grief."

"I'll be here at dawn."

Erik and Christine's carriage pulled up to the house before the first gray light of day. Benjamin was up and met them at the door. A different set of Jewish ladies waited in the parlor to affix black armbands to their coats. When the burial society arrived with a horse drawn hearse, Erik followed the men upstairs where the vigil of reciting scriptures had continued in shifts throughout the night. Dispirited and silent, Benjamin and Erik helped carry the coffin down the stairs to the doleful chanting of Hebrew. As they slid the casket onto the floor of the hearse, the sky was awakening with brilliant shades of pink and orange, but they felt none of its unsympathetic promise. Benjamin and Erik rode in the first carriage with the men from the *Chevra Kaddisha,* while a second carriage containing the women, including Madame Giry and Christine, followed behind.

A frail, gray breaded rabbi met them at the cemetery. As the procession formed to carry the coffin to a bier spanning the opened grave, the lament of the prayers recommenced. The service seemed too simple. Words of gratitude were spoken for Abraham's good deeds as a physician, a few more Hebrew prayers were chanted, and the coffin unceremoniously lowered into the ground. Tearfully, Benjamin picked up one of several shovels and dutifully began placing dirt upon his uncle's casket. He stopped when inconsolable crying blurred his vision. Sob after pitiful sob wrested his slender frame. Christine and Madame Giry moved to comfort him and passed the shovel to Erik, who in turn brought dirt to cover the thin shell of wood that separated them from Abraham. When the other Jewish men moved in to join Erik, the ladies guided Benjamin to a seat, holding both his hands and offering words of encouragement. After the coffin was encased, the Jews handed the shovels to the cemetery workers to complete the burial.

Benjamin and the ladies moved up the walk toward the carriages, but a demoralized Erik remained at the graveside. Christine came back to stand beside him, trying to persuade him to leave the cemetery but Erik would not budge. With downcast eyes he watched every scoop of earth that entered the hole, enclosing the body of his friend in its grave. He had the insane impulse to jump in with the dirt and let the pain come to a final, anticlimactic ending.

Christine hurried up the path to Benjamin. "I cannot get him to leave. He doesn't respond to me. His eyes look despondent, almost insane. I've never seen his eyes like that."

"Insane or full of grief?" asked Benjamin. "Stay here." He returned to the graveside and spoke tenderly to Erik. "You know, I was so happy when I finally met you in our home. My uncle loved you so much. You and I are the sons he never had. Come sit *sheva* with me, we can observe the ritual at the chateau if you like. Let me hear your music. I haven't had the opportunity. You can play something for my uncle, something that would have thrilled him if he'd heard it. I'll tell you about his life...he knew first hand the anguish and dejection people can suffer. He was married once. On the way to the honeymoon, ruffians waylaid the carriage taking Abraham and his bride to their wedding night. They kidnapped his wife, wrenched her from his very arms and dragged her out of the coach. He was still searching for her and her abductors, when I came as a teenager to live with him. I helped him make hundreds of inquiries. Believe me when I tell you that he tasted the assault of loneliness and the pain of futility all too often. After years of failed searching around the city of Lille, where we were born and raised, we got a tip that she'd been taken to Paris. We had no family but each other, both my parents died of influenza when I was fourteen, so we came here and ended up staying. We never found her."

Erik listened to Benjamin and after a minute sighed deeply. "Life is a curriculum of pain, with periods of respite if we're lucky enough to be blessed."

"Come, Raoul, let's pay honor to him, sit *sheva* with me."

Erik's eyes were sorrowful, pleading for the pain of this reality to somehow stop. Benjamin wondered sadly if his own eyes appeared the same. He reached over and opened the top of Erik's cloak. Taking hold of the lapel of Erik's jacket, he said, "I, who have placed the goodness of God before my eyes, perform this act of *keriah* for you." He tore the stitching leaving the side of the jacket's collar free of the garment. Then took a handful of soil from the grave, and as Erik bowed his head Benjamin released the dirt over it.

Erik blinked as the cloud of dust around him blew away. "What is God that He would tear this precious soul from us?"

Benjamin responded, "Blessed is God the righteous judge!"

Erik ordered his throat to repeat the words. "Blessed is God the righteous judge."

Tears were sliding down the tender face of the music teacher. "Difficult words to utter in the face of this loss." Benjamin put his hand on Erik's upper arm and turned him toward the walkway. "We will see

Abraham again, the *Kabbalah*, a book written by Jewish mystics says we will." They walked to the carriage reluctantly. "My uncle's generosity was as large as the human landscape is wide. I will miss him."

"I find it so hard to leave him here. He knew the truth about me and never judged where the boundaries of human law should exist. Where will I ever meet another like him?"

"He was a man of great depths."

"What was his young wife's name?"

"Feigel-Evie. Rossman was her family name, and then of course, DeVille."

Erik bent over as if someone had hit him square in the stomach. His hands went to his knees to brace himself.

"What's wrong? What's the matter?" The alarm in Christine's voice reached his ears as if she were far, far away.

Still with his face toward the ground, he asked Benjamin, "That's an unusual name isn't it?"

"No, not among the Jews it isn't. Why, do you know someone with that name? Today she'd be in her early sixties."

The reply, spoken to the ground, was void of any emotion except for a hollow bitterness. "Did know, I did know someone with that name. She's dead to the world – and to me. With a little investigating we can find out if she was Abraham's wife. If she was, I may be able to lead you to end of the story of what happened to her."

Benjamin's expression moved from profound grief to dazed astonishment. He felt as if his life were being slammed about at the whim of a tempest. His ears were roaring. Bewildered he gazed at the top of Erik's head and wailed, "Who are you?"

The man in the elegant funeral suit and black silk cravat straightened, squaring his shoulders with social grace. With the flawless ease of inbred aristocracy he lifted his head, and drew the corner of his cape over his left shoulder, protecting his chest against the chill of a winter's day. Like a polished dancer, he turned on the ball of his foot and looked directly into the eyes of Detective Edwards, who had just arrived and stood about twenty yards away – safely out of earshot.

In a voice rippling with the strength and smoothness of the finest French rapier, Erik answered. "Why Benjamin DeVille, you know me. I am the grand Count Raoul de Chagny, the former Phantom of the Opera and Christine Daae's paramour." *For her sake I am no longer the freak inside the mirror, I have become the breathing distillate of French nobility.* "The current and abiding Phantom of the Chateau is at your service," he confidently took Benjamin by the arm and they strode to the carriages.

Edwards thought there was something oddly familiar about the way the taller man moved. *He's majestic, almost fluid in the sunlight, yet he seems strangely tranquil, detached. Not Raoul at all, but something rather like...that elegant priest escorting Louisa through the rain. Yes, that priest in the rain!* Thomas squinted his eyes and concentrated on every detail he could absorb of the man. *Well hello, Father Raphael! We haven't met, but we will. Oh, we will!*

30 *INSPECT MY FACE*

Losing no opportunity to be of comfort, Christine and Madame Giry alighted from the carriage containing the mourners as soon as it arrived at the chateau. They hastened to the kitchen to attend to lunch. The cook told them everything was near ready to be served and that Imel was in his room reading. Madame patiently asked a persistent Grace to stop tagging along at her skirts and see if she could keep herself occupied for just a little while longer. Obediently, Grace sought out the men and found the Count with Benjamin in the southern salon.

The Count placed his favorite moppet on his knee and introduced her to Benjamin, but no sooner had she made herself comfortable than he asked her if she could go play until lunch. "We want to talk finances... very boring for little girls. Where are your dolls?"

Grace informed him resolutely, "The dolls are in my room." A bit miffed, she climbed off his lap and went to explore. On the second floor she discovered Raoul's door unlocked and decided to seek new adventure in the Count's realm. She tiptoed to his armoire and opened the drawers. *Men's underwear, ties, handkerchiefs...not much exciting in here!* Next she explored his closet, which was more a room than a closet. It had an interesting smell. *Hmm, cedar I think!* Here she found Raoul's coats and jackets hanging neatly, and a section of lovely vests of silks and brocades. His shoes were dusted and lined up neatly on wooden racks. She reached for a pair of brown calfskins with square chiseled toes and hard leather heels. They were highly waxed and shiny, interestingly smooth to the touch of her little fingers. *I've never seen the Count wear these. His feet are long and narrow; these shoes are for big wide feet. They probably don't fit him anymore.* She slipped off her pumps and playfully put her feet into Raoul's shoes. The heels of her greatly over-sized footwear thwacked annoyingly against the floorboards as she walked around the closet floor, so she thumped her way over to the carpet where the sound was less like the clopping of a country horse. Giggling, she paraded herself in front of the full-length mirror. She could barely see the cuffs of her lavender socks – her feet were so swallowed by the enormous, heavy shoes. *Goblin feet…I have goblin feet! The Count used to have goblin feet too, but the dragon's fire changed them.*

Meg, Jean and Claude arrived with the Daroga in tow. A flurry of greetings and condolences were showered onto Benjamin. Everyone was at a loss trying to accurately express grief over the death of Abraham. As they settled in the dining room, Jean tried to scoop up the two-and-a-half year old Claude, who was busy chasing Grace around the enormous table. The boy had great traction on the sculpted patterns of the immense Chinese carpet, and occasionally Grace slowed down to let him grab her skit – creating a backward pull against her run with resulting peels of laughter from them both.

"Calm down," ordered Jean. "You two are like wild banshees set loose from a swamp."

The cook served an aromatic lunch of Spanish Chicken with olives and rice. The rich smells of garlic and chili filled the room. Christine placed several baskets of bread on the table and praised cook's culinary arts. "Your food is always excellent, Marie! You have a southern influence hidden in you somewhere, I think."

"Thank you, Mame. It does make a pretty dish doesn't it?"

Madame Giry entered with a platter of steaming winter squash and turnips. Jean twisted his nose as the vegetables passed, "What's for dessert?"

"Chocolate cake," announced Meg as she walked through the butler's pantry door with a platter of green beans and pearl onions. "Cook's prepared a feast for us! Thank you, Marie."

Marie gave a tiny courtesy to Meg and informed Benjamin knowingly, "I made sure there's no dairy in anything, Monsieur DeVille. Just don't butter your bread. I've set out crushed garlic and olive oil for you just there. You can have all that you like."

"How kind of you, Marie."

As they passed the dishes and started to eat, Louisa commented on what a wonderful, kind man Abraham had been. "There will never be another like him, I'm afraid."

"He was a great uncle and an amazing model for me to follow. I shall miss him everyday." Benjamin's voice bore such exquisite sadness that Meg's kind heart went out to him.

"Mama," Meg redirected the subject, "please tell all of us what you're thinking regarding Grace's future."

Madame Giry wiped her lips with a linen napkin, but before she could speak Grace announced, "I live here now! Don't I?"

Louisa smiled at her. "Well, as you can all see, over these last months our Grace seems to have adjusted quite well to her new family. I'm considering keeping Grace as my full time ward. Would you like that Grace?"

"Where would we live?"

"Would you like to live here some of the time and at Meg and Jean's for the rest?"

Before she could answer Imel interrupted, "How do you go about making her your ward?"

"I'm not sure of the legalities. I plan to make inquiries of Monsieur Toussaint if Grace is agreeable."

"I like both places," Grace diplomatically informed them. "There's plenty of room to roam around, and the boys are fun to play with, well not Ariel, but Claude is good for tag…and Michael is walking, so I'll teach him to play hide and seek."

Christine's face registered astonishment. "What do you mean Michael is walking?"

"He walked this morning, all by himself, then he went boom," she pounded her fist into her palm, "right down on his bum, but he didn't cry. He thought it was funny. When the nanny came into the play room she asked what Michael was laughing about and I told her, but she didn't believe me either."

"We believe you, Grace," soothed the Count. "We'll bring Michael downstairs after lunch and see if he'll walk for us, too."

"I haven't caused any trouble have I?" Grace squirmed in her seat.

"No, you haven't caused any trouble. It's just that a baby's first steps are an occasion for joy."

"Good. The Angel of Music says I should not cause trouble, but I like to explore and hunt around. That's not trouble is it?"

"Hunt around where?" Louisa asked anxiously.

"Did you know that the Count's feet shrank in the fire?"

Christine's fork dropped to her china plate with a clang. "What do you mean shrank?"

"All his shoes and boots are big, this way." Grace put her palms together then drew them apart, "And today his feet are this way." She brought her little hands back together. "The dragon took his goblin feet away!"

A deep, thirsty laugh sprung from Erik's gut, it rose uncontrolled from his throat and echoed in the vaulted ceiling of the room. No one had heard him laugh since December. It was blessed music to everyone's ears. Christine's shoulders eased down and she started to laugh as well. A contagious wave of amusement moved round the table, and a perplexed Grace stammered. "It's true! The Count is going to need all new shoes. Is it funny that his goblin feet are gone?"

"No, Sweetheart, it's good his goblin feet are gone," Madame Giry said. "We're laughing because the Count is laughing and we haven't heard him laugh in a long time."

Christine wiped her eyes and added, "Yes, well…we should bundle up all the clothes and shoes that don't fit him any more and give them to the Sisters of Charity, shouldn't we."

Louisa added, "Let's make it a rule to lock all the doors in the house for a time. It seems we're in for an epidemic of curious cats."

Erik tried to constrain his laughter, but it was like a treasure chest finally cracked open – its precious goods spilling out upon the ground for everyone to see. "I'm getting full," he finally managed. "I hope there's not another course." He winked at Christine.

After lunch the Daroga, Imel and Jean went to play billiards in the game room. Erik and Benjamin retreated to the cellar to discuss music and introduce Benjamin to the massive black and gold organ housed there. Benjamin let out a low whistle of admiration. "She is a beauty. We're supposed to sit *sheva* in a well-lit room and there are no windows down here…but this is where **she** abides. I vote we stay here!" He ran his fingers lovingly across the sets of keys and admired the rows of gleaming pipes. "The acoustics in here must be phenomenal."

"Yes, Christine tells me the floors of the first level vibrate when I play. And I believe that cook leaves all the doors open so she can hear the music better. Sometimes I play just for her amusement. Did you hear how the laughter enveloped the table at lunch? Interesting crescendo."

"To be honest I didn't pay attention to its timing or the volume, only that it spread. Please play something for me. Where is your opera? The 'Don Juan Triumphant' you want me to read?"

Erik dipped behind the organ and returned with a leather portfolio full of handwritten music. "I've worked on this for over twenty years."

"I'm honored to hold it, maestro." While Erik played sample passages from the scores and interludes of his opera, Benjamin leafed through page after page. As he reached the end of the folder, Erik brought the music to an expressive close, softly repeating the final bars as if to sound an aching refrain through an empty canyon of love and betrayal.

Benjamin spoke enthusiastically, "This is magnificent! The subtleties, the flavor…the variances in structure are so persuasive. They engage the listener in a tempting caress, then dissuade with a dynamic slap against the cheek. It's an opus to be proud of...imagine if we heard it played by an orchestra, the way you intended."

"It has promise doesn't it?"

"Promise isn't the word. In the right hands it will become a classic. Thank you for sharing it with me. We should arrange to have it presented, it's worthy of the *Garnier* or *LaScala*." Benjamin's fingers held the work tenderly, but his mind was buffeted to a sadder reality, one of severe grief.

"What is it? Is it Abraham?"

"His search never found a triumphant ending. We failed to uncover even a hint of his wife's true location. Please, tell me about the Feigel-Evie you knew."

"She was my woeful excuse of a mother, and this is what she did to her son with the monstrous face." Without vehemence, Erik spent the next few minutes describing his childhood years under his mother's care.

"Maybe she was Abraham's wife, but even if she wasn't, we can search together for the truth and perhaps learn how she met your father. How old are you? When were you born?"

"I'm forty this year. I was born in thirty-six when my mother was twenty. She'd be just sixty if she were alive. How old was Abraham's wife when he married her?"

"She was nineteen. They wed in thirty-five. The timing is right. We could go to Rouen if you're up to it. Make inquiries or send letters, look at marriage certificates, birth records. Do you know her maiden name?"

"No, I never knew it. There's nothing wrong with me, Benjamin, but thanks for wondering if I'm up to the trip. Your comment pays true complement to my performance here." He swept his arm through the air indicating the chateau.

"You're right! I forget that you weren't the one burned in the fire. You're an amazing thespian."

Erik left the organ's bench and came to where Benjamin sat on an upturned keg. He rolled another keg upright and took a seat beside him. Leaning closer he spoke in confidence. "D'Angelus is a name I adopted. I haven't told anyone my real surname in decades."

"So you're a man of many characters. Shakespeare could have used you as an ambassador for the stage."

"Does anyone in your family have eyes like these?"

"Not that I know of, and I seriously doubt that Abraham would have been intimate with her out of wedlock. She came from an honorable Jewish family and he respected her virtue as a good Jewish woman. Not that engaged Jews don't indulge in pleasure, I just don't believe Abraham would have. Abraham told me that the three rogues who stole her were tall, strong men, their faces covered with black cloths...but he had the most peculiar impression that one of them knew her, that it wasn't a chance abduction. While one of the men held Abraham at gunpoint, another kidnapper grabbed his bride's wrists to pull her from the coach. In the tumult, this second assailant actually paused to release her hem from her heel so she wouldn't trip. Abraham found that odd bit of courtesy almost surreal. The picture of it stayed vividly in his mind. He anguished over it for years. Believing they meant her no injury, he waited for a ransom demand but none ever came."

Erik studied Benjamin's eyes very carefully. "Do you think the scoundrel could have been someone outside the Jewish community? Someone who had seen her and wanted her for himself?"

"Yes, but even if he proclaimed love for her, she probably rejected him if he wasn't Jewish. She was raised in a very proper family."

"What if she became pregnant without Abraham knowing about it...but the man knew, or suspected it."

"Yes, I see where you're going. Maybe we need to talk to **her** family, not yours. Someone there might know something. What do you know of your father?"

"Tall, black and gray hair...I was told I have eyes like my paternal grandfather's, only much brighter."

"They are definitely unusual eyes. What color were your father's?"

"I believe they were hazel green, something like Christine's. Talking about my parents brings a queer apprehension. It stirs up bitter emotions. What if my mother was Abraham's bride and my own father stole her? He was a master mason in Rouen...are there any special prayers we should be saying for Abraham?"

"Are you changing the subject? Yes, I have the prayers with me. We can skip the Hebrew and read the French translations. If you are the son of Abraham's wife, then in some very weird way...and brace yourself for this...you are Jewish and we are kinsmen. What I really want to do is rush from here, and for my uncle's sake, go out and discover the truth. This is the best lead we've had in years!"

Upstairs, Detective Edwards stood at the front door paying his promised visit to the chateau. Joseph ushered him in, asking him to wait while he announced the officer's arrival to his mistress. Christine and Louisa hurried to the front reception area.

"Ladies," Edwards bowed, "unfortunately I am here on official business. Raoul's sisters made an interesting report to the police and I need to make an inquiry. Louisa, all the girls, including my Kate, sorely miss their ballet lessons. I hope you will consider reopening the studio at some point in the future. How are you doing out here?"

"We are managing quite well, Sir. Thank you for asking."

He listened thoughtfully to her response then turned to Christine. "Madame le Countess, might I inquire if you plan to rebuild your house?"

"No detective, my husband expects to put the land up for sale within the next month. If it doesn't sell, we might rebuild and then try to sell it."

"How is your husband?"

"Much better, thank you, the major damage is located in one area of his face and on top of his head. The rest of him seems to be healing to the best of our expectations. Would you like to speak with him?"

"Perhaps in a little while. I'd like to talk to the staff first, then to the Count."

"I'll assemble them for you. Would the kitchen be an acceptable spot? You could take some refreshment."

"That would be fine. How many servants are there?"

"A nanny, two maids, a cook and a driver, all are in the house today."

While Edwards greeted each staff member individually as they entered the kitchen, Louisa and Grace brought the babies into the library. Christine fetched Erik and Benjamin up from the cellar – and Jean's group, when they heard they were being investigated at the sisters' prompting, wanted to join in too. When the adults and children were gathered in the library, Christine explained, "Raoul met Inspector Davier in this room when the police investigated Victor's disappearance. This seems like the most appropriate place for us to assemble." Everyone agreed.

Sitting in the kitchen, Edwards told the staff, "I'm making a follow-up inquiry about the disastrous fire that injured your employer. In general how are things going? Is there anything peculiar you'd like to report? Don't be shy, I want to hear whatever you have to say."

The nanny spoke right up, "I, for one, am very grateful for the job. The Count and the mistress are kind and considerate people."

"Yes, I'm grateful as well, but the Count is a strange one, likes to be alone, and doesn't like wine anymore," retorted the downstairs maid, Blanche.

Marie immediately scolded her. "Hush now, there's nothing wrong about wanting to keep your wits about you after being involved in a fire like that. Madame says he never drinks, or takes drugs of any kind, because they impair his judgment. That's how he got hurt. I guess he'd been drinking pretty heavy."

Edwards agreed, "It's hard to offer an argument against sound reasoning like that, you should all respect his privacy."

Blanche informed him with a smirk, "The Countess tells us she'll dismiss anyone who doesn't respect his privacy, or interferes with his life in any way."

Edwards responded firmly, "It's very difficult to defend yourself against household gossips, especially if one is trying to recuperate from a devastating burn."

"Right you are, Sir," the upstairs maid, Antoinette, concurred. "I'm for protecting the Count and helping him get back on his feet. This is a lovely place to live and they're good to us. Just last week the mistress gave all of us new clothes and new shoes. We could wait a month of Sundays to get things that nice from some estate owners."

"Yes indeed," said Joseph. "They've been through a rough patch here. It's our job to help them get re-established as quickly as possible. The Countess could easily have been a widow, fighting the world alone with two little babies."

Blanche stirred the pot in the reverse direction. "But why does he always have to wear black? It's too depressing...like everyday is a funeral, not just today."

Marie gave the back of Blanche's hand a sound, motherly tap with a wooden spoon. "Oh for goodness sake! Give the man a chance. He's in mourning for his face and his head." She looked at Edwards with chagrin. "What a mess, Sir. You never saw the like of it in all your life. I swear it's like a potter pounded on clay, then walked away for lunch and let the disarray set anyway it chose."

"Yes, well no need to swear," counseled Edwards. "We're not in court and we've no plans to go there in the future. The old Count Raoul is dead. He came through the fire and made it out alive. Let him wear any clothes he wants. Yes?" Everyone was silent. "Good. Is there anything else?"

Feeling more charitable, Blanche offered, "Well, he plays music in the cellar a lot but it's beautiful music. If we prop open the doors, it fills the whole ground floor with its lovely qualities."

Edwards asked, "Does he sing?"

"No, not that we've ever heard," offered the nanny.

"Maybe he'll try it out. You should give him a chance to find his voice if he attempts it." Edwards' expression was difficult to read.

Joseph thought him official but really rather sad. "That's exactly what we'll do, Sir. If the Count wants to sing, we'll encourage him. The mistress says they'll build a chapel attached to the house someday. He won't always be playing down in the cellar."

Antoinette sounded excited. "The Countess wants an arboretum too, with lots of trees!"

Edwards pushed his chair back. "This is splendid news. It sounds like you are all doing an admirable job for your employers." He admonished Blanche by adding, "Watch your comments, Madame, or you'll find yourself on the outside looking in, wondering that you didn't understand how well you had it."

Cook folded her meaty arms across her chest and nodded resolutely. "That's good advice, Blanche. I'd take it."

Edwards made a request, "Could someone locate the mistress of the manor for me?"

Joseph jumped to his feet. "Yes, Sir." In a few minutes he returned. "They're waiting for you in the library, Sir. I'll show you where it is."

Edwards smoothed his hair and brushed off his lapels before rounding the corner to the library. He had expected to see Christine and Louisa in the company of whoever was playing the part of the Count, but found himself also greeted by Imel, Meg, Jean, a man introduced as the Daroga, and Benjamin DeVille. "My, we have quite a gathering in here. Are we missing anyone?"

From the end of a long reading table near the window, Jean elaborated on the known census. "My son Claude is on the floor back here, coloring with Grace and Raoul's oldest boy, Michael. The Count's second son, Ariel, is in a bassinette over here as well."

Edwards bowed and took a seat in an empty chair by the door. "Monsieur le Count, I am sorry to tell you that your two sisters paid a visit to the police station Monday. They believe that you are not yourself, to be precise, they think you're someone else entirely."

Erik sat between Jean and the Daroga; the window directly behind them was closed but unlatched. He made no attempt to alter his voice and sound like Raoul. "I'm sorry to hear that they troubled you, but it's not unexpected. In truth, I am not the same man I used to be. Unfortunately you've come at a very sad time for us. Our dear friend and physician, Abraham DeVille, has passed away and we are in mourning."

Surely the man must know the effect his voice has on people. I'd like to hear him speak for hours...and sing...oh yes, please sing. I believe you have a voice to lift the souls right out of hell, Father Raphael, or whoever you are. "I'm so sorry to intrude upon you this day of all days. I was at the cemetery toward the end of the funeral. Monsieur DeVille, please accept my most profound condolences. I extend my sympathies to you all. The doctor's passing is a loss to our entire community. Abraham DeVille was a remarkable and generous man." Edwards looked around to each of them. "What do you believe the sisters perceived that gave them the impression Raoul is an imposter?"

Louisa responded without hesitation. "Lucille and Jacqueline cannot cope with the deformities thrust upon their brother...he's disfigured now, thinner, less abrupt. The sisters are royalty and indifferent to true suffering. Instead of compassion, they respond with self-righteous indignation, taking affront over food and their brother's fatigue."

"Inspect my face for yourself, detective." Without bravado, Erik removed his mask and wig. "*Ecce Homo,* behold the man that I am today." He let the officer grasp the full splendor of his abnormalities.

Edwards was shocked at the extent of the damage, but to his credit maintained a professionally calm expression. *You poor mutilated being, with your pound of putrid flesh attached to living bone.*

"As you can plainly see, nothing can be done about this area except to cover it up." Erik passed his hand over his right face and across his frightening, whimsical clumps of hair.

Sitting to the left and somewhat behind the detective, Benjamin was out of the officer's line of sight. He allowed himself the levity of a brief smirk, well viewed by the others in the room, who all managed to remain uniformly placid. If this interview did not unfold well, the plan was for Benjamin to shove Edwards in his side, while Jean and the Daroga launched Erik out the window. They had assured Benjamin that Erik was more than capable of an acrobatic tumble to the ground below, and would land adroitly on both feet. A saddled horse stood tethered to some bushes just to the side of the library's windows.

Edwards addressed his next questions to Christine. "And you, Madame, do you think the fire has changed your husband? Excuse my bluntness, but are you revolted by his appearance? Do you wish to return to your home on *Rue du Renard*? Could you leave freely if you wished it?"

"My husband is kinder and gentler than he has ever been. I think he values life more. I doubt that he will ever go hunting to kill an animal just for sport, and he enjoyed that very much before the accident. All of us seem to be more precious to him. Dr. DeVille wanted him to play music to exercise his hands, Benjamin has been teaching him."

Benjamin picked up the hint and continued. "I can attest to the depth of his sensitive nature. I'm amazed at it. He's a fast learner as well, and will be a gifted musician in his own right if he pursues it."

"Please, Benjamin, you flatter me," offered the Count who seemed utterly composed and strangely removed from the group.

"You are too modest. Many of my students pray for a tenth of the innate musical ability laying dormant in your little finger."

"You are too kind."

Edwards ended the weirdly received 'Fest of Praises' by pushing the issue with Christine. "Please Madame, I need to know for a certainty, are you safe? Could you leave here if you wanted?"

"Yes, I am safe. Raoul would let me go if I wished it, but it is my desire to stay with my husband. We are going to have another child."

Louisa smiled broadly and placed her hands over her heart.

"Mazel Tov!" exclaimed Benjamin, clapping his hands together.

Christine asked the young DeVille, "Is there a feminine form of Abraham, because we're hoping for a girl this time."

"I believe Sarah would be most appropriate."

Edwards rose to leave. "I am going to report that everything seems to be in order here. I am quite satisfied." He shook the Count's gloved hand – each returned the other's grip firmly. "I shall tell your sisters they are lucky to have you alive. Blessings and a hastened recuperation back to your place in the world, whatever you choose it to be."

Louisa took the detective's arm and showed him out, as they walked to the front door Thomas leaned in closely to her. "I'm of the opinion that Blanche's loyalties are questionable. She'd like to stir up trouble if she could...probably just for the drama it would create in the house. You've most likely had your fill of the dramatic these last few months. I've truly missed you, Louisa. Would you consider an invitation to dinner? You name the date and time."

"I'm needed here, Thomas, but please come back, and not on official business. I'll tell the others I've invited you."

"You love that Count in there don't you?"

"With all my heart...for years...he is closer to me than my own blood brother."

Edwards kissed her fingers and left to report to Davier that he thought the de Chagny sisters outrageously smug and over-bearing.

31 *CARNIVOROUS RATS*

Over cups of cocoa brought in by Marie, they tarried together in the library to discuss their impressions of the interview with Edwards. Louisa told them the detective's last comments to her before leaving – they were impressed that she had conjured up an invitation for him to return.

"Bold stroke, Mama," praised Meg. "What shall we do about Blanche?"

"We'll replace her in the morning," answered Christine as she rocked Ariel in her arms.

The Daroga reached up and locked the window behind Erik's head. "Let's move to a more comfortable room."

"Benjamin and I still have some things to accomplish. We'll join you in a few minutes." Erik loosened his tie and took the seat next to Benjamin.

Louisa gathered up the children's coloring. "I asked Joseph to stoke a fire in the southern salon so we might visit comfortably in there."

The group moved to the cozier parlor where flames leapt cheerfully in the baroque fireplace. In the library Benjamin took the prayers out of his pocket. "Normally there are ten men to say these but is God counting? I doubt it." Together they read the passages and at their conclusion Benjamin vocalized frustration. "This is so unsatisfying. I don't attend synagogue regularly. I do want to fulfill my obligations to my uncle's memory, but I truly think I can best sit *sheva* for him by trying to learn the truth."

"So you'll go to Lille?"

"Yes. I'm thinking by rail, early in the morning. Maybe, you should stay here in case there's any trouble replacing Blanche tomorrow, and since Detective Edwards has an eye for Louisa, he could always return for a follow-up visit." Benjamin squeezed Erik's shoulder. "As you said, you're supposed to be in a delicate state of healing at the moment. It would probably seem suspicious if you were caught gallivanting across the countryside with me."

Before daybreak Benjamin boarded the train traveling from Paris to Lille, a textile city one hundred forty miles away on the Deule River in the Nord-Pas de Calais region close to the Belgium border. At the chateau, a sleepy Erik followed Christine into her rooms, asking lightheartedly when she thought they might combine their two suites of bedrooms into one domain.

"When we have the money to throw at remodeling," Christine smiled. "It does please me that you don't want me moving further down the hall, you want me closer. Be patient, remember we have another child on the way." She started to dress.

"Don't," coached Erik. "Don't dress yet. I'm bored. Entertain me."

"Entertain you? What with? A dance?"

From behind, he wrapped his arms around her, "Perhaps."

"How about later this afternoon? We'll meet back up here in my room for a change of scenery and I'll dance for you. I'll even sing. You can critique my vocalization and movement. I'll listen to your instructions with rapt attention, I promise. We haven't sung together in a long time. What are your plans for the day?"

"Benjamin's gone to Lille and I'm anxious to know the results of his trip. While you're in Paris searching for a new downstairs maid, I'll learn more about the shipbuilding trade, but I'm going to hold you to your tantalizing proposal of an afternoon's liaison. Don't think I'm not aware of your provocative tease."

She emerged from the closet. "Let me comb my hair and go downstairs to release Blanche. We might as well launch the day with the crash of cymbals."

By noon Benjamin found himself on the narrow streets of the Vieux Lille, the oldest section of the city. The architecture of the homes surrounding him bore a strong Flemish influence. Quaint and practical, they were built tightly up against each other with steep tiled roofs and shuttered windows. He'd already been to the Town Hall searching through birth records, and to the local synagogue to inquire about the Rossman family. He'd pieced together that no one remained of the Rossman's except for one elderly widow, a woman named Hemdah Zevah Rossman-Stendal. He was scrutinizing the numbers on the houses – hunting for hers even now. At the top of the street his search was rewarded. He knocked smartly with the brass knocker on the heavy wooden door. In a minute, a stern faced housekeeper, with her hair combed severely into a puffy white cap, answered his persistent summons. He introduced himself politely, asking to speak with the mistress of the house on urgent business regarding a possible relative, and mentioned Feigel-Evie Rossman's name.

The housekeeper's face registered nothing except annoyance at having her chores interrupted. "Wait here – I'll speak to my mistress."

When she returned, she directed him into a front room where she stiffly instructed him to stay put. "Madame Stendal wishes to speak with you." Benjamin tried to bottle his anticipation and wait patiently, but could not control an insistent tapping of his foot. He rose when a silver haired woman entered the room, using an elaborately carved, wooden cane to steady her steps. She wore a soft-blue wool day dress and a cream colored cashmere shawl, a string of perfectly matched pink pearls hung below the folds of her small throat. He guessed her to be about sixty and was drawn to her sweet smile before she spoke a word.

"Monsieur DeVille, it's been many days since anyone has come to visit this house. You've entered my day with some welcomed diversion. I am Hemdah Stendal."

"Benjamin DeVille at your service, Madame. Please, allow me to assist you to a seat."

She settled daintily into a mauve colored arm chair. "I knew of your family, Benjamin. You're named for your grandfather's father are you not? Your father was Aaron DeVille? His older brother a physician called Abraham?"

"Yes. I can't thank you enough for seeing me. I need to speak with you…"

"Have you eaten young man? You seem entirely too thin to me. I may be an old withered apple, but my eyesight and my brain are both functioning splendidly."

"I ate on the train early this morning as it left Paris. I'm not…"

"Up before dawn for the five-thirty rail, that was hours ago. Elise, Elise, come in here." She thumped the cane on the floor. The housekeeper instantly appeared beside the green velvet drapes surrounding the arched entrance to the room. "Please prepare lunch for two and tell us when you have it ready. We'll eat in the dining room." The somber faced housekeeper offered only the beginnings of a curtsy in response. No doubt disgruntled at having her eavesdropping foiled.

"That is too kind of you, Madame Stendal. I've intruded on your privacy and can hardly expect you to feed me."

"Nonsense, you'll eat and I'll hear nothing less. Please call me Hemdah. When your parents passed you went to live with your uncle, Abraham. How is he?"

"He died peacefully in his sleep, we believe of a heart attack. I am here about his young bride of many years ago…Feigel-Evie Rossman. Are you related to her?"

The woman breathed in deeply through her nose, expanding her chest. Holding her breath, she placed her fingers on her pearls before letting the air out her nostrils. Benjamin thought she must have been exquisitely beautiful in her younger years. Her blue-gray eyes still sparkled in a soft, lustrous face of gentle wrinkles. She held her back perfectly straight with her dainty knees drawn together. The tiny, white silk Chinese slippers visible below the hem of her dress, spoke of refinement and comfort.

When she finally answered him, her voice carried a tone of sadness. "I knew Feigel-Evie quite well, better than most. She is my older sister, but I have not seen her, or heard anything from her in many years. Do you know something of the accursed tragedy that befell her?"

"I know she was abducted as she traveled with my uncle Abraham on the first night of their honeymoon. She was removed from their hired coach on the road outside Lille. I want to tell you that my uncle searched for her all his life."

"I can well imagine. Abraham was always a sincerely compassionate man, but when I knew him, he had a remarkable streak of perseverance running straight through him. An admirable characteristic, I suppose, but my sister's disappearance must have caused him endless discomfort. I extend my sympathies at your great loss."

"Thank you. It is so ironic, so painfully peculiar, that here after his death I may have uncovered a solid clue as to what happened to Feigel-Evie. I would like your permission to speak to you freely of private matters."

"How private?"

"Was there anyone else romantically interested in your sister besides my uncle? Perhaps a non-Jew?" The old lady's eyes grew wide for a moment, and then she closed them completely, deliberately shutting Benjamin and his words out of her mind.

"Hemdah." Her eyes opened. "I can imagine that you are reluctant to tell me of your sister's private life, but I beg you to open your heart to me. I **too** have spent years trying to locate her. I watched my uncle suffer profoundly. He condemned himself for not fighting off the criminals who stole her. You could very well end a great deal of my own personal pain. After so many years, and my uncle's death, what could come of my knowing her history...except for the blessing of a little peace?"

"My father's father immigrated here from Germany...a very industrious man. He built a successful textile factory and passed it on to my father before he died. Under my father's management the business flourished. He ended up owning two factories. The one here in town manufactured cotton cloth, and the one he built outside of town, in Roubaix, produced woolens. He hired a gentile architect and his son to build the one in Roubaix. My father had only us two girls for children. He planned to leave each of us, along with our future husbands, a factory apiece to guarantee our livelihoods. From the time we were children, Feigel-Evie favored your uncle for a spouse. She met him in the synagogue and waited patiently when he went to medical school. When he returned on his last summer break from the hospital's academy, they formalized the engagement. Abraham planned to practice medicine in this area, so she chose to inherit the newer plant, leaving me the one that was already well established and profitable. In the fall, when your uncle left to complete his studies, my sister started going to the building site for the new factory several times a week. She wanted to check on its progress and make sure the construction proceeded on schedule."

Hemdah paused with her hands resting on the head of her cane. Benjamin urged her to continue, explaining that if what she knew corresponded with his information, they might both be enlightened. Hemdah, obviously uncomfortable, nodded in agreement. "It was some kind of infernal madness. The architect's son was a handsome young man. He fell in love with her almost from the moment he laid eyes on her. When she refused his advances, explaining she was betrothed, he was not the least bit deterred. In fact, he seemed more fueled with determination as she withdrew. She stopped going to the construction site all together, and the scoundrel began following her, spying on her as she went to the stores or the synagogue. His own father fired him off the job site and sent him home to Rennes. Feigel-Evie thought he'd left, but he was only biding his time, forming a plan. One day when she went out to shop, he saw his opportunity. He cornered her in the street and dragged her into an alley. She told him she was a proper Jewess, she begged him not to sully her for she was promised to another. Her betrothal was of no concern to him. He acted like a barbarian, breaking the lock off a door and forcing her inside a vacant yardage shop. When he had her safely confined, he fingered her and set his lips upon her... claiming her, demanding her. She protested and tried to resist him, but she'd never been confronted with such a willful flood of passion...and Abraham was away. She stopped fighting and gave in to him." Hemdah sighed. Her silvery crowned head had developed a mild tremor.

"When Feigel-Evie finally made her way home she swore me to secrecy, begging me to advise her. What could I do but help my sister? She wanted to be Abraham's bride, so she hid inside the house. I bought the goods to sew her wedding dress, planned the reception with her from her bedroom, and went to the *shul* to see the rabbi. We heard nothing from the young man again and hoped he'd finally given up. All the wedding arrangements unfolded exactly as we'd planned them, except that our father insisted on walking her by candle light to the synagogue to be wed. You know, the old-fashioned tradition. It was Chanukah and she was getting married! He scolded the two of us for not being happier at such a luminous time. When the procession set forth from this house, she and I walked out in dread. At every doorway and corner we expected the man to spring on her...it was frightful...the most gruesome processional I'd ever been in. Even at the *shul* we were frightened. We didn't relax until both the ceremony and the reception were over without an incident...and you know the rest! If the young architect stole her, I can only guess that he waited until after the wedding because he held no respect for the ceremony, or perhaps because she was the most defenseless then with fewer people around her...in the cover of night...outside the city on that doleful road."

"Did you know the man's name?"

"Oh yes, but I think he may have changed it. I was never able to find either of them, and believe me I tried. What was I to do? Tell Abraham his bride may have been tainted, when I didn't even know for sure myself how far she'd gone with him...or let it go and wait for her to contact me. She did have feelings for the gentile, of that I'm sure, terrifying, hellish feelings, but feelings none the less. I've struggled with this all these years...never losing hope that with God's grace she'd contact me, or that Abraham would somehow find another and forget the bride that was stolen from him. I still don't know if I did the wrong thing. I could have told our father, but he would have forbidden the marriage to Abraham and forced her to be a spinster. Until this very afternoon I've kept my word to her. I'm telling you because I'd like to see my sister, and you may well hold the key, young Benjamin."

"She may have been taken to Rouen. If she is the lady I am thinking she might be, she died years ago. I am friend to her son and only recently learned something of his childhood."

Huge tears filled Hemdah's eyes. "Her son? She had a son? You must give me his name, Benjamin."

"I don't think that I can, he is a recluse. He was born facially disfeatured, his mother shunned him."

Exasperated, Hemdah stomped her cane into the floor. She tried to stand and walk to him, but was too weak to rise and remained in her seat. "You don't understand. Our father left the both of us a fortune. Her half has been sitting in the *Banque de France* accumulating interest all these years. She never reappeared to claim it and I have no need of it! Three times I carried children in my womb. All three were dead at birth. They didn't take so much as a single breath in this world! The tragedy of it wore on my husband all his life, he died in sadness. If Feigel-Evie had a son he is my only heir. Where is this boy?"

"He's thirty-nine years old and lives in Paris. Do you have any likeness of her? A painting, a tintype? We need to be cautious, he has suffered greatly."

"No, I have no likeness of her, but she had a birthmark that I didn't have. It was a reddish brown circle on the bottom of her lower right calf, a couple of inches above the ankle."

"Why do you say she had a birthmark that you didn't have?"

"Because she's my twin."

A gasp escaped Benjamin, he nearly fell out of his chair. Crowded thoughts shot from his mouth almost simultaneously. "How's your health, Hemdah? Can you travel? Can I bring this man to you? When could you leave? How quickly could I return to Paris to fetch him here?"

Hemdah delicately wiped her tears with a lace handkerchief. "Slow down Benjamin DeVille, I'm an old woman and you're speaking much too fast for me to follow you."

Benjamin sprung to his feet in declaration. "You said she was your older sister!"

"Yes, older by twelve minutes. She was born first."

Benjamin plopped backwards into the chair, holding his head. "This is too much, Hemdah. I need to catch my breath."

As planned, Christine and Louisa released Blanche from her employment in the morning. The maid had asked for another chance, promising she would watch her tongue, but Louisa had cautioned Christine that should those words be offered, they were only a temporary platitude to maintain her position. Given time, Blanche would be unwanted trouble. So Joseph helped Blanche pack her few belongings and took her to Paris, returning promptly to conduct Christine to the employment agency in the city. In the mid-afternoon, Joseph drove the carriage carrying Christine and the new downstairs maid to the front of the chateau. Louisa met them in the entranceway and offered to get the new girl settled into her quarters before giving her a tour of the house and an outline of her duties.

Anxious to bring Erik up to date and furnish him with her promised rendezvous, Christine asked, "Where is the Count?"

"He's spent the better part of the day in your room. I think he's probably reading in there."

Christine hurried up the stairs but found her bedroom door secured. Intrigued and happy, she knocked. *How ironic, now I'm the one in the hall asking for admittance at my own door. He must have prepared some clever surprise within.* When she recovered the keys from her pocket and unlocked the door, a macabre sight met her eyes – but only for a second. A bright light immediately blinded her. Someone had yanked down the heavy drapes covering her windows, flooding the room with brilliant sunlight. She squinted, painfully trying to regain her vision. As her assaulted pupils accommodated, she gasped in revulsion. The furniture had been pushed away from the walls, and the wallpaper painted, from floor to ceiling, with the images of rats, hundreds of rats. Rodents with brilliant yellow, protruding eyes stared maliciously at her from every inch of the walls. Erik was nowhere in sight! She closed the door and after relocking it, ran to find Louisa.

Tremulous, the two women quietly entered the bedroom and locked the door behind them. "What is this?" asked Christine. "Could one of the servants have done this?"

"I doubt it. I've seen everyone off and on all day except for Erik."

"Did he take lunch downstairs?"

"No, Imel brought the meal to him. See there on your desk...the empty dishes." Louisa scanned the morbid artwork. "These are Erik's creations."

"Who is in the house that could help us search for him?"

"Only Joseph and Imel...and I don't know where either is at the moment."

"Then this is for us to handle." They moved from her bedchamber to her bath. No Erik and no rats. They looked in her closets, then went to the door of her sitting room, turning the knob with trepidation. The furniture of her private parlor had been stacked haphazardly into the center of the room. Across the room they could see the back of Erik. Dressed and wearing his cloak, with the hood pulled over his head, he held his arms outstretched. He was side-stepping slowly, his face and abdomen pressed tightly against the wall, as if he were listening and feeling for something with his white-gloved fingers. The bizarre nature of the scene stunned them. He rounded the corner and kept proceeding to his right, intent on the pursuit of this strange occupation.

Christine's voice trembled. "What is this? It looks like he's been doing this for hours."

"I don't know. I've never seen this before. Erik. Erik?"

He stopped and turned his head to the left, but remained pressed to the wall with his arms fully extended, almost as if he moved along a ledge and to turn completely around would cause him to fall off a precipice. Louisa and Christine walked to him timidly. Christine touched his shoulder. He turned cautiously, in a circle confined to the area of his feet, ending with his back firmly against the wall.

Christine let out a muffled shriek of horror. His face was covered in a blood streaked skull mask – his eyes almost invisible to them behind the tiniest of holes in the eye sockets. "Erik, whose blood is this?"

Louisa pointed to the palms of his cotton gloves. "He's punctured his own hands."

Christine believed she would faint, the room was spinning.

"Stay strong, Christine," ordered Louisa. In the most soothing voice she could manage, she asked, "Erik, why have you covered your entire head? Why, love? Come, let us see you." Gently Louisa lowered the cape's hood. Erik struggled to keep her hands away by moving his head violently from side to side, but remained rigidly in place, as if some unseen entity pinned him to the wall. Louisa slipped her hand behind the mask and removed it. Nothing on his face had been further damaged, but he snorted like a pig rooting at the ground. His eyes were clouded and unfocused – spittle trailed from the corners of his mouth. When Louisa took her handkerchief to wipe the saliva, he once again tried desperately to avoid her touch. His eyes wild with terror from a threat in the room they could not see.

"Some form of insanity has seized him. He was fine before I left this morning," Christine sobbed.

"His skin is cold to the touch and yet he sweats. Go get Imel. We'll see if together, we can get him to his room and look to these wounds. Hurry child, I'll stay here with him."

After a great deal of coaxing, the three managed to pry him from the wall and take him to his bed. Christine asked Imel to bring some juice while they checked Erik's body.

Erik snatched Louisa's hand, whispering almost incoherent words. "Raoul is here." She managed to free herself from the powerful grasp, and as Christine tried to put a cool wet cloth to his forehead, he screamed as if it burned him. "Raoul…Raoul!"

"He's not here, Angel. He's gone. He died." Erik seemed to calm a bit and let them take off his gloves. A single, round puncture hole rested in the middle of each palm – placed perhaps by the tip of a feather pen, or a sharp drawing pencil. They could find no other wounds but everywhere they touched seemed to terrify him badly.

"Maybe he injured himself to streak the mask with blood," offered Imel, as he set down a large glass of apple juice. "American Indians sometimes streak their faces with blood to prepare for battle."

Louisa's eyes remained focused on Erik. "Please leave us, Imel. I need to look after him and try to untangle what's happened."

"He's made quite a knot of things, hasn't he? But Christine is his wife. She should tend to him. What do you want me to tell the new maid?"

"That we'll start her obligations in the morning. Go, Imel, go…and thank you for the juice. Tell Joseph I want every door in this house locked. When someone enters a room, I want them to turn around and relock the door behind them, no exceptions."

About ten o'clock Erik became somewhat coherent. Neither Christine nor Louisa had left his side. He still refused the juice but had allowed them to wipe his face.

"Raoul is here. He's lurking in the shadows over there, waiting. Waiting for Philippe. They're coming to take me with them."

Christine kissed his hand repeatedly. "Erik, he's not there. We swear it. Raoul is in the earth. We could dig him up and show you…he's not in here! Some strangeness has descended upon your mind."

Erik raised his head off the pillow. "Raoul thinks I killed Philippe. He thinks I bashed in his brother's head. I told Raoul the truth except for one detail."

Louisa asked, "What detail? How did Philippe die?"

"Philippe came to help Raoul rescue Christine. I didn't touch him." He clutched at the cascade of lace gathered below Louisa's throat. "But I let him see my hideous face. When he saw it he stumbled in fright and hit his head on the rocks."

"You didn't kill him. It was an accident." As he let go of the lace, Louisa tried to ease him back but he was inhumanly strong. She brought the juice to his lips and he swallowed, gulping down the liquid.

"Rest, please, rest my love," begged a miserable Christine.

"Kiss me. Do you love me at all? Kiss me." His words started to slur, "Don't be porcelain...be pregnant."

She shuddered and looked at Louisa deeply frightened. "He sounds like Raoul."

The wind began howling wildly outside, banging window shutters against the chateau's stone exterior all across the mansion. Louisa went to the windows. "Tonight of all nights! The last northern storm of the season I hope. It's as if the demons in hell are hammering fiendishly, clamoring for freedom so they can prey upon Erik and the rest of us."

Christine brought the two middle fingers of her right hand to her thumb. Pointing the protective horn-signal toward the gale, she commanded, "They shall come no further!"

Erik pushed her off the bed with a growl and bolted to his feet. He ran to his desk and overturned it. With a fierce grunt he commenced dragging the heavy piece across the carpet.

"Does he mean to barricade us in?" screamed Christine.

Louisa held up her hand. "No, he's going to put it in the center like he did before." Indeed, Erik had left the desk and picking up its chair, placed it on top of the desk's ornate edge, where it rested precariously. "He's too damn strong for us to stop him! Go get Imel and Joseph. We'll need their help...and bring a rope. I hate to tie him, but he could exhaust himself and drop dead from fatigue before he stops!"

Grateful not to watch her husband perform this bizarre mission, she ran to Imel's room and pounded on the door. Dispatching him to the Count's bedroom she went to find Joseph. "Joseph, I need you to come with me. We need rope, quickly...where?"

"The stable has rope, Mame. It's the closest place. I'll go get it. What's wrong?"

"No. I'll get the rope. You go to the Count's rooms and do whatever Madame Giry directs."

Through the wind and heavy falling snow, Christine made her way to the stable. She scanned the supplies necessary for affixing horseshoes to the animals' hooves, and found several coils of rope near the saddles. Quickly, she grabbed the rope, two horseshoes, a mallet and four nails. Shivering from her exposure to the storm she returned to Erik's door. She dreaded going in. On the left doorframe she hammered a horseshoe with the opening upward, to catch whatever luck there was to be had, then nailed the other on the right. Fortifying her resolve to defeat whatever foe lay beyond, she summoned her courage and opened the door. She stood aghast at the preternatural sight before her. The furniture was piled in the center of the room. Even Raoul's massive bed had been pushed, or somehow hauled, toward the middle. Imel and Joseph stood next to the furniture, observing. Their hands were tucked into the pockets of their trousers. Her eyes ran wildly in the direction of their stare. *Heaven protect us!* Erik was again pressed against the wall with his left cheek to the wallpaper and his arms outstretched. Louisa was stationed right beside him in the same exact position, but with her face turned to Erik. Madame was side-stepping to her right. Unable to see where she was going she used her fingers to tell her when they approached the corner. Rounding it she continued on with Erik following her. Appalled, Christine started to weep. "Whatever has taken Erik has Louisa as well!"

"Don't cry, Christine. Come here," requested a lucid Louisa.

Christine tiptoed to where they slowly crept around the wall, dragging their bodies in an aching progression of exactitude. Erik's breathing was rapid, he panted like a dog with his lips apart. Balls of foamy white saliva clung once again to the corners of his mouth.

"You're not mad as well?"

"No, but he does think we're doing this together. He told me there are hundreds of carnivorous rats around us. They're all over our feet, hungry, biting at our legs. That's why we're moving at this pace. We're trying not to agitate them into overrunning us in a frenzied feeding."

"Why are you pressed against the wall?"

"We're in the caverns, seeking the secret passages to escape. If we step away from the wall we'll fall and be hurt."

"He's hallucinating," declared Imel.

"Yes, I'm afraid he is," answered Louisa. "And I don't know why."

"He's lost his mind, poor man," Imel diagnosed from the sidelines.

"Send the men away," Louisa whispered to Christine. "I don't think we'll need them. Lock the door behind them as they go."

Christine did as she was directed and came back to stand behind Louisa. "Do you think you know what's going on?"

"I'm not sure, but this is very peculiar. He was getting better and suddenly deteriorated. He's worse but the delusions are not escalating."

"How long are you going to walk the walls like this?"

"As long as it takes."

By dawn they had Erik lying down in his displaced bed. The women were frazzled and mystified. A foot of snow had fallen in the long hours of the night. The world outside seemed clean and magical, but inside it resembled the aftermath of a fearsome earthquake. Louisa held Erik's hand as he slept and Christine stood up, stretching. "I want to try something Erik told me about. We have no idea what we're dealing with and it couldn't hurt."

"I'll wait here with him. I'm at a loss, I don't know what else to try. If only Abraham were still with us. He'd probably take one look at Erik and know exactly what to do."

Christine went into the horror of her newly redecorated bedroom and changed into riding pants and a jacket. Going down to the kitchen she found Joseph and the female servants.

Genuinely concerned, Joseph inquired, "How is the Count this morning?"

"He's asleep for the moment. I want you to come with me. I'm going to do something strange, and I don't want any of you to ever repeat it to anyone outside this house. If you do speak of it, I'll fire you the instant I hear about it. Do you all understand?"

Her employees nodded in somber agreement.

"Something we don't comprehend yet is attacking this house, and I'm going to see if I can bring it to an end. How long will it take to get a sheep, Joseph?"

"Half an hour, Mame."

"Bring one to the backdoor, a female please, and dress warmly. We'll be outside for a while."

"Yes, Mame."

Christine brought another rope from the stable and waited just inside one of the backdoors for Joseph. When he arrived with the ewe they led it away from the house onto the snow-covered lawn. The female servants watched from the kitchen windows trying to guess what the mistress planned to do. Christine had Joseph tie one end of the rope to the sheep's left hind ankle, she cut off twenty feet of rope with her dagger, and they tied the other end to the remaining back leg. Christine went to the ewe's head and rubbing her between the ears, thanked her. Then she stood to the side of the animal and quickly slit its throat – the bleeding was profuse. The women inside let out little cries of bewildered surprise. Joseph and Christine started dragging it. An eerie trail of crimson blood followed behind them in the shallow ditch created by the weight of the animal's carcass.

"Tell me if she stops bleeding and we'll cut into her to produce more," Christine instructed. "I want a circle of blood around the entire chateau." Joseph nodded. As they pulled the sheep Christine prayed.

"Oh, Anubis, I ask for your protection and enlightenment. I call upon you, *Anpu,* great jackal god. You are the opener of the way, the guardian of the veil, guide to the spirits of the deceased. Hear this orphan's cry, for you are the patron of orphans, father to the lost souls, the personification of time itself. Show compassion to me and protect him whom I love. Hear my message, god of magic, let it reach the entire underworld, then carry it into the heavens on high. For you are the diplomat with the dark and sardonic nature, the Changeling, the one who is not what you appear to be. Breach this madness and enlighten me, expose its cause and its cure. I am your warrior and will always serve you well."

As a unified group the female servants moved from room to room inside the mansion, watching in wonder as the pair hauled the lifeless body of the sheep. When the trail of blood dwindled, Christine and Joseph stopped and cut off a front leg, carrying the appendage as they went to drip more blood upon the snow. A little further they sawed into the ewe's soft underbelly.

Antoinette pulled her shawl around her shoulders, murmuring, "This is creepy."

Marie chastised her. "I think it's really sweet. Don't the priests do the same thing, sprinkling holy water and incense all over the place? She's doing what she knows to do. She loves her man. God cannot sit complacently blind to the fact."

Antoinette sniveled, "How could He miss it? What a barbarous, unholy mess."

Near the edge of the woods a large black wolf appeared and sat down in the snow. Joseph pointed to it and Christine explained, "It's a sign...our prayers are being heard. Thank you, *Anpu*. We are grateful for your assistance."

Benjamin's carriage pulled up and from the window he saw the trail of blood across the front of the mansion. Fearing mass murder, he ran after the trail and found Christine and Joseph set into their task. "What on earth are you doing? Have you gone mad?"

"Good morning, Benjamin. We're not mad, but something dark and terrible has overcome the Count's mind."

"And you are...?"

"Pleading for help and blessing the house."

"I see...then let me help pull. Wouldn't it be better to walk barefoot, out of respect? More of a sacrifice."

"Yes, you're right." Christine sat in the snow and pulled off her boots. "Joseph, you don't have to do this part."

"Begging your pardon Mame, I want to. I saw the Count's condition last night."

Inside the female servants clutched each other. "What are they doing now? Heaven protect us! They'll freeze for sure. If the wolf attacks they'll never make it safely away."

Barefoot, Benjamin looped the rope around his shoulder. Like a horseless farmer harnessing himself to a plow, he bent into the chore. Christine walked beside him and continued her chant of supplication to Anubis. When the circle was complete she told Joseph to take a break and then burn the carcass completely. Joseph suggested that he take the ashes and sprinkle them over the blood trail as well. Christine immediately understood the wonderful harmony of his thinking, and gave the astonished man a grateful hug of consent.

In the kitchen, Marie wrapped their feet in warm towels and dried their socks and boots near the stove. When they were prepared, Christine took Benjamin upstairs. Outside Erik's room she explained. "He's gone insane and we're consumed with worry. He sees Raoul in the room, and hundreds of hungry, menacing rats. He crawls along the wall striving to find a way to escape."

"I've been gone for less than a day-and-a-half! How could he have lost his mind so quickly? Without a precipitating factor, people don't usually jump into mental illness, they slid into it over time."

"See for yourself." She started to turn the knob but he stayed her hand. From around his neck he took a gold chain with a filigreed charm.

Christine held it in her palm. "What is this?"

"It's a *hamsa,* a Jewish amulet. It represents the protecting hand of God. Wear it around your neck to ward off evil."

"Better that we place it around Erik's neck. I still have my wits about me." They went into the room and found Louisa standing by the mass of chaotic furniture. Erik's bed was empty. The window was unlatched and wide-open. "Louisa, it's freezing in here! Where's Erik?"

"Gone. He woke up and refused to take any nourishment. His eyes seemed almost perceptive. He asked me what happened and I told him, sparing no detail. He complained that his head hurt terribly, then he quoted a scripture. 'The truth shall set you free.'"

"I think that's from the eighth chapter of John. Did he say anything else?"

"He said, 'Tell Christine to inhabit the void where love pricked her.' Whatever that means, and I should prepare myself. We've been betrayed by the rats. I'm at a loss to tell you if he's really any better. Do you know where he wants you to go?"

"I think so."

Benjamin closed the window. "How did he leave the estate?"

"In your hired carriage."

He asked the women, "Do you want me to get Joseph and go after him?"

Christine sighed, "Where's he's going is his world. He knows it well. I want a nap, a bath and a meal, but I'll settle for your explanation of what happened in Lille. Then I'll follow him down his hole of degradation, into the dark abyss where love germinated."

Louisa spoke with reservation. "Its halls can confound the mind and ensnare the will. Do you want the Daroga with you?"

32 *UNDERGROUND*

Fortunately Christine warned him before she took him upstairs. He actually thought himself prepared, but until Christine opened the door of her bedroom, Benjamin had never, in all his life, viewed such an unnerving sight as the walls of rats. The enormity of the paintings, the astounding amount of energy expended to generate the hundreds of rodents, the vicious quality of their life-like eyes, as if with singular purpose they endeavored to attack all in their path, simply overwhelmed him. Fighting off a primitive, instinctual urge to turn and run, he forced himself to stagger into the wreckage of the room.

Deeply affected by the hopelessness of the situation, he pulled his fingers through his curly hair. "Madness poured out in visual proliferation," he moaned. "Erik saw himself surrounded by these vermin, perhaps devoured. What will you do?"

"As he requested. I will go to the nether world, to the place where love invaded me like an army of pillaging Saxons. My husband has an interesting way of understating my experience. He said love pricked me. It was more like love ravaged me, for I've not been the same woman since the conquest took place." Removed from the shock of the initial discovery, Christine folded her arms across her chest and studied the paintings more calmly.

Benjamin wondered if any female would ever speak of the effects of his love in such a fashion. "Where did he get the paint to do this?"

"All the unused materials to decorate this house are in the attic. Cloth, wallpaper, paint...all in abundance up there. No regard to containing expense was ever considered when the chateau was constructed. These depictions are actually quite realistic, aren't they?"

"Too realistic. Why would he paint them?"

"To confront them...remove their threat. In defeating them he defends his right to choose for himself. He's battled all his nightmares by painting them."

"So he planned to negate their power?"

She answered as she strolled the perimeter of the room. "Yes, like in a sword fight...if you're overwhelmed and loosing ground you employ a tactical diversion...a twirling cape, smoke, a loud noise of some kind. Your opponent doesn't anticipate the trap you're setting for him, or the unexpected exit you're providing for yourself."

Following the alley of space created by the disordered collection of furniture piled in the middle of the room, she came to the window where her desk had been situated. There on the ledge stood a lone candelabrum. In the confused panic of yesterday she had missed its presence. "He seems to have clung to slivers of reality. I have to prepare myself and leave."

Hidden from the world above, the Phantom laid his exhausted body in the coffin. With a final growl of contempt for the entire human race rumbling through his chest he closed the lid – a sweet fog of sheltering seclusion descended over him. *Safe in the sepulcher at last!*

She could taste the foul moisture in the air before she reached the boat. She'd forgotten the mephitic character of the lake. A lantern held in her right hand directed her careful steps down the slimy stairs of stones. In her left hand she carried a basket of bread, cheese, boiled eggs and fruit. It had taken her three hours to leave the chateau and reach this point. If she was lucky, he'd entered his underground lair through the quickest route, the trapdoor into the torture chamber, leaving the doree tied to the little dock for her to use. She located the boat, as expected, and started to row across the lake.

From the vantage point of a crevice high up in the stones the Phantom squatted like a gargoyle on a ledge. Misty blue lights shone on the waters below, other worldly to most, but home to him. He heard her determined efforts to propel the boat before he saw her, and knew her to be genuinely tired but still strong. After she entered the house, he lowered himself gracefully down a rope to the shore, and moved secretively around the embankment to an alternate entrance hidden in the rocks.

Inside she choked on the thick air of decaying mold and dust. *No magic here, just neglect.* A huge gutted-out cavern greeted her where his beautiful organ used to stand. She set the lantern and the basket on the kitchen table and waited, absolutely sure he was aware of her arrival. The whisper of her name softly repeated, and muffled through the walls, reached her ears. She sang his name back to him. "Erik. Let's sing together. We have so much of life to live. Come to me, Bright One."

"Erik will not come! He will not do it just because you call him!"

His voice seemed distant with an odd echoing quality to it. *Hollow stones!* She ran her fingers across what appeared to be a solid wall of rock and found a section of screen, so masterfully painted that the only way to discern its presence was to touch it. She could hear him breathing on the other side as she pushed gently against the mesh with her finger. The malevolent hiss of a snake warned her not to advance. "Here you are, I've found you! You are so sneaky...truly the craftiest, the most artful sneak I have ever met." Standing with only the thin screen between them, she realized that he must be able to see her.

He thought to affect a quiet retreat and slip away like a vapor of smoke, but she took off her hat and her gloves and laid them on the floor. Unbuttoning her coat and opening its front she let him see the pretty dress of lavender velvet with the cream colored lace for a collar. She unfastened three of the buttons on its front and waited patiently. No response.

Instead of employing the solemn adjurations he expected, she teased him and teased in a way that only a lover could. She unbuttoned more of her top, exposing the cleavage of her bosom above her camisole. Taking her pregnant, swollen breasts in her hands and lifting them upward, she pressed on her nipples with her thumbs.

She set her lips into a pout. "If I cannot have you back, the aching inside me will grow impenetrable…and I ache for the Master of Rascals! Come penetrate this aching."

He wiped the sweat off his upper lip with his index finger. "Erik's rawness does have a need to worship at your body."

"I know it does and I'm glad for its appetite. Erik's seeds grow here," she drew her hands seductively over her lower abdomen. "One grows within me even now. *Enceinte!* It will take little work to place me in the house of pleasure." She stepped back a few feet and lifted up her ruffled petticoat, showing the inner part of her left thigh to the screen. "Come, my prince, and bring your orchestra to play at my altar. Take your tongue and your mouth and reverently place them on me in adoration." She brushed her hand up and down her thigh. "My skin tingles at the thought of you plying your offerings into me." She took another step backward and waited. Unpinning her hair, she let it fall about her shoulders, and thinking him still inside the screen let her coat fall to the floor – prepared to undress completely and let him watch from the shelter of his hidden alcove.

His dark shape manifested in the shadowed light of the lantern, but over to her right and up on the landing in the area that had embraced the organ. "At last you appear!" She could not see his face. "Thank God you are a deeply sensual man. I have no qualms appealing to the readiness of your salacious nature."

"Licentious goddess, does it bother you that Erik plays Raoul? Do you miss your former Count?"

She spoke firmly but in kindness. "I do not miss Raoul. There were strange moments when he first died…I would turn a corner at the mansion and expect to see him there, but those have stopped. Are you sorry that you became Raoul? How could you not be?" He didn't answer and his reticence to speak troubled her. Tenderly she entreated, "Will you come forward a little so I can see you better?"

"Everyday I perform. It's an act and I do it for you. But I am no longer safe...someone is trying to unravel my mind. I've been poisoned. I know it. Just being here, away from the estate my mind is clearing."

Her arms reached up to him, her voice incredulous. "Poison? Someone is poisoning you?"

Still positioned in shadow, he answered, "With a noxious mixture of chemicals and without my consent. I cynically considered that it might even be you."

"It is not me, Erik, I could never hurt you! I love you so much. I would be devastated without you. Don't go back to the estate! Pursue your music, abandon the notion of building ships – just survive!" She crossed her arms over her chest to quell her rising anxiety. "Who is doing this and how are they giving it to you?"

"I don't know who's doing it, or how. No one's ever tried to destroy me so insidiously. Every other attack involved capture and physical torture."

She came to the foot of the stairs with the lantern, but he kept himself sequestered in the darkness above her. "Have you considered Raoul's sisters? Could they be paying the cook to poison you?"

"I believe Marie is one of the sweetest creatures alive. Murder takes a strong will. The sisters' maliciousness is easy to read. They enjoy complaining and being pampered too much. Besides, they think the children are Raoul's. I doubt they'd bring poison into the home of his little ones and risk them being accidentally harmed."

"Then who? No one else has stood against you."

"Who was with me when I awoke this morning?"

"It's not Louisa! She loves you as much as I do! From the moment she saw you ill yesterday, she never left your side. The second time you crawled along the edge of the walls she even crawled them with you!"

"What do you mean the second time?"

"What do you remember?"

He leaned against the rock in apprehension and she advanced up the stairs like thickened honey, trying to get to him without alarming him.

"I remember Raoul waiting, snickering…wanting me dead and rotting in the grave with him. Rats, thousands of rats, trying to eat me. When I lived down here they were an unavoidable addition to my world. Sometimes they were my only audience when I played my music, but they never attacked me."

"Even they respected the Angel of Music! This is my fault. I should have known someone would try something. Everything was going too smoothly. I should have protected you."

"Stop where you are and tell me about the second time."

She halted. "You spoke around ten o'clock. You sounded like Raoul, asking if I loved you, ordering me to kiss you, but you were speaking. Louisa was able to get some juice into you and you deteriorated again."

"Who brought the juice into the room?"

"Imel."

"And Imel gave me lunch about eleven o'clock." She lifted the lantern toward his figure to get a better view of his face. The glow of it bothered him and he raised a trembling hand to his forehead, covering his eyes. "Why did you come here? I didn't call you."

"Call me? Like with your mind? No, you didn't call me. You told Louisa where I should go and I understood your meaning. It's the poison, Erik. Try to fight it. Try to stay with me. It has to be Imel. Cook would have been asleep when he poured the apple juice."

She came right up to him and set the lantern on the floor. Dark stubble adorned his chin, the crow's feet of his left eye and the vertical folds of flesh above his nose were pronounced with worry. The expressive nature of his intelligent, disarming eyes dulled from malady. He straightened and tried to grasp the meaning of her words, but swayed dramatically to the side.

Alarmed, she steadied him with her hands. "Erik! You're still weak. Stay with me. Who am I?"

"You are my persistent, disobedient wife. I told you to halt!"

She smiled wearily. "Your skin and lips look very dry. You need to drink something. When did you eat last?" She placed her hand lovingly on his cheek. His face was ashen, the skin sticky and glutinous beneath her touch. "Whoever's poisoning you doesn't have the slightest notion of how physically strong you are. Sit down, please. I brought some food."

Descending the steps together, he moved to a chair with her. In a low, shaking murmur he asked, "Where did the food come from?"

"I brought it from our pantry. I'll throw it out and go get more."

"No, give it to me if you packed it yourself." Then he regarded her sadly. "You're not speaking to Erik through a mutinous, rebellious mouth are you, princess?"

"I am the Black Queen, thank you, and you may well be the death of me...not I of you."

As she opened the wine he thought outloud, "I wonder if Imel used my own tricks against me. If he got to my vials, I doubt he would know the lethal dosage. I'm still alive."

"We won't do anything until you are well. Then the Daroga and I will drown him near the boathouse."

"And what will we do with the body once you're a murderess? I want an end to the piles of corpses surrounding me. There was a time in my life when no amount of violence frightened me, now I abhor it. I have too much at stake. I dream of growing old with you, of seeing our sons take on a profession and fathering children of their own. Dreams I never dared to embrace, even in the blackest of Satan's nights." He drank the wine and spoke of despair. "Why hope for anything when you believe you'll die young?"

"Be strong, we can still be happy together. There will always be trials."

He slammed his fist weakly onto the table top. "You made me dream these dreams!"

She handed him a slice of bread with cheese. "I'm not going to apologize for loving you. You are breath itself to me."

He took several bites, studying her face in the light of the lantern. "Would you have stripped yourself bare in front of the screen?"

She nodded willfully. "And performed, anything to draw the trickster forth."

"Well, we've gained one thing of value from my poisoning." He watched her lift her left eyebrow in question. *My God, she's mimicking one of my expressions perfectly.* "If this is what insanity feels like, then I know I haven't been insane all these years. I've just been..." He swallowed for emphasis.

"You've been what?"

"Sick with loneliness and in desperate need of spiriting you off for a vigorous probing."

Smiling in relief, she went to kiss him but he stopped her. "I smell of sweat and something very strange, almost putrid."

"Is it the poison? Can you taste what's still left in you?"

"No."

"Maybe it's coming out through your skin with an odor. Eat and I'll prepare a bath. Let me wash you and your clothes."

"Stay here."

"Yes, of course. We'll go together to prepare the bath, but I doubt if we'll see Raoul lurking about in there. Can I start heating the water?"

After he finished eating they went to the tub. He watched her roll up her sleeves and move about in her preparations. When she was ready, she stood him up and slipped her hands beneath the notched lapels of his black jacket. "You did this once for me, turn about is fair play." She undressed him and steadied him as he lowered himself into the water. As she sponged his shoulders and rubbed his head, she suggested, "When we confront Imel you will control the situation for us. Where, how, who should be there...is for you to decide."

"Hmm."

"Can you call to me, call me in your mind like you used to do?"

"I doubt it."

"I hope it returns. What we share is very unique. How I feel about you is no transitory thing. It's lasting, Erik, and will out shine the stars. All I want is for us to be together. I meant what I said. Give up shipbuilding and stay with your music. If you're ever refusing to eat or drink, I'll know Raoul is around somewhere tormenting you."

"That's not comical, not even vaguely humorous."

"Sorry, I meant for it to be funny. I'm not handling all this very well. Nothing matters to me more than you and the children. I'm so grateful that they'll know their true father." She pushed the tears welling in her eyes back down. *Don't be maudlin, Christine.* She squeezed his shoulders and kissed the back of his neck. "My emotions are a tangle of knots." He leaned back as she started to lather his hair. "When Michael and Ariel reach manhood, they won't be pressing me to identify the person they've caught glimpses of all their lives – a man – always remaining at a distance, never engaging them in conversation. I won't have to tell them the truth from my deathbed, pleading with them to respect our privacy, ordering them to offer thanksgiving for the father who gifted them with their prestigious lives. We'll raise them together...nurturing what is most noble and discreet in their characters, teaching them to love with the same boundless determination you possess."

"We will raise the boys de Chagny, as Raoul requested, and tell them the truth of the matter before we die." Erik's face contorted in deprecation. "We missed the depth of Raoul completely. All those months he suspected the truth and allowed our relationship to exist. We were never disturbed...never blocked in any way from seeing each other."

"That is the one dimension of his generosity I cannot comprehend. He actually blessed our meetings with privacy."

"Without the protection and assistance of Raoul...and our brave Louisa, we'd still be confined to clandestine meetings in a cemetery."

Christine could not resist, "We seem to have made remarkable progress. We're right back here in a cavern five cellars below the theater. Erik?"

"Yes."

"The children don't have to know the truth about their parents. Think about it. We could let the nightmare end with us."

He snorted. "You're right. Why send their minds into disarray explaining the snarl of roots they come from? This confabulation is nothing they need know. They'll have their own lives and families to occupy them." Erik lowered his entire head into the water and popped back up a few moments later. "This feels good, a cranky ghost thanks you." Christine's fingers relaxed on his arm. Without turning to look at her, he reached for her hand and kissed it. With his eyes still on the water he apologized. "I'm sorry. I do know that I am no ghost to you."

Steam no longer rose from the bath, so she got up to retrieve the pots from the stove. "I'll warm the water again." As she poured carefully around the sides, she broached the subject of Benjamin's news. "Benjamin thinks you have an aunt but is not completely sure. He found her in Lille. He says she is very kind, a widow." She sighed deeply. "Could you bear to see your mother again?"

"She's dead."

"This woman may be your mother's twin sister. How old was your father when you were little? He died when you were quite young didn't he? Benjamin thinks the man you knew as your father may have actually been your grandfather. That would mean you have your great grandfather's eyes."

"So my father might still be alive?"

"Maybe. Benjamin thinks your father stole your mother from Abraham, and when your grandfather tried to return her, she refused to go because she'd been shamed. The passionately obsessed young man who stole Feigel-Evie was the son of a master mason."

"Thinking about this gives me a headache. Who cares?" He stood up and she wrapped him in several towels.

"There's more."

"I'll just bet there is," he kissed her forehead and shivered. "I'm weary. Let's sleep."

"I still don't feel like I really know you…know who you are inside." She rubbed his head with a towel.

He moved her toward the door. "Isn't some mystery good, keeps you coming back for more?"

Hours later she awoke beneath him. He lay with his legs between hers and his chest angled off to the right. In this position the bulk of his weight did not prevent her from breathing comfortably. She could tell he was asleep with his face turned away from her. She started to speak softly to the air above them, telling him that she would rather live in a hole, any hole, than live without him. "You are my very existence, Erik. I want to remain in your presence even if it means we live in madness." She longed to stroke his head or his back, but knew that needed sleep would heal him. "We will find out who's poisoned you, and how they've managed to do it." She felt his muscles harden between her legs. He turned his face to her. She kissed his deformed cheek and breathed softly into his ear. Her hips swelled up in greeting. Moving her hands across his upper back, then down his spine to the firmness of his buttocks, she nuzzled her head into the hollow of his shoulder.

She spread her legs further apart but he pulled his hips away from her. She wondered if he was repositioning himself to gain better access. Instead, he went to his knees. Wrapping his arms around the small of her back, he lifted her lower half, hugging her pelvis reverently to his chest. "The first time I made love to you was in this bed," he whispered in the dark.

She encircled him with her legs. "Oh, I think you were making love to me long before that weren't you? Your skin's not so cold anymore."

"Hmm." Sensing her readiness, he kissed her curls, and separating her cheeks from behind began to explore with his long fingers, gently circling the warm smoothness of her feminine structures.

Her brain issued a clarion call to respond and she shuddered with silky invitation, inhaling sharply.

But he hesitated to have her. "Please...tell me," he asked.

"I love you. I love you," she murmured. He let her rest on the sheets. "I want you...always. *Inamorato*, you are my heart's undoing...god to my soul...ugh...yes!"

"Do you feel how delightfully tight you are around me? I could drag my fingers over the keys of an organ a thousand times and it would not do to me what one *glissando* within you does. We fit so well together."

"I was made for you."

He held himself still within her, suspended in purity, but her body could not bear the cessation. It screamed for movement, for gratification.

In a will of its own, her pelvis eased away from him and then rejoined him, only to ease away again and rejoin once more. Arching her back, she managed to slide him out completely.

"What are you doing?"

"Drawing you into the act. Compelling you back into my already impregnated body. Pierce me. Please. I am in physical pain without you and pleading for relief. I want the sweetness of you fully inside me."

"Like this?" He took the initiative and drove himself deeply into her pelvis.

"Yes, like that. More. Abandon analysis, Erik. I am starving for you!" She purred out the word, "Husband."

He surrendered to her sexual pleas, and her profound tugging on his arms each time he pushed inside her, urging him deeper. He would always and forever marvel at her enthusiasm for his body and his mind. *You were wrong, Mother. I have a bride – a living, breathing wife and she craves me.*

As he picked up the cadence and brought her into orgasm, she cried out into the hair upon his chest. "Erik, my sweet magnificent Erik."

"I love you," he said breathlessly and turned his face away again, returning swiftly to the sleep of exhaustion.

33 *LIXIVIUM*

Under Christine's vigilant eyes, he received the things he needed most, sleep and nourishment. They disappeared from the chateau for three days. During the long hours of their absence from the estate they were visited several times by the Daroga, who gladly took on the responsibility of taking messages to Louisa, and helped to formulate a strategy to uncover the culprit guilty of feeding poison to Erik. Christine insisted they not return to the mansion until their Count felt strong and completely healed. Erik settled for enough vigor to fight if it were necessary.

On the afternoon of their return, Jean and Meg entered the wine cellar and strategically placed four small kegs in a semicircle in the area directly in front of the organ. At two o'clock Louisa brought a perplexed Imel to the basement.

"Why are we meeting down here and not upstairs near a warming fire?"

Louisa responded lovingly, "We have family business to discuss. Would you rather meet upstairs where they adorned everything with eighteen carat gold leaf or down here where earthen floor speaks to grounded truth?"

The Daroga came down the stairs first, the bulk of his cape thrown casually over the shoulder of his woolen jacket. Then Christine descended, radiant in a shantung silk dress of dark ochre to accent the eyes of the husband who followed. At last, a pair of black suede boots appeared at the top of the stairs. As the Phantom climbed down into the wine cellar, his heels resounded solemnly on every stone they hit. He looked glorious in the light of the candles. A stately Lord dressed in an immaculate black suit. A diamond stickpin twinkled in his white silk cravat, and then his face appeared – the upper portion covered in a mask of solid gold! He held his head high and looked through eyes no longer haunted by the madness drugs. He went to Christine where she stood in front of the organ and took his place to her left.

"Raoul you've returned!" exclaimed Meg brightly, almost childlike.

"We've missed you, Count," said Jean as he stood to shake Erik's hand.

When Madame Giry saw the fully alert, glittering amber lights in his eyes she came tenderly to his left side and linked her arm in his, staying in close attendance.

A chagrined Imel inquired, "How are you feeling, Erik? Better I trust."

"No worse for wear I suppose. A good deal wiser and obviously not dead."

Imel stomped his heel onto the stones. The thump made an echo. "Obviously! Good for you."

Words of hatred squeezed their way through the Daroga's teeth. "I am not a man to be trifled with, Imel Grey. I wish you to declare yourself. You are either with us or you are against us. We found the vials of potions in your room this morning while you took breakfast."

Imel made no attempt to conceal his aversion. "The two of you," referring to Khalil and Erik with snobbish jerks of his nose, "are void of any pleasing qualities – Mr. Foolish and Mr. Ghoulish. So you discovered my chemicals and my secrets are out, so what?" Imel's laughter held no mirth. "You're a pair of sniffing dogs, that's all!"

The sound of water dripping from the melting snow as it leeched its way down into the ground, through the stones of the walls around them, filled the silence that followed.

Meg spoke on a cue from Erik. "Why would you do this after we've welcomed you into our lives and our homes?"

"This is an insane asylum, my dear. This imposter," he jeered at Erik, "would arrogantly stand on Raoul's unmarked grave and sanctimoniously call himself a Count."

Christine added calmly, "But that is exactly what Raoul asked him to do, and you know it well."

Erik savored the intensity of Meg's skeptical questioning and Christine's contempt. His own hubris was deliberate and intended to goad Imel. "Raoul was my adversary, my rival, and in the end my benefactor. I was willing to let him raise my own children. Had I the opportunity, I would have called him friend."

Christine continued, "We owe Raoul a tremendous debt. One we can only repay by raising the children as de Chagny's – as he requested!"

Louisa's tone was deceptively smooth, prodding. "There must be more to this than self-righteous indignation over Erik taking Raoul's place. You haven't told us all your insidious motivations, have you? What else is there, Imel?"

"Yes uncle, what else do you resent?"

"To be a part of this charade, I've been obliged to shed my own good name. Tell me, Louisa, where does this deep affection, this unreasonable devotion for Erik come from? Do you hang so persistently at his side to shelter him, or to protect the rest of us?"

"I stay because I love him, and because I want to ease the effects of an obscenely callous world! You've never seen the gruesome scars in his flesh but I have."

Erik gently set his right hand on Louisa's where it rested on his arm. His sincerity and respect were unmistakable. "Louisa's ability to love me speaks of her great heart, not mine."

"You got that right, fraud. She is loving and protective while you are odiously shrewd. You think you're so resourceful, don't you...using their pity to weasel your way into their affections. You'll probably evade your just desserts, and learn how to make a success of shipbuilding too. You're like a cat, always landing artfully on your clawed feet!"

"Did you bring the poison with you from America?" asked Jean.

"He's not the only one who knows how to trick the mind with chemicals. The American Indians have been using herbs and mushrooms for years to alter reality. I'll let you in on a little secret, Jean. I've poisoned him many times, but his constitution is so damn strong he kept brushing off the effects. When they fired that sweet girl, Blanche, I'd finally had enough. I upped the ante and got the effects I wanted."

"And yet he's still not dead!" declared Jean.

Meg challenged Imel's actions with disdain. "You could have left, or gone to the police...turned us all in. What held you here, uncle? Why use poison?"

"He's got you hoodwinked, Meg. Even if I went to the police, he'd slither right out of the arrest. You're too willing to help him. When he was crawling along the walls and drooling like a baby, Louisa and Christine wanted to be with him all the more. They wouldn't even leave his damnable bed to get some sleep for themselves." He turned to Louisa, "The man's heartier than a bull. He doesn't need your help to get better, or to survive, and yet you fawn over him like he's some kind of spectacular trophy. You disgust me!"

Jean stood up and heaved an aggravated sigh from his chest. "I want to understand what you're saying with perfect clarity. You didn't mean to just incapacitate Erik...you meant to kill him. You wanted him dead and rotting with the worms, because he took Raoul's place and your sister cares for him. Is that correct?"

Imel folded his arms across his chest and fumed, refusing to answer.

The Daroga loosened his cravat. "You make my bones ache!"

Jean mimicked Imel's defiant posture by folding his own arms. "Or was it something else entirely? What about Grace? Who's the real imposter, Imel? Why don't you tell us about Grace?"

"I don't know what you're talking about," he sneered.

"Oh, I think you do. Grace loves the Angel of Music doesn't she? With all her heart she loves him. Every night she hopes he'll come and sing to her. And every night you steal shamefully into her room when he finishes singing, and wake her right back up don't you?"

Meg screamed at the top of her lungs and successfully distracted the culprit. "Scum! You're a vile lecher!" While she stood to cast her vilifications, the Daroga moved to the bottom of the stairs to block Imel's path should he try to flee. "You're a disgusting slime oozing down the halls of this house!"

"You've lost sound reason, Meg. I wouldn't touch that sweet child for anything!"

"You will never get your treacherous fingers on Grace again, Imel. She told us everything you do to her!"

Instead of pronouncing her own litany of curses, Louisa sprang forward and slapped Imel soundly across the face. He was caught off guard. Unprepared for the assault, his legs and arms swung precariously in the air as he tried to keep his balance on the keg. He gave up trying to remain seated for their inquest and leapt to his feet.

He reached for his sister. "Louisa, you can't believe that I…"

"Keep your filthy paws away from me!"

"You've caused all this," his words to Erik were so vehement that flecks of spittle blew from his mouth as he cursed him. "Filthy corsair!" Like a nefarious wood tick sinking a bite into unprotected flesh, he drew the gun he kept concealed inside his waistcoat and aimed it at his sister's chest, demanding, "Move over and let me out of here!"

Jean let out a low whistle to get his attention. "I don't think you want to point that gun at my mother-in-law, Imel."

"And why not? I'll do as I please, thank you."

"Because I have a gun pointed at you." Imel glanced over his left shoulder and took in the accuracy of Jean's statement. Indeed, Jean's pistol was aimed directly at Imel's head. In the second that it took for Imel to look at Jean, Erik deftly swept his body in front of Louisa's, holding her behind him with the vice-like grip of both his hands. When Imel turned his face back to Louisa and saw Erik in his sights he fired, cracking the air in between the stonewalls with the sound of the blast. A split second later another ear shattering shot went off.

Erik staggered backward, sprayed with arterial blood as Imel's hand, still holding the gun, fell to the floor. Clenching his wrist, with his life's blood pumping out of him, Imel turned and looked into Meg's frosty eyes. Her sword had delivered the amputating blow in the blink of an eye. Standing next to his wife and still pointing his pistol at Imel, a trail of smoke rose from the barrel of Jean's gun. A noxious sulfuric smell filled the air.

For the space of a jagged breath, time seemed to standstill with everyone frozen into position. Then Imel dropped to his knees, still conscious but choking with Jean's shot lodged in his throat. The transgressor looked quizzically at Erik who appeared to be unhurt. Grimacing, he fell straight forward crashing his face into the floor. He exsanguinated in a matter of seconds and no one moved to help him.

Christine fell backwards in a faint and the Daroga caught her, easing her head onto his lap as he sat on the floor.

Screaming wildly, Louisa spun Erik around to face her. "Are you hurt?"

"That was a point blank shot, Louisa. Don't you think I should be?" From behind the mask Erik seemed to restrain a smile of acceptance, vexing her woefully.

"Where are you hit?" Maddened by his nonchalance, her hands moved frantically across his chest and arms. She failed to locate the strike point of the bullet, no blood seeped from him anywhere! "Oh, Erik," she wailed. "Oh God, save us. No! Not this! Not like this!"

"Louisa, the biggest risk was not to me…it was to you. I had to hold you behind me to keep you still and protected. I apologize that I held you so tightly, but I had no intention of letting you die today."

"I simply could not let you die today either," said a resolute Meg.

"Where is the bullet?" Louisa's plaintive hands still traveled over Erik, searching desperately, her mind refusing to accept that he was in one piece.

Meg wiped her blade with a handkerchief and sheathed her rapier. "Mama, I could never let anyone shoot the Angel of Music, the maestro… the man who taught me the sword. I had Imel's hand off the instant he pulled the trigger. The bullet is lodged somewhere around us."

Erik took Louisa's hands gently into his and placed them firmly over his heart, assuring her that the hunt for an injury was futile. She clenched her eyes shut, still believing he had taken a ball of lead intended for her. He spoke tenderly trying to calm her. "Listen to me, Louisa. Meg sliced cleanly through Imel's wrist joint where it articulated to his hand...just as he pulled the trigger. Her timing was precise. She struck like a viper, with deadly accuracy. With her blow the joint bent downward, taking on the shape of the letter 'V', forcing the shot to go upward, off target."

From the floor the Daroga added, "I think it hit the door at the top of the stairs. I heard wood shatter just as Jean fired his gun."

Relieved, Louisa looked in wonder at Erik. "You're all right? That was incredibly brave and very, very stupid!" She pounded her fist weakly into Erik's chest. He kissed her forehead and she asked meekly, "What shall we do with this body?"

Christine opened her eyes and the Daroga nodded in satisfaction. Erik turned Louisa toward the organ and pointed. "We don't have God to save us. We have a more worldly agent."

Louisa stared in disbelief as Detective Edward's stepped out from behind the organ. "I heard everything and I understand perfectly, most enlightening Count. My report will read that in a moment's insanity he tried to shoot you. I believe he took his own mushrooms seeking spiritual enlightenment and probably consumed too much."

"Thomas? Thomas is here?" Louisa put her hand on her throat. "How long have you known?"

"Since yesterday. Khalil brought me to the underground house, where the four of us had a most enlightening chat. It seems my services were finally needed. They had little choice but to bring me into the inner circle of this tight little group."

Louisa sobbed, "Please, don't take him. He's suffered terribly. You've no idea..."

Edwards stepped forward. "Shh, Louisa. The only one I want to take is you and it would be straight to an altar if you'd consent. Erik is safe. I know...really I understand." He pulled her affectionately into his arms, patting her on the back. "You've had years of hiding, years of doing what you had to do to help him survive. Imel sealed his fate the moment he fired the gun. It's enough. Let it end here."

"How much do you know?"

"I know we need to take this body to a morgue and send for a medical examiner. That I have to fill out pages of appropriate paper work to document the death of Richard Grey."

Louisa started crying uncontrollably into Thomas' jacket.

"My, my…I believe I'll just have to keep you under the watchful eyes of the law."

EPILOGUE

Silently I inch my way down the hall to the southern salon…my favorite room in this fabulous kingdom. My father broke through a window and built a large arboretum attached to the house for my mother. She loves it in there, with her trees and her plants. I love it because it contains a wealth of places to hide. Ah, you ask who am I. I am Michael de Chagny, the midnight pirate who strikes unawares and steals their property with cunning! At the accomplished age of six my shrewd talents dazzle my victims – and my pursuers. For no treasure, no matter how safely hidden, is secure from me. Come men, I'll lead you to our next prize. Peek around the corner with me. Steady...steady. Quiet now, like brigands on Sunday we invade! See, there on the couch. My father rests with his pockets full of booty. But lo, mates, look there! My Aunt Louisa sits in a chair nearby. A formidable guardian but she will not deter us. She is my jewel of great price…my secret informant, always looking out for me. You dare to ask why she takes such risks? Naves full of idiots! Because I am her favorite, of course! By the skull and cross bones you know nothing. He spoke in gestures to the German Shepherd who followed stealthfully, playfully behind him.

Louisa rocked in her chair and covering her lips with a handkerchief, suppressed a smile. *He is such a scallion, thinking I don't know he's in the corridor, but I always know where he is. His vivacious little face is as beautiful as his mother's, but his eyes and his hair…all Erik. My sweet Erik, almost asleep here on the couch, only just returned from Lille. He has finally convinced his Aunt Hemdah to come live with us. He leaves again in two days to help her close up her house and bring her here permanently – such an endearing woman. I've gone to see her myself. Here he comes, my precious onion, pillowcase for a cape, wooden sword clutched in his hand.* "You have a visitor, Erik."

"Hmm, I heard our prowling young thief as he crept down the stairs with the dog. What an imp. I'll lay here and let him think he's caught me unsuspecting." *I hear my Christine and our Sarah in the arboretum too. Sarah's in the dirt again, probably just out of her mother's sight. What a treat your baby has for you, Mama! The soil Christine uses for her flowers smells so good to me – fresh, wholesome. Benjamin will be here soon and we'll discuss Hemdah, music…*

An unmasked Phantom opened his eyes the barest of slits. He rarely wore the facial covering inside the chateau anymore, no need to hide the fire's damage except from guests. His face reflected peace and contentment as the young marauder approached, traveling behind the backs of chairs to conceal his attack. *The rascal's wearing my skeletal mask of death again! How does he always manage to locate it? I'll bet his mother helps him find it, or maybe Louisa. I should find out who's aiding him. A blooming conspiracy is afoot here.* He closed his eyes completely. The point of the toy sword came close to his throat and he feigned a grimace. "Have you come to dispatch me, Monsieur? Are we to repeat the battles of before? Who can say which one of us will survive this day?"

The demand of the young plunderer was absolute, unbending. "Chocolate or beware, the confines of the brig are yours."

"I feel honor bound to tell you, young ruffian, I am prepared to defend myself! I will not easily surrender my treasures to you. You must fight for them." Michael held his ground and brought his left arm back behind him in the stance of *en garde*. "I see your mother has been practicing with you." Michael studied his adversary with cold vacant eyes. *I wonder if that is my expression, it's certainly not Christine's.*

The robber's attack stance ended abruptly. "Come on, Papa, put on your mask and play with me. You always have candy in your pockets for us. You know you do."

"Where is your brother? He's not a pirate today?"

"He's in the kitchen with Marie. They're baking chocolate biscuits and we get to have **all** of them, because I'm the best pirate ever. I plan to steal every last one of those cookies right out from under their noses!"

"You do? That's rather brazen!"

Michael scrambled from the room shouting over his shoulder, "Catch me if you can, Papa!" His laugh was something like a hurried squeal, followed by a frantic giggle as he whisked down the hall with his shipmate at his heels.

Erik sat up and throwing his legs over the side of the couch said to Louisa, "That plum colored dress looks magnificent on you, Mrs. Edwards. Thomas doesn't stand a chance tonight." Louisa blushed. He cracked his knuckles gregariously and she frowned in response. Pleased at his intended annoyance, he asked her, "Does any carnival freak have a right to be this happy?"

Christine stood in the doorway of the arboretum with a very dirty little girl in her arms. "And what would you say to heaven's messengers, to the celestial beings roaming among us? Remember, they see with most discerning eyes...all our truths unmasked before them. Have they not proclaimed something entirely different about you?"

Louisa leaned forward in her chair and touched his face. "You are true beauty, Erik. All the rest of us are the freaks!"

Here begins the Season of the Witch

Printed in the United States
201686BV00005B/82-93/A

9 781425 994921